Dianne Blacklock has been a teacher, trainer, counsellor, check-out chick, and even one of those annoying market researchers you avoid in shopping malls. Nowadays she tries not to annoy anyone by staying home and writing.

Also by Dianne Blacklock

Call Waiting
Wife for Hire
Almost Perfect
False Advertising
Crossing Paths
Three's a Crowd
The Right Time
The Best Man

The Secret Ingredient

Dianne Blacklock

First published by Macmillan Australia in 2011
This edition published in 2017 by Dianne Blacklock

dianneblacklock.com

The Secret Ingredient

EPUB format: 9781925579628
Print on Demand format: 9781925579635

Cover design by Red Tally Studios

Publishing services provided by Critical Mass
www.critmassconsulting.com

To Joel, Dane, Patrick and Zachary

Prologue

'Why did you introduce me to that man as your "current" wife?'

'Huh?' Ross glanced across at Andie before returning his attention to the road ahead.

'That man . . . oh, what was his name? From the London office.'

'Alistair Campbell?' said Ross. 'The whole reason we were there tonight? The cocktail party was in his honour. Jeez, Andie, keep up.'

'Sorry, okay.' She took a breath. 'The thing is, you introduced me to him as your current wife.'

'So?'

'Well, I'm just wondering why you would call me that?'

'Because that's what you are,' he said smoothly.

'But . . .' Andie hesitated. 'Don't you think "current" implies . . .'

'What?' he said after a while, his eyes not leaving the road.

'Well, it implies "right now", for the present, at the moment. It doesn't sound very permanent.'

'You'd prefer me to introduce you as my permanent wife?'

'No.' She was beginning to feel flustered. It was pretty obvious what she meant. She wished Ross wouldn't do this, it made her feel stupid. 'I just don't understand why you need to say anything beyond "wife". I am your wife, pure and simple.'

'For better or worse,' he muttered.

Andie shot him a look.

'Oh, Andie Pandy,' said Ross, giving her knee a squeeze, 'you read too much into things.'

The Corner Gourmet

'You do, you know.'

'No, I don't,' Andie protested. 'I don't read anything into anything.'

'You read plenty into plenty,' said Jess. 'Especially where Ross is concerned.'

'Why do you say that?'

Jess glanced at her friend; she looked apprehensive. Damn, she shouldn't have said anything. 'Oh, you know,' she said, trying to sound offhand. 'You can just be a little paranoid sometimes . . .'

'You think I'm paranoid?' Andie frowned, biting her lip.

'No, I don't think you're paranoid,' she corrected. 'I said you can *be* a little paranoid. Sometimes.' Like now, Jess wanted to say. Instead, she picked up a wheel of cheese and lugged it over to the slicer.

'You're right. I think I used to be a little paranoid,' said Andie, leaning back against the bench. 'Early on, with Ross. You know, you can't help thinking that if he was capable of leaving his wife for you, then what's to stop him doing it again?'

Jess nodded. 'How much of this Reggiano do you reckon we should put out today?' she said, hoping to change the subject.

'But that was ten years ago,' Andie went on, oblivious.

So much for that.

'I don't think I'm paranoid any more. Ten years is a long time, we're established, secure, we're an old married couple, for goodness sake . . . Which is exactly why I thought the term "current wife" was odd. It seems so . . . transient, or temporary or something. But I wasn't saying it means . . . What exactly do you think it means?'

'I don't think it means anything, hun,' said Jess, cutting into the rind. Lately Andie seemed to be obsessing rather a lot about what Ross did and what Ross said. Jess didn't like seeing her thrown off balance like this. Bloody Ross, heaven help him if he was up to something.

'You don't think what means anything?' Donna asked, coming in from the back.

Jess frowned. 'I have no idea how to answer that question.'

'Hey, Donna.' Andie smiled. 'I didn't realise you started early today?'

She blinked. 'Oh, maybe I don't? I better check the roster,' she said, turning back again.

'Don't worry about it,' said Andie, 'you're here now.'

That was just like Andie. The deli operated almost like a sheltered workshop for her friends. And friends of friends. Anyone who needed a job was welcome to it, and Andie basically let them choose – even dictate – their hours. Jess took advantage as much as anyone. She had to give priority to any chef work that came her way, but that was patchy at best. The restaurant sector, particularly fine dining, had suffered a battering since the GFC, but Jess was able to take any work she was offered because she could fill the gaps working at the deli. This haphazard approach to rostering meant the place was seriously overstaffed at times, but Andie didn't seem to mind; it wasn't as though she was dependent on the income, and the shop turned a profit regardless. A gourmet deli, in what was perhaps the most salubrious of the eastern suburbs, had a licence to print money. And that was even before the *MasterChef* phenomenon had turned every other person into a wannabe cordon bleu. Jess remembered when a large part of their trade was in ready-prepared hors d'oeuvres for platters and sides. People wanted to impress their friends when they entertained with conspicuously expensive, modish fare, but they couldn't be bothered actually *making* it themselves. Now it was *all* about the making, and Andie was forced to keep the place stocked with a plethora of exotic or otherwise rare ingredients; she virtually ran a hotline to her favourite suppliers on Monday mornings to source ingredients for the latest *MasterChef* challenge.

'Since you are here, Donna,' Andie continued, with a glance in Jess's direction, 'let me ask you something. How would you feel if Toby introduced you as his current wife?'

Donna looked confused. Stumped even. She always tried superhard to say what people expected her to say. Jess, on the other hand, had no such compunctions.

'Um . . . why do you ask?' Donna said tentatively.

'Because Ross introduced her as his current wife and now she's being all paranoid about it,' said Jess.

'I'm not being paranoid,' Andie defended. 'You're the one who suggested it means something, I wasn't even thinking that.'

'Then why did you bring it up?'

Now Andie looked stumped. 'You know what,' she said finally, 'you're right, I shouldn't bring up stuff like this with you. You always think the worst of Ross.'

Jess could hardly argue with that. Truth was, she didn't like Ross, for any number of reasons, but mostly because she didn't like what had happened to her friend since he came into her life. Jess and Andie had met at TAFE training to be chefs. They were excited, ambitious, full of big ideas about the brilliant careers they were going to have, maybe even opening their own restaurant one day. A little pie in the sky, but if you can't have pipedreams when you're twenty, what's the point of being twenty?

They graduated in their checked pants and chef's hats and started looking for jobs and a place to share. Chefs were better off living with other chefs, no one else would tolerate the crazy work hours and the stress and the obsession. Then reality began to creep in. The only jobs they could get were in the bistros of various clubs – the kind where the carpet was about as tasteful as the menu, and the ubiquitous chicken kiev and veal parmigiana weren't even made on the premises, which meant the chef did little more than heat and serve. Things were looking up when Andie got a call back after she applied for a position at Lemongrass, the 'it' restaurant back then. But it turned out they didn't want her in the kitchen, they wanted her front of house. Andie regarded it as a foot in the door, and though it was that, almost literally, Jess was not so sure. What Andie didn't seem to understand about herself, or at least refused to acknowledge, was that she was way too decorative to be hidden out of sight in the kitchen. Jess eventually got her break as a line cook in the restaurant of a five-star hotel, while Andie remained front of house at Lemongrass for another couple of years. Until she met Ross. He'd frequented the restaurant with clients, never his wife of course, and it wasn't long before he began to pay Andie special attention. She started to drop his name more and more often. Jess noticed and ribbed her about it. Andie coyly denied. It was all typical flatmate banter. Until the night she brought him home after a shift, and Jess saw that not only was he an old man – at their age anyone over forty was old – he was wearing a big fat gold wedding band.

She'd dragged Andie into the kitchen. 'He's married!'

'Oh, yeah, kind of.'

'What does that mean?'

'Well, it's been over a long time.'

'But he still wears his wedding ring?'

'Well, yeah, he's still married to her.'

'You mean they haven't got a divorce yet?'

'I mean they haven't even separated yet.'

'What?'

'He's got kids . . . it's complicated.'

'No shit.'

Jess had been confounded at the time. What on earth did her friend see in an old guy like him? Okay, he was good-looking – for his age – and he had money, though Jess was not so sure how much he'd have after he went through a divorce. That's if he ever did, and she'd had her doubts. And yeah, sure, there had hardly been any prizes among the guys they'd been dating. Andie and Jess used to take turns holding the tissue box for each other when their hearts were broken by yet another dropkick. Well, they weren't really broken, just bruised a little, but with monotonous regularity. Jess got through the tumultuous twenties by toughening up and hardening her heart. She decided to play like a boy: just have fun, not get attached, not have any expectations so they couldn't get shattered. She had never really had misty pictures in her head of her wedding day. Marriage was a bit of a crock, human beings weren't built for monogamy, so as far as Jess was concerned, everyone should just get over it. And the idea of children freaked her out a little, quite frankly. So maybe all these commitment-phobe guys were onto something, and Jess decided if she couldn't beat them, she might as well join them.

Andie plunged headlong in the opposite direction. She kept the faith, believing in true love and soulmates and all that hokum. But any half-decent guy – one with the slightest bit of self-awareness, a little depth, and not too much ego – would assume he was out of her league and not even have the gall to approach her. So that just left the wankers who wanted a trophy girlfriend. And Andie was certainly stunning. You could tell her eyes were green from across the room, and she had a mane of golden hair that was so thick she had trouble restraining it under her chef's cap. But Andie was dismissive of her looks, even contemptuous. She used to say, 'You know, Jess, people are either only attracted to you for the way you look, or they hate you for it. Either way, you lose.'

That was the thing about Andie, despite an outwardly sunny nature – she was one of those people who was nice to everyone – there was a sadness underneath, something wasn't quite right. Jess finally got it out of her one night, after a few drinks. Her brother died tragically when she was in her second year at uni, and her mother fell ill soon after. Andie dropped out of uni to take care of her, until she died about a year later. So by the time Andie started at TAFE she was a few years older than everyone who had come straight from school. But Jess had always felt like the elder; Andie had a vulnerability about her that made her seem much younger.

So when Ross swooped into her life – with all the expertise of an Older Man – Andie was caught off-guard and vastly unprepared. He smothered her with an ardour she had never experienced before. He knew what a prize she was, and he didn't squander it like lesser men before him.

Jess was witness to it all, and to some extent it wasn't difficult to see why Andie fell so hard, particularly given the great, gaping hole left in her life by the loss of her brother and mother. But something about Ross had never sat right with Jess, and it wasn't because he'd left his wife for Andie. That was none of her business, and besides, Jess was firmly of the school that, just as oppositions don't win elections, a third party doesn't break up a marriage.

No, what bothered Jess was that while Ross trowelled on the charm, he always seemed to get his own way. Even this shop – it wasn't Andie's dream to run a deli, no matter how much of a foodie's haven it may be. But Ross didn't like her working restaurant hours, so she never did make it into the kitchen at Lemongrass. She quit instead.

Then seemingly out of the blue, Ross spotted the deli for sale and decided it would be perfect for Andie. Andie wasn't sure at first, but as usual, she came around to Ross's way of thinking, and ended up believing it was the best thing ever.

'You're always so suspicious about Ross and his motives,' Andie was saying.

'Huh?' Jess stirred now, looking up from the slicer.

'Ross, you always think the worst of him.'

'That is patently unfair,' said Jess. 'I was actually agreeing with Ross that you read too much into things . . . if you remember back to the beginning of this conversation.'

Andie folded her arms. 'Okay then,' she said, 'you're going to have to solve this for us, Donna, once and for all.'

Donna looked startled. 'Oh, don't ask me to solve anything, you know I'm no good at solving things. Oh gosh, look at the time! Shouldn't we be opening?'

'I'll get the door,' said Andie, walking around the counter. 'But just tell me what you think, Donna, I'd really like to know. How would you feel if Toby introduced you as his current wife?'

Donna glanced warily from Andie to Jess, and back to Andie again. 'Okay.' She took a breath. 'How would I feel . . . Well, the thing is, I suppose I am Toby's current wife, so there's nothing exactly wrong with him calling me that. But I don't think Toby would . . . Yes, that's it, I just don't think Toby would put it like that. Not that there's anything incorrect about it, per se.'

That evening

'So, Toby,' Donna began, while they were washing up after Max had been put to bed. 'How do you refer to me when I'm not around?'

'What do you mean?'

'Well, you know, if you were talking to someone who didn't know me, and you had to mention me for some reason, you wouldn't just say "Donna" because they wouldn't know who you were talking about.'

'You mean like I don't know what you're talking about now?'

'Toby!' She didn't want to have to spell it out. 'You'd say I was your wife, right?'

He shrugged. 'Yeah.'

'So, is that all you'd say?'

Now he was frowning. He picked up a pot off the rack. 'What's this about?'

'Just humour me, please,' said Donna. 'If you were referring to me, would you just say "wife", or would you use an adjective?'

His face broke into a broad grin as he leaned back against the bench, wiping the pot with a tea towel. 'Ah, I get it now.' He cleared his throat ceremoniously. 'Whenever I talk about you – which is all the time, of course – I say, "My *beautiful* wife, Donna", or "My *wonderful* wife, Donna . . ."'

'Oh sure you do.' Donna smiled, elbowing him. 'I wasn't fishing,' she said. 'I was just wondering if you'd ever call me something like . . . your "current" wife, for example.'

He frowned. 'Why would I call you that?'

'Because I am your current wife.'

'Yeah, but that sounds like I'm going to trade you in some day,' he said, sliding open the pot drawer. 'Like a current model car.'

Donna sighed. 'Hm, that's what I thought.'

'What brought all this on?' asked Toby.

'Oh, nothing,' she said vaguely. 'I was just talking with the girls today . . .'

Toby shoved the pot drawer closed. 'So Ross called Andie his current wife?'

Donna's eyes grew wide. So much for being vague. 'How on earth did you jump to that conclusion?'

'You were talking with the girls,' he said. 'Jess isn't married, so that only leaves Andie, which means it had to be Ross.'

'Oh.' She should have thought of that.

'God, that guy's such a wanker,' Toby was saying. 'Why would he call her that?'

Donna shrugged. 'Well, it's not like it's incorrect exactly —'

'Was Andie upset? What did she say?'

'She wasn't upset, we were just talking —'

'The bastard's getting ready to up stakes and move on,' he said. 'You mark my words.'

'Well, now you are jumping to conclusions,' said Donna. 'There's nothing wrong with him referring to Andie as his current wife, especially as he did have another wife before her.'

'How could I forget?' he muttered.

'It all happened such a long time ago, Toby, you can't keep hating Ross forever just because he left his wife. He did leave her for Andie, after all.'

But Toby could never think badly of Andie. He had been best mates with her brother, Brendan, right through school, ever since kindergarten. Brendan and Andie were the closest brother and sister Toby had ever known. Although she was older, if only by a year, Brendan was fiercely protective of her, always threatening guys twice his size if they were ogling her, because she did get ogled quite a bit. On the other hand, Andie was forever getting Brendan out of scrapes and covering up for him.

Not that he would ever have really copped it from his parents – he was their beloved only son, their golden boy. Everyone made excuses for Brendan, and allowances for him, and in the absence of consequences he became a little too fearless for his own good. So when he saw a fight break out outside a nightclub, he decided he was the one who would be able to calm everyone down. But instead he was king-hit, his head cracking on the gutter as he went down. He died before an ambulance made it to the scene. Of course, Andie blamed herself for leaving the nightclub earlier without him. But Toby was there, he knew Andie had tried to talk him into going home with her, but Brendan was not easily persuaded, even by his adored sister. So Toby told her it would be all right, he'd stay with him. And he did, until the end, until his best friend died in his arms.

Toby and Andie shared the loss keenly and a tight bond had formed between them, so much so that when Toby first started dating Donna, she thought he was in love with Andie, and she said as much to him. He was horrified, and a little grossed out. He didn't think of Andie that way, he insisted, she was like a sister to him. And she could do no wrong in his eyes. So Ross was a cheating bastard, but Andie was completely innocent – it wasn't her fault that the love of her life turned out to be married, and anyway, he was the one who left his wife, Andie didn't do anything wrong. Donna tried to argue Ross's side – he may have been married, but apparently they were only staying together for the sake of the kids, and appearances. Then he found the love of *his* life . . . wasn't he as entitled as Andie to pursue it?

Toby didn't see it like that. He tolerated Ross, but he had never grown to like him, and certainly not to trust him.

'He left one wife,' Toby was saying, 'what's to stop him leaving another when he's ready to upgrade again. Like I keep telling you, a leopard —'

'— can't change its spots,' Donna chanted. That was Toby's favourite saying about Ross. 'Except that's a myth, you know.'

'Since when?' he asked.

'Since there was a study recently that showed it's not true.'

He looked doubtful.

'Seriously,' Donna went on, 'I heard it on the radio. They found that leopards can change their spots depending on their environment. They adapt. So isn't it possible that Ross has adapted to his life with Andie?'

'No.'

'How can you be so sure?'

'Because,' he said grumpily.

Donna smiled, drawing close to him. 'You know, Toby, sometimes I think you *want* them to break up.'

He didn't have anything to say to that.

'And imagine how devastated Andie would be?' she said. 'If you care so much about her, and you don't want to see her hurt, it seems to me you should be doing everything you can to support them both, rather than finding fault with Ross all the time.'

Toby sighed deeply and leaned his forehead against hers. 'You can be so annoying, you know that?'

'Why?' she protested. 'I thought that made a lot of sense.'

'It does,' he agreed. 'That's what's so annoying.'

Friday

'*Mu-um*, Andie's on the phone.'

The journalist clicked off her recorder. Joanna smiled apologetically. 'Sorry about that.'

Brooke burst through the doorway, waving the phone. 'Oh, crap. Sorry, I didn't realise you were with someone.'

'That's okay, sweetheart,' said Joanna. 'This is my daughter, Brooke.'

'Ah, the one who's following in Mum's footsteps, I hear,' she said. 'You're in your third year of architecture, right?'

'Yeah . . .' Brooke said warily.

'Darling, this is the journalist from *Design* magazine,' Joanna explained. 'Rachelle King.'

'Oh, right,' Brooke nodded. 'You're interviewing Mum about the businesswoman award thing?'

'Designing Woman of the Year,' Rachelle corrected with a smile.

'Did you say Andie wants to speak to me?' Joanna asked Brooke.

'It's just about Sunday, I'll say you'll call back. Sorry for the interruption,' said Brooke, slipping from the room.

'My first grandchild's christening is this Sunday.' Joanna turned back to the journalist. 'Lauren's baby, she's my eldest.'

'And her husband is James, right?' said Rachelle, flicking through her notes.

'That's right.'

'And your son is Matthew.'

'Yes, he's nineteen, in his first year at uni.'

Rachelle looked up at her. 'So Andy is . . . ?'

'Oh, no,' said Joanna, smiling. 'Andie is actually Andrea, she's Ross's current wife.'

'You mean your ex-husband, Ross?'

'The one and only.'

'How long has he been remarried?'

'About as long as we've been divorced. He left me for Andie.'

'Oh . . .' Rachelle appeared momentarily lost for words. 'But you're on speaking terms with her . . . with Andie?'

'Of course,' Joanna dismissed. 'I used to despise the girl, but time heals, as they say. I did the work, learned a lot about myself, my marriage . . . moved on.'

Rachelle clicked the recorder back on. 'What did you learn?'

Joanna cast her mind back; it was such a long time ago now, and so much had changed. At first she'd hated poor Andie, and she was just a kid, Lauren was older now than she was at the time. But Joanna was the woman scorned. All their friends sided with her – Ross was the one having the affair, the full weight of blame rested on his shoulders. Joanna got off scot-free, and she got all the sympathy. But she had no self-esteem. Her whole identity became that of the victim, the martyr. If she'd kept going down that path she was destined to become a bitter, lonely old woman, she was never going to grow or change. She had to fess up at some point and accept that she had let the side down as well. The marriage had become stale and she had to accept her share of the responsibility for that. Of course she had her defence – she was looking after the kids, her life was consumed by their needs – but in reality, they both had just stopped trying. When you're married that long, you think it's going to take care of itself.

Joanna stirred as Rachelle cleared her throat. She was still waiting for an answer, but Joanna had forgotten the question.

'I'm sorry,' she said. 'What was it that you asked?'

'You were saying that you learned a lot about yourself through the breakdown of your marriage. I was wondering how you achieved that?'

'Well, therapy, of course. When you're of a certain age, in a certain income bracket, you're going to take the therapy route eventually.'

'And it helped?'

Joanna nodded. 'It did, just to have someone to talk to who didn't let me get away with bullshit, basically. There wasn't any blinding moment of insight. My therapist just made me tell the truth. And the truth was that the marriage had died, buried under the weight of the kids and the mortgage and the bills, Ross's job, his long hours. We were no different to most of the couples we knew at our age. That weariness you feel around each other. The eye-rolling when you hear the same old jokes, the TV in the bedroom so you don't have to talk to each other. The "can't be botheredness" of it all.'

'So you forgave your husband?'

'I don't know that *forgave* is the right term,' said Joanna. 'I still think it's disappointing that the father of my children could only leave on the arms of someone else – it shows a lack of courage at the very least. But I do forgive her . . . Andie,' she added to clarify. 'Like I said, I hated her at first, but that was just a waste of emotion. What did she know? She was still in her twenties, and Ross, oh, he can turn on the charm all right. He would have had her believing she was saving his life. What girl's head isn't going to be turned by talk like that?' She paused. 'Anyway, eventually it became clear that the kids were spending more time with her than their father – he was still working very long hours – and they were torn, out of loyalty to me. Someone had to be the adult. I pretty quickly worked out Andie wasn't a scheming jezebel, she was just a bit naive, really. She was actually a nice person, I liked her. And I wouldn't be in her shoes for anything.'

'Why do you say that?'

'Well, I wouldn't put it past Ross to do it again.'

'You mean leave her for another woman?'

He'd done it once, and it worked out, why wouldn't he try it again when things went stale? Which they inevitably would. From what Joanna could see, Ross hadn't learned any other way to deal with conflict, so if they hit a rough patch, she didn't imagine him trying to weather it.

But she just waved her hand. 'What do I know? They'll probably grow old together. I only know if it was me, I'd never be able to trust him again. But Andie's not me.' Joanna looked directly at Rachelle, becoming serious. 'Hey, that's all off the record, right?'

'Oh, of course, if you say so. It is an interesting angle to your story, though.'

'You can use the angle that I picked myself up after my divorce and made a new life, success is the best revenge, all that. But don't mention Andie, all right? That wouldn't be fair to her.'

Joanna could afford to be generous now. Besides, she wasn't exactly proud of some of the things she'd done back then.

'So,' said Rachelle, 'after the divorce, that was when you started the business?'

'Not right away,' said Joanna. 'I had to go back to work, and my qualifications were out of date. A degree in architecture is what it is, but the industry had moved on and I'd been left behind. Plans and drawings were all being done on CAD programs and I didn't have any experience. So I had to find a way to use the skills I did have.'

'From your original degree?'

She nodded. 'My head was still full of design ideas, and I believe I was good at communicating them. I single-handedly supervised both our home purchases and the subsequent renovations, Ross was just too busy,' she said. 'What I learned at uni was only a part of it. Being a mother of three married to such a busy executive meant I had to be organised, manage my time, manage my kids and their schools and their activities, keep track of dozens of details, and juggle dozens of demands, often on a daily basis. It seemed to me that I had all the skills for project management, but I couldn't get anyone to take me seriously without formal qualifications or workplace experience. So I decided there was only one way to go, I started my own business.'

'And you've never looked back?'

'No, I never have.' A small smile formed on her lips. 'I guess you could say that Ross leaving me for another woman was the best thing that ever happened to me.'

Paddington

'Andie?'

'Short for Andrea,' Tasha explained to the hairdresser. She had Gia today, she liked Gia, she was a good listener. Much better than . . . whatsername – Alicia? Alanna? Whoever she'd had last week. That girl couldn't stop talking about herself.

'She's his current wife. He was married once before as well.'

'That doesn't bother you?'

'Why should it? The first wife is ancient history now. She was old-school, you know, stayed at home, had the babies . . . *Boring!* Ross totally outgrew her. He's so dynamic, so *young* for a forty-nine year old. I mean, I don't even think of him as that age, he's, like, only a couple of years younger than my dad. But he's, like, a whole other generation.'

'Just tilt your head forward,' said Gia. 'That's it, great . . . So he's forty-nine, did you say? That's not so old, not for a guy.'

'Exactly. For a guy, it's like his prime,' Tasha agreed.

'So what went wrong with the current wife?'

'Well, Ross totally believed this "Andie" was his soulmate, but she's turned out to be worse than the first. She used to be ambitious, it was one of the things that attracted him to her, he told me. Apparently she was this amazing chef with loads of potential, but now she just works in a shop.'

'Really? What kind of shop?'

'It's a deli, gourmet foodie place. You know the kind of thing. Ross had to buy it for her to give her something to do.'

'All right for some.'

'I know, right?' said Tasha. It was so good to talk to someone who totally got it. 'It gets worse. She absolutely vowed to Ross that she never wanted kids. That was the agreement when they got married. And now she's gone and changed her mind, just like that.'

'No!'

'Yes,' Tasha confirmed. 'I mean, how could you do that to a guy? Totally sucks. He's shit-scared she's going to trick him, stop taking the pill, and it's not like he can wear a condom without her knowing.'

'So they're still having sex?'

'Oh, hardly ever,' she dismissed. 'He's trying to avoid it as much as he can without her getting suspicious, you know? He tells her he's working late, or he's at the gym, when he's with me. And he's not drinking at the moment, so he's got his wits about him.'

'Sounds totes stressful.'

'Tell me about it. I just say to him, I say, Ross, baby, walk away. You can move in with me. But you know, it's not that easy. The first wife sucked him dry, and it's taken him ten years to get back on his feet. If he leaves the current Mrs Corcoran, well, he'll get screwed all over again.'

'Didn't he protect himself this time around? Like, he didn't put the shop in her name, did he?'

'He didn't have a choice,' Tasha insisted. 'They had to put it in her name because of taxes and that, even though he bankrolled the whole business. The thing is, it's not like he planned for this to happen. He's so not like that, he's way too trusting. So she'll get the business, as well as half of everything else.'

Gia frowned, looking at Tasha's reflection in the mirror. 'But wouldn't he get half of her assets as well? I think that's the way it works.'

'Not according to Ross,' Tasha maintained. 'Like with his first wife, she got way more than half of everything, yet she's this kick-arse property developer, making a fortune.'

'The first wife?' said Gia. 'I thought you said she was old-school, stayed at home with the kids?'

What was this now, an inquisition?

'Well, yeah, while she had Ross to support her she stayed home and did nothing. Seriously, all he's ever done is try to look after the people he loves, and they've taken advantage of him, again and again. I say to him, it's a wonder you want to take the risk again with me.'

Gia just nodded as she combed a hank of Tasha's hair upwards. Was she even listening?

'But then he says he's never met anyone like me,' Tasha said loudly. 'He's never felt so alive. He said he feels like he's twenty years younger and all his life's ahead of him. Because of *me*,' she emphasised.

'Wow . . .'

'I know, right. Wow,' she said.

'So do you get to spend much time together?'

'Enough, for now,' said Tasha, inspecting her nails. 'I'm seeing him tonight, as a matter of fact. He told his wife he's going to the gym, but he has to be home later for something or other,' she dismissed. 'So he's coming to my place for a drink, and, you know . . . whatevs,' Tasha smiled suggestively.

'Hm, doesn't that feel like . . .' Gia seemed to be searching for a word.

'What?'

'Well, you know,' she shrugged, 'a booty call?'

Tasha was beginning to think she was better off with whatsername. Gia had a weird take on things. Envy did strange things to people.

'Ross's situation puts limitations on him that have nothing to do with how he feels about me,' Tasha insisted, reciting the exact words Ross had said to her so many times. 'And yes, we'll have sex when he comes over later, but that doesn't make it a booty call. I want it as much as he does, believe me. Have you ever had sex with an older man, Gia?'

'You mean *much* older?'

Tasha didn't like her tone.

'It's amazing,' she said. 'Being with an older man – not that I think of Ross as *older*, like I said – but it's so different to being with a guy your own age. They're so into themselves, sex is just a way for them to get off. They don't think about your needs.'

'Oh, I don't know —'

'Well I do,' Tasha interrupted flatly. 'You said you haven't slept with an older man, so you can't really make a comparison, can you? Whereas I have, so I can, you know, make a comparison.'

Gia nodded. 'Of course. Go ahead.'

Tasha took a breath. 'Younger guys don't know the first thing about how to treat a woman,' she said. 'And I'm not just talking about manners and that. What Ross knows about the female anatomy would curl your toes, *literally.*'

Tasha could tell from the expression on her face that Gia was impressed.

'But you want to know the best part?'

Gia was waiting.

'All men lust after younger women, everyone knows that, it's fact,' said Tasha. 'So in Ross's eyes, I'm like a fantasy come to life. I'm a decade younger than the current wife, and God, a lifetime younger than the first one. Can you imagine what it's like for him to make love to me? He just *adores* me, I can see it in his eyes. And I have to say, that's a real turn-on.'

Roseville

'Dad, it's me,' Andie called as she let herself in through the front door. There was no reply, but she could hear the TV going. He was home. Where else would he be? He never went anywhere, except to Mass and doctors' appointments.

Andie came down the hall into the living room, where her father was manning his regular station in front of the giant flatscreen TV. Andie didn't understand why he bought such a huge screen and still sat so close to it.

He was struggling to get up out of his recliner. 'Andrea,' he puffed. 'I wasn't expecting you, dear.'

She usually came Fridays, and if she wasn't going to be able to make it, she came earlier in the week instead. But her dad was forgetting what day it was lately.

'How's my girl?' he asked, once he had got to his feet and sidled around the chair. 'Let me look at you.'

She smiled at him as he held her by the shoulders and examined her face. This was his ritual every time. 'Still as beautiful as ever,' he declared, before wrapping her in a big hug and planting a warm kiss on her cheek.

Andie held up the bags she was carrying. 'I brought you some things.'

'What are you doing bringing me stuff?' he tutted, following her out to the kitchen.

She put the bags down on the table. 'I like to bring something when I come.'

'You only have to bring yourself to make your old man happy,' he said, reaching for her hand and giving it a squeeze. 'Now, let me give you something for it,' he added, patting his pockets for his wallet.

'Dad, don't be silly,' Andie chided. He was always trying to give her money. 'I brought all this from the shop.'

'Still costs you something.'

'It's fine, Dad,' she dismissed. 'It's just some bread —'

'Oh . . . what kind of bread?' he asked carefully.

'Don't worry, it's not the same as I brought you that other time. I know you didn't like it.' She had found the entire loaf moulding in the bread box the following week.

'Oh, it's not that I didn't like it, I just think it might have been stale.'

'It wasn't stale, Dad, it was sourdough. It has a different texture. You might have found it a bit too chewy.'

'Hm.'

'Anyway, this is nice and soft in the middle. And I brought you some cheese —'

'You know we don't eat the strong stuff.'

He still dropped in and out of the plural, without even realising. It worried Andie a little, after all this time.

'Yes, Dad, I know you don't like strong cheese.' He preferred that awful fake stuff wrapped in plastic. 'This is a mild cheddar, and I shaved it so it's nice and fine.'

'I always seem to use more when it's shaved,' he remarked, shaking his head.

'It doesn't matter how much you use, Dad, I'll bring more if you like it.'

'Oh, you don't want to be wasting your money on me.'

Andie looked at him, bringing her hand up to touch his cheek. 'It's not a waste if it's for you, Dad.'

He smiled at her, patting her hand.

'And lastly,' Andie added, turning back to the bag, 'fruit salad, fresh cut today.' She reached in and lifted out a large container.

'Oh my, all that? It'll go off before I can eat it.'

'Well, it was going to be thrown out anyway,' she said. 'We make it fresh daily, so whatever's left gets tossed if no one takes it home.'

He looked a little doubtful. 'We're not big fruit eaters.'

'I know you're not,' said Andie. 'But you should be, it's good for you, Dad.'

'You shouldn't have too much, though,' he said. 'I saw it on the telly, it can muck up your sugars.'

If he was that worried about his sugars, he shouldn't be eating all the packaged biscuits and snacks he was so fond of. 'Any doctor would recommend a couple of pieces of fruit a day, Dad.'

He still looked unconvinced.

'I worry about you,' she said. 'Do it for me?'

He took hold of her hand and gave it a kiss. 'When you put it like that, how can I refuse?'

'Thank you.'

Andie put the container in the fridge and looked around the kitchen, the dishes piled up on the sink, the sticky benchtops covered in crumbs. Since she had been paying for a cleaner, her father didn't seem to bother to do much for himself. 'Dad, how long has this been out?' she asked, lifting the lid off a pot on the stove.

'It was left over from last night,' he said. 'I heated up some for lunch.'

'Has it been out since last night?'

He just shrugged.

Andie crouched down to find a container in the plastics cupboard. 'Dad, you can't leave meat out overnight, it's not safe.'

'Oh my dear, you worry too much, we're not running a restaurant here.'

Andie didn't want to argue with him. She finally located a container and a lid that matched, and proceeded to transfer the contents of the pot. It was some kind of savoury mince; it looked okay she supposed, she hoped. He was getting worse. Andie didn't think it was dementia as such, more that a kind of atrophy had set in. He couldn't seem to be bothered doing anything, or going anywhere, he just sat mesmerised in front of that massive TV, day and night. Sometimes she worried that he was depressed, perhaps he just needed more outside activities to keep him interested, some company occasionally.

She had tried to talk to Meredith about it, but her older sister acted as though she was the only woman in the history of the world who had to work and organise a family. She couldn't possibly be expected to run around after Dad, she claimed, she had enough on her plate. 'You have no idea what it's like, Andrea, you only have yourself to worry about.'

And a husband. And a business. But they obviously didn't count in Meredith's reckoning. Andie made the weekly trek to see her father, but from what she could make out, her sister only occasionally called in, and Philippa and Tristan rarely saw their grandfather, even though Killara was barely ten minutes from Roseville. Meredith had not ventured far from where she had grown up. Why would you live anywhere else, she maintained. The north shore had the best schools, a better class of neighbours, real estate that consistently appreciated in value. Meredith was a snob; south of the bridge might as well be another country as far as she was concerned.

'Why don't you go watch your show, Dad?' said Andie. 'I'll straighten up in here.'

'No, no,' he said, shuffling over to the sink. 'I'll help you.'

'Dad,' she chided, 'go and sit down.'

He hesitated, looking at her. 'Well, okay, but I'm going to sit down right here. I'm not watching the telly when my girl's visiting.'

She smiled. 'All right, then I'll make you a nice cup of tea.'

Andie put on the kettle, surveying the mess with a heavy heart. Her mother would be horrified. Maybe she should have someone take over a few afternoons a week at the shop; she could come over more often, cook him some decent meals, keep him company. She felt guilty, if he really was only in need of some company, surely it was up to family to provide it. But what if it was more serious – depression, dementia – how much longer could her father be left on his own? Sometimes Andie wondered if it was grief, but if so it was a very delayed reaction. At the time of her mother's death he had appeared to grieve appropriately for a man of his generation, which, granted, was rather restrained. But he still had his work then, he was only in his fifties. Andie had dropped out of uni to care for her mother, but she didn't mind, she didn't even know what she wanted to do with her life at the time. Well, she did, she wanted to cook, but her mother said that when she got married and had a family she'd have plenty of opportunity to cook, for now she should get an education. Faye Lonergan had been very big on her girls getting an education, making up for what she'd missed out on. Her own father had died young, leaving her mother to bring up the family on her own, and Faye had no choice but to leave school as soon as she was old enough to start earning money. She had brains, but she'd never had opportunity. Her daughters were not going to be permitted to squander theirs.

Little wonder that she had a blue fit when Andie announced she would leave uni to care for her. 'Over my dead body,' she had declared, which was an unfortunate choice of words.

'I'm only deferring, Mum,' Andie had insisted. 'I'll go back after . . . as soon as you're better.'

'I'm not going to get better,' she'd returned. 'And I know you, Andrea, you won't go back without me here to push you . . .'

And on she went. Andie knew the lecture by heart, she'd heard it so many times. *A woman needs an education . . . Good looks will only get you so far . . . God knows you weren't blessed with your sister's brains.*

Meredith had just joined a graduate program at a major pharmaceutical company, so she couldn't be expected to help out, her dad had to work to support them, so in the end her mother didn't have any choice but to accept the situation. She lingered on another eight months, and was put to rest beside her son, barely a year after he was buried. But she never stopped saying until her dying breath, almost, that Andie had to return to her studies.

So it was not without some guilt that Andie enrolled in TAFE instead, but she really did not want to go back to uni, the business degree had been her mother's choice, not hers. Her dad quietly encouraged her. 'If we've learned nothing else from these last few horrible years, it's that life's too short, my darling girl. You should do what makes you happy.'

Andie placed his tea in front of him, and turned back to the sink.

'I'm sorry about the mess,' he said. 'I'm not real good with the housework, your mother always looked after all that.'

'I know, Dad. It's okay.' Andie looked over her shoulder. 'Do you miss her?'

'Your mother? Of course,' he said matter-of-factly, stirring his tea.

She leaned back against the sink, wiping her hands on a tea towel. 'Do you ever get sad?'

He blinked, looking up at her. 'It was a long time ago, Andrea.'

'But still . . . losing Brendan, and then Mum, in one year. That's a lot to cope with.'

'It was a lot for you to cope with too,' he said. 'Your mother would have been proud of what you've made of your life.'

Andie doubted that very much. 'I don't know, Dad. She wanted me to go to uni.'

'Still . . .' He stirred his tea. 'She was always worried you were too soft, that you put everyone ahead of yourself. But look at you now, you own your own business. You're successful, and you're happy, aren't you, dear?'

'Of course.'

'That's all she wanted, for you to be happy.'

Andie turned back to the sink. She couldn't remember her mother ever saying anything like that. That she was soft? Weak, maybe. But had she really thought Andie put everyone first? She tried to imagine how she would have put that to her father . . . She tried to imagine her mother being proud of her now.

Andie finished cleaning up the kitchen, topping up her dad's tea while he chatted away in the background. Eventually she wiped down the benches and laid the cloths over the sink.

'I'll have to get going now, Dad.'

'Oh . . .'

She couldn't stand the look in his eyes. She was sure he was just lonely. She wished she didn't live so far away.

'You won't stay to have some dinner?' he said, getting to his feet.

'Oh . . . um . . .'

But he took hold of her hand and squeezed it. 'What am I saying? The footy's on tonight, I'll be no company anyway.'

'What if I make you some dinner before I go?' she suggested.

'No, no, thank you anyway, darling,' he assured her. 'I'm not hungry yet. And you need to get on the road. S'pose himself will be expecting you?'

Her father rarely referred to Ross by name, didn't refer to him at all if he could help it. He hadn't even come to the wedding, said that while he wished her all the happiness in the world, he couldn't on principle – it not being in a church and all. He had lowered his voice, as though his dead wife might hear him. 'Your mother never would have stood for it, you know.'

Oh, Andie knew. But they couldn't have married in the church regardless – Ross was divorced, and he wasn't even Catholic. Besides Andie had long since lapsed, as had Meredith, but nonetheless her sister decided she'd better show solidarity with her father and so declined to attend as well. Ross's kids didn't want to be a part of it, out of deference to their mother, even though she told them she didn't expect that. There were friends who had long since turned their backs on both Andie and Ross, and others who just felt uncomfortable attending their wedding. So in the end, only Jess and Toby and Donna came, and they did their best to be happy for her. Andie tried to hide her disappointment at the time. She had always wanted a proper wedding; it didn't have to be big, she didn't care about that, she wouldn't have wasted her money on anything too extravagant anyway. But the cold little ceremony – if you could call it that – at the registry office didn't feel like a wedding. Ross tried to make it special; he booked a suite for them at the Park Hyatt, had it filled with flowers and French champagne, and she loved him for that . . . but it still didn't feel the same.

'Ross won't be home yet,' said Andie, as they walked up the hall. 'He was going to the gym.'

'What's an old bloke like him doing at a gym? Having a . . . what do they call it? A midlife crisis?'

'Well, if that's what it is, he's doing the right thing and trying to get himself fit.'

'He's probably just trying to keep up with you,' he said, turning to look at her at the front door. 'My beautiful girl.'

*

Ross was hardly too old for the gym, but Andie wasn't going to admit to her father that something about it didn't sit quite right with her either. Ross had allowed his membership to lapse years ago, early in their marriage. At the time he said he wanted to get home to her, not spend another hour after he'd finished at the office, slogging it out in a room with a bunch of sweaty blokes. So why had he suddenly decided to go back to the gym now? Andie had wondered aloud. Ross had dismissed it, saying he'd been feeling a little soft, and at his age he needed to make more of an effort if he was going to keep up with her. And since he'd signed up for Dry July, he was a bit fidgety when he couldn't have a drink after work, so the gym provided a welcome distraction. Which Andie didn't any more, obviously.

Dry July was a whole other thing. Ross liked a drink, but he didn't often drink to excess. So why the need to give it up for a whole month? For a good cause, he'd insisted. Now, Ross was as benevolent as the next overpaid executive, and was more than happy to write a cheque for any number of good causes. But to go to the trouble of getting sponsors and collecting pledges? Not his style at all.

Andie mulled it over all the way home. Jess would probably say she was being paranoid, and she had a point. But Andie couldn't help thinking it had something to do with The Baby Issue. She was beginning to wish she'd never brought it up. Actually that was not altogether true, if she was completely honest. She had to let Ross know what she was thinking sooner or later, she had to plant the seed at least.

They had agreed early in their relationship that there would be no children. At the time Andie wasn't interested; Ross was all she needed. She had felt so lucky to have found someone who loved her the way he did that she had been quite happy to forego the idea of children. And really, they weren't much more than an idea back then. She hadn't ever had a boyfriend who had struck her as good father material, or even good husband material for that matter. And she was still quite young at the time.

Before they got married, Ross had talked her into leaving Lemongrass. He didn't want her showing him and his clients to their table, he wanted her at the table as his partner. Andie all but gave up on being a chef after that. Ross's job involved such long hours they would never have any time together if she worked nights. Their relationship was more important. Sometimes it was hard for her to remember the girl she was back then. Why would it have ruined the relationship to work some nights? Why had she let herself get talked into that?

She did try working days at a couple of different cafés; Ross wasn't particularly thrilled, but he acknowledged that she needed something to occupy her time. She didn't admit to him that making salads and toasted focaccias wasn't exactly rattling her chain either.

Until she became interested in coffee – 'interested' being an understatement; in fact, calling it an understatement was an understatement. Andie became completely obsessed, learning about the different beans, where they were from, which produced the best shot of espresso, the best crema. She practised until her arms ached and she could produce the perfect cup in every variation that enjoyed its fifteen minutes in the spotlight. Cappuccino, latte and espresso endured, and Andie could make them blindfolded. So obsessed did she become, she seriously considered entering a statewide barista competition, but that was when Ross put his foot down. If she won – which Andie thought was highly unlikely, Ross was just being typically biased – anyway, if she won, she'd have to go on to the national championships, which were to be held in Melbourne that year. Ross didn't mind that so much, but if she was successful there, she'd be off overseas after that. And it was only coffee, he'd pointed out.

Ross worked for a global finance company as a management consultant. Andie had never really understood what it was that he actually did; it seemed very abstract when he tried to explain it. She just knew that he went to a lot of meetings, and was always hopping on a plane to somewhere or other for more meetings: team meetings, client meetings, management meetings, breakfast, lunch and dinner meetings. Would their relationship work if they were both off travelling all the time?

'But look, I don't mind taking a back seat for a while,' he insisted. 'I could be a kept man for a change, might be nice,' he added with a glint in his eye. 'Of course, you would have to bring in the kind of money I do, darling. I wouldn't want to cause any problems with Joanna, we'd have to maintain child support at the same rate.'

Andie couldn't hope to match anywhere near what Ross earned, certainly not making coffee. He did have a point. Coffee wasn't that important, and Andie eventually got over her obsession. And soon after that, she got over working in cafés.

She was back to where she started, with no career and nothing to fill in her days. So she tagged along with Ross on his business trips. Andie would shop in Melbourne, relax by the pool in Queensland or Western Australia, more shopping in Hong Kong and Singapore, sightseeing when they were further afield. But filling her days with shopping and facials and massages was, frankly, mindnumbing.

The only thing that did get Andie excited when they were abroad was the food. She would scour travel guides for out-of-the-way restaurants, meet local chefs and discover the regional specialties and delicacies, and then try to reproduce them when she got home. But she was always stymied in her efforts by the dearth of imported ingredients back then.

Then one day Ross came home all fired up about something. He'd had a lunch meeting in Double Bay and had noticed a 'For Sale' sign on the shop next door when he arrived at the restaurant. He proceeded to ask the maître d' about it, for conversation's sake more than anything, he told Andie. Turned out the maître d' was beside himself that the gourmet deli was up for sale. The deli actually supplied many of the restaurants in the immediate area; only for small orders, one-off specialty items, that kind of thing. The location was ideal, the hours regular, and there was already a loyal and built-in clientele.

'It's the perfect fit for your skill set, Andie,' Ross announced.

'What?' she said, confused.

'Isn't it obvious?' he said. 'You're a chef, it's a gourmet deli. It's ideal.'

'But Ross, my training didn't prepare me for running a shop, just because it sells food.'

'You also did two whole years of a business degree, don't forget.'

'How could I forget, I hated it.'

'Oh,' he chided, 'that was only because it wasn't your choice.'

'No, Ross —'

'Just hear me out,' he interrupted her. 'I was thinking what a great avenue this would be for you to source ingredients from overseas. You're always saying you can't get what you need here.'

Andie was listening.

'I'm only suggesting that we go and take a look,' he said, drawing her into his arms. 'What's the harm in that?'

She shrugged. 'I suppose . . .'

When she stepped inside the shop door a little bell rang, and Andie started to fall in love from that moment. It was a bigger space than she had pictured in her mind. The curved glass display counter stretched the length of the shop, as expected, but there was a lot of floor space that wasn't being fully utilised. Shelving units and racks cluttered the area, stocked with the kind of ingredients that used to be considered exotic – tins of broad beans and sauerkraut, jars of artichokes and packets of couscous – but which were all readily available from supermarkets now, at probably a fraction of the price. What they really needed to stock were ingredients you couldn't get anywhere else, at least not around here, like truffle oil, tamarind paste, pomegranate molasses . . . Andie wandered through the shop, her head filling with ideas. The counter was enormous, there was plenty of room for a coffee machine. She knew this area was probably already overcaffeinated, but being able to pick up a takeaway coffee with your deli order might just work. And if she cleared out some of these shelves, there would be plenty of room for a couple of small tables, should anyone want to take a load off. The back of the shop was, again, much bigger than she expected. A storeroom, small laundry and toilet all came off a large space with kitchen facilities and an office area. It wasn't a commercial kitchen, but it was well-equipped, and it presented Andie with possibilities . . .

Then it hit her – this would be entirely her own, she could do what she wanted, carve out something for herself. She had always been vaguely uncomfortable about being a kept woman, it went against the grain of everything her mother had tried to impress upon her. She had a little money saved, so she could finance part of the purchase herself, and Ross was happy to make up the difference. Andie agreed, as long as it was only a loan. The shop was so successful that she paid him back, with interest, after a few years. Ross said it was one of the better investments he had ever made.

The Corner Gourmet was a thriving, happy little place to work, and Andie had plenty of challenges to keep her interested in the first few years. She was clearly prone to obsessions – cheese became her first at the deli, then bread, organic produce, truffles, foie gras . . . She held tasting nights that were a huge success, and gave her the chance to connect with other foodies from the local area. They began swapping recipes and ideas, and gradually Andie focused on sourcing rare and unusual ingredients from importers, as well as stocking sweets and delicacies from all across Sydney and beyond. Macarons had been the latest fad, again courtesy of *MasterChef*, but their star was already beginning to wane.

And lately Andie had felt her own interest waning – there weren't any new challenges, only variations on the same theme. There was a huge difference between supplying and creating; and Andie missed creating. The kitchen wasn't equipped to handle much more than takeaway salads, sometimes soup in the winter. She got caught up for a time making sauces, pesto, relishes, that kind of thing, but while they were a hit, she couldn't stock them in viable quantities or on a regular basis. Andie was becoming frustrated by the limitations, being so close, close enough to almost taste the dishes her customers would tell her about, or that the chefs along the strip were adding to their menus. She'd try things in her own kitchen, but half the time Ross had already eaten out, or he'd come home late and the food would be spoiled. So then Andie stopped cooking much at all.

She was beginning to feel like she was just an accessory to Ross's life. She didn't tell him that, it would only get him worked up, and he'd start trying to solve the problem. It wasn't his responsibility. She had to find her own way . . .

Then something strange began to happen. Slowly, intermittently, and quite unexpectedly, Andie began to hear her biological clock ticking away quietly in the background. She ignored it at first, she refused to be that cliché; she did not need to have a baby to be complete. She just needed goals, direction . . . But the ticking became louder, compelling her, creating an urge she had never felt before; it was almost primal. All of a sudden Andie was seeing babies everywhere – and they really did seem to be everywhere: at the gym, in every café and restaurant, parks and shops and beaches. Whenever a pram nosed its way through the door of the deli, Andie found herself drawn to it, barely noticing the mother struggling to manoeuvre it while she cooed and made faces, doing that weird voice thing that adults reverted to when they talked to babies, the emphasis all distorted. 'Aren't *you* a beautiful girl, oh *yes* you *are*!'

Andie had always believed she could talk to Ross about anything, and she certainly wasn't worried about broaching the subject of babies with him. He was dismissive at first, but then he became angry when she persisted. This was not part of the deal, he said. 'I've already had my family, I'm done.'

'But I haven't had mine.'

'Well, you made that choice back when you married me, you can't renege now.'

'So there's no room for changing my mind?' Andie had declared. 'People do change their minds you know, Ross. People change, they grow up. They want different things.'

'So you're saying you want something different to this marriage?'

The resolve in his tone had shocked Andie at first. What exactly was he suggesting? When the shock subsided, she found a dozen reasons to explain away his attitude. He just needed time, he loved her, he had always wanted her to have whatever made her happy . . . hadn't he?

Potts Point

Andie had enjoyed a good run back across the bridge, going against most of the peak-hour traffic. She'd called in to her favourite butcher to pick up the lamb shanks she'd ordered earlier – they were Ross's favourite, and he'd promised to be home at a reasonable hour this evening so they could have a quiet night, just the two of them. He'd even had his secretary put it in his schedule so that nothing would get in the way. They hadn't had much time together lately, and they hadn't had sex for quite a while . . . Andie worked out it must have been weeks. Ross always seemed so tired, and it was beginning to niggle. She'd never thought very much about the consequences of marrying a man who was older; Ross had always been so vital, his sex drive rapacious. But Andie didn't really know what happened to men in their fifties. Maybe their libidos did slow down, though popular wisdom would have it otherwise.

As she walked into the apartment, she tossed the keys on the hall table and kicked off her shoes, glancing at the clock on the wall. She had to get dinner on straightaway, lamb shanks needed to cook slowly. She dusted them with flour before setting them to fry gently in a heavy pan, while she chopped onion and celery and carrot. She added the vegetables to the pan along with crushed garlic and her own homemade stock that she always kept on hand, plus a little wine and some fresh herbs. Andie sealed the pot and set the heat low, glancing at the clock again. They wouldn't need to be touched for at least an hour, she'd do the mash later. She wondered how much longer Ross was likely to be. Whatever, it was wine o'clock and there wasn't any point in waiting for him, he wasn't drinking anyhow.

She poured herself a glass of wine and walked over to the window. Their apartment was part of an old warehouse complex that had been gutted and reconfigured into a lofty, open-plan space. Ross had fallen in love with it immediately. He had been so desperate to get away from four-bed two-bath, lawn-mowing, gutter-cleaning, suffocating suburbia, as he described it.

Andie, on the other hand, had taken a while to get used to living in Potts Point, which was Kings Cross by any other name. But she did appreciate the convenience, though she craved peace and quiet occasionally. They used to get away for weekends whenever they could, down the coast, to the mountains or the Southern Highlands. They always ate out, trying new places, or returning to old favourites. They had even talked about moving away from Sydney when Ross retired, Andie opening her own place . . . But they hadn't had a weekend away in ages.

Andie sipped her wine, gazing out the window across rows of terraces towards the city skyline. Lately her life felt like she was just passing the time. She knew it was affecting Ross too. She probably wasn't much fun to be around, no wonder he'd joined the gym. They were in a strange, unsettled, uncomfortable place, and Andie didn't like it. She wanted it back the way it was.

But she also wanted a baby.

Maybe there had been an agreement, but Andie had given up her dreams again and again for the good of their relationship, wasn't it time for some compromise on his part?

She heard a noise in the outer hall and turned around to see Ross letting himself in through the door. He was still in his exercise clothes, juggling his gym bag and his briefcase as he fumbled to extract the key from the lock.

'Hi darling,' he said without looking up, in that expansive, commanding voice of his that still sent a shiver up her spine. 'Sorry I'm late. Something smells good.'

Andie took a deep breath as she approached him. She had to make an effort, reconnect . . .

'Hello you,' she smiled, drawing her arms around his neck, but he pulled back.

'Andie, believe me, you don't want to get any closer until I've had a shower.'

She reached up and brushed her lips against his. 'I could join you.'

Now he physically shrank from her, taking a step back. 'I'm all sweaty from the gym, I just want to get clean.'

'But I don't mind getting dirty.'

He looked slightly vexed at that. 'Please, Andie, can you just give me one frigging minute to myself?'

She stepped back immediately. 'Of course.' What the hell?

'Won't be long,' he called, striding away from her across the living room to the bedroom.

Andie walked back to the kitchen bench, picked up her glass and drained it. What was that about? The phone rang and she reached over to pick it up from its dock.

'Hello?'

'Hi, Andie, it's Joanna.'

'Oh, hi.' She still felt nervous talking to Joanna, like she was talking to the principal at school. A reasonable, quite pleasant type of principal, but the person in authority nonetheless. Andie always felt young and inexperienced, and somewhat awkward, like she'd been caught out where she shouldn't be. Fooling around with her husband, to be precise.

'I'm returning your call,' Joanna prompted her. 'From earlier today?'

'Oh, yes, of course.' Andie cleared her throat. 'I was ringing to let you know . . . Well, the thing is, I don't think I can make it to the christening on Sunday.'

'And Ross?'

'Oh, no, of course he'll be there,' Andie said quickly. 'He wouldn't miss it for the world.'

'I should hope not.'

She took a breath. 'It's just . . . well, I don't know if it's my place . . . you know, it's a family thing.'

The truth was, Lauren had never warmed to Andie the way the other two had. Andie was good mates with Brooke and Matty now, that's all she'd ever tried to be. But Lauren had never dropped her guard. She was older when the split happened, she was close to her mother and, as the eldest, extremely protective of her. Andie envied their relationship and she respected it, she would never have done anything to undermine it.

There was a measured pause before Joanna responded. 'Well, whatever you think's best.'

Good, that was good. It's not as though Andie expected Joanna to talk her out of it. Why would she? 'So, anyway, I wanted to send a platter —'

'We're having it catered.'

'Still, I'd like to contribute.'

'Andie, it's being catered,' Joanna repeated calmly. 'I assume you've organised the gift? Ross certainly wouldn't have thought to.'

'No . . . I mean yes, of course, there's a gift.'

'Then, there you are, you've contributed. Lauren will appreciate it.'

Andie suddenly had the urge to ask Joanna what she would make of Ross's behaviour – had he had periods when he'd withdrawn from her? Joined the gym out of the blue, given up drinking? Did any of that happen before he left . . .

Hell, where did that come from?

'Was there something else, Andie?' Joanna was asking.

'No, no, that's it. I'll let you go,' she said quickly. 'Thanks.'

Ross wandered out into the living room as she hung up. He was rubbing his head with a towel, making his hair stick out in all directions. It made him look boyish, even at his age. Blond hair didn't show the grey much so he really didn't look like he was over fifty. He was still a handsome man, his eyes as blue as the first time they looked into hers when he asked her for her name.

'Feel better now?' Andie asked him tentatively.

He smiled, walking towards her. 'Much better, thank you.' He sighed loudly as he drew her into his arms. 'So, where were we?' he murmured as his lips came down on hers and he kissed her soundly.

And just like that, it was over. This was happening too often lately, small flare-ups that went nowhere, truncated discussions –

especially anything to do with a baby – and just general avoidance of conflict, and each other. It wasn't only him, Andie knew she was guilty of it as well.

'How was your day?' he asked after a while, drawing back to look at her. 'Did you see your dad?'

'Hm.'

'How is he?'

Andie sighed. 'The same. I think he's just lonely. I'm wondering if I should go over more often, maybe have dinner with him one night a week.'

'You should, you know,' he said. 'That's a good idea, actually.'

'You wouldn't mind?'

'Of course not.' He released her and walked around the kitchen bench. 'I have to work back so often lately, you might as well go and keep your old man company.' He opened the fridge door and peered in. 'Was that the phone I heard before?'

'Oh, yes, it was Joanna.'

He looked back at her, frowning. 'What did she want?'

'It was about the christening,' said Andie.

He picked up the bottle she'd already opened. 'Do you want a top-up?'

'Oh, not if you're not drinking.'

'I'm not drinking, darling, but that's no reason for you not to.'

'Okay.' She gave him a smile, sliding her glass across the benchtop towards him. 'Thanks.'

Ross poured the wine. 'So, what about the christening?'

Andie hesitated. 'Oh, well, Joanna was returning my call, actually.'

He raised an eyebrow, waiting for her to go on.

'I phoned her earlier today, she was busy.'

'Andie, would you just get to the point?'

She took a breath. 'I was just letting her know that I don't think I'll go on Sunday.'

'What?' He passed her refilled glass back to her.

'I think,' Andie said slowly, 'that this is a family occasion —'

'Oh, for Chrissakes, not this again, Andie?'

She flinched.

'I'm so tired of going over the same ground every single time,' he said. 'You've known these people for ten years. You are my wife, Emily is your step-granddaughter.'

Andie groaned inwardly. She would never forget a particularly angry dressing-down she received from Joanna after she'd overheard Brooke referring to Andie as her stepmother. 'I don't know what you're telling them, but you are not my children's step*mother*,' she had said through barely-gritted teeth. 'Just because their father decided to update his wife doesn't automatically give you quasi-mother status with his kids. If I died, then maybe. If the kids were younger, and they were splitting their time equally between us, perhaps. However, my children have a mother, who has, incidentally, never walked out on them. Their father's new wife does not, never will have, and moreover doesn't *need* to have a maternal relationship with them. It's insulting to me, and completely unnecessary.'

'Ross, I think calling her my step-granddaughter is a bit artificial,' Andie said carefully. 'I'm no blood relation whatsoever to the baby, and Lauren and I aren't even that close.'

'And you're not likely to get close if you don't bother to show up for her daughter's christening!' he cried, glaring at her.

Andie wanted to say she thought it was a bit late to be expecting them to get close. But she kept that thought to herself, she didn't want to make him any more annoyed than he obviously already was. He stood for a moment, his head bowed, cupping his forehead in his hand, before finally he let out a deep sigh and looked up at her again.

'You are my wife,' he said, but his tone was gentler now. 'You are my family, you belong with me at something like this. Please come, Andie, I feel bereft when you're not beside me.'

Andie softened. Ross had a way with words, he could always talk her into anything. She walked around the bench and into his open arms. She leaned her head against his chest, she could feel his heart drumming.

She would go to the christening. Of course she would go . . . she'd do exactly what Ross asked of her. Just as she always had.

Sunday

'Do you want me to let you out here?' Ross asked, slowing the car as they went to drive by the church. 'I reckon I'll have to park at least a couple of blocks away.'

Andie surveyed the gathering on the church steps and breathed a sigh of relief. The blue suit had been the right choice; she didn't want to compete with anyone or stand out, but she didn't want to look inappropriate either. And she most certainly did not want to have to hover at the edges alone waiting for Ross to join her.

'Oh, no, I'll stick with you, thanks,' she told him.

He eventually found a park and took hold of her hand as they walked along the tree-lined streets back to the church. As they drew closer Joanna broke through a gap in the crowd, coming towards them. 'Ross, good, you're here.'

He dropped Andie's hand and stepped forward to kiss Joanna on the cheek. All very modern and amicable.

'Lauren has been asking for you,' said Joanna.

'I'm not late, am I?' Ross frowned, consulting his watch.

'No, you're not late,' Joanna assured him, taking him by the arm, 'but you know your daughter. Come on, let's find her so she can relax and we can get this show on the road.' Finally, she turned to Andie. 'Hello, Andie. You decided to join us after all?'

Andie's face dropped. Ross promised he was going to give her a call. 'Didn't you tell Joanna I was coming?' she asked him.

'Yes, he did,' Joanna assured her. 'I'm just saying . . . nice that you could join us. Now let's find Lauren.'

She drew Ross with her, her hand cupping his elbow, as Andie followed in their wake. She remembered why she generally didn't like going to these affairs. Lauren's wedding had been the worst, because she actually told her father point-blank that she didn't want Andie there. That had been fine with Andie, considering the way Lauren felt about her; the tension had barely lifted since the property settlement had been finalised, and the children subsequently reassured that their mother wasn't being ripped off. Ross was adamant, however, and had gone so far as to say that he would not go to the wedding without Andie. She loved him for that, she just wished he would have made his stand over something else. Joanna had stepped in at that point and assured Lauren that it was the right thing to do, and that she was completely fine with it.

Of course she was. Ross was part of the bridal party, naturally, so he had to escort his daughter to the wedding, while Andie had to make her own way to the church, and sit alone. Between the ceremony and the reception, Ross remained with the bridal party for the extended photo shoot, while Andie waited it out at a nearby café. She didn't feel comfortable joining the other guests at the bar in the reception venue; she didn't know anyone, the only people she did know were in the bridal party. And of course Ross was required to sit at the bridal table, so Andie had been put on the singles' table. The entire thing had been excruciating – especially when anybody asked which side of the family she was with.

Time passed, things had gradually become more relaxed, but it was still difficult at more formal family occasions, where Ross had a role but Andie did not.

'Dad, you made it,' Lauren exclaimed as they walked up the aisle of the church towards her.

'I'm not late,' Ross insisted with an indulgent smile as he received her hug. 'What are you all stressing about?' He glanced down at the pram. 'Look at Emily, she's not bothered.'

Emily was sound asleep, and blissfully unaware, but everyone drew closer to gaze down at her. She was a very pretty baby; on the couple of occasions Andie had been around her, she always seemed placid and contented. Watching her now, Andie had to resist the urge to pick her up, bury her face in her neck and take in a deep breath. That baby smell was almost irresistible.

'Look how chilled she is,' Ross remarked.

'Hm, and now I'm going to have to wake her,' said Lauren.

'Why not just leave her sleeping?' said James.

'I'd rather get her up now, than just before she has her head dunked in water,' Lauren explained to her husband. 'I want to prepare her.'

'How do you plan to do that?' Ross asked. 'Are you going to give her a pep talk?'

'No, Dad,' Lauren chided. 'I'm just saying it won't be such a shock if she's already awake.'

She stooped to retrieve Emily from the pram, turning immediately to place her in Ross's arms. He was taken aback for a moment, but then his face broke into a broad smile as he gazed proudly down at his granddaughter.

Andie watched him, feeling torn. With any other baby she'd have swooped by now, cooing and patting and doing that voice thing. But she felt self-conscious – if she cooed too much, they might all think she was just putting it on. Then again, if she didn't coo at all, they might think she was uninterested. Andie would dearly love to have a cuddle of the baby, but that would probably make everyone feel uncomfortable. Certainly Lauren. And she doubted Joanna would enjoy the picture of her grandchild in the arms of her ex-husband's current wife. There was that expression again. But if Andie didn't ask if she could hold the baby, they might all think that she was cold and unfeeling.

Years ago, after the debacle of Lauren's wedding, Ross had tried to reassure her that it wouldn't always be this complicated.

No, clearly it could get even worse.

'All right, everyone, we'd best be seated,' said Joanna, taking charge as she usually did. 'Lauren and James and the godparents are in the front pew, of course. Family should sit directly behind.'

Oh, not again. Andie might as well walk to the back of the church now.

'Okay,' Ross was saying, 'so Andie and I will sit the next row back.'

Something passed across Joanna's face, but it was fleeting. 'Good, we're all set then.' She peered down the aisle. 'I better go see where Matty and Brooke have got to.'

Ross stood back for Andie to go ahead of him into the pew, and they sat down. She reached over and gave his hand a quick squeeze, and he glanced sideways and winked at her.

The ceremony proceeded as usual, with the requisite amount of mumbo jumbo, as Ross would put it. Losing his religion was part and parcel of moving out of the suburbs. Not that he'd ever been particularly devout, he'd told Andie back then. The way he saw it, the church seemed to function as little more than an ideal venue for important ceremonies, what with the acoustics and ample seating, and an MC on tap. And the stained glass added a touch of class to the photos. He and Joanna were married in a church – so whatever Andie's mother might have thought, much good it did them – and the kids had all been baptised. Apparently Ross had baulked at that at the time, but Joanna had insisted it was the done thing. They never set foot in the church much outside of those occasions, except for funerals. Again, it was all about the venue.

As Andie watched the ceremony, it did seem to have more than its fair share of mumbo jumbo – the priest prancing around shaking the incense thing, the candle lighting, the splashing of the magic 'holy' water on the baby's head. And these modern, cyber-connected, smartphone-wielding people were transfixed. There was something comforting in the ritual, something transcendent. Andie didn't begrudge them that.

The ceremony finally drew to an end, and Lauren rounded up all the usual suspects for a photo shoot around the baptismal font. The godparents with the baby, the parents and the godparents with the baby. The grandparents, the godparents, and the parents and uncle and aunty – all in various configurations – with the baby. Andie watched patiently from her pew. Ross looked fit and young for a grandfather; as did Joanna for a grandmother. But they were grandparents nonetheless, they would never be mistaken for Emily's parents. Ross looked at the baby the way a grandfather would, full of a kind of bemused pride, holding her in a slightly awkward fashion, relieved to pass her on. It dawned on Andie there and then, under the light filtering through the stained glass window, that Ross was at a different stage of his life. Entirely. She'd never been so aware that they were from different generations. And even if he gave in and agreed to let her have a baby, there was no guarantee he'd come around once it was born. So where did that leave Andie? Bringing up a child with a disinterested, detached father, or not having a baby at all?

'Now, I'd like the whole family all together,' said Lauren. 'Andie?'

She stirred. 'Yes?'

'Could you take the photo? That way we won't have to leave anyone out.'

'Of course.'

Outside the church, Andie hovered at the edge of the crowd, waiting for Ross as he shook hands with old friends and greeted relatives from the extended family. Most of them would be going back to the house. Andie was dreading it already – she thought about the dozens of photos that would be taken, how many times she would have to sidle away out of frame, how Joanna and Ross's old friends were never completely comfortable around her. They weren't rude; they were, in fact, incredibly polite, excruciatingly polite – they really didn't know how they were supposed to behave around her, particularly in Joanna's house. It was all a bit modern for them, and it was beginning to feel a bit modern for Andie.

The hard cold fact was she wasn't, and never would be, part of this family. They were still a unit, Andie was the interloper. And the other hard cold fact that just hit her was that she didn't have a family of her own. She still had her father, and Meredith, but without Brendan, without their mother, they were only a shadow, a remnant of a family that had once been.

So it was just her and Ross, and as much as he tried to insist she was his family, that didn't make it so. How could they be a family? They were a couple, two adults who had made a commitment to each other. That wasn't a family.

'I think I might not stay . . .' Andie finally spoke up on the drive to Joanna's.

'Hm?'

'I think I might not stay when we get to the house,' she said. 'I'm getting an awful headache —'

'You probably just need a coffee.'

'I had one before I left home.'

'Then you must be hungry.'

'Ross,' she said finally, a quiver of frustration coming into her voice.

'What?' he glanced at her briefly before returning his attention to the road.

'I just . . . The thing is, I was there for the important part. You know you never give me credit . . .' She paused.

'Are you really getting a headache?' he asked tersely.

'I am, actually. I'm getting a bit of a stress headache. From all the —'

'Stress?' he finished for her. 'What stress, Andie? Everyone was perfectly pleasant to you.'

She took a breath. 'Yes they were. But you don't see it from my perspective —'

'I made sure you and I sat together.'

'I know, and I appreciate that you did that, I really do,' she said. 'But all your relatives and old friends are going to be there . . .'

'Well, what did you expect?' Ross said, with growing irritation. 'Christ, Andie, we're old news. You think anyone even cares any more?'

Oh, she knew they did.

'Look, it's a family occasion,' she persisted.

'And you are my family.'

'We're not a family!' she cried.

Her voice reverberated in the car as Ross pulled over to the side of the road, turning to face her. 'What's that supposed to mean?'

'You and Joanna and your kids are still a family, Lauren and James and Emily are a family . . .'

He didn't say anything. He was clenching the wheel with one hand, rubbing his eyes with the other.

'So here we go again,' he muttered.

'Well, we haven't dealt with it,' said Andie. 'You won't talk about it.'

'Because there's nothing to talk about.'

'How can you say that?'

'We made an agreement,' he said grimly. 'You married me on the basis of that agreement.'

'You're saying that's the basis of our marriage?'

'Don't twist my words.'

'I didn't twist anything. That's what you're saying.'

'And you're behaving like a spoilt brat who can't get her own way,' he said harshly.

Andie blinked. She could feel the ache rising in her chest, her throat tightening.

'Look, I'm sorry, I didn't mean that.' He sighed. 'It's just that you're always flitting from one thing to the next —'

'What?' she said in disbelief. 'Flitting?'

'Exactly. From restaurants to cafés, from being a chef to a hostess to a barista, and now you're bored with the deli so you want a baby. And how long do you think it'll take before you get bored with that?'

Now it was his voice reverberating in the car.

'That's what you think of me?' said Andie, her own voice barely making it out of her throat.

'The evidence is pretty compelling.'

'And that's why you won't have a baby with me?'

He breathed out loudly. 'It was never part of the plan, Andie.'

They sat in silence. Andie's throat was aching, but she was not going to cry in front of him.

'Look, I'm expected,' Ross said eventually. 'You don't have to come. You take the car, I'll get a cab home later.'

*

Joanna walked around the terrace, picking up empty glasses, the odd cake plate, and placing them on a tray, slowly and deliberately taking her time. She glanced intermittently towards the house, watching Ross wandering around the empty rooms, the other guests having taken their leave a while ago now. He obviously didn't regard himself as a guest, even though this was Joanna's house and he'd never lived here. But he'd lingered on, talking to the kids, until Lauren and James left to get the baby home and settled, Matty went off to meet up with some friends, and Brooke had finally disappeared up to her room. What was he doing hanging around? When was he going to get the hint and just go home?

He finally meandered over to the drinks cabinet and reached for the Scotch bottle. Joanna groaned, picking up the tray and making her way inside.

'Oh, do you want a hand with that?' he asked, as she walked across to the kitchen.

'No, got it, thanks,' she said, depositing the tray on the bench.

'I was just helping myself to a drink,' he added.

So she'd noticed.

'Can I get you one?'

'No thanks,' she said, as she began to clear the tray. 'Shouldn't you be getting home, you said Andie had a headache?'

'Then no reason to be rushing home,' he said with a grin.

Inappropriate, Ross. Joanna sighed inwardly.

He strolled over and leaned against the bench, watching her stack the dishwasher. 'I suppose you guessed that Andie and I had words?'

No, she hadn't guessed. Surprise as it might be to Ross, what went on between him and Andie was not actually at the forefront of her mind.

'In the car, on the way here,' he said. 'You know, after the church.'

'Hm.'

Was he waiting for her to ask what happened? Seriously?

'Andie wants a baby.'

Joanna paused, holding a dish midair. Now she needed a drink.

'She never wanted one before,' Ross continued, uninvited. 'In fact, she was the one who insisted we not have kids.'

Joanna resumed stacking the dishwasher. She knew she was only going to get one side of this. And that was one more side than she cared to have. 'I would have thought that would be okay with you, Andie not wanting kids.'

'Yeah, of course, I've had my kids. So I was kind of glad that she felt that way.'

Why Ross imagined Joanna wanted to hear any of this was beyond her. Part of his incessantly self-absorbed charm, she supposed. It had been such a relief once Matty had finished school, when there was no more negotiating weekends and holidays and child support and all the rest. The kids had their own relationship with him now, made their own plans, Joanna kept out of it. She had lost a lot of respect for Ross during the split, some of the things he had done were frankly unforgivable. But she'd largely put all that behind her, for the sake of the children, and for the sake of peace. Once the divorce was final and the property was settled and there was nothing left to haggle over, Joanna had made a concerted effort to get along. But she really didn't think that meant having to counsel Ross on his relationship woes.

'Now I'm a grandfather,' he went on, oblivious, 'having another baby is the last thing on my mind.'

'Have you told Andie that?' She was, after all, the one he should be talking to.

'Of course,' he said. 'But I'm also trying to be understanding. You want to know what I really think?'

No, but he was going to tell her anyway.

'I think she's just restless, doesn't know what to do with herself next.'

Joanna looked at him. 'She wants to give up the shop?'

'Well, not that she's said in so many words. But, if she wants a baby, she can't be too interested in running a business.'

'God, Ross, you sound like a caveman.'

He blinked. 'What?'

'You deal with women who run multinational corporations, I assume some of them have children?'

'It's not the same thing,' he said. 'Andie's never said anything about wanting kids, never been interested. And she has tended to flitter around trying out different things. It just feels to me like a baby is the next whim.'

Joanna shook her head. 'I sincerely hope you think better of her than that.'

He looked vaguely uncomfortable.

'Ross, it's not unusual for a woman to get to a certain age and have maternal urges she hasn't had before. She couldn't have known in her twenties that she'd want to have a baby ten years later.'

'But she made an agreement.'

'Well, so? You made an agreement to stay with me till death do us part.'

He winced. 'Joanna . . .'

'All I'm saying is that people change, Ross. They break "agreements", they change their minds, they want different things.'

'So you think we should have a baby?'

Good grief, heaven forbid. 'Ross, it's actually none of my business,' said Joanna. 'I'm just saying that you shouldn't dismiss Andie's desire for a baby like that. It isn't fair. She gave up a lot for you . . . her career . . .'

'I gave up a lot for her.'

Joanna sighed. She really needed a drink now. She crossed to the fridge.

'Well, I did,' he persisted. 'You think it was easy for me to walk away from my family?'

'No one was forcing you, Ross.'

'I know that, I'm just saying . . .'

She picked up a bottle of wine and turned to look at him, leaning back against the fridge door to close it. 'Look, Ross, you really should be having this conversation with Andie, not me.'

'Trying to get rid of me, much?'

When did he start talking like that? What had he said about the baby earlier, that she was 'chilled'? He wasn't around the kids enough to be picking it up from them.

'So you think I should encourage her to go back to her career?' he was saying.

Joanna poured herself a glass of wine. 'I don't really have an opinion, Ross,' she said wearily. 'I don't know Andie all that well. I don't know what she wants. Maybe you should ask her.' She threw back half the glass.

'I guess though, if she had some goals . . .' he muttered half to himself. 'Something more fulfilling to work towards.' He looked up with a broad smile. 'It certainly gave you a new lease on life when you went back to work after we split.'

Joanna drained the rest of her glass. 'So, I'll call you a cab?'

The Corner Gourmet

'Sorry to make you wait back,' said Andie as she came through the door, setting off the bell.

'Are you kidding?' Jess exclaimed. 'We haven't caught up in ages. I even ducked out and bought some wine earlier,' she added.

Andie smiled. 'I brought some too.' She stood a cooler bag on the counter and drew out a bottle.

'Ooh, champagne,' Jess cooed, inspecting the label. 'And the good stuff. What's going on? Are we celebrating something?'

'I hope so,' said Andie.

'You're pregnant?' Jess gasped.

Andie ignored the faint pang she felt in her heart. 'Would I be drinking champagne?' she said.

'Hm, good point. And it would have been pretty quick,' said Jess, 'seeing as last I heard, Ross hadn't even agreed to it.'

Andie tore the foil away from the neck of the bottle and changed the subject. 'So, here's the thing,' she said, popping the cork. 'I am going back to work . . . as a chef . . . in a restaurant!'

She watched Jess's face for signs of excitement, something. But she just looked confused.

'What?'

'I'm going to be a chef again,' said Andie as she poured the champagne into flutes she'd brought from home. She handed Jess a glass and held up her own in a toast. 'Shall we drink to it?'

'But I don't understand exactly what we're drinking to.'

'My new career, or my reincarnated one, I should probably say.' Andie was still holding her glass up, looking at Jess expectantly. 'What's wrong?'

She sighed loudly. 'Oh, I'm happy for you, really, I am, Andie, I'm just being selfish. I mean, I understand, I do, I know you haven't been all that interested in the shop for a while, it hasn't been exactly fulfilling, so I'm glad really, I am genuinely happy for you, couldn't be happier. I just . . . well, it's completely selfish, me expecting this place to just be here forever, so I've got work whenever I want it —'

'Jess —'

'I've even daydreamed about taking over when you did have a baby, you know, just temporarily, so you could have maternity leave without worrying about the place. But I'm jumping the gun —'

'You think?'

Jess finally looked at Andie, taking a breath. 'It's just sometimes I get tired of always stepping into someone else's role, never being able to do my own thing.'

The casual arrangement she'd enjoyed at the shop had allowed Jess to build up a solid, varied résumé over the years, and she had a good reputation in the industry as an experienced, reliable chef. But she wasn't a star, she didn't have a name, she wasn't exactly sought after. She had got by the last few years mostly standing in for staff who were on leave – a three-month stint here, a regular weekend gig there. She had occasionally been given head chef duties at small but respected restaurants, when the owner-chef took a night off and needed someone with enough experience to run the restaurant in his absence. But if she wanted to work full-time as a chef, the only recourse left to her now was to open her own place. But she didn't have the money, and as there were more restaurants closing than opening, she wouldn't have a hope of getting financed.

'Well, this is perfect,' Andie was saying.

'What are you talking about?'

'You may just get the chance to do your own thing, because I wanted to ask you if you'd be interested in taking over here.'

Jess blinked. 'What?'

'If I'm working in a restaurant, I can't give enough time to this place. I need someone to manage it for me.'

'You're not going to sell it?'

'No, of course not.'

Jess let out a loud sigh. 'Well, that's a relief. I'll totally drink to that,' she said, raising her glass to clink it against Andie's.

'It's about time,' said Andie. 'I was getting RSI holding my glass up.'

'Okay, so tell me the whole story. You're going back to being a chef?'

'It's probably more accurate to say that I'm starting over,' said Andie. 'All I ever did was work in a few of those horrible club kitchens, remember, right after we graduated? When I was at Lemongrass, I used to stand watching them in the kitchen sometimes, breathing in the wonderful smells, feeling the nervous energy, aching to dive in and be part of it . . .'

'I hate to put a dampener on it, but it's not all it's cut out to be,' said Jess. 'The hours are long, the work is backbreakingly hard. All these celebrity chef shows have made people think it's glamorous, but it's not.'

Andie had folded her arms while she waited for Jess to finish. 'Allow me to introduce myself, I believe we did our training together, as chefs?'

'Sorry.'

'Come on, Jess, I'm not jumping on the latest bandwagon. You know I've wanted to do this since I was a girl.'

'I know, but you still have to be realistic. It's hard enough for me to get regular work, and I've kept my hand in all these years. There aren't that many opportunities out there. At least not in the really good places.'

'I realise, but I'll be going in at entry level, for one thing.' She hesitated before adding, 'And Ross has contacts, he's sure he can find me something.'

Jess blinked. 'Ross is going to help you get a job in a restaurant?'

'I know, isn't it great?' said Andie.

'But he's never been keen about you working nights, the whole deal.'

'And he's realised how selfish he's been. Isn't that great?' she repeated, topping up their glasses.

Jess narrowed her gaze. 'Andie, tell me the truth, is this some kind of consolation prize? Ross'll let you work in a restaurant if you drop the baby idea?'

'Jess,' she chided, 'I dropped the baby idea all on my own.'

'You did?'

Andie nodded. 'We were at the christening yesterday —'

'Oh, that's right,' said Jess. 'Wow, must have been some christening to put you off having a baby.'

Andie smiled. 'No, it was a perfectly nice christening. But I was watching Ross, holding his grandchild. His *grandchild*. And he looked like a granddad – I don't mean he looked old, there was just a . . . a generational thing, I guess you'd call it. His kids are adults now, his baby days are over. I don't think it's fair to ask him to go back to that.'

'But what about what's fair to you?'

'Well, Jess, the problem is, it takes two people to make a baby,' she said. 'And I'm the one who changed my mind. You might think he's being selfish, but I'm being just as selfish expecting him to switch suddenly. Admit it, Jess, if this situation was reversed, you would be totally on my side.'

'I'd be totally on your side whatever.'

Andie smiled then. 'I know, and you should realise that sometimes, and give Ross a break.'

'Oh, if I must,' Jess sighed dramatically, a glint in her eye. 'I just hope you're really okay with this. I don't get the whole baby craving thing myself, but you seemed to have it pretty bad.'

'You haven't ever felt even a slight flutter?' Andie asked her.

'God help me, no,' she said, draining her glass.

'What if the right guy came along?'

'One who can ejaculate, you mean?' said Jess. 'Most of them seem to be able to manage that without too much trouble.'

Andie grinned. 'I mean, someone you could see yourself having a child with,' she clarified.

'I can't see myself with a child, whether or not there's a bloke around has little to do with it.'

'You feel that strongly?'

Jess nodded. 'Look at Donna, she's constantly on a short leash, everything revolves around Max. And don't get me wrong, that's great for her and Toby, if that's what they want. But I enjoy my freedom too much . . . staying out late, sleeping in late, going out for a coffee because I feel like a coffee, not because it fits around the sleep cycle of a three year old.' She shrugged. 'Maybe I'm just selfish, I don't know.'

'It's not selfish to know what you want,' said Andie. 'It's smart. You know, the catchcry these days is that you can have it all, but you can't. Something or someone always misses out. I could probably guilt or harass Ross into having a baby with me, and then he'd be unhappy. I do really want a baby, but a lot of women really want babies and can't have them. Either they don't have a partner, or they have fertility issues . . . For Ross and me it's a timing problem. It isn't his fault, and he's always been one hundred per cent honest about it.'

'I suppose,' Jess muttered.

'The thing is, I could spend the next part of my life feeling sad and bereft that I can't have a baby, or I can get on with my life, and do the next best thing. Fulfil a dream I've had since I was a girl.'

'Fair enough, but I'm still wondering how you talked Ross into it.'

'I didn't have to, he jumped at the idea. He was so enthusiastic, I was shocked, to be honest,' said Andie. 'Apparently he got talking to Joanna after everyone had left, and she really stood up for me, according to Ross.'

Jess frowned. 'Why did she have to stand up for you?'

Andie had felt slightly uncomfortable about that at first, but she was rather pleased that Joanna had stood up for her, the way Ross explained it. He was so worried about her that he'd ended up confiding in Joanna after everyone had left. He said she told him that she had come to realise what a mistake she'd made giving up her career for the family, even going so far as to suggest, according to Ross, that perhaps she'd stagnated a bit, as a housewife, and that she'd never felt so fulfilled as she did now. Ross said he hadn't been able to stop thinking about it all the way home, how much Andie had given up for him, how essentially selfish it had been for him to expect her to fit in around his life and his work.

'But you do know what being a chef means,' Andie had said to him. 'We'll hardly see each other.'

'Maybe it's time I started fitting in around you,' he had returned. 'I could go to the office a little later some mornings, we could have breakfast together. We could make Sundays our exclusive day for each other. We can make it work, Andie.'

Jess had filled a plate with antipasto as she spoke and she set it down in front of Andie.

'Thanks, it looks wonderful,' she said, gazing at the glistening olives, the wedge of creamy brie, the red bell peppers stuffed with mascarpone, her favourite. 'I know I shouldn't complain, I get to work around food everyday, but it's not the same. Sometimes I feel . . . I don't know, like an artist surrounded by all these gorgeous tubes of paint, every colour I can imagine, but I never get to paint, I'm too busy sorting and selling the tubes. I look at all the produce as it comes in, as I'm spooning it out into the dishes, or slicing it up, and all the time I'm thinking of the possibilities. Customers tell me what they're going to cook, or what they did cook, and I'm envious . . . but what am I going to do? How much can I cook for Ross and me? It's frustrating.'

'So you're going off to become a Picasso in the kitchen?' said Jess, smearing some cheese onto a cracker.

Andie smiled. 'Well, that all depends on you.'

Jess looked at her.

'Listen, we have enough casual staff, you can still choose your hours. I just need someone I can trust to manage the place so I don't have to think about it. And I'll put you on a retainer, you'll have a regular income above and beyond the hours you do at the shop. And look, seriously, it's your show, you have my blessing to do whatever you want with it.'

'You realise you're making an offer too good to refuse,' said Jess.

'That's what I was hoping.'

August

'So you haven't said, Tash, what's the special occasion?'

Tasha had dragged her best friend to her favourite lingerie shop in their lunchbreak. She was planning a spree.

'Well, there's going to be a lot of special occasions, now that Ross is going to be free most nights.'

Kylie's eyes grew wide. 'Why, what happened? Did he ditch the bitch finally?'

'Not yet, but he did get her a job in a restaurant, which means she'll be working probably five nights a week, at least.'

'I thought they were, like, mega-rich and she didn't have to work?' said Kylie. 'Why would she want to be a cook, and work nights?'

'Oh, she was working already, when she felt like it,' said Tasha. 'Flitting about in the gourmet deli Ross bought for her, remember I told you?'

'Yeah, you said it was a place she just hung out with her friends?'

'Totes. But anyways, she used to be a chef, I told you that, didn't I? So somehow Ross got it into her head to get back into it. Maybe she's a fan of *MasterChef*, I dunno. I think it helped that he told her he'd find her a swanky restaurant to work in.'

'And did he?'

'Absolutely. Ross is, like, so highly connected. She starts next week at Viande.'

'La de da,' Kylie chanted.

'Hm . . .' Tasha slid the hangers along the rack, inspecting the lace baby dolls. 'I'm only worried it's out of her league. Let's just hope she doesn't fuck it up.'

'Wouldn't it be easier for him just to leave her?' said Kylie.

'Don't I wish,' Tasha sighed. 'But he has to play this very carefully, or he could end up financially screwed, again.'

'So how's this gonna help?'

'Well, you see, the courts have to divide up Ross's assets according to her future income. While she's doing nothing but working in a shop, she gets a big chunk of everything to make up for her "loss of lifestyle".' Tasha rolled her eyes.

'Seriously? They do that here? I thought you only have to pay alimony in America.'

'It's not alimony, it's just the way they divide up everything when you divorce. That's why we have to be patient. If things work out at the restaurant, she'll be less dependent on him. Then Ross said it'll be our time. You know, he's really a decent guy, he wants her to be okay.'

She lifted one of the hangers off the rack. 'Some of the baby dolls look a bit, well, baby doll. I don't want to be cute, I want to be hot. Maybe I should go for a corset.' She walked over to another rack and started flicking through. 'Have you ever worn one of these?' she asked Kylie.

'Nuh.'

'I wonder how hard they are to get off?' she mused, picking up a black corset laced all the way up the front. She checked the price tag. 'O-M-G!'

Kylie looked over her shoulder and gasped. 'You're not going to pay that just for undies, are you?'

'I think of it as an investment,' Tasha said with a sly grin, but Kylie was frowning. 'What's wrong?'

'Okay, I'm just gonna say it, I'm worried about you, Tash.'

'Oh, Kyles, you're the best. But you don't have to worry, I know what I'm doing.'

'But what if he decides to stay with his wife after all this?' Kylie persisted. 'Married guys do that all the time.'

'That's a myth,' Tasha returned. 'More people get divorced than get married these days.'

'Really?'

'Ye-ah,' she said, as though the word had two syllables. 'It's in the statistics. I told you, I know what I'm doing. If we can hold out just a bit longer, well, we can have it all.'

'Do you need it all but? I mean, as long as you're together . . .'

Tasha looked at her. 'Okay, Kyles, I'm going to explain something to you. Ross is rich because he's smart and he's powerful and he works hard. That is who he is, it's his appeal. I'm not saying I love him for his money, but it's part of the package, and I love the whole package. It's, like, I don't think Ross loves me for my body, but I know he really loves my body, and if I got fat, I wouldn't expect him to feel the same way about me.'

'Hm, that's true.'

'And what do you think I'm doing here?' she added. 'Enhancing my assets. I know what Ross likes, and I give it to him. Don't you think I deserve the same in return?'

'Totes.'

'See Kyles, we're both bringing something to the table. Ross gets this,' she said, picking up another corset that was almost entirely see-through. 'And I get everything that comes with Ross. It's only fair.'

Friday night

'I'm so not looking forward to this.'

Donna sighed. 'Toby, we're five minutes from the restaurant, buck up, okay?'

When Andie asked them out to dinner to celebrate her new job, Donna knew it wasn't going to play well with Toby. But Andie was so excited that Donna went ahead and made all the arrangements, lining up Max's favourite babysitter before she even mentioned it to Toby. And when she did mention it, she tried to do it by stealth. In the middle of a conversation she casually dropped, 'Oh and we have dinner with Andie and everyone that weekend.'

Toby had not missed her trick, unfortunately. The number of times things went in one ear and out the other with that man, but not this time.

'Who's everyone?' he'd asked immediately.

'Oh, Jess . . . Ross, of course.'

It went down like a lead balloon then, and he was still grizzling now.

'And you're absolutely sure Jess is coming?'

'As sure as I was last time you asked,' said Donna. 'And if she can put on a good face for Andie's sake, then so can you.'

He shrugged. 'I guess.'

'This is for Andie, Toby. Don't you want to celebrate her new job with her?'

'Yeah, of course I do. Just not with Ross.'

'Well, Ross is the one who got her the job,' Donna reminded him. 'It's a really great thing he's done for her. She's so excited, she's going to be working at Viande. This is a fantastic opportunity for her.'

'There has to be something in it for him.'

'What could be in it for Ross?' said Donna. 'She's going to have to work most nights —'

'Maybe that's it,' said Toby, as though he'd just hit on something.

'What's it?'

'Maybe he wants to keep her busy at nights.'

'Toby!' she groaned.

'What can I say? I just don't trust the guy.'

'Well, you're way off base. The whole reason Andie gave up being a chef in the first place was that Ross didn't want her to work nights, because they wouldn't get enough time together.'

'Then why is it okay now?' Toby put to her.

Donna didn't know how to answer that. 'You have such a devious mind,' she said finally as they turned a corner. The restaurant was on the next block. 'Please, Toby, you will behave yourself tonight, won't you?'

'When do I ever not behave myself?' he said, as he manoeuvred the car into place for a reverse park.

He had a point. Toby did always behave himself, he was wonderful company when they went out, charming and affable . . . with other people. But Ross just rubbed him the wrong way. Always had, and, Donna feared, always would.

'Don't worry,' he tried to assure her. 'Jess'll be there to share the pain. We can get drunk together.'

*

They were shown to their table, where they found Andie and Ross already seated, waiting. Toby was happy to see Andie at least, he was always happy to see Andie. Though it was bittersweet as well, she reminded him so much of Brendan. When they were kids, people often thought the two of them were twins. They were only a year apart, and physically they shared the same features, the blond hair, the striking green eyes. But it was the mannerisms that always got Toby – they laughed the same, at the same kind of jokes, they had the same expressions. Whenever he was around Andie, Toby was catapulted back to when the three of them would hang out together. As kids Andie was always included. Brendan never made a thing about it, but if they were going to kick a ball down at the local oval, Andie came too; if they caught a bus to the beach in the holidays, she was always with them. As they grew older, Toby and Brendan were her unofficial escorts to every school dance – or maybe bodyguards was more appropriate. With Brendan around, no guy would dare approach Andie, though there were plenty who wanted to. They shared their first illicit drink together, tried their first cigarettes, which they all found disgusting and promptly gave up. But as much as Brendan was protective of Andie, she was just as protective of her brother, in a different way, keeping a watchful eye on proceedings and always knowing the best time to leave. She'd tried to get him to leave the club the night he died, and she was devastated, blaming herself for not being there. But Toby had been there, and yet Andie had never blamed him. Despite her own grief she comforted him more than anyone else could. They drew together, trying to close the gap where Brendan had been. She was part of Brendan that would be with him always.

Andie jumped to her feet, her face lighting up as soon as she saw them coming. Then Ross stood up behind her, the trademark smarmy smile planted across his face. Toby wished he could like the guy, for Andie's sake, but he knew in his heart that Brendan would never have approved of Ross. And he felt certain that Andie wouldn't have ended up with him had Brendan still been here. But all he could do was watch over her now, and be there for her if – or when – it all fell apart.

'Hi guys,' Andie said, beaming. 'I'm so glad you could make it.'

She threw her arms around Toby's neck, and he gave her a warm hug, glancing at the table settings over her shoulder.

'Jess on her way?' he asked, drawing back.

'Ah no, unfortunately,' said Andie. 'She phoned earlier, she's been asked to stand in at Dalgety's. She could hardly refuse.'

'You don't turn down Dalgety's,' Donna agreed with a nervous laugh. She glanced sideways at Toby – his jaw was clenched so tightly a vein was pulsing in his neck.

Ross reached across the table to shake Toby's hand. 'So it's just the four of us,' he said, smiling broadly as he beckoned the waiter. 'How about we start with champagne?'

Toby felt Donna's hand on his arm, applying gentle downward pressure, in case he bolted. As if he'd do that to Andie. He was just going to have to make the most of this, focus on Andie, it was her night, after all. Ross always made a show about wanting to pay, so this time Toby would let him, and he'd order the most expensive dishes on the menu. He turned to Andie as they took their seats. 'So, tell me about the new job.'

'Well, I guess you've heard of Viande?' she said, bubbling over.

'Everyone's heard of Viande,' said Toby. 'Even a pleb like me.'

Viande was a longstanding Sydney establishment, like the grand old dame of fine dining. But over the last decade or so it had been usurped by all the new kids on the block, and it had gone from three hats down to one, and was in danger of dropping off the list altogether. There'd been some hullabaloo a few years ago when management had brought in a new executive chef at great expense; apparently the guy had been working in some of the most famous restaurants across Europe. Last year Viande had its three hats restored, and management was vindicated.

'So how did you land the job?' Toby asked, as the waiter returned with a bottle of champagne and proceeded to open it.

Andie turned to look at Ross, smiling. 'It was all his doing.'

'The owner is a client of mine, we've been handling his business for years,' Ross said, taking the floor, like he always did. 'He has a substantial portfolio of restaurants and hotels across the country, so I gave him a call, asked if he couldn't find something here in Sydney for Andie. The kitchen at Viande is big enough that they can certainly give someone a tryout.'

'So this isn't an actual job?' Toby asked. He hated to think Andie was getting her hopes up and this was just a furphy Ross had created, so that he could say, well, you tried . . .

'You don't just hand someone a job in a prestigious restaurant like this, Toby,' said Andie. 'Particularly when I have hardly any experience – I'm going to have to earn it.'

'Oh, you'll do great,' he said, giving her hand a squeeze.

'I don't know, it feels like it's going to be a very long interview.'

'That's exactly what it is, darling,' said Ross, taking her other hand possessively. 'The owner told me the executive chef likes to try people out on the job. He feels that just because someone's good in an interview doesn't make them good in a kitchen. So his philosophy is to throw them in at the deep end.'

'The deep end?' said Donna. 'That sounds ominous.'

'I know,' Andie agreed with a grimace.

'Nup,' Toby declared. 'You're going to knock 'em dead,' he said, raising his glass. 'To Andie!'

'To Andie!' everyone echoed.

'So when's your first shift?' Toby asked her.

'Thursday.'

Thursday

Andie couldn't remember the last time she felt this nervous. But that was the whole problem – she didn't do anything that made her nervous anymore, her life was devoid of challenges, and that was not a good thing. She had to keep telling herself that, because right now she would have done anything to get out of this particular challenge.

Ross had offered to drive her to the restaurant but she refused; he'd have to leave work early, and he'd have to come out late to pick her up. Besides, there was really no need. She was perfectly capable of driving herself, there was parking for staff, it was easy. And she needed the time in the car, on her own, to compose herself.

But Andie had a feeling she could have driven to Melbourne and back and she still wouldn't have felt composed when she turned into the staff carpark at the back of Viande. She glanced at her new chef's kit on the passenger seat; a gift from Ross when she'd despaired that her apprentice kit from her TAFE days would not be up to scratch. So yesterday he'd presented her with a top-of-the-range professional kit, and now Andie didn't feel up to scratch. But she was dressed in a new, double-breasted white chef's jacket and fine-checked pants, so at least she looked the part. She stepped out of the car and pressed the remote lock as she walked across the carpark to the rear entrance of the restaurant. She was to report to the executive chef, Dominic Gerou. Andie just wished she'd had a chance to talk to the man at least; she didn't even know what he looked like. When she'd googled his name she discovered a formidable reputation – which made it even more daunting – and a few indistinct images where he was just one in a group, standing at the back, usually looking away. He never appeared on *MasterChef* or any of the cooking shows – though rumour had it he'd been invited repeatedly – and he flatly refused to have anyone from the media visit his kitchen. He was therefore described as rather prickly. The couple of direct quotes Andie did come across stated that he was not a celebrity, he was a chef; as far as he was concerned those two words did not belong together. He took his work seriously, and he expected others to do the same. Prickly indeed. Andie had to wonder what it was going to be like to work in his kitchen.

No, enough of that, she had to think positively. It was going to be amazing. She would finally get the kind of experience she used to dream about. And it wasn't as though she was an indentured servant; if she didn't like it, she could always move on.

Andie walked up to what looked like a fire exit door with a plaque: Viande. Staff Entry Only. She smoothed down her jacket, took a deep breath and pressed a large red button on the adjacent wall. Her heart skipped a beat when she heard the corresponding buzz emanating from inside. This was it. Presently the door opened and a small-statured man of Asian appearance was standing on the other side, dressed in full chef's regalia. Andie hated referring to people as 'Asians', she was sure it must sound racist, but she could never tell exactly where someone was from.

'Hello?' he prompted her. 'Can I help you?'

He spoke in a broad Australian accent, so that was no help. Not that Andie could distinguish Asian accents either. She really ought to work on that.

'Oh, hi,' she said. 'I'm here for a tryout. I'm supposed to report to Dominic Gerou.'

She noticed a slight lift of his eyebrows. 'All right. Well, I'm Tang,' he said. 'Please follow me.'

He led Andie down a long, dimly lit corridor, past a couple of storerooms, and on towards the familiar cacophony of a commercial kitchen. Suddenly they were on the threshold. Andie paused in the doorway, taking it all in: row upon row of gleaming stainless-steel benches and shelves, pots and pans and utensils hanging from their racks; the banks of double ovens, deep-frying vats, grills and hotplates; the sizzling, hissing and clattering, the roar of exhaust fans, voices snapping orders; the smells, too many to differentiate right now. Andie felt the adrenalin pumping through her veins. She was at once excited and scared as hell.

'This way,' Tang said over his shoulder. They weaved their way around a veritable army of chefs at work, Andie counted at least a dozen. No one so much as glanced in her direction, they all appeared to be completely engrossed in whatever they were doing. And deadly serious.

Tang finally came to a halt at the pass, where the meals were plated up and passed over to the waiters to be served. There was a small group of chefs and waitstaff gathered around another chef – Andie assumed this had to be Dominic Gerou – as he bent over the bench doing . . . something, she couldn't see past everyone. But he had the group in his thrall.

'Excuse me, Chef?' Tang said tentatively.

'Not now, Tang,' the man said without looking around.

Tang stood very still, like a soldier at attention. Andie followed suit as Chef proceeded to explain how to plate up a dish.

'And so the confit of duck rests on the bed of almond nut soil,' he was saying, 'and is topped with the glazed quince. Carefully spoon the jus of red wine and port, star anise and juniper berries. With a light hand, please, don't drown it. The sour cherries, three precisely, are placed to one side, like so.'

Andie detected a slight plum in his mouth – she couldn't decide if it was the remnants of an English accent, or if he was just pretentious. She'd expected him to be French with that name.

'And there it is,' he said, straightening up. 'Is everyone clear? Come close, take a good look. It's fiddly and I want you to get it right.'

He stepped back out of the way as the assembled group drew in closer to inspect the dish.

'What is it, Tang?' he asked, finally turning to him.

'Sorry, Chef, this lady was told to report to you.'

He glanced beyond Tang to Andie, the irritation plain on his face.

She cleared her throat. 'My name is Andie Corcoran. I'm starting —'

'I can't deal with this now,' he cut her off. 'Just set her up, would you, Tang?'

'Yes, Chef.'

Tang turned to Andie and ushered her back through the kitchen and up the corridor again, to one of the storerooms they had passed on the way in. A row of lockers lined one wall, and Tang walked along beside them, checking for one that would open.

'Here you go,' he said, turning to look at her. 'What did you say your name was? Sandy?'

'Andie,' she said. 'Short for Andrea.'

He shook his head. 'Chef's not going to like that.'

He's not going to like her name? What was she supposed to do, change it?

'Doesn't matter, he mostly uses surnames anyway.'

'Oh, okay,' said Andie. 'Is Tang your surname?'

He smiled, flashing a perfectly even row of white teeth. 'Lee's my surname, but Tang is what comes last. Chinese,' he shrugged. 'Everyone here calls me Tang.'

'Okay, Tang.'

'You can leave that,' he said, glancing at the kit she was carrying. 'You won't need it. Chef personally selects all the equipment, he doesn't like anyone bringing their own gear into his kitchen.'

So Chef was a fascist as well as pompous. Joy. Andie sighed inwardly as she placed her kit, along with her handbag, in the locker.

'And you'll have to change your jacket, we have a uniform.'

'Of course,' said Andie. She hadn't even succeeded in looking the part.

Tang gave Andie a quick appraisal up and down, and walked over to a double-fronted cabinet, opening the doors back. He scanned the shelves inside, drawing out a folded jacket wrapped in plastic, then a hat from the top shelf.

'Here you go, these should fit,' he said.

Andie looked doubtfully at the pillbox-style hat. She'd already plaited her hair back at home, using about a thousand bobby pins to try to flatten it against her head. 'You don't have any of the snood-style hats?' she asked.

Tang shook his head. 'Chef doesn't like them, he thinks they look sloppy.'

Chef sounded like a pain in the arse.

'Come find me outside when you're ready,' Tang said as he headed for the door.

'Thank you, Tang.'

Andie changed quickly, shoving her things into the locker. The pillbox hat was a snug fit, but she eventually forced it into place. If this worked out, she really should think about getting her hair cut. Ross wouldn't like it, but it was impractical for a chef to have hair this long. Oh God, she was going to be a chef again. She hurried back out to the kitchen, relieved to see that Tang was hovering close by, waiting for her, and that the haughty Dominic Gerou was nowhere in sight.

'Okay, Andie,' said Tang, 'let's put you to work.'

He set her up at a station at the end of a bench, with a pile of onions in front of her. She sighed again, but quietly, to herself. This was an apprentice's job, a first-year apprentice at that. She realised she had to start somewhere, but why, oh why, did it have to be onions?

'Sliced or diced?' she asked Tang.

'Dice for now,' he replied. 'I'll keep an eye on you, let you know when you can move on to something else. Just depends which sections get busy. Don't hesitate to ask if you need anything, I'll be floating around.'

Andie turned to the pile of onions. She picked up a knife from the magnetic strip running the length of the wall behind, glancing along the bench. She was one of four chefs in the row, all dutifully chopping vegetables as though their lives depended on it. She reached for an onion and scored the outer layer. Andie really hated chopping onions, though she supposed nobody actually enjoyed it. It took her a while to get into a rhythm, chopping almost as fast as she'd learned more than a decade ago. She should have practised at home. Her eyes started to sting. She paused, pressing them together for a moment.

'Everything okay?' said Tang, passing behind her.

'Everything's fine.'

Half an hour later she had a tidy mound of chopped onions on her board, and tears streaming down her cheeks.

'Okay, that's enough.'

It was the plummy voice. Andie turned slowly and looked up. Chef was regarding her efforts with unconcealed disdain.

'How long has it been since you've worked in a commercial kitchen?' he demanded.

She swallowed. 'Oh, it's been . . . a while.'

Tang appeared beside him. 'Move her along, get someone to take over here,' he snapped, before walking off.

Thank goodness for that.

'Okay,' Tang said. 'Let's get you some practice.'

'I'd appreciate that,' she said gratefully.

'Practice' involved more chopping, slicing, tearing lettuce, transferring baked bread to a wire rack, and just about any menial unskilled task Tang could find for her. Chef appeared every so often, frowning at her and ordering Tang to find her something else to do. Andie was getting anxious, he seemed to be judging her without giving her much of a chance. Okay, so her speed wasn't great, but her technique was fine, and she was doing her best. It was only a tryout, after all, her first night. She needed time to get into the swing of things. At least Tang was kind and polite, but she could detect a hint of mild curiosity on his face, as if to say, what the hell are you doing here?

Andie was wondering the same thing. Her legs ached, her arms were sore, she'd forgotten how much plain, hard, monotonous work was involved in a commercial kitchen, especially one this size. The restaurant had a hundred seats, and there were two sittings a night. There were also private dining rooms and two function rooms, both of which had been booked for cocktail parties that night, so a small team was preparing canapés. Tang told her it was particularly busy for a Thursday. Once dinner service had commenced, Andie was stationed in front of vast vats of oil that kept spitting at her, lifting heavy racks whenever the timer went off, and hooking them on the edge to drain. She was hot and tired and dishevelled. She could be at home right now, relaxing with a glass of wine. What was she trying to prove? Maybe she was too old to go back to train as a chef. Jess was right, it wasn't everything it was cracked up to be.

'Andie,' Tang said from behind her.

Thank God, he was moving her on again. She turned around, pushing a stray strand of hair off her face.

'Now you'll have to wash your hands.' Dominic Gerou was standing beside Tang, glaring down at her. 'And fix your hat so it doesn't happen again.'

He charged off, and Tang cocked his head urgently for her to follow after him. She caught up with Chef at the sink, where he stood, barely disguising a scowl, his arms crossed in front of him. She looked up at him expectantly.

'So fix your hat first,' he said impatiently, 'then wash your hands.'

Andie started to readjust her hat, tucking her hair right up out of the way. Blasted hair had a will of its own.

'There's a very precise chain of command here,' Chef barked at her. 'I am at the top, and you are at the bottom, which means you take orders from everyone, and I mean *everyone*, in between.'

She nodded. It's not as though she'd been arguing the point with anyone. She finished with her hair and turned around to the sink, flicking on the tap.

'What's your name?' he asked.

'Andie.'

'What sort of a name is that?'

'I don't know, it's my name.'

'If you were an eight-year-old boy.'

'It's short for Andrea.'

'What's your surname?'

'Corcoran.'

She thought she heard him swear under his breath.

'I am a fully qualified chef,' Andie said. 'Just so you know,' she added timidly.

'What are you trying to say, that what you've been doing so far is beneath you?'

'No, I wasn't saying that,' she said, reaching for the paper towel. 'I just thought you should be aware of my qualifications.'

'Oh I should, should I?' he returned. 'Perhaps you don't realise what a trial is all about. I have to be assured that you can do all the basics, that you have the requisite skills.'

'I'm just saying, these seem to be first-year apprentice tasks.'

'And yet you're not handling them all that well.'

'I'm a little rusty, a little slow, that's all.'

He paused, considering her. 'So you can debone a chicken?'

'Huh?'

'A qualified chef should be able to debone a chicken,' he said brusquely. 'Follow me.'

Andie tossed the paper towel into the bin and scuttled after him.

'Cosmo,' he called ahead.

Cosmo, she presumed, turned around. 'Yes, Chef.'

'Corky here tells me she's a qualified chef,' he said. 'She can work your section for a while.' He turned and walked away.

Corky? Where did he get off?

'Hello, Cosmo,' she said. 'My name's actually Andie.'

He gave her a knowing smile. 'Okay, Andie. Let's get you set up.'

A few minutes later Andie stood contemplating a whole chicken on the bench in front of her, a deboning knife in one hand, and a lump the size of Tasmania lodged in her throat. Why did she have to go and open her big mouth? They had learned how to debone a chicken at TAFE. She recalled making a bit of a mess of it, but she'd passed her assessment and she'd never had to do it again. Well, she'd cut the flesh from a chicken before, of course, many times, to finish with eight to ten separate fillets. But Cosmo instructed that she had to end with a single, perfectly opened butterfly. Shit, she really should have put some practice in at home. But even if she had, she was doubtful that she would have thought to practise deboning a chicken. *Shit!*

Okay, Andie, let logic and common sense prevail. Proceed slowly, with care . . .

But her mother's voice echoed in her head . . . *If you just took your time and used your head, Andrea, you wouldn't make so many mistakes . . . You know the thing I find most disappointing? You never really push yourself, do you? It's all very well to be pretty, Andrea, but it'll only get you so far . . .*

Andie blinked back tears as she cut into the chicken flesh, trying to slide the point of the knife as close to the bone as she could manage. She wasn't that bad, she kept telling herself, she was just a little rusty, that's all . . . Dominic Gerou was an arrogant arse. This was too much pressure, she needed to ease herself in . . . a smaller kitchen . . . a nicer head chef. Where was Tang?

'What in Christ's name are you doing?'

It was Chef again, looming over her.

'You're supposed to debone it, not massacre it.' He snatched it up, almost waving the mangled carcass in her face. 'You've ruined it, look! The flesh is all bruised and hacked. We can't use this. Cosmo!' he boomed.

'Chef!'

'See if you can salvage anything out of this, some fillets maybe.'

'Right, Chef.'

'And you —'

But Andie was already walking away.

'Miss!' He called after her, but she pushed on, weaving and ducking around the other chefs as fast as she could without breaking into a run.

'Andie, where are you going?'

That was Tang, but she didn't stop. She didn't look back, she raced out to the storeroom, reefing off the jacket and dropping it on the floor. Her hands were shaking as she grabbed her stuff out of the locker. She ducked back over to the doorway, pausing to glance down the corridor, fully expecting to see the towering, glowering figure of Dominic Gerou bearing down upon her, but there was no one in sight. Andie didn't hesitate a moment longer, she made a dash for the exit, pushing down on the heavy metal rail. The door released, and she was free and clear.

Potts Point

'So, this is it,' said Ross, standing back as Tasha walked past him into the main room. He was visibly uncomfortable. 'Okay, you wanted to see the place, now you've seen it, so let's get going.'

Tasha considered him with an indulgent smile. 'Aren't you even going to offer me a drink?' she asked.

'What?'

'She won't be back for hours, Rossie, what are you so afraid of?'

'I'm not afraid, Tash. I just think we could be at your place right now . . .'

She raised an eyebrow.

'Fine, I'll get you a drink,' he surrendered, walking over to the kitchen.

Tasha was the one who'd insisted on coming here. She had so little insight into Ross's real life, she had been desperate to see if it lived up to her imagination. She wandered around, surveying the room. She liked the space. Converted warehouses were becoming passé, but a good decorator could bring it up to date. Some of the furnishings were a little conservative for her taste; that brown chesterfield would definitely have to go.

'Vodka tonic for the lady,' Ross announced, coming up behind her.

She turned around as he handed her a glass.

'You're not having one?' she asked.

He shook his head. 'I'm driving, remember, to your place, as soon as you finish that.'

She took a sip. 'Honestly, what *is* the rush? You haven't even shown me the bedroom yet.'

'No, I haven't.' He cleared his throat. 'But I will show you the view.'

She pouted as she let him lead her over to the window. It was an okay view of the city, but Tasha wasn't sold. Potts Point was full of old fags, artists and crazy people. The eastern suburbs were sexier. An apartment in Bondi or Tamarama, overlooking the beach, now that she could get used to. The very idea made her hot.

She turned to Ross, pressing her body into him and looping her arms up around his neck. She felt his hands slide down to cup her butt as she drew his head close and kissed him hard on the mouth.

'Let's get out of here,' he murmured against her lips.

'Okay,' she breathed. 'Let me just use the bathroom first.'

*

Ross had called out once already, she was taking so long. Next time he would come looking. Which was the plan.

Tasha fluffed out her hair and adjusted herself. Her tits looked great in this corset, they were almost tumbling out of it. The whole ensemble was a knockout. Ross hadn't seen it yet, she was about to blow his mind.

'Tash, what are you doing?'

She heard his footsteps approaching. She leaned back on her elbows and uncrossed her legs. She was perched on the corner of the bed – their bed – facing the doorway, her stiletto-clad feet planted on the floor.

Ross stepped into the room. 'Tash . . .'

*

Andie pulled into the garage of their building and her heart sank when she saw Ross's car. She'd been desperately hoping he wouldn't be home yet. He'd muttered something about catching up on some work, seeing as she'd be late anyway. She had thought about going somewhere else first, biding her time. But where? Jess had scored another shift at Dalgety's tonight, and Andie didn't want to bother Donna and Toby, it was probably Max's bedtime. In truth she just didn't want to embarrass herself any further. She wanted to crawl into bed and go to sleep before Ross got home. Or pretend to be asleep so she didn't have to deal with it tonight. She was mortified. She kept reliving the moment, all the possible alternative endings there could have been to this evening aside from just walking out. Not even walking, nothing so dignified or adult. No, she had run off like a little girl, a frightened, stupid little girl, hopelessly out of her depth.

Why couldn't she have just toughed it out? Dominic Gerou was not the first arrogant chef she'd ever worked for, though he was arguably the worst. But she didn't have to whine 'I'm a qualified chef' like a total twit. No wonder he put her to her word. She should have just shut up and taken it on the chin. Things would have got better, gradually, if she had decided to go back. Which was always her choice, after all. She could have taken the mature approach, left a polite message with whoever was appropriate – the owner probably, Ross's contact – thanking him for his trouble, but advising she was not going to continue. After all, it was only a trial, she was checking the place out as much as being checked out.

Ross was not going to be happy about this, and Andie couldn't blame him, she wasn't happy about it either. But after all the effort he'd made to set it up . . .

And now she had no choice but to face him. But maybe he wasn't home – he didn't always take his car to work, if he had an early meeting out of the office he often took a cab. She cast her mind back to this morning; he'd left before her, and he hadn't said anything about calling a cab . . . Andie sighed inwardly. She was only delaying the inevitable with wishful thinking. She was just going to have to walk in there and see the look on his face as it dawned on him that she was home a lot earlier than she should have been.

She quietly unlocked the door to their apartment, and tiptoed in. She didn't know why, it's not as though Ross would be asleep at this time of the night, it was barely eight. She supposed she was subconsciously trying not to be noticed. If only.

The place was in darkness, the only illumination coming from streetlights outside. She could virtually see the entire apartment from the entrance – it was all one space, except for the bedroom and bathroom. There was a dim light coming from under the bedroom door; Ross might be in the bathroom, or he might be lying on the bed working on his laptop.

She walked across the living area. 'Ross?' she said tentatively.

No reply.

She stepped closer, she could hear movement on the bed, then a voice . . . more of a grunt. He was here. She sighed. He'd probably nodded off over his laptop, stirring at the sound of her voice. She took a deep breath and opened the door.

It took Andie a minute – would it have been a full minute? – to comprehend the sight that confronted her as she stepped into their bedroom. It was the woman who grabbed her immediate attention, not surprisingly. She was straddled on the bed, stark-naked, bouncing up and down, her dark mop of hair flying all over the place, boobs jiggling in the breeze. It wasn't until Andie heard Ross's voice that she realised he was the thing she was straddling.

He said 'Andie', then he said 'Fuck'. Well, she thought that's what he said, he kind of gasped the words. He might have been having a heart attack for all she knew, because she'd already turned and fled from the room. It occurred to her, as she bolted back across the apartment to the front door, that this was the second time she had run away today, tonight, in the space of an hour probably. It was bizarre.

'Andie!' she heard again as she slammed the door behind her. His voice was louder and clearer that time, the woman must have dismounted so that he could breathe. Andie headed straight for the stairwell, she had to keep moving, not give him the chance to catch up. She had an advantage; Ross was at least partly naked, so he'd have to do something about that before he could follow her. Andie didn't want to be standing waiting for the lift when he did. She ran down the stairs, her legs trembling . . . God, don't trip, she told herself. Her heart was pounding in her chest as she made it safely to the garage and over to her car. She jumped in and started the engine, pressing the remote for the garage door at the same time. It was trundling upward as she approached; she nosed the car closer till it was up and out of the way, before accelerating out of there so fast her tyres screeched. Her phone started to ring but she ignored it.

Andie steered through the maze of cramped, claustrophobic streets, tears almost blinding her eyes. She wanted to get right away from here, she wanted to drive as fast as she was legally allowed. She finally made it out of the rabbit warren and onto New South Head Road. She could only do seventy, but she felt free. She didn't know where she was going, she didn't know where *to* go, she only knew she couldn't go back to that apartment. Ever.

She needed time to process . . . what exactly? The image loomed back into her mind's eye. The woman seemed young . . . she might have been a prostitute for all Andie knew. Did that make it okay? Certainly not. Was it a one-off thing? Conveniently taking place on the very first night Andie was at work? Doubtful. So was it an affair? Was it serious? How long had it been going on? Why did he bring her into their home? Why was he having sex with her *on their bed*? Andie's phone suddenly started to ring again, startling her. 'Bastard!' she yelled at it, before reaching over to turn it off.

She had slowed down, she didn't have much choice as the road narrowed, dipped down to the water's edge for a while, and then meandered back up into suburbia. Andie wasn't shaking any more, and she wasn't crying. She felt drained, and achingly tired, but she kept driving. Until she realised she would soon come to a dead end at the HMAS Navy base at the south head of the harbour, and she would have to double back.

Instead, she turned onto Old South Head Road feeling alone and bereft. She had nowhere to go – Jess was at work, and she couldn't show up at Donna and Toby's like this, Toby was likely to go storming off to find Ross and throttle him. She couldn't even go to her dad, she didn't want to upset him. Andie suddenly missed Brendan, like a sharp pain to the heart. Of course he'd have been as bad as Toby, they'd have probably formed a posse to go and punch Ross's lights out. But she also knew Brendan would have felt it as deeply as she was feeling it, that's how it was between them. He would have understood her pain and comforted her, and protected her, and made it all bearable somehow. But Brendan was gone, long gone, and Andie had never felt his loss so greatly.

She just needed someone to pour it all out to without judgement, or opinion, so she could sort it out in her head. Because for some reason, more than anything, she felt ashamed. She hadn't done anything wrong . . . had she? Still, it was shame she felt. Shame and embarrassment. And betrayal. At least that was valid.

Betrayal. That was it.

Andie didn't know why the idea even crossed her mind, but as soon as it did, she seemed to go on automatic pilot all the way to Bellevue Hill. As she pulled into the street, it occurred to her that this was crazy. But something compelled her to keep driving, right up to the house, the house where she would find the only other person who could possibly understand what she was feeling right now.

Andie cut the engine. She picked up her bag and stepped out of the car. The air was cooler now, and she was only wearing the T-shirt she'd had on under her chef's jacket. Christ, that had happened tonight as well. It paled into insignificance now. Andie looked up at the house. Crazy or not, she was going in.

The door opened a minute or so after she rang the bell. Joanna peered out. 'Andie? What are you doing here? What's happened?'

*

'Have you ever seen her before, did you recognise her?' Joanna was asking.

Andie had blurted out the whole thing right there on the doorstep, and Joanna had promptly ushered her inside, sat her down, and poured them both a stiff drink. Andie had tossed hers back without even tasting it. Joanna refilled her glass, and she'd done the same again, anaesthetising the pain. So Joanna refilled it a third time, and Andie finally slowed down, taking just a few sips before she set it down on the coffee table in front of her.

'I didn't even really see her face,' said Andie. 'Just black hair swinging about, and those jiggly, pert little breasts.' She sighed. 'Twentysomething breasts, you know. I used to have those.'

'You haven't had children,' said Joanna, 'then you can talk.'

'Gravity doesn't discriminate, Joanna.' She looked down at herself. 'I used to have breasts that jiggled. Now they dangle.'

Joanna considered her. 'Andie, why are you dressed like that? Aren't they chef's pants?'

She nodded. 'I had a trial run at a restaurant this evening. Ross organised it. He obviously had ulterior motives.'

'How did it go?' Joanna asked. 'At the restaurant?'

She really didn't want to talk about it. 'Oh, okay . . . not so great. Okay.' Oh God, could she be any more pathetic? 'You must think I'm crazy showing up here like this.'

Joanna shrugged. 'We've all done crazy things at one time or another.' She paused. 'Do you remember that time I confronted you? Came to your flat . . . Your roommate – what was her name?'

'Jess.'

'She wanted to call the police, do you remember?' She shook her head. 'Madwoman in full flight. She really thought I was going to do damage to something, or someone, namely you.'

'Well, you had every reason.'

'I don't know . . . My rage should have been directed at Ross, not you.'

Andie thought about it. 'But I get it, I do, Joanna. I feel so much anger right now towards that woman. I think if I'd been any closer I would have been tempted to slap her. And I don't even know her. I know nothing about her. And I have no idea what she knows. Maybe she doesn't even know he's married?'

'They were in your apartment, Andie,' Joanna said plainly. 'She knows.'

Andie gave a heavy sigh. 'And I knew Ross was married.'

Joanna didn't say anything.

'He said the marriage was over, that you were just staying together for the sake of the kids . . .' She stared out in front of her. 'He said I gave him his life back, that he felt young again, excited about the future. Because of *me*,' she emphasised. 'I wonder if he's saying the same things to this girl . . .'

Andie looked over at Joanna then, her expression was grim. Oh shit. What was she saying?

'I'm sorry, Joanna. I shouldn't have come here, I shouldn't have bothered you.'

She didn't respond. Andie picked up her glass and sculled the rest of her drink. She put it back on the coffee table as she got to her feet.

'I'm going now,' she said. 'I'm sorry, this was wrong of me.'

Joanna stirred then, looking up at her. 'You can't drive, Andie. You've just downed three of those in less than an hour.'

'Oh . . .' she hesitated. 'It's okay, I'll get a cab.'

'Where will you go?'

'I don't know,' said Andie, 'but that isn't your problem, Joanna. You've been incredibly kind, really, way beyond the call. And now I'll leave you be.'

Joanna stood up. 'Look, it's getting late, we have a sofa bed in the study.'

'No, I couldn't —'

'It's no big deal, Andie,' said Joanna.

'It is, it is a big deal!' she insisted, wide-eyed.

'It's not like I'm inviting you to move in. It's just a bed for the night.'

Andie took a breath. 'Well . . . I don't know. What about the kids?'

'They're both out, but if they were here they'd be insisting you stay, especially Brooke.' Joanna paused. 'I know how many times you drove out late at night and picked her up from parties and nightclubs when she'd had a bit too much and didn't want me to know about it.'

Andie opened her mouth to speak but Joanna held up her hand.

'Brooke always confessed to me later,' she said. 'I was only glad she had someone she could call.' Joanna walked over to the hall. 'So I'll get you some sheets, you can make up the sofa bed yourself if it makes you feel better.' She looked back at Andie. 'Well, are you coming?'

Morning

Andie blinked a few times, looking around. Where the hell was she? She didn't know this place. She gave herself a minute, and everything started to flood back . . . the fiasco at the restaurant . . . running away . . . Suddenly the image of the woman and Ross came hurtling into her head like a meteor crashing through the atmosphere. She sat bolt upright, breathing hard. She was at Joanna's, for godsakes! Had she lost her mind completely?

She had to get out of here. She shimmied off the bed and crept over to the door. She could hear muffled voices. She didn't even know the layout of Joanna's house all that well; she had only ever stuck to the main living areas. Andie closed her eyes to recall last night. They went down a hall off the family room, stopped at a linen cupboard, Joanna handed her some sheets. There was a bathroom on the left, the study straight ahead. She was at the back of the house, and this room did not open directly onto the family room. So she could risk opening the door without being seen, try to work out who the voices belonged to, and plan her getaway.

She turned the handle very slowly and inched the door open.

'You have got to be kidding, Mum.'

Andie's heart sank. That was Lauren.

'Seriously, what kind of a nutcase is she, showing up here? And then you let her stay?'

'Lauren, don't be like that. She had nowhere else to go.'

'She has a home. That she shares with my father, in case you'd forgotten that little detail.'

'Yeah, well, be that as it may, it wasn't an option for her last night.'

'What on earth happened?'

Bugger. The whole sordid affair was about to become public knowledge.

'It's not my place to say,' said Joanna. 'It isn't any of our business.'

'She made it your business when she barged into your house and stayed the night.'

'That's the thing, she came to *my* house, Lauren.' Joanna's voice was calm but firm. 'This actually doesn't have anything to do with you, darling.'

Andie closed the door again carefully. Wow, Joanna was shaping up to be quite the good stick. But Andie was still going to have to get past Lauren the guard dog to get out of here. Maybe she could just sit and wait it out. No, that was ridiculous, for all she knew, Lauren was here for the day. Andie picked up her bag off the floor and found her phone, checking the time. It was after eight already. Who was opening the shop today? Her brain was pretty scrambled, but she had a sickening feeling it was her. Bugger. She had no change of clothes, nothing, not even a toothbrush. Even her phone didn't have much charge left. She did have a charger in her car, so that was something. She couldn't risk going back to the apartment, she wasn't ready to deal with Ross, nowhere near ready, she didn't think she could even look at him without feeling sick. No, she needed to stay right away from him until she got her head together. Because Ross would have a story, and it would be persuasive. And Andie needed time to prepare herself for that.

It occurred to her that it wasn't even safe going to the shop. That was sure to be Ross's first port of call this morning when she hadn't returned to the apartment all night. Blast. Okay, think. Jess had worked a full shift last night so she'd likely still be asleep, Andie couldn't expect her to leap out of bed to go and open the shop. She could try Donna, but that would depend on Max. She could start with her anyway. But first she needed to get out of here so she could make some calls.

She'd slept in just her T-shirt, so she pulled on her chef's pants that had been lying crumpled at the end of the bed. She looked like a wreck, which was probably appropriate. It would just confirm everything Lauren thought of her already, but that was the least of her worries right now. As quietly as she could manage, Andie stripped the bed and converted it back into a sofa. She could still hear voices, and the baby occasionally, so hopefully their attention was occupied elsewhere. Andie folded the sheets and left them in a neat pile – the only evidence that she'd been here at all. She pulled on her big chunky work shoes and gave her hair a quick brush. There was no mirror in here, so that would have to do. She grabbed her bag, pausing at the door to take a breath, before she opened it and walked determinedly up the hall to the family room.

Joanna was standing in the kitchen, Lauren was sitting on a couch with Emily propped on her lap and Brooke was slumped beside them, bleary-eyed; she must have only just got up. The look on her face suggested she hadn't been brought up to speed yet.

'Hi everyone,' Andie spoke up. 'Um, I have to get going,' she said, moving past the kitchen. She made eye contact with Joanna. 'Thank you, so much.'

Joanna nodded with a faint smile. 'Take care, Andie.'

'I will,' she said. 'I'll see myself out. Bye,' she called over her shoulder, not looking back at the girls, as she strode up to the front door. She could only imagine the conversation that was going to follow; Andie hoped she'd get a chance to explain it to Brooke herself sometime.

She raced out to the car, jumped in and took off immediately, the dashboard beeping, insisting she put on her seatbelt. She drove around the block into the adjacent street and pulled over, cutting the engine. The beeping stopped. Andie rummaged in her bag for her phone and plugged it into the charger. There were several missed calls from Ross and some texts, but she wasn't going to read them. What the hell could he say in a text message? Her hand was trembling as she deleted them all. Then she rang Donna.

'Hi, Andie,' she chirped a moment later.

'Hi, Donna. Look, I have a favour to ask. I suppose you weren't opening this morning?' she thought to check first.

'Oh, no, I don't think so,' she said. 'Oh, was I? Oh no, I —'

'No, it's okay, Donna. I don't think you were. But is there any chance you could?'

'Oh . . .'

'It's okay, you've got Max?'

'Well, yes, I didn't think I was on today, so he doesn't have child care.'

Damn. 'That's okay.'

'Is something wrong? Did someone call in sick?'

'No, I think I was opening this morning,' Andie assured her. 'And something's come up.'

'Um, well, I could see if Toby's mum's available.'

'Oh, I couldn't ask you to —'

'Come on, Andie, you're always doing favours for me.'

'Thanks, but I need someone to open, and you can't organise Max and get there in enough time,' she said. 'And I wouldn't expect you to,' she added, over Donna's protests.

'Well,' Donna said, 'I seem to remember Steph is on today, maybe she can come in early?'

Double damn. Of course, Friday was their busiest day, there needed to be at least two staff on, and a third from lunchtime . . . though that was probably Jess. Andie realised she didn't want to be there at all today if she could help it. Ross could show up any time.

'Listen, Donna, if I get on to Steph, do you think you could make it in later? I don't mind what time, I don't mind if you bring Max in with you for a while, till Toby's mum can pick him up. Really, whatever's easiest for you.'

'Oh, sure, of course, I'll sort something out,' said Donna. 'Are you okay?'

'Yes, I'm fine,' she lied. 'I'll call you later and let you know what's happening.'

She hung up the phone and scrolled down her contacts. She came to 'Casual Steph' and pressed *Call*. She had to list the casuals that way or she'd never remember them. She'd only worked with Steph a few times; Jess had recommended her, she was the sister of a friend as Andie recalled. Anyway, she seemed like a good kid, Andie hadn't heard any complaints. Fortunately Steph answered almost straightaway in a bright, perky voice, and it didn't sound as though she'd just woken up.

'I hate to ask you this, Steph,' said Andie, 'but do you think you could open today . . . it doesn't matter if you're a little late.'

'Oh, sure, that's not a problem, except I don't have keys.'

Of course. 'Where do you live again?'

'Clovelly.'

Well, at least that made it easier. 'Look, I'm not far from you right now, I can drop keys around to you.'

'Great,' she said. 'Actually, the only thing that's going to hold me up is the buses. Seeing as you're coming past, if you can drive me to the shop I'll be able to open up on time.'

'Good idea.' It was the least she could do, but Andie really didn't want to go anywhere near the shop. She took down Steph's address and hung up. She sat for a moment contemplating her options. There might just be a way she could get this to work in her favour.

Andie pranked Steph's phone when she pulled up outside her apartment block, as they had arranged. Steph came running out soon after and jumped into the car.

'Thanks for doing this,' Andie said, pulling out from the kerb. 'You've got me out of a real bind.'

'No worries.'

'Look, this might sound weird, but I've got this whole surprise thing planned for Ross.'

'Aww, that's so sweet,' she said. 'What's the occasion?'

Bugger, she hadn't thought of one.

'Well, it's an anniversary . . . of sorts. Not of our wedding,' she added quickly. 'It's just one of those silly ones. I don't even think he'll remember, but I wanted to do something special.' It was a wonder she wasn't choking on her words.

'I love it,' Steph gasped. 'Dean and I had to make up our anniversary, because, you know, we didn't really have a first date, we just kind of hooked up at a party. And you know, then we were just kind of together. And I said to him one day, I said, Dean, what's our anniversary? And he said, why don't we make it today! And so we did! Ha.'

Andie smiled. 'Anyway, I left early this morning before Ross was awake, and I left a note for him to meet me at the shop, but I want to go back to the apartment and set up the surprise.'

Steph's eyes lit up. 'What are you going to do?'

'The less you know about the details the better,' Andie said with a wink. 'That way you won't give anything away.'

Steph giggled. 'Okay. Go on.'

'So, just in case, I'm going to drop you around the corner from the shop . . .'

'Uh-huh.'

'. . . and if Ross arrives as you open, and he asks you where I am, you can just tell him that I called and said I was on my way, and that he should wait. That'll give me time.'

'Got it,' said Steph. 'But then what? Won't he wonder after a while?'

'I'll call you as soon as the coast is clear, okay?' said Andie. 'Then you can tell him that I'm waiting for him back at our apartment.'

She grinned. 'This is so exciting! I hope I don't give it away!'

'Just stick to the script. You don't know anything else. You haven't seen me this morning, okay?'

'Okay.' Steph frowned. 'But what if he's not at the shop? You might show up at your place while he's still there.'

That was a good thought.

'I know,' said Steph. 'I'll call you, either way . . . No, wait, I'll text you if he's at the shop. That way he won't know.'

'Excellent. And remember, don't act as if you expected him to be there.'

'But you said I should tell him you called me and asked for him to wait.'

Thank God someone was thinking straight.

'Okay, so don't say that. Just say I called you to open the shop, and that I said I was on my way.'

'That'll work.' Steph grinned.

After Andie dropped Steph off around the corner, she headed for Potts Point. If Ross had decided just to wait for her at home, this was not going to work, whatever Steph said. But he had to leave the apartment some time, and when he did, Andie was going to get in and grab as much of her stuff as she could in one hit. She was pretty confident he would try the shop, though. Ross would want to spin the story as soon as possible. And he would count on her showing up at the shop eventually.

As she drove into their street, Andie felt sick in the stomach. The whole thing began to replay in her head again, however much she tried to blot it out. As she glanced at the entrance to their building she panicked. What if he drove out of the garage now? Her heart was racing as she accelerated past the driveway. But he could pull out behind her, right this minute, and there wasn't a thing she could do about it. She drove on, one eye on the rearview mirror. She turned out of the street again and drove around the block. Their building was surrounded by a circuit of one-way streets, so this time Andie pulled up short, around the corner from the entrance. Ross couldn't pass her without driving the wrong way up a one-way street, and there was no reason for him to do that. Andie would have to just sit here and wait for the message from Steph. She tapped her fingers on the steering wheel, her stomach churning. It occurred to her that life as she knew it was over. Nothing would ever be the same again. Ross had cheated on her, in her bed, with some tramp.

But ten years ago, that was her. And she wasn't a tramp, was she? She'd never slept with him in their family home, and certainly not in their bed. She'd never even been inside his house. Ross took her past one time when it was up for sale, on an inspection day. He asked her if she wanted to go in, and she said no way. It felt disrespectful somehow.

Why would he do it, why would he sleep with this woman in their apartment? Didn't he have any sense of how vastly inappropriate that was? Or did it give him some kind of perverse thrill? Like an animal, marking his territory. Then it occurred to Andie, perhaps the woman had been marking hers. Well, she could have it. Andie could never sleep in that bed again, she could never live in that apartment again. She didn't care what excuses Ross came up with . . . she could imagine them now – it was a one-off, it's never happened before. The truth was, he had cheated before, Andie knew that better than anyone. Because he'd cheated with her.

It was in his DNA. Toby, Jess, they'd always had their suspicions . . . turns out they had been right all along.

Jess. Andie was going to have to tell her. And she wanted to tell her. Regardless of the inevitable 'I told you so's', Andie was desperate to talk to her because she knew that, no matter what, Jess would be on her side. She would say Ross was a prick, and that Andie hadn't done anything to deserve this. Andie really needed to hear that. She also needed a place to stay, at least temporarily. She hoped Jess wasn't working tonight.

Her phone beeped to signal a text message. She picked it up.

Elvis has entered the building.

Steph was right into this whole covert thing. Andie started up the car. She had time.

She drove into the garage and parked, slipping her phone into her pocket. She wanted it on her at all times in case Steph sent any warning messages. She hurried up the stairs to their apartment, opened the door and closed it quickly behind her. She paused there for a moment, as a feeling of dread came over her. What if the woman was still here? Surely not? But there was a chance . . . Her heart was pounding as she crept across to the bedroom. She thought about last night, about the vision that had confronted her, and it turned her stomach. She pushed back the door. The room was empty, the bed immaculate, as if no one had ever slept on it. Not good enough, Ross. He would have to burn the bedding to remove all trace, and even that wasn't good enough.

Andie threw back the sliding doors of the wardrobe and dragged her largest suitcase down from the top shelf. She dashed around the room, emptying entire drawers of underwear and T-shirts, throwing shoes in haphazardly. She found her smaller overnight bag and took it into the bathroom. Andie felt a sick sensation. This was *her* bathroom, one of her most private places. Had the woman used the shower, the sink . . . Andie stared at herself in the mirror, imagining the woman fixing her hair, reapplying lipstick . . . She felt violated. She couldn't stay in here any longer. She swept all her perfumes and lotions and flotsam into the bag. Then she emptied the drawers – cosmetics and more flotsam clattered in. She'd probably end up tossing a lot of it. She had too much of the gunk anyway, and what good had it done her? All the creams and lotions and age-defying potions in the world would not make Andie twenty again. And Ross clearly had a penchant for twentysomethings. Andie glanced around for anything she had missed. She plucked her toothbrush out of the glass it shared with Ross's and tossed it in the bag. Thinking about it, she'd have to throw it out and buy herself a new one. She certainly wasn't going to use it again.

She went back into the bedroom and scooped up an armful of clothes on their hangers, lurching them over into the open suitcase. Then she squashed everything down and zipped the lid closed, just. She slid the suitcase off the bed onto its wheels and pulled out the handle. Thank God for wheelie bags.

Andie cast a final gaze around the room, spotting her phone charger, a book on her bedside table, another bloody tub of overpriced goop – hand cream this time – and tossed it all into the overnight bag. Out in the living room she ranged around, picking up random things . . . a favourite mug, a little crystal unicorn Donna had given her, a photo of her and Brendan together as children. She glanced at the remote control and momentarily considered stealing it out of spite, but that was petty. And this was so far past petty. She paused at a framed photo of their wedding. She didn't even look like a bride; she had heard her mother's voice in her head telling her she had no business wearing white, so she'd chosen a simple pale blue dress with a jacket. No bouquet either, she would have felt self-conscious. But they did look happy. Despite the pain and angst they had been through, that they had put everyone through, they had convinced themselves that theirs was a true, once-in-a-lifetime love, that they had a right to be together, and to get on with their lives. Ross had vowed to make it up to his kids over time, and he promised Andie he would do the right thing by Joanna financially. But, he had said, it was their time now.

And now he was probably spinning the same yarn to this woman. All those niggles she'd had about him rejoining the gym, giving up alcohol, going off sex – though, as it turned out, only with her – she hadn't been paranoid after all. It must have been going on for months, perhaps longer. How would Andie ever be able to trust him again? Ross didn't end his first marriage because he'd found true, once-in-a-lifetime love. He was a serial monogamist, and he had moved on to his next conquest. Andie turned the frame face down, and slid her phone out of her pocket.

Pls tell Ross I'm waiting for him at home, she texted to Steph. She picked up her handbag and the overnight bag, grasped the handle of the wheelie suitcase, and walked out of the apartment.

Newtown

'You're not going to be able to avoid him forever,' said Jess, pouring Andie another glass of wine.

'I know that,' she said. 'I just need some time.'

Her phone hadn't stopped ringing earlier in the day. Andie worked out it must have started around the time Ross would have made it back to the apartment and realised most of her stuff was gone. She had decided not to go to the shop at all – after the story she'd fed Steph that wasn't really an option anyway. So Andie instinctively headed north over the bridge to her dad's. She was calmer now, she had no intention of telling him what had happened, and she hoped he wouldn't guess anything was up, she didn't want to upset him. He'd find out eventually, but for now Andie wanted to keep a lid on it. She needed more time to get her act together, she still felt so mortified. The marriage everyone expected to be a failure had finally fulfilled all expectations.

Andie had to make some calls first, so she stopped off at a café on the way. Although she couldn't recall the last time she'd put food in her mouth, she still wasn't hungry, so she just ordered one coffee after another, until she began to feel wired and vaguely nauseous, so she had to stop. She managed to get on to Donna, who had just arrived at the shop after dropping Max off at Toby's mother's.

'Thanks so much for this, Donna. I owe you.'

'Oh, you do not,' she'd insisted. 'So is everything okay?'

She couldn't answer that. And she realised that Steph would give Donna her version of the events anyway. Andie might as well leave it at that for now, she didn't have the energy for any more intrigue.

'Look, I can't really talk now, Donna, I just wanted to check who's on the roster for this afternoon.'

'Okay, just a sec,' she said, obviously going to look. 'It's Jess.'

Good. 'So you'll be right for today?'

'Absolutely, don't worry about a thing here.'

She wasn't, the shop was the last thing Andie was worried about. She left the café and stopped at a supermarket to pick up a few things for her father, she never went empty-handed.

She drove around to the house . . . today it would be her refuge, but it hadn't always been that. It had been a place of rules and order and tough love – her mother ran a tight ship. Andie and Brendan had planned their emancipation; once he'd settled into uni, they were going to start their own share-house with Toby, and maybe someone else, depending on what they found to rent. After their neat and tidy childhood, Brendan was desperate to find somewhere as grungy as possible – he dreamed of a crumbling, dank terrace in a back lane in Chippendale. Andie was hoping she could talk him up from that, just a little.

She walked up the front path now, through the unkempt garden. It must annoy the neighbours, they were a very houseproud lot around here. Her father used to be houseproud too . . . well, her mother was, and her father did as she told him, keeping the lawn tended while she saw to the plants. Andie was never sure if her mother actually enjoyed gardening, it was just another necessary chore, part of keeping up appearances, which was very important here on the leafy north shore. When she was too sick to go outside she had berated Andie for not planting annuals at the right time, even though she would not be around long enough to see them bloom. It didn't matter, the neighbours would see them.

Andie gave a cursory knock on the front door before letting herself in as usual, announcing herself as she did. There was no answer, and the TV wasn't going either. She walked through the house, calling out to her father, but it was soon obvious he wasn't home. He must have had a doctor's appointment. In the kitchen the kettle was still warm, a plate of toast crusts and a half cup of tea sat on the table. Andie felt a little disappointed. She'd just needed a place to hide out for a few hours where she knew Ross wouldn't come looking for her, but she would have found some comfort in a hug from her dad.

At least now she could phone Jess; Andie hadn't wanted to call any earlier in case she woke her up. But Jess was due at the shop within the hour, so Andie was sure she'd be up by now. She dialled her number.

'I have something to tell you,' she began when Jess answered. 'But this is just between you and me for now, okay?'

*

'You know I'm impressed,' Andie said to Jess, picking up her glass. 'You haven't said "I told you so" once yet.'

Jess shrugged, refilling her own glass. 'Why waste my breath stating the bleeding obvious?'

Andie just smiled, sipping her wine. She was sitting on the floor of Jess's cramped little flat, leaning back against the sofa where she would sleep that night. She had ended up leaving her father's house this afternoon before he made it home. She was a little surprised he stayed out most of the day, but then, it was good if he was getting out and about more. Maybe she had been worrying about him unnecessarily.

Jess had insisted earlier that Andie stay with her, she didn't even have to ask. She knew where the spare key was hidden, so Jess told her just to let herself in if she wasn't home yet. Andie wanted to cook her dinner to thank her. Besides, her stomach had finally registered it was hungry, so she stopped in Newtown and bought the makings for a Thai tom yum soup – a favourite of Jess's – and a couple of bottles of wine. By the time Jess made it home from the shop, the smell of coriander and lemongrass filled the flat, and Andie had started on the first bottle.

'What I will say is this,' Jess went on, 'I don't understand why you left the apartment the way you did. If I were you, I'd have called a locksmith and had the locks changed.'

Andie sighed. 'Don't be crazy, Jess.'

'It's not crazy,' she said. 'That apartment is as much yours.'

'But I don't want it.' She paused, thinking of how to explain it to Jess. 'Have you heard people describe how they feel when their house has been robbed? They've had more than their possessions stolen, they've had their privacy stolen, their security. They feel violated . . . that's what it felt like today when I went to the apartment.'

Jess drew closer and gave Andie's arm a reassuring rub. 'Okay,' she said gently, 'I understand why you don't want to *keep* it —'

'I don't want to set foot in there ever again, if I can help it.'

'Well, you probably can't help it,' said Jess. 'You've been married for ten years, it's your home as much as it is his.'

'Pity he didn't take that into account when he had sex with his . . . his . . .'

'Is "slut" the word you're looking for?'

'Don't call her that,' Andie said seriously.

Jess held up her hands in mock surrender. 'Okay, I know that's not a particularly PC term these days, but a spade is still a dirty tool for digging, whatever you call it.'

Andie looked at her directly. 'That was me, ten years ago.'

'That was never you,' Jess cried indignantly. 'I knew you back then, remember, and you would never have done something like that.'

'You don't think so?'

'I know so!' She shifted to face Andie squarely. 'You were constantly riddled with guilt, always worried about his family, and not wanting his kids to get hurt.'

'Does that make it all right that I took their father away?'

'Andie, you didn't take him away, he went of his own accord.'

'That's why I can't put all the blame on this woman now,' said Andie. 'Who knows what lies he's telling her? I only know that I can't go through it all over again. From the other side.' She took a breath. 'So I'm going to leave him, free and clear.'

Jess shook her head. 'After ten years of marriage, you're entitled —'

'But I don't want anything of his.'

'What about the shop?'

Andie looked at her. 'I don't know . . .'

'That shop is yours – "free and clear".'

'But it was his idea.'

'So? You made it what it is today. And it's your livelihood.'

'Then I'll have to find another way to make a living.'

'All right,' said Jess, with a heavy sigh. 'I have to say it, this kind of talk really worries me.'

'Why?'

'It's too . . . extreme. You're reacting out of shock,' she said. 'I know you're upset, you've got every reason to be upset, Andie, but you're not thinking rationally. You don't just walk away from everything and never talk to him again, you're not teenagers.'

Jess was right.

'You've been married to him for ten years, Andie,' she said, her tone softening. 'You need to stop and take a breath.'

Andie's phone beeped. It was another text. The texts had started after Ross had given up calling. At first they were plaintive.

Andie, I'm worried about you, please call me, let me explain.

They'd progressed to annoyed.

You're being childish, we have to talk.

And now they were downright angry.

*Fu*k this. Call me.*

'What's that one say?' asked Jess.

Andie replaced the phone on the table. 'Same as the others. He's getting angry now.'

'Next thing he's going to show up here, you realise,' said Jess.

Andie pressed her lips together, frowning. 'Do you want me to find somewhere else to stay?'

'No,' she insisted. 'I want you to take control of your life. You've decided what you don't want, now you have to decide what you do want. You need a plan.'

Monday

Andie sat drumming her fingers on the table. True to form, Ross was keeping her waiting. At least that would make it easier to maintain the rage. She had arrived early to avoid any chance of finding him already sitting here, waiting, all posed and prepared with his best little-boy face, looking abject and crestfallen.

Jess was right, everything so far had been a knee-jerk reaction, and avoiding Ross had seemed like the best strategy. As much as he repulsed her now, Andie knew she still had feelings for him. You don't just stop loving someone overnight because they turn out to be a shit. But those feelings troubled her. Jess said she had to take charge of her life again, but Andie wasn't sure how to do that. Ross had controlled her life for the last ten years, though to be fair she had willingly handed over that control. And look where it had left her. Had he fallen out of love with her because she was so weak and obliging? Had she bored him into infidelity? She remembered him saying something along those lines about Joanna, but Andie had always cut him off. She didn't like to hear him putting down the mother of his children. It wasn't Joanna's fault, it was nobody's fault. Andie and Ross had fallen in love, it just happened.

And now it was happening again. His duplicity was breathtaking. Did he really arrange the job at Viande just to keep her out at nights? Did that mean he was planning to maintain a marriage and a mistress? What was in it for him to keep up the deception? Were men so shallow that a little extra sex on the side was worth all the palaver involved in covering it up?

Yes, said Jess, some men were that shallow.

She encouraged Andie to finally reply to the barrage of text messages. To take the reins, so to speak.

Ross, pls refrain from the constant texting. I will be in touch tomorrow, as long as I don't hear another word from you in the meantime.

That gave her the upper hand, if ever so slightly. The next step in her still fuzzy plan was to arrange to meet him. Jess said all she really had to do was listen, hear Ross out and understand the tack he was going to take, so that she would be better prepared to deal with him from now on. Andie couldn't deny that it hurt like hell to think that Ross didn't want her anymore, that he might have fallen in love with this woman, and was planning to leave her. But if he claimed it was just a fling, if he never had any intention of leaving Andie . . . not that she would want him back, but, well, it would be a little easier to take.

She didn't share any of those thoughts with Jess though. She didn't need to hear how insipid they were. Andie had to steel herself if she was going to get through this meeting with Ross. She knew what he was like. He would use his considerable – and in her case, quite effective – powers of persuasion to talk her around, so she had to guard herself against that possibility. Jess had offered to send texts every twenty minutes, timely prompts that would also serve to give Andie an out, should she need one. She could say it was something important and that she had to leave.

Andie sighed, leaning back heavily in her chair. With all the covert operations of the last few days, she was beginning to think she should consider a new career as a spy. That would certainly give her a whole new life – exotic locations, handsome co-spies, false identities involving fabulous wardrobe changes . . . But who was she kidding? She was frightened of fast cars, heights, guns – not that she'd ever even seen a gun in real life, but just the idea was enough to terrify her. So spying was probably not for her, after all.

Andie was jolted back into reality when she spotted Ross weaving through the stream of people on the boardwalk moving towards her. When she proposed meeting at Darling Harbour, Ross had baulked at first, suggesting they meet at the apartment. Andie certainly didn't want to be alone with him, she wanted to meet him somewhere busy and noisy, so they could talk freely without drawing attention to themselves. So when she proceeded to outline the rather obvious reasons why she didn't want to step foot in the apartment, Ross had quickly backed off and reluctantly agreed to meet her here.

This had all been done via text messages, Andie hadn't felt ready to talk to him yet. But now she had no choice. He was approaching her table, and she could see him arranging his features into an expression that read 'contrite'.

'Hello, Andie,' he said solemnly.

She just nodded.

'May I?' he asked, planting his hands on the back of the chair opposite.

'Of course.'

He made a bit of a production of pulling the chair out and arranging himself to sit. And then they were facing each other across the table.

'Have you ordered?' he asked.

'Not yet.'

'So what would you like to drink?'

'Just coffee for me, thanks.' She wasn't going to have anything stronger, she had to keep a clear head.

Ross raised his hand to beckon a waiter, and one came running immediately. He had that effect. And of course it was a woman. He gave her their coffee orders and after she left, he sat back in his chair, clasping his hands loosely in his lap, like he was waiting for something. But surely it was up to him to start?

'So, Ross?' Andie prompted him.

He released a heavy sigh, as if he had the weight of the world on his shoulders. He sat forward now, leaning his elbows on the table, and rubbing one hand across his jaw. 'Andie,' he said finally, 'I don't think there are words to express how sorry I am . . . I can't imagine what it must have been like.'

I, I, I.

'I know it probably won't mean much to you,' he struggled on, 'but I didn't plan for that to happen, I certainly didn't ask for it —'

'You seemed to be bearing up all right at the time.'

He closed his eyes for a beat, opening them again and fixing them on her. 'It was her idea . . . she ambushed me —'

'Oh for Chrissakes, Ross!'

'No, listen to me, it's the truth. We only called in to the apartment briefly, I had to pick up something. I wasn't even going to bring her inside, but she got out of the car before I could do anything. Then when we were about to leave she asked to use the bathroom. She didn't come out for a while, and she didn't answer when I called, so I went looking for her.'

Andie couldn't believe this was his defence.

He stared down at the table. 'She was just sitting there . . . barely dressed . . .'

Oh, the horror.

'And because you're a helpless male, you had no choice in the matter?' said Andie.

'That's not what I'm saying,' he snapped. 'Christ, Andie, are we going to talk about this like adults? Or do you just want to score points? Because you win, okay? The points all go to you. I forfeit.'

Forfeit? That was generous of him. Andie was surprised he thought he had any points in his credit in the first place.

Ross took a breath. 'So, all right,' he continued in a calmer tone, 'I'm weak, I admit it. But I did try to stop her, I said it wasn't appropriate, but she . . . persisted. Anyway, it was wrong. And if you don't think for a minute that I know it was wrong, then . . . you don't know me at all.'

How did he just do that? Did he expect Andie to say sorry now? He had a magician-like sleight of hand, only with his tongue.

Just then her phone beeped. 'Excuse me,' she said, fishing it out of her bag. It was from Jess.

Hows ur bullshit meter holding up?

Andie had to keep her wits about her. 'Ross, I think this is bigger than just what happened the other evening,' she said. 'Let's ignore that for a moment, shall we?'

His eyes narrowed, waiting for her next move.

'How long have you been seeing this . . . girl?'

'I've known her a few months,' he said. 'It didn't start out as anything.'

What did that even mean?

'She was just a pretty young girl in the office, flirting with the boss,' he said. 'I mean, it happens all the time, and it's hard not to be flattered by the attention when you're my age. I didn't lead her on, though, I certainly didn't mean to. I made it very clear from the start that I was married. Didn't seem to put her off, if anything it made me more of a challenge,' he muttered.

The waiter returned with their coffees, placing them on the table.

'Can I get you anything else?' she said to Ross, flashing him a dazzling smile.

'No, thank you,' he said, and she left.

'Go on, Ross, you were saying?' Andie prompted. 'You were put upon by this girl, helpless against her considerable advances —'

'Stop it, Andie!' he cried. 'Do you realise how hard this has been for me? I've been struggling with it for months. I didn't want to go through it all over again, the recriminations, introducing someone new, it would be so much easier to keep the status quo . . .'

What?

'But you pushed me to this, with all your talk about wanting a baby. I know how it feels to be betrayed, Andie. You betrayed our marriage as much as I did. You didn't give a damn about me and my wishes any more. You just wanted me to impregnate you.'

Andie's gob couldn't be more smacked. He saw his betrayal on the same level as hers? Really? *Really?*

'I didn't know what to do,' he said, his voice softening. 'Then I thought that maybe if you had a career, some goals, you would drop the idea of a baby, and we could pick up again like we were before. I was ready to do anything.'

The new chef set. The special celebratory dinner. Steel yourself, Andie.

'So the girlfriend was part of the plan, an interim measure to get you through?'

She said it snidely, but he didn't respond in kind.

'No, that's a mess of my own making, and I'm just trying to extricate myself with the minimum amount of damage.'

Andie frowned. 'To whom?'

'To you. Me. Tasha.'

'That's her name?' It seemed somehow appropriate. She'd been imagining Tiffany, or maybe Kimberley.

'The thing is,' Ross went on, 'Tasha's a bit needy. You might even say . . . unhinged.'

Something inside Andie – something she was not proud of – gave her a moment's delight at hearing that.

'So you bring her to our apartment,' Andie said, 'and succumb to her advances – that's how you "extricate" yourself from her?'

Ross was shaking his head. 'It's so easy for you to sit there and judge, isn't it, Andie?'

'Yes, it is, Ross,' she said evenly. 'It's actually very easy for me to sit here and judge the husband who I've discovered has been cheating on me.'

He looked sullen. 'Yeah, well, you can be as smug and superior as you like. You can lay all the blame at my feet. After all, I'm the cheating husband, in the eyes of the world, your rap sheet is clean. You don't have to look at yourself, or analyse your role in what happened. But if you honestly believe a third party could ever get a foothold in a strong, sound marriage, then fine, you can go away with a clear conscience.'

Andie's heart had begun to race as he spoke, and now she felt a little breathless. Her phone beeped again. Thank God. She picked it up and looked at the message without reading it.

'I have to go. There's a junior filling in at the shop, I have to close.' She picked up her bag and Ross quickly reached across the table to grab her hand.

'Andie, come home,' he said, his voice plaintive.

'No.'

'I'll move out,' he said. 'I'll go and stay in a hotel, you shouldn't have to leave the apartment.'

'Ross, I can't go back there, don't you get that?' She pulled her hand away and got to her feet. 'You really don't seem to understand how much this has hurt me.'

He stood up. 'I do, Andie, I understand, and I'm going to do everything I can to make it up to you. I'm not letting you go without a fight.'

She just looked at him. She didn't know what to say. She didn't trust herself to say anything. 'Goodbye, Ross.'

*

Andie didn't have to close up the shop, by the time she got there Donna would have closed and left already. But she was going to hide out for a while. She needed time to think, on her own, with no distractions. Of course she knew Ross was protecting himself, of course she knew a lot of what he said was bullshit . . . she just wasn't sure which parts, or how much. Jess would say it all was, she would write off everything he said.

And Andie would have a clean rap sheet.

As she made it to her car in the parking station, she heard the beep of another text message arriving. It was Jess again.

Whats going on?

Andie unlocked the door and sat in the driver's seat to answer it.

It's over. On my way to the shop to do paperwork.

No debrief?

Later. Glad I don't have to hide from him anymore. Thanks for making me do it. xA

There was a slightly longer pause before Jess replied.

Glad to. Talk later, take care xJ

*

Andie did feel some solace at the shop; it was the only place left that was hers now, where she wasn't a guest or an interloper. She was going to have to do something about her living arrangements; she couldn't stay on Jess's fold-out forever, her flat was way too small anyway to accommodate two people for any extended length of time. She got herself a plate from the kitchen, and went to inspect the containers in the fridge. She wasn't all that hungry, but she knew she should eat something; her jeans were sagging a bit around the bum, and her face looked wan staring back at her in the mirror. But she had a whole shop full of food and nothing appealed, like that poem, *Water, water everywhere* . . . In the end, Andie sliced some bread and made a simple sandwich of cheese and ham. But she couldn't eat it, she just sat in the quiet, semi-dark, thinking.

Andie didn't know what was going to happen down the track, but she had to do something now to prove to Ross that this was serious, and that it wasn't going to be fixed overnight. She wasn't going back to the apartment, so she had to find a place of her own. The idea was actually appealing – somewhere she didn't have to answer to anyone, or allow for anyone else . . . A small studio apartment would do, she didn't need much space, but it would be her space, and hers alone. A refuge.

She needed time out, to take stock, to decide if this was where she wanted to be. Whether or not Ross was telling the truth, if he ended it with the girl and had no intention of seeing her again, how would Andie ever be able to trust him again?

She wasn't falling for his hype, but neither could she absolve herself of some of his accusations. She knew how much the baby issue had thrown him. She had expected him to change his mind for her, to completely turn around on something he'd stated emphatically from the beginning of their relationship. There was nothing wrong with Andie's desire for a baby, that was natural, but to expect Ross to fall into line without question, well, perhaps that was unreasonable. A fifty-four-year-old man with grown children and a granddaughter had every right to recoil at the idea of starting all over again.

But to have an affair? He was drawing a rather long bow there. It didn't excuse him. Not that he'd said it was an excuse, or did he? Some of his double-talk had confused her. The big thing was whether to believe him on the matter of Tasha. And there was a part of Andie that really wanted to believe him, not to exonerate him, but so that she could differentiate herself from the girl. Ross had had an affair with Andie, but she was not unstable, or unhinged or whatever terms he'd used. She had not flirted outrageously, or pushed herself onto him . . . She hadn't been needy, had she? She had certainly never stepped foot inside the marital home. She had always made him do the decent thing by Joanna and the kids. In the murky moral morass of a marriage breakdown, Andie had tried to do the right thing. She was not like Tasha, and she did not want Tasha to be anything like her.

The ringtone of her mobile startled her.

'Are you all right?' Jess said as soon as Andie picked up. 'What's going on, where are you?'

'I'm fine,' she said. 'I told you I was going to the shop.'

'But what are you doing there so long?' she persisted.

'Well, I'm just having something to eat, and then I'm going to do some paperwork – like I said.'

There was a pause. 'Are you sure you're okay?'

'I am, Jess. Thanks for your concern, but really, I feel better since seeing him.' That was mostly true. 'You were so right, I couldn't avoid him forever. Now I can move on, start making some decisions for myself.'

'That's great.' She sounded a little tentative. 'What did he have to say for himself?'

'Oh, I don't want to go into it all now over the phone. We'll talk about it later.'

'Well, that's the thing,' said Jess. 'You know my friend, Alex, and some of the others? Well, they're meeting for a drink, she invited us along.'

'Oh, thanks anyway, but I think I'll pass,' said Andie. 'I'm feeling a bit drained actually.'

'Oh, okay, I'll stay in then, and wait for you.'

'No you will not,' Andie retorted. 'Jess, I'm perfectly fine. I'll probably just crash when I get back to your place anyway.'

Jess still hesitated. 'Are you sure? What if you need to talk?'

'We'll have plenty of time to talk, Jess. You should go out, have some fun.'

'Okay,' she finally relented. 'But I'll text you where we end up, in case you change your mind later.'

She wouldn't, but she said, 'Okay,' before hanging up. Andie was glad she wouldn't have to go over it all with Jess tonight. Her thoughts were still too chaotic.

Maybe it would help if she focused on something else for a while. Paperwork was not such a bad idea. She walked through to the back of the shop and sat down at the desk, switching on the lamp. She began to sort through invoices and orders and general correspondence, but after a while she realised she was doing nothing but shuffling papers around. She sat back with a heavy sigh. Clearly she wasn't going to be able to focus on anything else. She found herself putting pictures to the story Ross had fed her, imagining the dark-haired girl with the pert breasts flirting with him at the office, throwing tantrums when he made excuses not to see her, forcing her way into the apartment and stripping off before he could do anything about it.

It was like a bad soap opera, with Ross coming off as the hero, or at the very least, the victim. How much of what he said was true? Surely he couldn't have made up the entire thing; surely he was only stretching the truth? But by how much?

Andie groaned out loud and got to her feet, pushing the chair away. She was pacing around the room like a caged animal when she heard the beep of a text message. She rushed back out to the shop where she'd left her phone. It was from Jess, letting her know they were at a pub in King Street.

Maybe Andie should join them after all. She wasn't going to get any peace tonight, she might as well get drunk instead. She closed the message, which brought her back to Contacts. Joanna was listed directly after Jess. Andie's heart started to race. No, she couldn't do it again. It was out of the question. Joanna would undoubtedly have a very interesting perspective on what Ross had said today, Andie was sure of it. But, no matter, she was not going to bother the woman again.

She wondered what Joanna would have to say, though . . . It would certainly help clarify some things . . .

But no, it wasn't appropriate. Joanna had been so kind to her that night . . .

And Andie had never thanked her! That was very remiss of her. She should have at least called Joanna afterwards to say thank you. It was too late for that now.

Flowers! She could have some flowers delivered, with a thankyou message. That was an appropriate gesture.

Though it might seem a little distant, impersonal . . . And you send flowers when someone dies . . .

What if she bought some flowers now, and dropped them around to Joanna's house? She wouldn't even go inside, she'd just have a polite chat on the doorstep. In fact, even if Joanna invited her in, Andie would simply decline. It was the perfect solution.

*

Andie knew a place only a few blocks from the shop. They sold fruit and vegies, and lovely fresh flowers – a limited range, the owner only bought what caught his eye at the markets each morning. Today it was Singapore lilies. Andie bought two bunches which they wrapped together in tissue paper, then she set off for Joanna's house.

It would be overstating things to say that Joanna was shocked to see Andie when she opened the door. Surprised, most definitely, but not shocked. Though Andie was beginning to think that maybe she should have called first.

'I'm not staying,' she said quickly. 'I'm only here to give you a belated thankyou.' She passed Joanna the flowers.

'They're lovely,' said Joanna. 'You really didn't have to, Andie.'

'Oh, I did. You were very kind, I'm not sure how I would have made it through that night. I should have done this sooner, but . . .' She left that hanging.

'How's it going?' Joanna asked her.

Andie shrugged. 'Fine.'

'Did you go back . . . home . . . to Ross?'

'Only to collect my things, when he wasn't there.'

'Have you seen him, talked to him?'

'Not until today.'

Andie saw the realisation dawn on her face. 'Why don't you come in for a minute?'

'No, I promised myself I wasn't going to impose on you again.'

Joanna sighed. 'Look, I've been wondering how you were getting on. I was going to call, but *I* didn't want to impose on you.'

'You wouldn't have been imposing,' Andie was quick to assure her.

'And you're not imposing now. Come in, Andie.'

She hesitated. 'Is anyone home?'

'Only Brooke,' said Joanna, standing back from the doorway. 'And she's upstairs, cramming for an exam tomorrow. If we sit here in the front room, she won't hear us, she won't even know you're here.'

'Okay then, just for a minute.'

She followed Joanna into the sitting room. It was such a gorgeous room, Andie had always admired Joanna's taste. Plump sofas that had exactly the right number and combination of cushions tossed artlessly across them; warm timber bookshelves crammed with beautiful books . . . it was perfect without looking like a magazine spread. In fact it was probably more like a film set; one of those fabulous houses in a movie, where Meryl Streep or Diane Keaton might come walking out of the kitchen any moment.

'Sit down, make yourself at home,' Joanna was saying as she carried the flowers across to the doorway. 'I'll just put these in water. Can I get you a drink – hard, soft, hot, cold?'

'No, thank you, Joanna, I'm fine.'

Andie sank into the plush sofa that almost felt like it was hugging her. Joanna soon returned with the flowers in a simple glass vase, perfectly arranged.

'They really are beautiful, Andie. Thank you,' she said, placing them on the coffee table, off-centre, so they wouldn't be in the way. She sat down on the sofa opposite. 'So, where are you staying, if you don't mind me asking?'

'Of course not. I'm staying with my old friend, Jess,' she said. 'But her flat is tiny, I'm going to look for a place of my own.'

Joanna raised an eyebrow. 'So it's come to that?'

'I guess it has,' said Andie. 'I mean, I don't know what's going to happen down the track, but I think I need my own space while I work it out.'

Joanna nodded thoughtfully. 'How does Ross feel about that? You saw him today?'

'Yes. He wants me to come home. I told him no, I'm never going to be able to live in that apartment again.'

'Will you ever be able to live with him again?'

'He hasn't convinced me yet.'

'He's trying though?'

Andie realised Joanna didn't want to hear this. Ross had not been able to get out of their marriage fast enough.

'Oh, he's mostly just trying to save his own skin,' said Andie. 'He's blaming it all on the girl.'

Joanna shook her head with a wry smile. 'At least he's consistent, sticking with the same MO.'

Andie looked at her. 'Pardon?'

She hesitated. 'Oh, nothing.'

'Really, Joanna,' she urged, 'what do you mean by the same MO?'

'Well, you know, I'm sure it's no surprise that he did the same thing when he was caught out with you,' she said. 'It's pretty typical for a man in his position to try to shift the blame.'

That didn't make sense. Ross had always maintained that he had been the one to confront Joanna, that he had sat her down and explained he'd found someone else, that maybe they wouldn't be able to keep up the sham of their marriage until the kids finished school, that he had asked her if there wasn't a way they could do it amicably.

'You caught him out?' Andie eventually managed to say.

Joanna nodded. 'Of course, not in the same way you did. You'd have known about that.'

'Yes . . . but you found some damning evidence, some proof he was having an affair?'

'No, nothing that concrete,' she said.

'So how did you find out?'

She shrugged. 'It was little things at first . . . you wouldn't worry about any one of them on its own, but they started to add up after a while. He'd always worked long hours, but it got worse, he never seemed to be at home. And he began to stay away overnight more often. Before that, when he had to travel interstate, he did everything to wrap his business up in one day. I started to ask questions, but he always dismissed them, said I read too much into things.'

Andie's heart cramped painfully inside her chest. So not only did Ross not tell Joanna upfront, he actively denied it.

'Then he went on a health kick,' she said. 'He took up jogging, said he was getting soft, at his age he had to start looking after himself.' Joanna shook her head. 'In retrospect it all sounds so obvious, he was a walking cliché, going through the classic midlife crisis. Finally I confronted him. He lied and lied, but the more he lied, the more I knew for sure there was something going on. It took days to get it out of him.'

And now he was spinning the same lies to Andie, he wasn't even original. And he'd lied to her back then as well. In Ross's version, Joanna had freaked out and reacted completely unreasonably. He claimed she knew as well as he did that the marriage had no future, but she was suddenly concerned about keeping up appearances. She said the children were still too young . . .

'Once he knew he was cornered,' Joanna went on, 'he started blaming it all on you – swore he never led you on, that it was difficult to resist the advances of a pretty young girl at his age.'

Andie felt winded. Word for fucking word. And that's what he said about her to Joanna? She swallowed hard. 'Joanna, it isn't true,' she barely managed to squeeze the words out of her throat.

'Don't worry about it,' she said with a wave of her hand. 'Water under the bridge. It's a long time ago now.'

'But I need you to know that's not the way it happened,' Andie insisted, finding her voice. 'I didn't come on to him at all. I didn't flirt, you can ask Jess, I've never been a flirty type. I mean, I was flattered, we used to chat, have a laugh, but I didn't start anything. A lot of the businessmen – most of them – who came to Lemongrass regularly, well, they all flirted.'

Joanna was listening. 'Were they all married?'

'Mostly they were,' Andie admitted. 'So when Ross started coming on a bit stronger, suggesting an actual date, I reminded him he was wearing a wedding ring. He said it was only for appearances, that you two were just biding your time for the sake of the kids, till they finished school —'

She stopped abruptly, shaking her head. 'God, that sounds so flimsy now. I should have known better, I was too gullible, too ready to believe him.'

'You were young,' Joanna shrugged. 'And I know how convincing Ross can be.'

'It wasn't just that. I was so alone,' she said, remembering. 'I'd lost my brother, and my mum, only a couple of years before. My dad was withdrawn, my sister and I were like distant relatives. I had a few good friends, but my family was shattered.' Andie paused, looking across at Joanna. 'I'm not trying to make excuses. I should have known better, I promise you I was brought up better than to break up someone else's family.'

'Listen, Andie,' said Joanna, leaning forward. 'Things are never that simple. If Ross and I had been strong and happy together, he may have flirted, he's always been a bit of a flirt, but he wouldn't have risked his happiness, and the happiness of his family, on a flirtation.'

Andie wondered where she was going with this.

'Our marriage had definitely hit a flat patch,' she said plainly.

'You don't have to explain to me —'

'I want to,' she insisted. 'Now that we're in the same boat, I think I'd like you to hear my side as well.'

This was so weird. She and Joanna were in the same boat now? How had that happened?

'The marriage wasn't over,' Joanna continued, 'despite what Ross made out to you. Maybe in his head, but he certainly hadn't shared that observation with me. It's true, you couldn't say there was much passion any more. I don't know if you can have the kind of passion he was pining for after twenty-odd years of marriage and three children. It's replaced by something deeper by then. Or it's supposed to be. But instead of coming to me, and trying to work it out, Ross had an affair.'

Joanna looked straight at her. 'He did try to blame you, Andie, but I knew deep down, even if I didn't admit it to myself at the time, that he had the responsibility to the marriage, not you. It wasn't your fault, even if on some level I wanted to believe that.'

'What do you mean?'

'Don't you see? It's so much easier to believe that some kind of temptress has lured your husband away, almost beyond his will. Then it only means he's weak, not that he doesn't love you anymore.'

Oh God, they *were* in the same boat, Joanna knew exactly how she was feeling, because she'd felt it too. And even if she wasn't blaming her any more, Andie still felt some responsibility for putting her through that.

She thought about Ross's story that Tasha had seduced him in the apartment. He knew which buttons to push. 'Ross told me this girl is very clingy, apparently, he's worried she's a little unhinged . . .'

Joanna had an odd look on her face, but she didn't say anything.

'It's probably all lies,' said Andie, shaking her head. 'I just have to wonder what he's telling her. He couldn't use the same story he gave me, that you were staying together for the sake of the kids, seeing as we don't have any.' Andie drew her breath in sharply.

'What is it?' said Joanna.

She looked at her. 'I was pressuring Ross to have a baby . . . Well, I don't think I was exactly pressuring him, it didn't get that far. But he knew how I felt, and I'm not sure I was taking his feelings into account.'

'So that makes it all right for him to have an affair?'

'No, I guess not.'

'Of course not,' Joanna insisted. 'Andie, just because there were problems in our marriage, it didn't mean Ross had no option but to have an affair. That's the coward's way out. He didn't even give me the chance to work on the marriage, to meet him halfway. He was already gone.'

He hadn't come to Andie either, he hadn't told her he was unhappy. He was unhappy with the idea of having a baby, yes, but he hadn't said it was make or break . . . or had he? Andie's head was beginning to hurt.

'I should get going,' she said, standing up. 'I didn't mean to take up your evening.'

'It's all right.' Joanna walked her to the door. 'Stay strong, Andie, don't be afraid to stand up for yourself,' she said.

'I'll try.' She stepped out onto the porch.

'And keep in touch. The kids will want to know where you are.'

'Of course. Thanks.'

As Andie got to her car, her phone beeped. She took it out and read the text message. She was surprised that it was from Brooke.

I need to talk to you, can you drive down to the corner & wait for me? Pls.

Andie glanced up at the house. Brooke was standing at a window on the first floor. She held her hand up in a wave. Andie felt conflicted, she didn't want to do anything behind Joanna's back, all the more because of how kind she had been to her through all this. But she couldn't ignore Brooke. She would hear what she had to say, and make it very clear that she had to be honest with her mother. Andie raised her hand and nodded, and then got into the car. She drove down to the corner and waited.

It wasn't long before there was a tap on the passenger side window, and Brooke appeared. Andie indicated for her to get in.

'Thanks for waiting for me,' said Brooke, as she sat in the car and pulled the door closed.

'Hi,' Andie began carefully. 'It's really good to see you, Brooke, but I have to say, I feel a little uncomfortable about this. Couldn't you have come downstairs and talked to me in front of your mum?'

'It'd only upset her,' she said.

'But maybe you shouldn't be telling me something you wouldn't want your mother to hear.'

'It's not like that,' said Brooke. 'It's just, well, I heard a lot of your conversation tonight.'

'Oh?'

'I didn't mean to eavesdrop, really I didn't, Andie,' she said. 'I was coming down the stairs to get a drink, and I heard voices. I didn't want to interrupt, I have a bad habit of doing that, Mum gets a bit frustrated. So I stopped to listen to wait for the right moment, and, well, there wasn't a right moment. I heard everything.'

'Out of context, Brooke,' said Andie. 'You don't know the whole story.'

'Mum had to tell me a bit of what was going on, after you stayed the other night.'

'Then you should be talking to her.'

'I will, I'll tell her what I know, I promise. I'll even tell her that I've spoken to you. I just wanted to catch you before you left.' Suddenly her face dropped. 'I don't even know when I'm going to see you again, Andie.'

She reached over and squeezed Brooke's hand. She'd always been such a sweet kid, and open like a book. Andie had often seen the dilemma in her eyes; her natural inclination to get on with people, to love her dad no matter what, vying with the need to stand by her mother. Out of the three, she was the one who looked most like Ross; Lauren was a clone of her mother, and Matty was a blend of both parents. Brooke was like Ross in temperament as well, gregarious and full of life. But she was more sensitive than her father. Andie had always had a soft spot for her.

'Of course we'll see each other,' said Andie. 'You don't have to worry about that.'

'I'm not a child anymore, Andie,' she said plaintively. 'What is wrong with Dad? How can he keep doing this?'

Andie didn't know how to answer that.

'It took me such a long time to trust him again,' Brooke went on, 'to try to understand. Once Mum was okay, and I got a bit older, I worked out that parents aren't perfect, and people fall out of love, and they move on. I knew so many kids whose parents were divorced, we weren't anything special. And you were always so nice to us, it didn't seem fair to blame you for everything, the way Lauren did.'

'I think she still does, just quietly.'

Brooke gave her a small smile. 'What's going to happen now, Andie? Are we supposed to just accept the next one? Forget about you?'

Andie hadn't even stopped to consider the bigger picture. She didn't have children with Ross, so there was no blood tie between her and his children. But that didn't mean there wasn't a connection.

'Brooke, you're getting ahead of yourself. I don't even know what's going to happen from here.'

'Does that mean you want to get back with him?'

'I don't know,' she said. 'He's saying he wants me back, but . . .'

'He said the same thing to my mother,' Brooke sighed.

Andie reached over to touch her chin so she would look at her. 'Whatever happens, Brooke, you are a part of my life,' said Andie. 'And that's not going to change.'

'It will change.'

'Well, okay, it'll be different,' she allowed. 'But we can still see each other. And you can call me anytime, I'll always be there for you, in whatever way you need.'

Brooke gave her a brave smile.

'But right now, you have an exam to study for. You need to focus.'

'Okay.'

'And please talk to your mum, maybe not tonight, but after your exams are out of the way?'

'I will.'

Brooke leaned over and gave her a quick hug before she got out of the car. Andie watched in the rearview mirror as she bolted back up the street to her house, and the deep sadness resurfaced . . . she couldn't lose any more people who mattered to her. She didn't think she could bear it.

So she made some resolutions on the drive back to Jess's. Other people were affected, and Andie had to show Ross that she wasn't going to let him wheedle or charm his way back. She couldn't trust him right now, she didn't know if she would ever be able to trust him again. He'd lied to her from the very start. Andie would never have taken up with him if she'd known his marriage was basically sound, that the biggest problem he and Joanna were experiencing was that things had gone stale. Jess and Toby had had their misgivings, they'd tried to warn her . . .

But Andie had chosen to ignore them. Chosen to. Had she been kidding herself all along? Ross walked into her life at a time when she felt lost and alone in her grief. Perhaps she had been needy . . . but she wasn't unhinged. She knew that much.

And she would be needy no more. Andie had to grow up and start to rely on herself. She would find her own place, make her own life. She would 'extricate' herself from Ross, from needing him in her life in order to be a whole person. And if he really wanted her back, things were going to have to change. There would be compromises, many compromises. More than anything, he was going to have to find a way to make her trust him again. That was his responsibility. From now on, Andie only had a responsibility to herself.

The next day

Donna was obviously stunned. 'I don't understand . . . when did all this happen?'

Andie had arrived at the shop early so she could use the internet to start searching for accommodation. Donna was coming in at ten, and Andie had decided the subterfuge had to end. She had to be upfront . . . well, as upfront as was prudent. She wasn't going to tell Donna all the gory details, especially not the part about walking in on Ross and the woman.

'You're protecting him,' Jess said when she filled her in on her plans.

'Only from Toby,' Andie insisted. 'He doesn't need any encouragement to hunt Ross down and . . .'

'Punch his lights out?' Jess suggested. 'If you ask me, it'd do Ross good.'

'You know that's not true,' said Andie. 'And Toby would be the one who would end up paying for it. I'm protecting Toby from himself.'

'So what's your story going to be?'

'I'm going to say we've been going through a bad patch. That I want a baby, and Ross doesn't – which is the truth – so I'm taking some time to work out if I can live with that, or if it's too important to me.'

Jess was shaking her head. 'So you're making yourself the bad guy?'

'I don't think so,' Andie defended. 'You know how Donna feels about babies, she'll be totally on my side.'

And she was.

'Oh Andie, it's such a tough one. You shouldn't have to give up your dreams,' said Donna.

'Well, Ross shouldn't be forced into something he doesn't want either.'

'He'll come around.' Donna gave her arm a squeeze. 'He won't be able to live without you, and he'll give in.'

'But, I'm not trying to force his hand,' said Andie. 'That's not the way I want to bring a child into this world, or into the relationship. This is the best way for both of us to really work out what we want.'

'Well, I know my fingers will be crossed,' Donna said earnestly.

'And, Donna . . . please be careful about the way you put this to Toby. You know how he feels about Ross.'

She gave Andie a knowing wink. 'Don't you worry, I'll keep his muzzle on.'

*

Andie made several calls to real estate agents throughout the eastern suburbs. She'd had enough inner-city grunge, she wanted to live somewhere she could breathe the salt air, even if an actual view might be out of her price range. Her first appointment was at two this afternoon. As she drove away from the shop her phone started to ring. She didn't have it set up for hands-free, so she let it ring out, and waited to check it at the next set of red lights. She sighed. It was Meredith, of all people. She hardly ever rang Andie, and when she did it was only to complain about something. Andie really wasn't up to dealing with her now. She would have left a voicemail if it was important, Andie would check later. She had two appointments this afternoon and she was not going to be waylaid for anything.

But as soon as she pulled away from the lights the phone started to ring again. She could have kicked herself for not connecting the hands-free while she was stationary. Next red light. But typically, she didn't get another one before she arrived at the real estate agent, and the phone had rung out twice more by then. Andie parked the car and picked up the phone. It was Meredith every time. Four missed calls, only minutes apart. Her sister couldn't stand being ignored. Andie stared at her name on the screen, debating whether to call her back or just turn it off, when it rang again, startling her so she nearly dropped the phone. She fumbled to answer it, placing it to her ear. But before she could even speak, Meredith was shouting down the phone at her.

'Why didn't you answer your phone?'

'I was driving.'

'So you just ignore it? I rang and rang, didn't you think it could be an emergency?'

'That's why I pulled over,' Andie returned calmly, 'and I was just about to call you back. Now, what's the problem?'

'You have to get over here right away.'

'I can't do that, Meredith, I have an appointment at —'

'What did I just say, Andrea? This is an emergency!'

'Well, what is it?'

'I'm not going to tell you over the phone!'

Andie groaned silently. Meredith could be such a drama queen. 'Okay, I'll come straight after my appointment —'

'Andrea,' she interrupted in her best mother's voice. 'How many times do I have to say this is an emergency?'

Meredith's idea of an emergency could be anything from one of the children not getting a test score she thought they deserved, to just about anything. Their mother was the only one who could handle Meredith, they were on the same wavelength. Andie and her dad were at a loss. And Brendan used to steer well clear.

'Look, you're going to have to give me some clue of what this is about,' said Andie, 'if you expect me to cancel an appointment.'

'Fine. Let it go on the record that I didn't want to say this over the phone, but you left me no choice.'

'Okay, it's on the record.'

There was silence down the phone line. 'Meredith?' Andie prompted her eventually.

'I really don't like this —'

'Would you just spit it out!'

Andie heard a strange noise, like a strangled sob. 'It's Dad, he died.'

She couldn't have heard that right.

'What did you say?'

'Exactly what you think I said,' she said tearfully. 'Do you understand now why I didn't want to say it over the phone?'

Andie couldn't breathe. 'Dad . . . he died?'

'Yes.'

'But when . . . Did this just happen? How?'

'Look, you know what the emergency is now, do you mind if we continue this in person?'

'Yes, yes, of course. I'll leave right away. Which hospital are you at?'

'What? No, we're not at a hospital. Come to my house.'

'But I want to see him, will I get the chance to see him?'

'Andrea, just come to my house, we'll work it all out then.'

As Andie hung up the phone, tears welled in her eyes and her chest heaved. Her father was dead? She still couldn't catch her breath. How did he die? When? She was only there the other day. She began to sob, the tears pouring freely now. Her father was dead. She was never going to see him again. She should have waited for him to get home. Where had he been? Maybe the doctor had given him bad news? Maybe he'd had to go for tests, maybe he'd been admitted to hospital that very day? That's why he was gone so long. So why didn't someone call her then? Surely Meredith would have called her, she always called her. As the eldest she'd insisted that she was recorded as the emergency contact on all their father's important documentation. But whenever she was contacted about anything, she always palmed it off onto Andie, insisting she didn't have the time to deal with it.

So why didn't somebody call her?

She nearly drove herself mad on the way to Meredith's, trying to put together the pieces to understand what had happened, though there was no way she could until she spoke to Meredith. All she was doing was holding at bay the imminent tsunami of grief that was rising to engulf her. Her father was gone, what did it matter who called who, when, where and how? He was gone.

Andie pulled up in front of Meredith's house and rushed up to the front door, pressing impatiently on the buzzer. Neville opened it a moment later. He was a decent enough man, maybe a little dour, but who could blame him, married to her sister?

'How are you holding up?' he asked kindly.

She shrugged. 'I'm still in shock. I don't even know what happened.'

'Come on through,' he said. 'Meredith's anxious to see you.'

Andie followed him down the hall to the living room. Their home was stately and elegant, a well-preserved Federation, but the decor was stuffy and old-fashioned – drab colours and ugly florals, doilies dotted on heavy, dark furniture. Meredith was on the phone. She raised her hand and mouthed 'Hi' when Andie appeared, then held up a finger to indicate she would be a minute.

'Yes, we'll have to look into that,' she said into the phone.

Neville leaned in close to Andie, keeping his voice down. 'Can I get you a cuppa?' he asked. 'Tea or coffee?'

She nodded. 'Tea would be great, thanks.'

She mostly drank coffee, but tea felt appropriate right now. Her parents only ever drank tea. Her mother used to imply that coffee was vaguely immoral, in the same class as cigarettes, drugs or alcohol.

Meredith hung up the phone and turned around. 'Well, not the best circumstances,' she said, coming right up to Andie, grasping her by the shoulders and pulling her closer as she pressed their cheeks together. It was as close to a hug as Meredith was capable of. When she pulled back, her eyes were glassy.

'So,' said Andie, 'what happened?'

Meredith nodded gravely, leading her over to the couch. 'Come, sit.'

Andie did as she was told, turning to face her sister, who perched herself on the edge of the couch, her back straight, her hands folded on her lap.

'This isn't going to be easy to hear, okay?' she began.

Andie's eyes widened. 'What?'

Meredith took a breath. 'Dad was found in the garage. He'd been there . . . a few days, they don't know for sure. There has to be an autopsy.'

Andie's throat went dry, as the blood drained from her face. She felt dizzy. She dropped her head into her hand.

'Neville,' Meredith called, 'can you bring Andrea a glass of water?'

Andie didn't look up, didn't register anything until a glass materialised in her hand. She took a couple of sips, and put it down on the coffee table.

'Are you okay?' Meredith asked her.

Andie nodded. 'I don't understand. I was there, only the other day.'

'When?' Meredith frowned. 'Which day?'

'Um . . .' She closed her eyes, tracing back through the increasingly surreal events of the past week. 'Friday, it was definitely Friday.'

'Really? So how did he seem to you?'

'Oh, I didn't see him.'

'What do you mean you didn't see him?'

'He wasn't there, he wasn't home.'

'Are you sure, did you check everywhere?'

'I checked around the house, I called out for him.'

'Did you check the garage?'

'Why would I check the garage?'

'Oh, I don't know, maybe because *you could have saved his life*!'

'Meredith,' Neville cautioned, as he walked back into the room carrying a tea tray.

She looked perplexed. 'I just don't understand, weren't you concerned?'

'I . . . I thought he must have had a doctor's appointment,' said Andie, her voice breaking. 'When I got there, the kettle was still warm, there was half a cup of tea on the table, toast . . .'

Neville poured the tea as Meredith sat there, wringing her hands and shaking her head. 'Well, he did have an appointment, as it turns out, with his GP. They said they rang when he didn't show up. You didn't hear the phone?'

Andie felt addled. 'I don't know, I don't remember.' She had been in such a state, but she wasn't going to tell Meredith about any of that right now.

'Then yesterday,' Meredith went on, 'he didn't turn up for another appointment – with the radiologist this time, he was booked for a scan. When he didn't arrive, they called his GP. Thank God the receptionist was on the ball. She tried Dad at home and when he didn't answer, she called me to find out where he was. Well, of course, I had no idea. I called you, but it went straight to voicemail. There was no answer on your home phone, and at the shop they didn't seem to know where you were. Then I tried Dad's . . . of course there was no answer. I decided the best course of action was to call an ambulance and meet them there. They were waiting for me when I arrived.' She paused, taking a deep breath. 'We went right through the house, looked in every room. One of the ambulance officers suggested we check the garage. I opened the door for them . . .' Her voice broke, and she covered her face with her hands.

Neville sat down beside her, slipping his arm around her shoulders. 'The car door was open,' he said quietly, 'your father was slumped, face down, across the front seat. It looked as though he collapsed getting into the car. They suspect a coronary, or an embolism, heart, brain . . . They won't know until they've completed the autopsy.'

Andie brought her hand to her mouth as tears sprang to her eyes, spilling over onto her cheeks.

No one said anything for a while . . . minutes probably. The mantle clock ticked in the background like a heartbeat.

Meredith lifted her head and dabbed at her eyes. 'It must have happened on Friday.'

'We don't know that,' said Neville.

'Of course we know that,' she retorted. 'The kettle was warm, Andrea said so herself. She was there, in the house, as my father lay dying!'

'How was I supposed to know?' Andie cried.

'Why didn't you check everywhere? How could you go to visit him and just assume —'

'Okay,' said Neville over the top of them. 'This isn't doing anyone any good. It's not going to bring him back.'

'But she could have saved him,' Meredith shrilled at him.

'You can't —'

Andie cut him off. 'How do you know that? It might have happened hours before.'

'The kettle was warm!'

'So go see how long your kettle stays warm,' said Andie. 'Even if it was only an hour, there's nothing I could have done.'

'You don't know that.'

'You don't either, he might have died instantly.'

'Or he might have been lying there, gasping for breath while you were inside, pottering around —'

'Meredith, that's enough!' Neville was a quiet, composed kind of man, so when he raised his voice, even slightly, it had an impact.

His wife began to sob. 'My father died like someone who didn't even have family. Like those sad, lonely people you see on the news, discovered weeks later.'

They all sat in silence, reflecting the awful reality of that. The blasted clock kept ticking in the background. Andie couldn't take it anymore, she had to get out of there. She stood up. 'I have to go.'

'No, Andrea . . .' Neville said, getting to his feet.

'It's okay,' she said. 'I really do have to go. We'll talk when we know something.'

Meredith didn't get up, didn't even look up. Andie grabbed her bag and walked into the hallway. Neville followed her.

'You know, it's just the grief talking,' he said, holding the front door open for her.

Andie gave a faint nod. 'Please let me know if you hear anything, anything at all.'

'Of course.'

She walked briskly out to the car and got in. She had an overwhelming need to call Ross. Nothing else mattered now. He was her husband. Her father had died. He had to be told. She took out her phone and rang him.

She could hear the surprise in his voice when he answered. 'Hi, Andie, I'm so happy to hear from you.'

She swallowed. 'Something's happened,' she said, tears rising in her throat again.

'What is it? What's wrong, darling?'

'My father died.'

'Oh my God,' he breathed. 'When? What happened?'

'They don't know. He collapsed suddenly,' she said in a strangled voice. 'They have to do an autopsy.'

'Oh, Andie, I'm so sorry. Are you all right?'

She couldn't answer.

'Of course you're not all right,' he said gently. 'Where are you now?'

'I'm just leaving Meredith's.'

'Okay, come straight home, I'll meet you there.'

'No!' The thought of that place . . .

'Andie, don't do this now, come home.'

'I won't go there, Ross, it's not my home anymore.' She didn't have a home. She had nowhere to go. Damn him.

'Come on, Andie —'

'No, just . . . forget it!' she shouted into the phone. She wished she could slam it down, stupid mobile. Instead she hung up and threw it onto the passenger seat. It started to ring seconds later. 'Leave me alone!' She picked it up and turned it off, tossing it aside again. She started up the car and drove down the street and around the corner. But her tears were blinding her, her whole body was shaking with sobs. She couldn't drive. She pulled over to the side of the road and wailed, beating the steering wheel with her fists.

Suddenly there a knock on the window beside her. Andie looked up, startled. A woman was peering in at her. She mouthed, 'Are you all right?'

Andie nodded. The woman indicated for her to lower the window, which Andie did, reluctantly, and only part of the way.

'I've just had some bad news,' she explained to the woman. 'I'm okay.'

'Can I call someone for you?'

She shook her head. 'I'll be right in a minute.'

'Maybe you shouldn't drive . . .'

'I'll be all right. Really.'

The woman hesitated. 'Are you sure?'

Andie took a deep, calming breath. 'Yes. Thank you for your concern. I'll just sit here a minute, and then I'll be fine.'

The woman still hesitated, frowning down at her.

'I called my husband,' Andie added, 'he's waiting for me.'

That seemed to satisfy her. She nodded. 'Okay then, you take care.'

Andie watched in the side mirror as the woman walked away, looking back once over her shoulder. The kindness of strangers. Andie only had to stop and cry on the side of the road and a Good Samaritan had appeared out of nowhere to see if she was all right. Why hadn't anyone been there for her dad?

Because he didn't know his neighbours anymore. There weren't any left from Andie's childhood days, or even her young adult days, for that matter. Some had died, others had been shipped off to nursing homes. Houses had been sold, new people had moved in, but her father tended to keep to himself. His wife had been the talker, the instigator, without her he didn't know what to do with himself.

Could he really have been dead, or worse, dying, the day Andie was at the house? The idea was almost too unbearable to contemplate. Maybe Meredith was right, she should have checked everywhere, but it hadn't even occurred to her. She didn't suspect that anything was wrong, only that he was out. She had to admit it was rare not to find him at home, maybe that should have alerted her. But usually Andie visited him later in the afternoon, so she wasn't at all concerned that he wasn't home in the middle of the day. She remembered it vaguely crossing her mind as she prepared to leave, that it was odd he was out so long . . . If only she hadn't been so caught up in her own problems, she may have thought to check outside. But would it have done any good by then?

Her eyes filled again, and she wept until there were no more tears left, until she felt empty. She leaned over and grabbed tissues out of the glove box. She wiped her eyes, her nose, her whole face. She should go. But where? She couldn't remember if Jess was working somewhere tonight, after she closed the shop. Andie couldn't bear to go back to that little flat if Jess wasn't there. Then it struck her. Toby. Of course. He'd known her family. He knew her father. They had grieved together for Brendan. It didn't matter what he knew about Ross, Toby wouldn't let that get in the way now.

She started up the car and pulled slowly away from the kerb.

Kensington

Toby and Donna lived in the dearest little cottage they had been renovating for a few years now. Toby dropped out of uni after Brendan died; he said he couldn't focus, that he didn't want to live inside his head anymore, that he wanted to work for a living. But that was only part of the reason. The boys had been doing the same engineering course, Andie knew Toby wouldn't be able to continue, that going to class every day would only make Brendan's absence all the greater. He had to do something completely different. He applied for an apprenticeship as a carpenter and had stuck with the trade ever since. He had almost entirely rebuilt much of their house, as well as adding a big, airy, family room extension off the back, opening directly onto a small yard. Andie loved their little house, she always felt at home there.

When Toby answered the door, she dissolved into tears as soon as she saw his face. He drew her inside and closed his arms around her in a brotherly hug. It was exactly what Brendan would have done, exactly what she needed.

'What's the bastard done to you now?' Toby asked after a while.

Andie looked up at him. 'No, you don't understand, this has nothing to do with Ross. It's my father . . . he died, Toby.'

That only brought on another wave of tears, and Donna appeared from the back of the house to see what was going on. Together they calmed Andie down, and comforted her, and listened while she poured out the whole story, including Meredith's accusations.

'Look, you can't let her get to you,' said Toby. 'I know she's your sister, but she's always been a bit of a hard case.'

'Toby,' Donna chided. 'But he's right, Andie. You can't let it get to you. It wasn't your fault.'

'I know it wasn't my fault,' she said, 'but I might have been able to do something if I'd found him . . . if I'd only looked for him.'

The concertina doors that ran across the back of the house were opened all the way, and Max was playing just outside, within earshot.

'I'm going to take Max upstairs,' Donna said, getting up.

'Oh, sorry,' said Andie.

'Nonsense, it's time for his bath anyway.'

After Donna had scooped Max up and left them alone, Toby sat next to Andie and placed his arm around her. She rested her head on his shoulder.

'Look, Andie,' he said, 'it's very unlikely you could have done anything to save your dad. If it was a massive heart attack —'

'We don't know that it was. It might have been something milder.'

Toby took a breath, shifting to look at her. 'Andie, if your father keeled over as he was getting into the car, it must have been sudden and acute. It could have even been a brain haemorrhage, and there's really nothing anyone could have done about that, even if they were there right as it happened.'

Andie sighed deeply. She'd just have to wait for the autopsy report and hope that what Toby was saying was right, that it would prove beyond question that there was nothing she could have done. That should get Meredith off her back . . . But that wasn't all. Andie had to be certain her father hadn't suffered so she could find a way to live with herself.

'This is how I felt after Brendan died,' she said quietly. 'If only I'd been there . . .'

'I was there, Andie,' Toby reminded her. 'And there was nothing I could do to save him, nothing anyone could do.' He paused. 'Brendan would never have blamed you, or held you responsible, you know that.'

'I know.'

'And if he was here now, he wouldn't have you talking like this. And he'd have put Meredith in her place.'

That made Andie smile. 'Hm, he was the only one who ever could.'

'I reckon,' said Toby. 'He'd be gutted about the old man.'

He would. Her father was typical of his generation, and he wasn't given to displays of affection towards his son. But they shared a strong bond as the men of the family, and when Brendan decided to go into engineering, like his dad, he could not have been more proud.

'So, you're staying here, right?' said Toby. 'Until the funeral, and after that, as long as you want.'

'Thank you.' Andie had some decisions to make, but they could wait, and she honestly couldn't think of a better place to stay in the meantime. It was a real home, and she needed that right now. 'How am I going to get through another funeral?'

Toby drew his arm around her tighter. 'With me right beside you, and Donna, and Jess.'

She hadn't even spoken to Jess yet to tell her what had happened. Andie hoped she wouldn't be offended if she stayed here. But Jess was not easily offended, and she was canny enough to understand that Andie should do whatever she needed to get through this.

Donna was about to start preparing dinner, and she wouldn't hear of Andie helping. She suggested instead that she take a nice long shower and wind down, while Toby made up her room. Donna offered to lend her some clothes, but Andie remembered she had a lot of her stuff with her. It was too crowded at Jess's to leave her giant suitcase in the middle of the floor, but there was nowhere else to put it, so it had ended up living in the boot of her car. Toby went to fetch it for her, and Andie was relieved to find clean underwear and enough clothes to keep her going for now. She felt a lot better after her shower. They put her in the small third bedroom, which doubled as study and guestroom, with one of those couches that folded out into a futon – Andie was becoming quite the connoisseur of convertible bedding. It was a nice little room; it felt cosy and safe, and it gave her some privacy. She'd be able to come in here whenever she needed to be alone. Despite every rotten thing that had happened over the past week, at that moment Andie felt blessed to have friends like Toby and Donna, and Jess. Which reminded her, she needed to ring her.

When she fished her phone out of her handbag, she realised she'd forgotten that she'd turned it off after she spoke to Ross. She turned it back on, and sure enough, there were six missed calls from him, and a few messages. Andie went through them; they all pleaded for her to call him back, not to ignore him at a time like this, that he was worried about her. She was calmer now, she supposed she could handle talking to him.

She heard the relief in his voice when he answered. 'Thank God, Andie, I've been worried sick about you. I didn't want to start ringing around your friends in case you hadn't told them about your father. I didn't want to alarm anyone.'

'I'm okay, Ross, it was all just too much for me before.'

'Of course, I understand. Where are you now?'

'I'm at Toby and Donna's. Toby knew my family.'

'Yes, I remember.'

'They said I can stay until the funeral.'

There was a pause. 'Andie, don't you think I should be with you at a time like this?'

She sighed heavily. 'Up to a week ago, I would have said yes, absolutely.'

'Then how is it different now?'

'How is it different?' she said, raising her voice. 'Do you really have to ask that?'

'Okay, okay, I'm sorry. Don't get upset, I didn't mean to upset you, that's the last thing I want to do.' She heard him take a breath. 'The thing is, Andie, I am still your husband, and you are still very much my wife, and I want to be there for you, in whatever way I can.'

Andie couldn't help it, when Ross spoke like that, she just wanted to feel his arms around her at the same time.

'I really want to see you,' he said carefully. 'I need to see you, Andie. We need to talk.'

'Ross, I can't deal with all that now.'

'I know, I'm not talking about any of that. I just want to see you, make sure you're all right.'

She was thinking about it. 'I don't know, Ross. It might make Donna and Toby feel uncomfortable. And it is their house.'

'They know . . . about us?'

'Actually, they don't, not the whole story, not the worst of it. But you know how Toby's very protective of me.'

'What if I come by and pick you up and we go somewhere to talk?'

'Donna's making dinner.'

'Well, what about later?'

'I don't know . . .' She hesitated.

'You say the time, whatever suits you.'

Andie finally agreed that he could come at eight thirty, but that he should wait for her out front, in the car. Then she had to break it to Toby.

'He just wants to make sure I'm okay,' she explained over dinner.

Toby didn't say anything.

'Of course he does,' Donna said, reaching over to pat Andie's arm. 'And it's right that he should, and that you should see him, and talk to him. Toby . . .?'

He shrugged. 'Well, I'll wait up for you.'

'That's not necessary,' said Andie. 'I don't want to put you out.'

'We'll be up anyway,' Donna said.

'I won't be that long,' she assured them.

*

Andie looked out the front door a few minutes past eight thirty, and Ross was already waiting. That was a first. He jumped out of the car when she appeared and came around to greet her, taking both of her hands in his.

'I'm so sorry about your dad, Andie.'

She nodded. He leaned in send kissed her cheek. She didn't flinch or pull away. She liked the feel of his face close to hers. Andie knew if she took half a step towards him she could be in his arms, and right then she was aching to feel those arms around her.

But she had to restrain herself. She had to be careful. When she came out of this awful fog of grief she didn't want to find herself back in that apartment, as though nothing had ever happened.

Ross opened the car door for her and she got in.

'Where are we going?' she asked when he climbed in behind the steering wheel.

'Wherever you want,' he said.

She shrugged. 'I don't know.'

'We won't go far then,' he said as he started the engine.

They drove past the racecourse and through Randwick, and then Andie stopped paying attention. She settled back into her seat as the houses and shops and streets flickered by in the window. And then they were turning into a carpark by the beach. Andie looked around to get her bearings. They were at Bronte, and Ross was pulling into a spot overlooking the water. There was barely anyone about, being a weeknight in late winter.

'Why are we stopping here?' she asked.

'I thought this would be more private,' said Ross, turning off the engine. 'You won't have anyone gawking at you. You can relax.'

She was frowning at him. 'Did you plan this all along?'

'No, I promise,' he insisted. 'Give me some credit, Andie, you just lost your father. I'm not a complete animal.'

'I know that.'

He sighed. 'Look, I don't want you to feel uncomfortable. If you'd rather, we can go somewhere for coffee, or a drink . . . just say the word.'

Andie rested her head back against the seat and gazed out at the ocean. Ross was right, they could talk here, she could cry . . . she could yell at him if it came to that.

'It's fine here,' she said eventually.

'Are you sure?'

'I'm sure.'

He took his hands off the steering wheel and shifted in his seat, turning to face her. 'So, how are you feeling?'

'Numb, I guess. You know I went to Dad's house last Friday?'
'Oh?'

Andie looked at him. 'I wasn't going to tell Dad what happened, obviously. I just needed . . . somewhere to hide out for a while, I guess.'

'That was after you went to the apartment?' asked Ross.

'Hm.'

'Where did you go the night before? You know . . . after . . .'

Shit. She stayed with his ex-wife. Andie turned away, staring out the window beside her.

'Sorry, it's none of my business,' he said.

'So, anyway,' she continued after a while, 'on Friday, Dad wasn't home, or at least, I didn't know he was.'

'What do you mean?'

Andie swallowed, she could feel tears rising in her throat again. God, there must be some kind of limit to how many tears you can produce in a given period? And she must be getting close to it.

She cleared her throat, but her voice was thin and wavering when she eventually spoke. 'He collapsed in the garage. It must have happened that day.'

'Oh, Andie.' He reached over and placed his hand on hers. 'You couldn't have known.'

She turned to him, tears pooling in her eyes. 'But if only I'd checked . . .'

Her voice broke, and Ross drew her slowly and tentatively into his arms, but she didn't resist. She leaned her head against his chest while he stroked her hair and shushed her.

'It's not your fault,' he said quietly. 'It's just something that happened, you couldn't have changed it. It was his time.'

After a while, Andie drew back. She wiped her face with her hands and Ross passed her a handkerchief. He liked to carry a pressed white handkerchief. Andie had always thought it was quaintly old-fashioned.

'Thanks,' she said, taking it from him. She breathed deeply. 'Anyway, we'll know more after the autopsy.'

'So they suspect his heart?'

She nodded. 'Or maybe an aneurism. They can't tell for sure.'

'How long will the autopsy take?' he asked.

'I don't know. A few days, maybe . . . I really don't know.'

'But it will delay the funeral?'

'I guess.'

He reached over and took her hand, enclosing it in both of his. 'Andie, we have a lot to talk about, but now is not the time. So I'm not going to make excuses, or promises, or ask for forgiveness, or anything like that.'

She turned her head to look at him.

'I just want to say this. You said yourself that even just a week ago, my place would have been with you. We can't change what happened, and I completely understand why you don't want to go back to the apartment. But I want to be with you through this. So, I booked us a serviced apartment in the city —'

'Ross —'

'Just hear me out,' he said. 'Can't we put this aside for now – not behind us, I know it's not going away – but just to the side? Let me support you through this. I want to stand with you at the funeral, as your husband. Andie, you've lost so much, you've only got Meredith left, and you two have never been close. I'm your only other family.'

Andie stared straight ahead. The moon was low over the water, casting a shimmering silver trail before it. Ross was still holding her hand. It was comforting.

'I don't want to go to a serviced apartment,' she said finally. 'It would be like staying in a hotel.'

'I'd be there with you.'

'Not all the time,' she pointed out.

'Are you sure you wouldn't feel more comfortable in your own home?'

She drew her hand out of his then. 'I don't have a home now, Ross. You've taken that away from me.'

'I wish you didn't feel that way.'

'Well, I wish you hadn't done what you did,' Andie returned sharply.

'Okay, okay,' he said. 'I'll drop it.'

She breathed out. 'I'm comfortable at Donna and Toby's, I want to stay with them.'

'All right, whatever you need,' said Ross. 'But will I be able to see you, a little? Will you let me come with you to the funeral?'

Andie thought about it. 'I suppose, but I'm not making any promises, Ross. If I change my mind, or I feel differently, for whatever reason . . .'

'Okay.' He nodded.

'And you can't harass me.'

'I won't, of course I wouldn't harass you, Andie.'

'No demands, is what I'm saying.'

'I won't make any demands of you,' he vowed. 'I'm just asking you to keep me in the loop. Call me, anytime, day or night.'

Andie looked at him. In this light he was still the man she'd fallen in love with, her husband of ten years . . .

'You know I love you, Andie.'

She turned away. 'I'd like you to take me back to the house now.'

A week later

'I don't understand why you have to go to the funeral with him,' Jess was saying. 'I would have taken you.'

Andie had already been through this with Toby. 'It just makes it easier if I go with Ross,' she said. 'Meredith doesn't know that I've left the apartment, I don't feel like going into it all with her right now.'

The last thing she needed was more of Meredith's disapproval. Nothing Andie did to help with the arrangements was good enough, nothing she said was the right thing. Even the results of the autopsy had done little to appease her sister. Their father had suffered a massive heart attack – an 'acute myocardial infarction' as it was described in the report. Had he actually been in a hospital when it had happened, they might – *might* – have been able to save him. As it was, he didn't stand a chance. It was still horrible to think that he was lying dead in his car while Andie was in the house, even more horrible to think that he had lain there for days afterwards. But she couldn't be held responsible for his death.

Neville had been decent, under the circumstances, though if Andie heard 'It's the grief talking' one more time she thought she might scream. They were both grieving, but even though they were burying their father together, they couldn't share that grief, they were too distant from each other, and it broke Andie's heart that she wasn't close to the only surviving member of her family.

So no matter how tenuous the tie that bound them, Ross was still Andie's husband, her next of kin, and she couldn't get through this without him.

'Well, I'm still coming,' Jess was saying, 'if that's okay?'

'Of course it's okay,' said Andie. 'I really appreciate it, thank you.'

*

Meredith insisted on the full Requiem Mass, at least they agreed about that. Their father was a card-carrying Catholic of the staunchest variety. Andie was sure he found comfort in the strict adherence to rules; it suited his engineer's logical mind, not that any religion could be considered logical in Andie's mind. But in Catholicism there were actions and consequences, sin and repentance, a lifetime of guilt in return for an afterlife in heaven, at least after a spell in purgatory to pay for your wrongdoings. Andie had heard they'd dropped the idea of purgatory, clearly even the Almighty had to adapt to modern mores. But as far as Andie knew, her parents never got that memo and still held firmly to the doctrine. Penance was obligatory. Punishment was essential.

Such a long ceremony in such a voluminous, near-empty church only served to emphasise the pathos of her father's passing. Neville's mother and sister came, which was nice of them, but Andie didn't recognise anyone else; she guessed they were parishioners of the church. She wondered if they really knew her father or if it was just their official duty, like a modern version of wailers, only silent.

So Andie couldn't muster up much emotion at the church, but the cemetery was a different matter. She hated the place, she hadn't been back since her mother was buried, not even to visit Brendan's grave. It just didn't feel like it had anything to do with him; he didn't belong among all these stone monoliths, grim and sombre against the backdrop of the container terminals. It was such an ugly setting, and Andie had argued vehemently about the decision to bury Brendan here. She thought he should be cremated, and they should scatter his ashes somewhere that had particular meaning to him. He was a surfer, and he had a few favourite breaks. Toby would know the best spot. But her mother had thought she was disgraceful even to suggest it. Their own parents had been buried here, and they were adamant that family should be together in their final resting place. Andie watched as her father's coffin was lowered into the ground in the same plot as his wife, reunited at last. Tears filled her eyes, and she thought of her brother, her beautiful, vital, young brother, sealed in a box beneath a couple of metres of earth, right under where they were standing. He'd be nothing but bones now.

That did it. Andie finally broke down. She felt Ross's arms close around her, holding her up as she sagged against him, and she just let it all out, she didn't care. She was grieving for Brendan, for the life he never got to live, and she was grieving for her mother, for a life so unfulfilled. And now her father's life was over too. Her family, all dead and buried.

*

'People grieve differently, you know, Andrea,' Meredith said, catching up to her as they made their way through the cemetery back to their cars.

'I know that, Meredith.'

'I'm just not the type to burst into tears in public . . . that doesn't mean I'm not devastated.'

They arrived back at the cars. Meredith had instructed the funeral directors to provide a limousine for the family, but Andie told her she and Ross would follow in their own car. She was fairly certain Ross was not counted as family anyway. Philippa and Tristan were climbing into the funeral car. Andie barely knew them, and yet they were her closest blood relatives after Meredith. She wondered if anything would change, or if they would grow even further apart now that there was nothing, no one, to hold them together.

'There are things to discuss, to settle,' Meredith was saying. 'The will, what we're going to do with the house.'

Andie nodded. 'Of course.'

'I'll call you next week.' Meredith stooped to give Andie a perfunctory kiss on the cheek and turned towards the waiting limousine. Neville was holding the door open for her and he lifted his hand in a wave, before climbing in after his wife. There wasn't going to be a wake. Meredith said they were in bad taste, Andie thought it was just as well they wouldn't have to spend another couple of strained hours in each other's company.

Ross had discreetly dropped behind when Meredith caught up with them; now he came up next to Andie, resting a hand on the small of her back. 'Are you all right?'

She looked at him. 'I'm glad it's over, to be honest.'

He nodded. Jess and Toby and Donna drew up alongside her.

'I really appreciate you coming, Ross,' said Andie.

'That sounds suspiciously like I'm being dismissed,' he said.

'Well, it's just that I can go home with Toby and Donna,' she said. 'There's really no need for you to go out of your way.'

'I want to go out of my way for you,' he insisted, drawing his arm more firmly around her waist and leading her to his car.

Andie looked over her shoulder at the others. 'See you at home then.'

*

'I don't know why she couldn't have just come with us,' Toby grumbled as they tailed Ross's car out of the cemetery. 'We were standing right there, there's room for her in the car. I hate the way he just takes over.'

'God, you don't think he's going to come in, do you, back at your place?' Jess asked from the back seat.

'I didn't invite him.'

'Oh, come on, you two,' Donna said sternly. 'Don't start. Andie's father died, she needs all the comfort and support she can get.'

'We're here for her.'

'And Ross is still her husband,' Donna reminded them.

'Hm,' Jess grunted, staring out the window. 'She said a funny thing to me, it's been playing on my mind ever since. She said that she wanted Ross to come to the funeral because Meredith didn't know she'd left the apartment.'

'Yeah, she told us the same thing,' said Donna.

'Meredith's a real piece of work,' said Toby. 'I do totally get why Andie wanted to keep up appearances in front of her.'

'That's not my point,' said Jess. 'I mean she's saying "left the apartment" not "left Ross".' Jess waited for that to sink in. 'I'm worried that this obsession she has about not going back to the apartment is a smokescreen.'

'I don't understand,' said Donna.

'A smokescreen,' Jess repeated, 'stopping her from seeing things clearly.'

'Oh,' said Donna, nodding thoughtfully. 'So you think Ross is never going to agree to having a baby?'

'What's a baby got to do with it?'

Toby pulled up at a set of lights after Ross and Andie's car had slipped through on the orange. Both he and Donna turned around in their seats to look directly at Jess.

'What do you mean?' Toby asked.

Jess saw the bewilderment on their faces. Andie still hadn't told them? She was staying with them for fuck's sake! Now Jess was even more worried. Andie had created such an effective smokescreen it was keeping everyone in the dark.

'Jess?' Donna prompted. 'What do you know?'

'Nothing,' she said lamely.

'Bullshit, Jess,' said Toby. 'There's something more to this . . . I knew it,' he said, turning back around in his seat and giving the steering wheel a thump, just as a car beeped them from behind. The lights had turned green.

Toby took off through the intersection. 'Spill, Jess. We have a right to know.'

'Not if she didn't tell us herself,' said Donna.

'She has a point,' Jess said.

'He's fooling around on her, isn't he?' said Toby.

'Thank God you guessed.' Jess sighed with relief. 'I didn't tell you, right, guys?'

'Why didn't she tell us?' said Donna.

'Bastard!' Toby clenched the steering wheel. 'If I get my hands on him . . .'

'There's your answer, Donna,' said Jess. 'She was protecting Ross – not just from Toby, but from either of you thinking badly of him.'

'Too late for that,' Toby muttered.

Donna was frowning. 'He's cheating on her? Poor Andie, how did she find out?'

'The worst possible way,' said Jess.

'What do you mean?' Toby glanced at her in the rearview mirror.

'Oh . . . I really don't think I should tell you this part.'

'God, she didn't find them together, did she?' He grimaced.

'You're good,' said Jess.

'Oh no,' Donna exclaimed. 'Poor Andie, how awful.'

'Wait a minute,' Toby said. 'She walked in on them at the apartment, didn't she? That's why she doesn't want to go back there.'

'Brilliant deduction, Dr Watson.'

'What sort of a fuckw—'

'Toby!' Donna chastised. 'Still, why would he take a girl back to their apartment? That's . . . well, it's just wrong. And it's a little creepy.'

'A little?' Jess said. 'He tried to blame it on the girl somehow . . .' She held her hands up in defeat. 'I gave up trying to follow the logic.'

'Does Andie believe him?' Toby asked her.

'No . . . and yes, I think, a little,' said Jess. 'She's not excusing what he did, but she's partly blaming herself because she wanted a baby and he didn't, and it was causing friction between them.'

'So it's all right for him to go and have an affair?' said Toby. 'Fuck that.'

'You said it.'

'I have to talk to her —'

'No!' Donna blurted.

'Why not?' Toby glanced at her.

'Well,' she said, thinking about it, 'Andie didn't want us to know, and not just to save Ross's face, but maybe to save her own as well. Rightly or wrongly, she's probably embarrassed, and humiliated. We should let her hold on to her dignity.'

They drove on in silence for a couple of blocks.

'I just don't know if I can sit back and do nothing,' said Toby after a while. 'I don't trust the bloke. She's just lost her dad, she's grieving, she's more vulnerable, he could so easily take advantage.'

'Well, she was on her way to see a real estate agent when she got the call about her dad,' said Jess. 'She was looking for a place of her own. Let's hope she still goes through with that.'

'She's welcome to stay with us as long as she likes,' said Donna. 'We'll have to make sure she knows that.'

'That's really good of you guys,' Jess said, 'but it's still a temporary arrangement, and it makes it easier for her to go back to Ross anytime. Getting her own place is a more permanent step, I wouldn't talk her out of it.'

'She's right, Donna,' said Toby. 'The best way we can help Andie is to do everything we can to help her to find her own place.'

Spring

It was strange coming back to the house. Andie hadn't been able to face it before now. Neville had had the presence of mind to go over a few days before the funeral and clear out any perishable foodstuffs, take rubbish out to the bins and put them on the kerb for collection. Then he made sure the house was secure, checked that all the windows were closed and locked, that sort of thing.

Today Andie was meeting Meredith to begin 'discussions'. Her car was already there, parked in the driveway. Andie left hers out front and walked up the path to the house. She had a key, but she didn't know whether she should knock. This was weird.

She ended up doing both, just as she'd always done when she visited her father – a knock to announce herself before letting herself in.

Meredith appeared at the end of the hall. 'You're here.'

Was it always going to be so awkward between them? Andie walked towards her as Meredith put her hands on her hips, surveying the living room. 'I only got here a few minutes ago,' she said. 'I've been looking around, there's so much to sort through.'

Andie nodded. 'A lifetime's.'

'Just look at this room,' Meredith went on, 'it's barely changed in twenty years.'

'Except for that,' Andie said, cocking her head at the television.

'What was he thinking?' said Meredith. 'It's so gauche.'

Andie wouldn't have used that particular term, but at least they agreed on something.

'Why don't I make us a cuppa?' Andie suggested.

'I'd love one, but there's no milk.'

'Yes there is,' said Andie, lifting a carton out of her bag.

At least that brought a smile to Meredith's face. They made the tea and sat at the kitchen table, facing each other.

'Well,' Meredith began, 'I assume you agree the house should be sold?'

Andie nodded, sipping her tea.

'But we can't put it on the market like this. It's going to have to be cleaned out sooner or later, so I think it's better if it's done before it goes up for sale.' She paused. 'I just don't know where I'm going to find the time . . .'

Meredith prattled on about her busy life and the kids' busy lives and Neville's busy life but Andie wasn't really listening. She was having an epiphany of sorts.

'I'll do it,' she said suddenly, interrupting Meredith's monologue.

'What?'

'I'll do it,' she repeated. 'I'll clean the place out, get it ready for sale.'

'Well, granted, you have more time than I do,' said Meredith. 'But you live on the other side of the bridge, how often will you be able to get over here? I don't want this to drag on.'

'No, I'm saying I'll move in for the duration.'

Meredith was frowning. 'What will your husband have to say about that?'

Oops.

'Look, it's only temporary,' said Andie. 'Ross works such long hours, he travels, and I can always spend weekends with him. I don't know, we'll play it by ear.'

'But what about your shop? It's a long way to travel back and forth every day.'

'Oh, I've been pulling back from the day-to-day running of the shop lately.' Andie had managed to staff the shop almost entirely without needing to be there ever since her father's death, and even the days leading up to it. Jess was alreadly acting as manager; Andie only had to drop in, do the pays, oversee the ordering, but really, Jess could handle all that now anyway. 'I have enough staff to run the place, I don't need to be there all the time.'

Meredith was regarding her suspiciously. 'I hope you don't think this will give you squatter's rights.'

Andie groaned inwardly. 'Of course not, Meredith.'

'I just think we should be upfront,' she said. 'If things aren't said out loud there can be a lot of misunderstandings. People get weird after a death in the family, you know.'

Yes, Andie was certainly getting that idea.

'So when is the reading of the will?' she asked.

'I made an appointment for next Wednesday,' said Meredith, taking out her phone and touching the screen. 'Ten am. Does that suit you?'

Bad luck if it didn't; she'd gone ahead and made the appointment without asking first. 'Suits me fine,' said Andie.

Wednesday 10 am

'Well, ladies, I think you'll find the will is quite straightforward,' said Mr Hodge, after giving them both a copy to look over. 'Your father changed it after the death of your mother, and I believe his circumstances have remained the same ever since. He wasn't a wealthy man, but he was very secure financially. He'd invested wisely for his retirement, so there are shares and fixed investments to be distributed. And I'm sure you're aware that the family home is quite a valuable piece of property, given its location.'

'Did he take his grandchildren into account?' Meredith asked, flicking through the papers.

'Yes he did. If you look over on page two, he has set up a trust fund for both Philippa and Tristan, which they can access at age twenty-one. Apart from that, he made several modest bequests, to the church, and to a couple of Catholic charities. But the bulk of the estate is to be divided equally between the two of you.'

Meredith and Andie continued to scan the papers in front of them.

'I think you'll find this is a textbook scenario,' said Mr Hodge. 'But please don't hesitate to contact me if you have any questions.'

Meredith seemed irritated, Andie could see it in her body language. When their business was complete, she charged out of the office with a curt goodbye and was standing waiting at the lifts, her arms crossed, tapping her foot, when Andie caught up with her.

'It's nice that he set up that trust fund for the kids,' Andie ventured to say.

Meredith snorted. 'It won't even buy them a car by the time they reach twenty-one.'

Which was more than either of them were given at that age.

'I would have thought that he'd want to contribute to his only grandchildren's education at least,' she added, 'considering how important education was to them. I'm sure Mum would have insisted had she been alive.'

'If Mum was alive, it would be a moot point,' Andie reminded her. 'The estate would all go to her.'

Meredith just humphed in reply. The lift doors opened and they stepped in. Meredith pressed the button for the ground floor and Andie turned to her as the doors closed.

'Meredith, is there a problem?'

'What do you mean?'

'Well, I think we're both going to end up with a very generous sum after the house is sold and everything's worked out. I'm sure it will cover the kids' education, and a whole lot more besides.'

'What's your point?'

Andie hesitated. 'Is there something you're not telling me?'

'What?'

'Well, is everything all right . . . financially?'

Meredith's head spun around, her eyes ablaze. 'What are you implying?'

'Nothing, I —'

'How dare you!' she boomed. 'In case you've forgotten, or more likely haven't been paying attention, Neville is the executive director in charge of Australasian operations, and I am a senior director of the research facility.'

'Then I don't understand why you seem to be upset about the will. I think it's fair.'

'Of course you think it's fair,' she sniped, 'because you've always expected to have everything handed to you on a platter.'

Andie was bewildered. 'What exactly have I had handed to me on a platter?'

'Oh please, you've barely worked a day in your life, Andrea,' said Meredith, crossing her arms. 'You steal someone else's husband, and then make hay on the proceeds, pottering about in your little hobby shop that apparently you don't even have to show up at every day.'

'Even if that were true,' Andie said, trying to keep calm, 'why does it bother you so much? What have I done to make you so angry, Meredith?'

She shook her head. 'Nothing, Andrea. You've done absolutely nothing. While I've had to work hard for every single thing I've achieved,' she said. 'I actually completed *my* university degree. Then I worked my way up in my career, as did Neville, and we gave Mum and Dad their only two grandchildren, while you carried on an affair with a married man almost twice your age. Thank God Mum didn't live to see that. You've sailed through life using your looks as a meal ticket. But you should realise that looks fade, Andrea, and that husband of yours left one wife when something younger and prettier came along, don't think he won't do the same thing to you.'

'He already has.'

'What?'

'Ross has been having an affair,' Andie said plainly. 'And I've left him.' The lift doors opened and she stepped out.

Meredith followed her, looking a little dazed. 'That's why you want to stay in the house.'

'Meredith!'

'Don't be offended, Andrea,' she returned. 'I was wondering why you were so keen. Now I understand, that's all.'

Andie shook her head. 'No, Meredith, I don't think you understand the slightest thing about me,' she said, before she turned on her heel and walked away.

That night

Tasha stood glaring at Ross, her hands planted on her hips. 'How long is she going to keep using the excuse of her father dying? She knows about us now. Does she really think she can hang on to you forever?'

She was so over this limbo they were living in at the moment. Ross spent most nights with her, so she wanted to know why they were keeping two apartments, why they couldn't move in together, to either her place or his, Tasha didn't care. Though, Ross still had to pay the mortgage on his apartment regardless, whereas if Tasha gave up her apartment, she wouldn't have to pay rent anymore. That seemed like the most sensible way to go. According to Ross, his wife was refusing point-blank to ever set foot in the apartment again, so why should it just sit there empty most of the time?

'Tash, this is a sensitive time,' Ross was saying. 'We have to be patient for just a little while longer. Andie was going to the reading of the will today. If that turns out as I expect it to, she's going to be a lot better off, and that puts us in a better position.'

'What do you mean, *she* will be a lot better off?' said Tasha. 'You're entitled to half her assets as well. You're still married.'

Ross looked uneasy. 'I don't know, Tash, it doesn't feel right to go for a share of her father's estate.'

'Why? She'd take it from you if it was the other way around, in a shot.'

'My parents are long gone, Tash.'

'That's not the point. It sounds to me like what's yours is half hers, while what's hers is all hers.'

'Look, I've been through this before,' he said, 'and I don't want that shitfight all over again.'

'So you expect me to just wait around?' she demanded. 'For how long, Ross?'

'For as long as it takes,' he said, raising his voice.

Tasha didn't like it one bit. 'Well, what if I'm not prepared to do that?'

'Look, I don't know what you expect of me,' he said angrily. 'I couldn't have foreseen her father dying.'

'Fine, but enough's enough. She knows about us now. I don't understand what you're hiding from.'

'I'm not hiding from anything, I just don't think it's appropriate right now.'

'I'm so fucking sick of hearing that word!' she cried, her head starting to pound.

'Look, you were prepared to be patient before,' he said. 'I'm really beginning to wonder what your motives are here.'

'What exactly are you saying, Ross?'

'You know what I'm saying.'

She narrowed her eyes. 'Well, why don't you just spell it out?'

'If Andie hadn't found us that night . . .'

'You'd be happy for us to still be sneaking around?' she finished for him. 'How long do you think I would have put up with that?'

'You agreed at the time, for as long as it would take.'

'But things have changed. She knows about us,' Tasha insisted for what felt like the billionth time. 'The shit has already hit the fan. So what are we waiting for? Let's just move in together and take it from there.'

He turned his back on her and walked over to the window. He was clenching his forehead, the way he did when he was frustrated.

'You don't even know if you want to move in together, do you?' she accused him. 'You talked the talk while you could fuck me on demand. Now you're getting cold feet when the only thing in the way of us being together is out of the way. I have to wonder if you ever planned to leave her for me.'

She waited for him to protest, to argue the point, something. But he just stood there at the window, perfectly still.

'Get out, Ross.'

'What?' He turned around.

'I'm not going to be used like this anymore.' She walked over to the door and held it open. 'Get out.'

'Tasha . . .'

'I mean it, Ross,' she said coldly. 'When you make up your mind what you want, then give me a call. Though I can't promise I'll pick up.'

Roseville

Andie let herself into the house with her key; she'd almost gone to knock as well until she remembered, with a faint pang, that she didn't need to do that anymore. She wheeled her giant suitcase behind her, propping it upright near the wall in the living room, then she carried the hamper of food she'd brought from the deli to the kitchen. She'd only packed enough to get her through this evening and breakfast in the morning. She would do a proper shop tomorrow.

She put the milk and some other things in the fridge and closed the door, staring around the room. It was unnaturally quiet. She gazed out the window, she could see the roof of the garage from here. She would have seen it that day too, without really looking at it, without knowing . . .

Andie started to wonder what had possessed her to do this. Everyone had tried to talk her out of it.

'We meant it when we said you could stay here until you got your own place,' Toby had told her, with Donna nodding in agreement beside him. 'I don't like the thought of you staying all the way over there on your own, Andie.'

'It's so nice of you guys,' she said. 'And I will get my own place eventually, but it's better if I stay at the house in the meantime. It'll be easier that way, there's just so much to do before we can put it on the market.'

Toby looked uneasy. 'You're not going to let Ross move in there with you, are you?' he asked.

'Of course not. What made you think that?'

Ross had had his own objections.

'You don't need to stay all the way over there, Andie,' he said. 'Can't we do something about this? I know you don't want to come back to the apartment, so why don't we get tenants in, and rent ourselves somewhere else while we work through this?'

'Because I don't want to live with you while we work through this.'

'But I'm not even seeing Tasha now.'

Andie groaned. 'And is she aware of that?'

'What do you mean?'

'Never mind,' she said flatly. 'I need to stay at the house, Ross, it'll be so much easier to organise everything that has to be done.'

'What about us?'

'There is no "us" at the moment.'

'But . . . I thought, since the funeral and everything . . .'

Andie sighed. 'I appreciated your support, truly, I did. But what did I say to you, Ross? No demands. I need time, I need space. Don't pressure me.'

The fridge motor started up suddenly behind her and Andie jumped. Okay, she had all the time and space she could want, and it was creeping her out. She walked into the living room and dropped down onto the settee, picking up the remote. She turned on the TV and cycled through the stations, but the screen was so big it was like sitting in the front row at the movies. Andie went to switch it off, but then she thought better of it. She needed some background noise. Instead, she turned over to the news, and got up to go and inspect the bedrooms. She had to decide where she was going to sleep.

She stood at the door of her parents' room, but she didn't go in. The bed had been hastily made, probably by Neville. There were some clothes slung over the chair, shoes kicked aside. Everything would have to go, the bedding, all her father's clothes, all his belongings. She noticed a thick, hardcover book on the bedside table, a bookmark poking out about halfway through. He never got to finish it. She reached for the handle and pulled the door closed. She'd have to work herself up to this.

She walked up the hall and pushed on the door of her old bedroom; there was something in the way, so she couldn't open it right back. She poked her head around. It was the smallest room in the house, and now it was filled with junk, by the looks of it. Andie had taken everything she owned when she moved out, even the bed. Obviously her dad had only used the room for storage ever since. Andie suspected she was going to find a lot of her mother's stuff in here. She backed away and closed the door again. Another day.

Brendan's room was like a shrine; no one had been allowed to touch or move or take anything from it while her mother was alive. She hadn't even let the grandchildren sleep in there when they stayed over. Andie walked over to the bed and sat down, smoothing her hands across the dated, brown-striped quilt. She gazed around the room, trying to feel some sense of her brother here, but it was no use. Her mother used to insist on cleaning his room for him, regardless of his protests to give him some privacy and leave his things alone. So it was pristine, and it didn't feel like Brendan's room, it felt like a room in her mother's house where he had slept.

Andie swivelled around to lie down on the bed, staring up at the ceiling, the same ceiling that Brendan would have stared at. She had been missing him more keenly of late. She wished he was here to talk to, to tell her what to do next, though Brendan would never tell her what to do. He'd say, 'Andie . . .' – he was the one who'd first called her Andie when he was little and couldn't pronounce Andrea, and while their mother always tried to correct him as he got older, the name stuck, though he was the only one in the family who called her that. If he was here now he'd say, 'Andie, you know what to do, you have to stop listening to the outside voices and listen to your own voice, the one inside your head that knows you better than anyone. Even better than me.' He was barely a teenager when he said that to her, yet he could be so wise sometimes.

Andie wondered about the man he would be now, if he would have married, had any kids. She could have had a real, honest-to-goodness relationship with her nephews and/or nieces, and Andie was certain she would have got along brilliantly with his wife, her very own sister-in-law. Andie imagined barbecues with Toby and Donna, all the kids running around, the adults watching them, laughing together, happy . . . but strangely, Ross was never in the picture. Andie had always had the feeling that things wouldn't have got very far with Ross if Brendan had still been alive. She could cope with Jess and Toby and just about everyone else's disapproval, but she could never have coped with Brendan's.

She sat up again. She didn't want to sleep in here, it would only make her melancholy. So it would have to be Meredith's old room, which had long ago been stripped of all things Meredith and converted to a guestroom. It would do for Andie.

She went back out to the living room for her wheelie bag, when she thought she heard knocking. She wasn't used to the noises in the house yet, it was probably nothing. She picked up the remote and turned down the sound on the TV. Then she heard it again, this time it was unmistakably someone knocking at the door. Andie sighed; the only person she imagined it could be was Meredith, and the only reason she could imagine she'd come around was to start giving her orders.

But when Andie opened the door, it was not Meredith standing on the porch, but Ross, flowers in one hand and a bottle of wine in the other.

'Ross,' she said, 'what are you doing here?'

He shrugged. 'I'm allowed to visit, aren't I? You didn't say anything about not visiting.'

Andie just stood there, pressing her lips together.

'These are for you,' he said, thrusting the flowers at her. 'I thought you might want something to brighten up the place.'

She looked down at them. They were beautiful, of course, his secretary knew the best florists in the city. 'Thanks.'

'So,' he said after a while, 'are you going to invite me in?'

She hesitated. 'I don't know . . .'

'Come on, Andie,' he cajoled. 'I drove all this way.'

Why did he drive all the way over here? What was he hoping for? Andie had avoided being alone with him wherever possible, she didn't trust him . . . much less herself.

'Look, it's not as though I'm moving in. Let's just have a drink,' he said with a wave of the bottle.

'Okay,' Andie finally relented, taking a step back as he walked past her into the hall. Don't be a wimp, you can handle this, you just have to stay in control, keep your wits about you. She closed the door after him and followed him into the living room.

He was looking around. 'I've never been inside this house, you know.'

'I know.'

'It's a little . . .'

'Stuck in a time warp?' she finished for him. 'Come through to the kitchen and I'll get us some glasses.'

Ross opened the bottle and poured the wine, while Andie searched for a vase for the flowers. She couldn't find anything appropriate, so in the end she stuck them in a plastic container so at least they were in water.

'I guess I should have brought you a vase as well,' Ross said with a smile as he handed her a glass of wine.

'Last thing I need is more stuff around here,' she muttered, bringing the glass to her lips.

'Hold on,' he stopped her. 'Shouldn't we drink to something?'

'Like what?'

'To new beginnings,' he said, raising his glass.

'I think it might be more appropriate to drink to endings right now.'

'I hope you're not referring to us.'

Andie shrugged. 'I guess we'll have to wait and see.'

Ross threw back the contents of his glass almost in one go, and picked up the bottle again. 'Top-up?'

'I've barely started on this one,' said Andie. 'Aren't you driving?'

'Yeah,' he said, filling his glass again.

If he was going to drink that fast, Andie had better get some food into him at the same time. 'I don't have much to eat here at the moment,' she said, opening the fridge door. 'I was going to do a big shop tomorrow.'

'It's okay,' he said. 'I could take you out to dinner, if you like?'

'Thanks anyway.'

'Then we'll order in.'

Andie turned to look at him. 'I thought you were only staying for a drink?'

'Why don't we play it by ear?' he said, flashing her one of his stock smiles – category: charming. He took off his jacket and hung it over a chair, then he sat down, loosening his tie.

Andie put out a wedge of brie and some crackers, but Ross didn't touch them as he guzzled down another glass. He better not be planning to drink himself over the limit so that he couldn't drive. Well, that wasn't her problem, there were such things as taxis.

'So, how's it coming along?' he asked.

'I only got here about an hour before you, if that,' she returned.

'You'll have to show me around later,' he said. 'I'd like to see where you slept when you were a girl.'

'It's a junk room now, there's not even a bed in it.'

'Still, there must be beds in other rooms,' he said with a suggestive wink.

Andie winced. 'Ross . . .'

'Sweetheart, we haven't talked, properly, in weeks.' He reached over and covered her hand with his. 'There are so many things I want to say to you.'

'Like what?'

'Like I miss you.'

Andie didn't respond.

'Don't you miss me,' he asked, 'even a little?'

'That's a difficult question to answer,' she replied.

He treated her to his forlorn face.

'Ross, I miss what we had, or what I thought we had. I don't know anymore. The rug's been pulled out from under me and I don't know what's real and what's not.'

'What's real is that I love you. We've had ten years together, that's what's real.'

She sighed. 'Is it, Ross?'

'What are you trying to say?'

Andie wasn't sure she wanted to start dissecting their whole marriage right now. She wasn't prepared. Ross would have too many clever answers and, well . . . she just wasn't prepared.

'Never mind,' she said.

'No, Andie, I want you to tell me what's on your mind,' he said earnestly. 'We should have it all out. Say whatever you've been wanting to say, give me a chance to defend myself.'

'I don't know, Ross,' she said. 'You have an art.'

'Well, that's hardly fair,' he protested. 'You're going to dismiss everything I say because I have a way of saying it?'

She shrugged, and he took hold of her hand now and drew it to his lips, planting a kiss.

'Ross —'

'No, listen to me,' he urged. 'I know I've made mistakes, huge ones, but I've come to realise through all this that I love you more than anything.'

He was stroking her hand, gazing at her with those vivid blue eyes of his. It had been ages since . . . Andie couldn't even remember the last time they made love. Why was she even thinking about that now? He pressed his lips into the palm of her hand and it was as though a jolt of electricity passed through her body.

She had to stay in control. She jerked her hand away and got to her feet. 'You've had your drink, Ross, in fact you've had two. Time to go.'

'Andie —'

'Really, Ross, I want you to go now.'

He stood up and she backed away from the table, right into the corner of the kitchen. Well, that was stupid. Why didn't she head for the doorway? Was this some kind of Freudian slip? Now he was right in front of her, blocking her. She would have to physically push him out of the way to move to the door, and that was hardly going to look like she was in control. She'd like to maintain some dignity.

She folded her arms in front of her. 'Ross, enough, I'm asking you to leave. Politely.'

'Andie,' he said, bringing his hand up to cup her face. 'I've missed you so much.'

Screw dignity. She went to brush him off but he caught her up in his arms, holding her tight.

'Ross, let me go,' she said firmly.

'I don't want to let you go,' he said, 'that's what I've been trying to tell you.'

He brought his lips down onto hers and kissed her hard, his hand cupping the back of her head so she couldn't pull away. Andie steeled herself not to respond, but it was useless. His lips prised hers open as his tongue plunged into her mouth. Andie began to dissolve into him . . . oh God, she was losing it. They hadn't had sex in ages, certainly not sex like this. It used to be like this all the time, tearing the clothes off each other in the kitchen, the living room, wherever, their passion too overwhelming to wait till they got to the bedroom. But no longer. Andie had begun to doubt he was even interested any more, and she had switched off, because what else was she going to do? Live in a perpetual state of frustration? Now she was so achingly sensitive to his touch that she felt like she was all nerve-endings. His hands slid down to grasp her hips, propping her up onto the bench behind, and drawing himself in between her knees. Andie wrapped her legs around him, it was like a reflex action. She wanted him inside her, she wanted him to lose himself in a rage of desire, to realise what he'd been missing . . . She arched her head back as his lips slid down her neck and his hands grasped her breasts. And she saw the woman, straddling him on the bed. Andie opened her eyes and was jolted back into the reality that was her parents' kitchen. And Ross.

'No, Ross,' she breathed, grabbing his shoulders.

'It's okay,' he murmured into her neck.

'No, it's not!' She pushed against his shoulders now, slipping down off the bench. 'It's not okay at all.'

'What's the matter, Andie? What's wrong?'

She sidled away from him and around the kitchen table, putting more distance, and an obstacle, between them. 'I can't, Ross. I can't be with you.'

'Why? Come on, Andie, it's obvious that we still want each other,' he said.

'So what, Ross?' she cried. 'Two dogs passing in the street "want" each other.'

He grimaced. 'How can you say that? Are you going to tell me you have no feelings for me, beyond some kind of Pavlovian sexual urge?'

'Ross —'

'No, tell me, Andie, I want to know. Because what I feel for you is so much more than that.'

'Then why did you have to go and sleep with another woman?'

He sighed, dropping his head. 'That's what this is about?'

'Yes, Ross,' she cried. 'I can't get the image of you and that woman out of my head.'

'Well, you have to try,' he urged, 'for the sake of our marriage, Andie, you have to put this behind us. I may have "wanted" someone else – for a brief, stupid, careless moment – but it's you that I love. I've never stopped loving you, and I could never stop loving you.' He paused, his eyes searching hers. 'I can't bear this, Andie. Remember how much we went through to be together? And now you want to throw everything away because I made one mistake?' He paused again, for effect. 'It just feels like it can't have mattered as much to you as it has to me.'

Andie stood there trembling . . . How could he turn the tables on her like that? It was her responsibility now to fix the marriage? But then, if what he said was true, if this was just a . . . a lapse on his part, was it bad enough to give up everything? She'd read the magazines, affairs didn't always ruin marriages, sometimes they saved them, or at least alerted the couple to problems and got them working on the relationship. Was it really wise to throw away ten years on a 'careless moment', as he'd put it?

The problem was, the image of that 'careless moment' was burned into her brain, the thought of it made her sick. And Andie was just not sure of her own feelings any more, if she even had it in her to work on the marriage.

Ross was watching her, she wondered if he could read her mind.

'I'm not seeing Tasha, I told you that,' he said. 'She was a mistake, Andie, I swear to you. She got through to me when my defences were down, and she was relentless . . . I was even a bit afraid of her at the end . . . I think she might be a bit unhinged . . .'

His voice faded and Andie suddenly remembered the look on Joanna's face when she'd said that word. Something snapped inside her. 'Is that what you said to Joanna about me?'

'What?' He was clearly stunned. 'What's this got to do with Joanna?'

'You made the same excuses to her,' she accused. 'You blamed everything on me.'

'No, I didn't.' He looked confused. 'Where are you getting this from?'

'Joanna.'

'What?'

'You've been reading from the same script, Ross, but I guess you never planned on your current wife and your former wife comparing notes.'

'What the hell?' he said. 'What were you doing talking to Joanna?'

'It doesn't matter, and it's none of your business who I talk to anyway.'

'This is crazy, Andie,' said Ross. 'I don't know what Joanna's been telling you, but you actually trust her word over mine? You don't think she might have an agenda to get back at me?'

Andie groaned. 'Why would she do that, Ross, after all this time? She has nothing to gain.'

'Except revenge. And sticking it to you. Are you really that naive, Andie?'

She bristled. 'Joanna didn't have any reason to lie to me, Ross. She said things unwittingly . . . she didn't know that you'd fed me a completely different line. The fact is, you lied to everyone – to me about Joanna, to Joanna about me, and now you're lying to me about Tasha. And you're probably lying to Tasha as well.'

He was just glaring at her. 'This is bullshit. Andie, honestly, you'll believe anything.'

'Yes, apparently I will.' She was getting pissed off now. 'I almost believed you just then, that I'm the big love of your life, that you'll never stop loving me. Well, I don't know about you, Ross, but I couldn't sleep with someone – for months – if I was in love with someone else. I just couldn't. So,' she paused to catch her breath, 'it seems to me there's definitely plenty of bullshit going around, but it isn't coming from me.'

Her voice reverberated around the room for a second, and then there was silence. He obviously had nothing to say to that.

'Now would you please leave,' said Andie.

'Gladly.' He strode over to the table and picked up his jacket, then he grabbed the bottle of wine.

'Ross, don't be an idiot,' she said. 'You're driving.'

'Don't act like you could give a shit, Andie,' he threw back at her as he marched out of the room. Eventually she heard the front door open, and then a loud slam as it shut again.

Andie stood there trembling. What had she done? She shouldn't have told him she'd spoken to Joanna, she had no right to give up a confidence like that. And now Ross was driving off into the night, angry, with half a bottle of wine in his hand, and most of the other half in his bloodstream.

She hurried up the hall and pulled open the front door, but his car was already gone. She stepped out onto the porch in time to see it swerve around the corner and out of sight.

*

Joanna had made plans to go out tonight, but it had been one of those days, and she'd felt a headache coming on the closer the clock ticked over towards five. She would have to leave no later than that to get home in time to get ready to meet the girls . . . it made her tired just thinking about it.

As she texted her girlfriend to bow out, she readied herself for the onslaught she would receive in reply. Her friends all thought she worked too much and played too little. And they probably had a point. But Joanna liked her work, she revelled in it, most of the time it didn't even feel like work. Okay, so today had been hectic, and frustrating, and stressful, but she had made it through, problems solved, or well on the way to being solved. Joanna felt a sense of accomplishment in her work that she had rarely felt with anything else before in her life.

That was all well and good, her friends would say, but she needed to get laid once in a while. Joanna didn't disagree, necessarily, but she was not interested in a relationship and all the complications that went with it. Her friends said they weren't talking about a relationship, they were talking about sex, pure and simple, while Joanna maintained there was no such thing. She hadn't exactly been a nun, it had been ten years after all. Friends had set her up, which nearly always proved to be a mistake, if not an outright disaster. At Lauren's insistence, she'd even given internet dating a whirl. But Lauren said it didn't count if she only ever exchanged emails and didn't actually arrange to meet anyone. Joanna simply could not be bothered. Any vaguely interesting, accomplished men – though who knew for sure, they could make up anything online – were only interested in women who were ten, even twenty years her junior. She gave up, she told Lauren she didn't need to resort to the internet because she met plenty of men through her work; she was in a male-dominated industry after all. However, they all seemed to be intimidated by a woman succeeding on their turf, and felt the need to go to extraordinary lengths to establish their superiority. That was just tiresome.

Joanna decided eventually that she was not built for the midlife dating scene. The truth was, though she'd never breathe a word of it to another soul, she often just wished her marriage had weathered the storm and survived. That's the way she was, it was in her DNA. When she married Ross, it was forever. She knew the relationship had seen better days, but she'd assumed it would come good again as the children grew in independence and they moved on to the next stage. She envied long-married couples, free of kids and babysitters, going out to restaurants and the theatre, travelling together, enjoying their grandchildren. She would have been quite content with that kind of life.

Oh, she was well and truly over Ross, the man; she wouldn't have him back now if someone paid her. It wasn't him, it was the concept that she missed – the security and ease that came from the knowledge you would be with that person for the rest of your life. Some people, a lot of people, found that stifling. But Joanna had found it an enormous comfort, and she suspected she was never going to find that same level of comfort with someone else. If she did, it would have to come along when she least expected it, so she had stopped expecting it.

Her headache eased as soon as she'd sent the text and was off the hook for the night, at least once she'd dealt with the flood of messages trying to talk her into changing her mind. Finally she was on her way home, listening to Paul Simon on the car sound system, looking forward to a glass of wine and a bath. All on her own. Bliss.

But when she arrived home she was confronted by a trio of noisy boys playing video games in her family room. They were actually young adults now, but they reverted to noisy boys when they were playing those damn things, and Joanna could have screamed, until she was informed they were only waiting for Matty to get ready and then they'd be 'out of here, Mrs C'.

Her bath would have to wait, so she kicked off her shoes, shrugged off her jacket, and poured herself a glass of wine. Joanna couldn't stand the sound of video games, so she went out onto the terrace, and before she'd finished her glass Matty had come out to say goodbye. When she heard the doorbell only a few minutes later, she thought he must have forgotten something. It was his usual trick, he never seemed to be able to make a clean getaway, that kid. It was probably his keys, which would explain why he was ringing the doorbell.

But to Joanna's considerable surprise, it wasn't Matty at all.

'Ross, what are you doing here?'

'What kind of welcome is that?' he said.

'Well, I wasn't exactly expecting you to show up at my house on a Friday night.'

'I need to talk to you,' he said. If she wasn't mistaken, Joanna thought she detected a slight sway in his stance.

'Have you been drinking?' she asked him. 'And driving?' she added, noticing his car parked out front.

'Joanna,' he chided, 'I was fine to drive, I've only had a couple.'

She wasn't so sure. His speech was a little slurred as well, it wasn't like Ross.

'So, are you going to invite me in?' he asked.

She hesitated. 'I have plans later.' A bath, a night in peace . . .

'I won't keep you from them,' he insisted, as he propped one arm against the doorjamb. Joanna wondered if he was holding himself up. She better let him in, she might have to call him a taxi.

'All right, come on in.' She stood back and he stepped inside, leaning over to kiss her on the cheek before she realised what he was doing. It was more of a smooch than a peck, and Joanna could smell the wine on his breath. She turned away from him to close the door and wipe her cheek. This was going to be interesting.

'So,' she said as she followed him into the kitchen, 'what did you want to talk about, Ross?'

'Steady on, aren't you at least going to offer me a drink?'

'Sure. What will it be – tea, coffee, water?'

He pulled a face as he headed for the liquor cabinet. 'I meant a real drink,' he said over his shoulder.

'Seems to me like you might have had enough.'

'Joanna —'

'If you want to drive home, is all I'm saying.'

'I can look after myself,' he said, reaching for the Scotch bottle.

She was getting an uneasy feeling about this. Joanna had picked up her glass to refill it, but she decided to leave it for now. One of them ought to stay sober.

'What's up, Ross?' she prompted him again. 'What did you want to talk about?'

'Andie and I are . . . we're on a break, did you know?' he said, pouring the Scotch into a glass.

'I'll get you some ice.' Joanna slotted a glass under the ice maker and watched the ice tumble into it. Things must be getting more serious if he'd decided to tell her. Maybe Andie had found her own place.

Ross came over to the bench and parked himself on a stool. Joanna slid the glass of ice towards him, and he dropped a couple of cubes into his Scotch.

'What happened?' she asked.

He looked up at her. 'I think you might know already.'

Shit. Joanna felt the heat rise into her cheeks. She had such a bad poker face.

Ross took a swig from his glass. 'You've been talking to Andie.'

'Well, that's between me and Andie,' she said coolly.

'Joanna, I don't care that you've talked to her,' he said. 'Mind you, I give up trying to understand women. You two were archenemies in the past.'

That was overstating it just a tad.

'But that's beside the point,' he went on. 'Andie said some things that you told her I said, and I don't remember saying them at all.'

'Such as?'

'Ahh . . .' He closed his eyes and rubbed his forehead, as though he was straining to remember. 'Something about . . . when you and I split up, I put the blame on her.'

Joanna was waiting. 'Yes?'

He looked up at her then. 'I didn't blame Andie, our marriage was already over.'

'That's debatable, Ross, but we won't go there now. You certainly did, however, try to put some of the blame on to Andie.'

He frowned. 'And you told her that? I don't understand, how did it even come up?'

Joanna hesitated. 'You don't know the context, Ross.'

'Well, why don't you fill me in?' He threw back the rest of his Scotch and made a return trip to the liquor cabinet.

She sighed. She hated lying, but she felt an obligation to protect Andie, even though Andie had clearly not felt the same towards her. But she shouldn't judge, she didn't know what kind of spot Andie had been put in.

'Andie was meeting Brooke here, Brooke was late, she and I got to talking, she was upset . . .' She watched Ross as he joined her again at the kitchen bench, his glass refilled, double. 'Getting the picture yet?'

'I suppose.' He shrugged. 'But I still don't get women.'

Joanna decided to turn the conversation around. 'What are you doing, Ross?'

He looked at her. 'Sitting here having a drink with you. Hey, why aren't you drinking?'

'Ross,' she chided, 'you're throwing away another marriage. How many do you plan on going through?' She paused to let that sink in. 'What are you doing, Ross?' she repeated.

'You want to know the truth?' he said quietly. 'I don't even know anymore. I feel like everything's going to crap around me.'

'How old is she?' Joanna asked. 'And please don't tell me she's not older than Lauren.'

He just gave her a baleful look.

'Ross,' she sighed, shaking her head.

'It was just a stupid fling, I swear. I was frustrated about Andie and the whole baby thing, I didn't know how far she was going to push it. I saw myself at sixty taking a kid to kindergarten, and it was freaking me out a little, to be honest.' He took a breath. 'Then this girl starts flirting with me at work, and —'

'— she's young and pretty,' Joanna finished for him. 'It's hard not to be flattered at your age, right?'

Ross was just staring at her.

'But you never led her on. Next thing you know, she won't leave you alone, she's needy, maybe even a little *unhinged* . . .'

'How do you know all that?'

'Don't be a complete boofhead, Ross. You said the same things about Andie to me, a decade ago.'

His eyes widened. 'Is that what you told Andie?'

'Don't worry, I kept the worst of it to myself.'

'Thanks.'

'You needn't think I did it to protect you, buddy. It only would have hurt Andie, and it would have just made me sound like a bitch anyway.'

He was shaking his head. 'I don't know why I would have said that. Andie wasn't unhinged, she's nothing like Tasha.'

'That's the new girl?'

He nodded. 'She's giving me all these ultimatums, making demands. Andie never made any demands. She's still not making any,' he added wistfully.

'What about her wanting a baby?' Joanna reminded him.

'But she never demanded . . .' He raked his hands through his hair and groaned. 'God, it's all such a fucking mess.'

'And who do you think made the mess? Ross, you have to start taking some responsibility for your actions.'

He met her gaze. 'I'm trying, but I don't think Andie's ever going to forgive me. She can't seem to get past it.'

'Well, can you blame her? I never had the misfortune of catching you two in the act, but I imagine it'd be a pretty tough mental picture to erase,' she said. 'And it was in your apartment, in your bed . . . her bed! Honestly, Ross, what were you thinking?'

'I didn't plan it . . . it was Tasha . . . she ambushed me.'

Joanna just stared at him, her eyebrows raised in disbelief. Her little fantasy about growing old with Ross was just that, a fantasy. He had to grow up before he could grow old, and Joanna had a suspicion that was never going to happen.

'Oh God,' he groaned, raking his hair again. 'How am I ever going to fix this?'

'You can start by going home and sleeping it off.'

'Don't make me go, Josie,' he pleaded.

Uh-oh, he hadn't called her that in a very long time.

'I told you I had plans tonight,' she reminded him.

'Well, that's okay, I can stay here while you're out, can't I? It's not like I'm going to break anything.' He sighed. 'I don't want to go home to that bloody apartment on my own, Josie. Can't I stay on the sofa bed?'

Joanna picked up the phone. 'I'm calling you a cab now, Ross,' she said. 'And you are going to go home, drink lots of water, and go to bed. Things will look better in the morning, I promise you.'

Saturday morning

Andie felt hungover, and she'd only had about three sips of wine last night, she'd poured the rest down the sink after Ross had stormed out. But she'd had a fitful night's sleep, worrying about the way he took off, bottle of wine in hand. What was he thinking? If anything happened to him . . . Andie knew it wasn't her fault, but she'd still find it difficult not to blame herself.

Maybe she had been too hard, too unyielding. She had suggested before this that a reconciliation was possible, that she just needed time and space. Now she didn't know what she wanted. Maybe she wasn't being fair. If Ross wanted to work on the marriage, shouldn't she be prepared to meet him halfway? And wouldn't that involve seeing each other, dating, maybe even having sex . . . But then again, without a proper break, how was she ever going to get the perspective to work out what she really wanted?

No wonder she couldn't sleep. She kept thinking she should call Ross, but then she worried he'd take the call while he was driving, which would only make things worse. In the end, she didn't call, but every time she closed her eyes she had horrifying visions of Ross lying dead on a road somewhere.

Or else she dreamed of having sex with him in the kitchen . . . on the bench . . . on the table . . . up against the wall . . . She kept waking up in a lather of sweat, her heart pounding.

At daybreak she gave up trying to get any more sleep, but it was too early to call Ross to make sure he had made it home all right.

So Andie paced through another couple of fretful hours, gulping down coffee, until she thought it was reasonable to phone, even if he wasn't up yet.

Hearing the ringtone after she'd dialled his number gave her some immediate relief – at least his phone wasn't smashed to pieces inside his wrecked car. But Andie wasn't prepared for what happened next.

'Hello?' said a woman's voice.

Andie couldn't find hers for a moment. Then all that came out was a stuttering, garbled string of syllables approximating: 'Oh, is that . . . I was after . . . I'm not sure . . .'

'This is Ross Corcoran's phone. He's in the shower right now, can I give him a message?'

Andie hung up, shaking. Who was that? It could have been a nurse, he was in the hospital . . . No, that was unlikely. Andie would have been contacted by now, wouldn't she? She was his next of kin. Maybe he'd been picked up for drink-driving, and he was in some kind of lock-up facility? So who was answering his phone? They confiscated personal items and stored them separately, or at least that's what they did on TV; whatever, Andie doubted some police officer stood there fielding incoming calls.

While the detainee was in the shower.

She had conveniently overlooked that little nugget of information. She was just stalling, kidding herself, denying the inevitable. As her heart sank deep down into her gut, Andie knew that was Tasha who'd answered. And Tasha most certainly would have known it was Andie. Her picture appeared on the screen when she called Ross's phone, along with her name. Tasha had answered fully aware of what she was doing, which was to make it indisputably clear where Ross had spent the night.

Andie was angry now, furious, she felt it rippling through every fibre of her body. How could he do this to her after everything he'd said last night? He'd lied, barefaced, again and again. He was a compulsive liar. And Andie had swallowed it all. She was angry with him, but she was also angry with herself. She had desperately not wanted to be like Tasha, needy and unhinged, but how desperate and needy she must have been all these years, like a loyal puppy, only needing to be patted and she would accept whatever she was told, however she was treated.

She'd given everything to him, she had abdicated all choice – maybe that wasn't all his fault, Andie had been all too willing. They weren't a partnership, Ross was the CEO making all the decisions, getting everything his own way. She couldn't have a career, she couldn't have a baby . . .

Andie blinked, looking around, like she was coming out of a trance. Right, she had to get on with it, clean out this house, sell it and move on. She would find a place to live, her own place, and she would work out what she wanted to do with her life, because it was, in the end, her life.

She stared down at the phone in her hand. And as for you, Ross Corcoran, if I don't see you for as long as I live, it won't be long enough.

*

Ross sauntered out of the bathroom with a towel around his hips, his skin still damp, his hair ruffled. He had a good body still, maybe he wasn't quite as buffed as some guys her age, but he'd kept himself in pretty decent shape. Tasha stretched out on the bed, her arms above her head, the sheet artfully arranged across her body for maximum effect.

'You're awake?' said Ross, coming to sit on the bed and planting a hand either side of her as he leaned in closer.

'Hm,' she murmured lazily. 'The phone woke me. Both your ex-wives have called already.'

He frowned. 'I only have one ex-wife.'

Tasha raised an eyebrow at him.

'Officially,' he relented. 'You didn't answer it?'

'I did.'

'Why did you do that, Tash?' he said, sitting upright.

'Because it was ringing.'

'Well, what did you say?'

'Not much,' she shrugged. 'Joanna was cool, she just wanted to remind you that your car's at her place.'

He nodded.

'So what is your car doing at her place, Ross?' Tasha asked.

'What?'

'Why is your car at your ex-wife's house?'

'Oh . . . um, it was Matty, he asked me if he could borrow it last week.'

'Hm.' She supposed that sounded reasonable. 'So why isn't he dropping it back to you?'

'I don't know,' Ross dismissed. 'I'll have to give him a call, organise something. You said both ex-wives?'

Tasha rolled onto her side, propping her head in her hand. 'Yeah, your latest . . . she was not so cool. Bit of a freak, actually.'

Ross frowned. 'What do you mean?'

'I don't know, she ummed and aahed and couldn't even put a sentence together. Then she just hung up.'

He turned away from her to sit on the edge of the bed. 'I think it's best if you don't answer my phone in future, Tash,' he said after a while, his back to her.

'Uh-uh.' She shook her head slowly and rose up onto her knees, allowing the sheet to drop away altogether. She pressed her naked body into his bare back. 'We have a deal, Ross.'

He had showed up last night out of the blue, no phone call, no warning, she hadn't heard from him since the day he walked out on her over two weeks ago. She was getting ready to go out when she heard the knock. When she saw it was Ross, she left the security chain in place and stared at him through the chink in the door. She had no intention of making it easy for him. He begged her to let him in, said he had to talk to her, that he missed her. It was like he'd been drinking too much, which was strange for Ross. He liked a drink well enough, but Tasha had certainly never seen him drunk. He was obviously really broken up, and she softened. She told him he could have ten minutes.

That was more than ten hours ago. He completely broke down after she let him in, he was a mess. He told her he thought he was doing the right thing, trying to make up with his wife, but the whole time he hadn't been able to stop thinking about her. He said he'd come to realise through all this that he loved her more than anything, and he knew he could never be happy again without her. He only feared he'd lost his chance forever to be with her.

Tasha was moved – she wasn't made of stone, after all. But she was wary too; what was to stop him caving next time Ms Andie clicked her fingers? So there were going to have to be some conditions. Ross told her to list them, that he'd do anything. She knew he was a good man, and that he could never turn his back on his ex altogether, Tasha was not completely heartless. But she was not going to put up with him running around after her; her father was dead and buried, enough already. And Tasha refused to be hidden away like a guilty secret any longer. If Ross wanted to be with her, then she had to be his girlfriend, out in the open. She was not going to be his mistress any more.

Ross had agreed to everything, eagerly, without question, he just wanted her back. They spent half the night having the best make-up sex ever. Tasha was sure of one thing, he couldn't have been getting any with the former missus; he was like a man dying of thirst in the desert who had come across an oasis.

'Remember, Rossie,' she said now, her lips close to his ear. 'No more secrets, no more lies. No more hiding anything from me. You promised.' She brought her arms around him from behind, stroking his chest with her fingertips. She could feel his breathing becoming laboured under her touch.

'Now, what do you want to do?' she said in a low voice. 'Worry about some silly phone call, or . . .' Her hand slid down his torso. '. . . I have a much better idea.' She slipped her hand under the towel. She really had him now, in every sense. She might have taken him back, but he'd had to beg. And now she owned him.

Roseville

Andie had to get out of this house, at least for part of the day; staying indoors and trawling through her parents' belongings would only make her depressed, and there was more than enough going on to make her depressed without adding to it. She needed to go shopping for supplies and that was as good a reason as any to get out, so she set about doing an inventory of the kitchen cupboards. Neville had disposed of all the perishables; the refrigerator was almost empty. Apart from the few things Andie had brought with her yesterday, there was a jar of jam and one of pickled onions, possibly dating back to the seventies. As there was no use-by date, that was highly likely, so Andie turfed it, and the jam, along with most of what she found in the cupboards. There were canisters of weevil-ridden flour – both plain and self-raising. When was the last time either had been used? She couldn't imagine her father doing any baking. There were years-old packets of breadcrumbs and jelly crystals, and skim milk powder that had set rock-hard. Andie found stale saltines and Milk Arrowroots in the bottom of a pair of biscuit barrels, tucked right at the back of a cupboard. Her father had probably forgotten they were there. She tossed cans of food that had dents, or signs of oxidation around the rims, or that she wouldn't eat anyway – there were four tins of rice cream that only brought back bad memories of bland childhood desserts. In the end, all she kept was a couple of tins of baked beans that appeared to be relatively new.

Finally, as she stood on a chair to reach into the back of a cupboard above the fridge, Andie discovered a stack of cookbooks. She had never seen her mother use a cookbook or follow a recipe. She stuck to plain, unfussy food and made a variation of the same dinner, week in and week out, pretty much the whole of their childhoods. She was very much a graduate of the school of meat and three veg.

Andie dumped the books on the kitchen table and started to flick through them. They were very dated, and very Anglo – there were no Asian dishes here, not even any Italian. The books all harked from before the days of silly experimentation, when the height of sophistication was half a pineapple studded with cheese and gherkin toothpicks. Ingredients here were simple and largely unadulterated; nothing was processed, or wasted for that matter – there were an awful lot of offal recipes. But it was the method that really grabbed Andie's attention: detailed and exacting, often an art in itself. There was a respect and understanding of the properties of food and rules for handling that read like sacred doctrines. As Andie turned over page after page, she came across handwritten notes in a lovely, old-fashioned script next to some of the recipes; corrections, additions, ideas . . .

It eventually occurred to Andie that these books must have belonged to her grandmother, her father's mother. She died when Andie was quite small, maybe five or six, and so her memories were fuzzy at best. But she did remember the kitchen of her simple weatherboard house in Ashfield. Her grandmother had the purest white hair, and she always wore a pinafore-style apron over a flower print dress. Andie could see her now, standing at her kitchen table, the big round mixing bowls, striped blue and white, wooden spoons laid out, and one of those wonderful old Mixmasters that were a designer must-have these days, and cost a bomb. She used to let Andie sit on a stool and watch as she cooked. She showed her how to measure ingredients and add them to the bowl, she let her sift the flour and stir everything together. She talked to Andie the whole time about what she was doing, why you needed eggs for cakes but not biscuits, why cakes rose in the oven, why she added certain spices – a touch of ginger to a teacake, for example. And when it was cooked, she'd ask Andie if she could taste the ginger.

These weren't just books of recipes, they were manuals about how to cook. They featured simple, unadorned photographs to clearly illustrate each step, not glamorous shots of celebrity chefs in state-of-the-art kitchens. There were no such things as microwaves and fan-forced ovens, measurements were still imperial. Andie was mesmerised. She reached for her notepad and began to make a list.

Sunday

Jess parked out the front of the Lonergan home in Roseville. She'd been here a few times when she and Andie were at TAFE together, but she'd never stayed long. The place used to creep her out then. The ghosts of Andie's dead mother and brother seemed to hang over everything; Jess could only imagine it would be worse now, with her father gone as well. As she started down the front path, she noticed the overgrown garden, and that the front facade of the house looked faded and shabby. She remembered it used to look neat as a pin – a little soulless, but always immaculate.

Jess was worried about Andie, rattling around in the big empty family house, all on her own, it couldn't be good for her. She'd called yesterday to see if she wanted to do something last night, but Andie had declined. Jess suspected that Ross was hanging around so she asked her straight, but Andie assured her she had nothing to worry about on that front, Ross was gone for good. It was over. And that was all she would say about the matter.

So, what now? Was she just going to hide away in the old family home and never go out again, like some kind of twenty-first century version of Miss Havisham? Jess realised the metaphor was strained – Miss Havisham had been stood up on her wedding day – but the fact remained that Andie was in danger of becoming . . . well, maybe not a recluse, but heading down that path. She'd hardly stepped foot in the shop for weeks, and Jess doubted she was going be any more actively involved now she was living way over on the other side of the harbour. Jess was worried that she might easily sink into a depression. It was creepy that she was back here at the house. Her father had never been able to move on, and Jess was not going to just stand by and watch that happen to Andie.

She stepped up onto the porch and knocked loudly on the door. After Andie turned her down last night, Jess informed her she would come for a visit today. She didn't ask, she just told her she was coming over.

Andie opened the door a few moments later, looking weirdly like a housewife from the fifties. She was wearing one of those pinafore-style aprons, her hair tied back in a ponytail. And was that flour smudged across her cheek?

'Hi, Jess!' she said. Her eyes were bright, maybe even a little manic, and she had a wide smile on her face. 'Come on in.'

Jess followed her down the hallway past the living room while Andie prattled on, barely stopping to take a breath. She had made a discovery, she was so excited, she'd been up half the night, and had got straight into it again first thing this morning.

'I know what I have to do,' Andie declared as they walked into the kitchen. 'I'm going to start cooking again.'

Jess surveyed the room. Every available surface was covered with racks of cakes and slices cooling, trays of biscuits jostled for space on the sink and two large stockpots bubbled away on the stovetop.

'Well, looks like you already have,' she said.

Viande

Andie had been carrying out surveillance from her car since first light. She had a plan, which, granted, wasn't much of a plan, but it was too late now – she was here, she was going to have to just sit it out. Luckily she had brought supplies: a large coffee she'd picked up on the way, and a container of her scones. *Her* scones! Which were, if she said so herself, not bad at all. Making them had felt like a sheer labour of love; kneading the dough, rolling it out flat, and marking the scones out with a glass, just as she remembered her grandmother doing. She made batch after batch until she got it right, until they tasted exactly the way she remembered. Taste was such an evocative sense; Andie had closed her eyes, with the scone melting in her mouth, and been transported back to her grandmother's kitchen, biting into the same warm scones . . .

She had almost lived in the kitchen this past week, rediscovering what she loved about cooking, what she had always loved – the magic, the alchemy that happened when you took raw ingredients and transformed them into something not just edible, but delicious and sustaining. Nourishment was nurture.

Her mother had never seen it that way. Cooking was just another household chore, which explained the perennially bland meals, desserts out of a tin, and always a shop-bought cake for their birthdays. Andie had begged her once to let her make a cake for Brendan's birthday. She'd eventually agreed, on the strict condition that Andie clean up afterwards. So she went ahead and made the cake, icing it meticulously, even piping his name on top. Brendan made a huge deal over it, of course; even her father chimed in, saying he hadn't tasted cake like that since his mother died. Buoyed by her success, Andie asked if she could bake another cake the following weekend, but her mother became annoyed. 'Cooking is for housewives, you have better things to do with your time. Haven't you got homework anyway?'

During the week, Andie had gone out to buy cooling racks and biscuit trays and cake tins because her mother had never had much call for such things. She wished she'd thought to collect some of her kitchen gear from the apartment, but it wasn't really a priority on the day. At least she'd held on to her chef's kit, so she had decent knives and utensils.

'Do you know how fast these would sell at the deli?' Jess said as she perused the kitchen on Sunday, sampling the fresh-baked goodies.

Andie shrugged.

'I'm serious, Andie,' she said, holding up a lemon slice. 'You said you want to get back into cooking, you already have an outlet at your disposal.'

'I tried all that a few years ago, remember?' said Andie. 'The shop's just not set up for food production. It was all too much of a hassle.'

Jess leaned back against the bench and folded her arms. 'I've been thinking about that. Really, all you need is a commercial-grade double oven, in addition to what's already there. Some of the other equipment might need to be upgraded, and we could definitely use more bench space. But the area's so big, there's plenty of room for a huge island bench, and that would allow three or four people to work at it at once.'

Andie looked at her. 'You really have been thinking about this, haven't you?'

'Since I've been there more often, I can't help it,' said Jess. 'I just think there's so much more we could be doing with the shop. I'm getting sick to death of the casual gigs, and now you've got your cooking groove back. I know last time it got a bit much on your own, but if we did it together . . . Think about it, Andie, we're both chefs, and you own your own deli – we have all the ingredients at our disposal and the skills to do anything we want with them . . .'

Andie didn't know how to tell Jess that she couldn't work up much enthusiasm for the deli, especially right now. It was a symbol of her chronic acquiescence to Ross – she'd wanted to be a chef, instead she owned and ran a shop that sold food.

'You should look into it,' said Andie.

'Seriously?' Jess said. 'You're open to the idea?'

'Get Toby over to give you a quote.'

Andie was happy for Jess to check it out, but right now, she wanted to plot her own path, which was why she was sitting in her car, gazing across the carpark to the back exit of the restaurant. She was waiting for Dominic Gerou to arrive for work, she needed to get to him first thing. He was the type of man – no wait, she hardly knew what type of man he was – he was the type of *chef* who did not brook interruptions, and once his day got underway, Andie was quite sure she wouldn't be able to get anywhere near him, and she needed his full attention in order to state her case effectively. She knew it was a long shot, but at the moment it was all she had. If he refused to give her a second chance, she'd have to start applying for work through the normal channels, and Andie didn't like her odds. She was too old to be starting out, her qualifications were dated, she was out of practice – despite her cooking frenzy of the last week. She doubted anyone would give her a look-in. Dominic Gerou probably wouldn't either, but he was the only contact she had, no matter how tenuous. And besides, she kept telling herself, what did she have to lose?

A compact black BMW swept around the corner of the building and pulled into a reserved space not far from the entrance. Andie's heart began to race. It may not be him, it could be the owner. She watched anxiously as the car door swung open and a leg appeared. There was a moment's delay before the rest of the body followed, and Andie breathed again. It was him. He reached into the back of the car and lifted out a satchel-type bag, hooking it over one shoulder before closing the door and heading for the entrance of the restaurant. Andie watched as he paused at the door, fiddling with keys, until finally he unlocked the big, heavy, *security* door. Bugger, she'd forgotten about that. He pushed the door open and went inside, and it swung closed behind him with a loud clunk that Andie could hear all the way to the other side of the parking lot. Damn, she was going to have to press that buzzer and summon him back to the door, and that was probably going to be as far as she would get. So much for her plan.

But now the door was opening again. Gerou appeared, dropped some kind of block on the ground, and then kicked it under the door to wedge it open. Then he walked back inside. Andie could hardly believe it. He must be waiting for a delivery, or maybe he did that to avoid going back and forth, letting staff in as they arrived for work. Whatever the reason, it didn't matter . . . a door had opened for Andie, and the symbolism was not lost on her. She couldn't let the opportunity be lost either.

She locked her car and darted over to the door, slipping inside. She really felt like a spy now. As she started down the long corridor, sidling along the wall, she thought about the last time she was here, running for all she was worth in the opposite direction. Little had she known what she was running towards that night or she may not have been in such a hurry. Her whole life had changed. She wondered where she'd be right now if Dominic Gerou had not given her a hard time, and she hadn't fled, and she hadn't arrived home early that night. She'd probably still be with Ross, oblivious to what he was getting up to, except for those niggling doubts, which he would have just kept dismissing. She may even have continued at the restaurant, giving him all the time in the world to carry on his affair.

Maybe she should be grateful to Mr Gerou – if he wasn't such an arse, none of this might have happened.

A quiet rage had been slowly building inside Andie since the night Ross had turned up at the house, or more accurately, since the fateful phone call the morning after. She'd had enough of bloody men with bloody enormous egos, the kind whose needs and wants and opinions outweighed everyone else's. They weren't all like that – Toby wasn't, or Brendan, or her dad. Having a penis didn't automatically make you a dickhead, but it certainly helped.

So she wasn't going to let Dominic Gerou intimidate her. Mentally she had to cut him down to size so that she could pull this off.

Andie came to the end of the corridor and shrunk back against the wall, peering around the corner into the kitchen. It was quiet, there didn't seem to be anyone around. Good. That much at least was going to plan. Now she had to find Gerou. She crept into the kitchen and over to the side wall, skirting along past the rows of stainless-steel benches. She knew very little about the layout of the place. There was an office over the other side, but it was still in darkness. Directly ahead was a set of double swing doors, which she assumed must lead into the restaurant proper. Andie surveyed the kitchen again; there were no other exits. Apart from the back corridor, there was only one way for her to proceed. She tiptoed over to the doors, carefully easing one open just enough to peer inside – into an airlock, as she suspected. Beyond was another set of doors with the standard porthole windows. Andie saw Gerou pass on the other side, a phone to his ear. She ducked her head down and crept into the airlock, flattening herself against the wall. She could hear him talking, but his voice was muffled. Andie pushed on the door to open it a crack.

'Be that as it may, when I am told twenty-four hours I expect the produce to be delivered in that time.'

Great, he was already in a bad mood and it was barely eight o'clock. She eased the door closed again, and shrank back out of sight. The muffled voice had stopped, but she could still hear his footsteps. They didn't sound like they were coming this way, but they might any minute, and it would be much worse for him to discover her here, hiding like a thief.

Music started up suddenly, mid-song, probably a radio. Andie raised her head to look into the restaurant again, but she couldn't see him now. There was a bar off to one side, stretching away from her. She realised she had no choice but to walk in there and find him. She had nothing to lose, she told herself for the umpteenth time. She straightened, took a deep breath, and strode determinedly through the doors and right into the room. Andie scanned the area and spotted Gerou, over behind the bar. He was staring at a computer screen, his head down; he hadn't noticed her.

Andie cleared her throat and walked towards him, treading heavily on the polished timber floor so he would hear her coming. He looked up.

'Where did you come from?' he said abruptly.

'Um, through the kitchen,' she said. 'I came in the back way.'

'That isn't a public entrance.' He frowned, studying her for a moment. 'Do I know you?'

'My name's Andie,' she said. 'Andie Corcoran . . . Lonergan, it's Andie Lonergan now. I had a trial here, in the kitchen, about a month or so ago.'

He considered her for another moment. Her hair had been tucked up under a chef's cap when he'd last seen her, Andie wasn't surprised he didn't recognise her.

'You,' he said finally, his expression not giving anything away. 'What are you doing here? We're not open for a few hours yet if you were after a meal.'

Smart arse.

'I came to see you, actually,' Andie said, unperturbed.

'Well, you're looking at me.'

'Do you have a minute?'

He gave a loud sigh and glanced at his watch. 'Roughly,' he said, returning his attention to the computer screen.

'So . . .' She took a breath. 'I came to ask for my job back.'

He didn't look up, but a smirk formed on his lips. 'I wasn't aware you ever had a job here.'

She was expecting him to say something like that.

'That's not quite true,' she said.

He did glance up at her then, briefly, before looking back at the screen. 'It was a trial, not a guaranteed position. And as you only lasted half an hour —'

'It was closer to three hours actually.'

He shrugged. 'So you lasted a couple of hours. You had your trial. And you've had your minute,' he added, turning away.

'Hold on,' she blurted. Keep your cool. Don't lose it in front of him. Again.

He turned around again slowly. 'Look, miss, I'm very busy —'

'I was promised a trial,' Andie persisted. 'I think you should hold up your end of the bargain.'

He shook his head. 'You have got gall, I'll give you that much. But I've already given you your trial,' he said, finally meeting her gaze, 'and you failed.'

'Because you were impatient and you didn't give me a chance,' she said brazenly.

He narrowed his eyes. 'Did you imagine everyone was going to pussyfoot around you?' he asked. 'Make it easy for you? Then you have no idea, Miss . . .'

'My name is Andie.'

'A kitchen is a busy, stressful, hectic place,' he went on, ignoring her. 'We don't have the space or the time for someone who can't function in that environment.'

'I can cope with the stress and the workload,' she said, 'but I don't see why I should have to put up with plain bad temper.'

'And I don't see why I should have to put up with you,' he retorted. 'Oh wait, I don't have to.' He turned on his heel but then he stopped, turning around to face her again. 'And you can get off your high horse, because I know exactly how this all came about in the first place. You're married to a rich successful businessman and you're bored. You think you might like to try being a chef, just like the ones you've seen on television. You have a word in your husband's ear, and he has a word in the ear of an old friend who happens to own a restaurant. You stroll in, right past all the kids, the hardworking kids who would kill to get a chance at a place like this. But they don't get the chance, and what do you do with yours? Run away when it all gets too hard.'

Andie met his gaze directly. 'Mr Gerou, I wasn't a bored wife looking for a hobby. I'm a trained chef, but I hadn't been in a commercial kitchen for . . . some time, and I wasn't prepared for the pace. But I don't think I deserved to be treated that way.'

'Then it's just as well you left, because that's the way it is.'

'Why?'

He frowned at her.

'Why does it have to be that way?' said Andie. 'I mean, what is it with chefs and this arrogance? They don't train it into you. What happens to turn you all into . . .' He could fill the blank in himself.

'Maybe it's because we have to work with people like you?' he suggested.

Andie bristled. 'You don't even know me, so please don't judge me,' she said. 'You prepare and cook food to *serve* to people. This is a service industry. In previous eras you'd be called servants. So when did being a chef become a licence to be arrogant?' Maybe she should have shut up, but she was on a roll. 'It's such a cliché. How can you think it's a good way to run a workplace, verbally bullying everyone into submission so they're scared of you?'

He was glaring at her now. 'That is not how I run my kitchen.'

'It's certainly how it looked that day.'

'Well, you don't know what was going on that day, do you?' he said. 'Perhaps you shouldn't be so quick to judge me. Bill didn't clear it with me that you were coming, or I would have told him it wasn't a good time. We were introducing a new menu and I already had to train existing staff, let alone someone who had never stepped foot in the place.'

'Well, if it was such a bad time, then you really do owe me a second chance.'

'I don't *owe* you anything,' he shot back.

'So you've never screwed up, Mr Gerou?' she said. 'You've never needed help along the way to get to where you are? No one has ever given you a second chance?'

He seemed to be thinking about that. Andie wondered if she'd finally struck a chord.

'So why should I give you a second chance?' he asked.

'Because I don't think you're as big a jerk as you make out.'

He lifted an eyebrow. 'What makes you think that?'

'Because no one could be that big a jerk.'

Andie wasn't sure, but it looked like he might have been suppressing a smile. He leaned back against the bench behind him and folded his arms across his chest.

'Why the delay?' he asked finally.

'Pardon?'

'If this means so much to you, what made you wait so long to come back?'

Andie took a breath. 'It's been . . . well, it's just that a lot of things have happened,' she said. 'My father died. I had to move —'

'You lived with your father?'

'No . . . it's complicated, and it's personal,' she said. 'The thing is, a month ago I didn't really need this job, but I wanted it. Now I really need it as well.'

He was watching her closely, and something twigged in his eyes. 'Look, Miss . . .'

'*Ms* Lonergan, it's Lonergan now. But you can call me Andie.'

'Well, Ms Lonergan, this isn't the place to get over . . . whatever it is you're getting over.'

'Why not?'

'Pardon?'

'Why not?' she repeated. 'It's as good a place as any.'

He frowned. 'What do you mean by that?'

'You have to move on, whatever life dishes up. Seems to me you have a better chance of doing that if you're busy and focused and passionate about something. You might as well pour all that emotional energy into something useful.'

'I don't need you crying over my stockpot.'

'I'm not going to cry over your stockpot,' she said plainly. 'I'm not going to cry over anything, except maybe chopped onions, and I don't think you can blame that on a broken heart.'

He was staring down at the floor, but he was listening. She nearly had him, she was sure.

'Mr Gerou . . . Chef, this was always my dream. I was one of those kids who would have given anything to work in a place like this, and I didn't get the chance. And then . . . circumstances took me in a different direction. I let go of my dream, and I regret that I did.' She paused. 'I know I screwed up that day,' she continued, 'and I must have seemed pretty hopeless to you. But I know I can be good at this. I am good. And I'll prove it to you, if you give me another chance. Like I said, I was just unprepared.'

He was still staring down at the floor. Finally he lifted his head to look at her. 'Are you going to be prepared this time?'

'You can count on it.'

Roseville

'Oh my goodness,' said Donna. 'Why are there so many chickens in your fridge?'

'Ahh,' said Andie, coming up behind her, 'they're the reason we're gathered here tonight.'

'I thought we were here for a slumber party?' said Jess.

Andie had invited them over to put their minds to rest, more than anything. They both called every day; if it wasn't Donna, it was Toby, and Jess always found some work-related excuse to call, not-so-subtly adding at the end of the conversation, 'So, how's everything going there?'

Andie had the feeling they were worried she was going to become a mad recluse, locking herself away in the deceased estate like . . . she was thinking Miss Havisham, but that wasn't right, she'd been jilted on her wedding day. Andie had been jilted ten years later. In fact the term jilted didn't even apply really.

The truth was, she had been absolutely flat out. She had to begin work on the house, because once she started at the restaurant there wouldn't be time. So she had got over her squeamishness and started clearing out the bedrooms. Her dad's had been the saddest, packing up his clothes and belongings as though a whole life could be contained in a few boxes. She held on to some of his things, his reading glasses, his rosary beads. She even kept the book on his bedside table. It wasn't her preferred genre – a big fat spy thriller – but she'd taken to reading it at night when she went to bed, hearing her father's voice in her head as though he was reading it to her. It made her feel closer to him.

She forced her way into her old bedroom, and, as she expected, it was filled mostly with her mother's things. Her father had obviously not been able to part with them, and now she knew how he felt. She didn't go through all the boxes of clothes and shoes and handbags – what would be the point? They'd been packed away for more than a decade, they wouldn't be in any state to keep. Meredith had instructed her not to toss anything until she had a chance to have a look, but she'd been too busy to come over and go through it all. So Andie stacked them along the wall in the hall. But there were a couple of boxes of documents and old photos, other mementoes. She would have to go through it all carefully, and she simply didn't have the time. So she stored those boxes away in the wardrobe in the room where she was sleeping. If need be, she'd take them with her when she left, worry about them then.

In the meantime she called a real estate agent to come out and inspect the place, and the woman made a list of suggested repairs and improvements. Andie asked Toby to take care of all that; she could trust him to come and go from the house when she wasn't there, and she knew he'd do a good job. At least Meredith had given the go-ahead for that, and Toby would be starting in earnest next week.

So Andie had decided to have the girls over tonight, have some fun, and show them that she was absolutely fine. More than fine. And in the spirit of killing two birds, or at least deboning them, she had an ulterior motive.

'We are having a slumber party,' Andie reassured them. 'But I also need your help with something, Jess.'

'Does it have to do with those chickens?' she asked warily.

'Yes, as a matter of fact, it does,' said Andie. 'I want you to teach me how to debone them.'

Jess frowned, bending over to peer into the fridge. 'How many are there?'

'Twelve.'

She turned to look at Andie. 'We're going to debone twelve chickens?'

'No, I am, with your expert guidance.'

'Sounds like a fun evening,' Donna muttered, still clutching the bottles she'd been planning to stow away in the fridge. 'You know I don't get out much, what with a toddler and all . . .'

'We're going to have fun, I promise,' Andie said, with all the enthusiasm she could muster. 'I've made a heap of food, and we can gossip, and drink – well, I won't be drinking until I get through all these chickens. Keep a bottle out, Donna, I'll get some glasses.'

'Okay,' said Jess, 'I know you've been on this whole cooking frenzy, but why chickens, and why tonight?'

Andie smiled as she placed the glasses on the table in front of them. 'Imaginary drum roll, please,' she announced. 'I have another trial at Viande. I start on Tuesday.'

'Wow,' Donna said, pouring the wine. 'That's great.'

'I don't understand,' said Jess. 'After what happened . . . Did they contact you?'

'No, of course not,' said Andie. 'I walked in there myself and more or less demanded it.'

'You did?'

'Well, it'd probably best be described as a cross between begging and demanding,' Andie said wryly.

'Good for you,' said Donna, raising her glass. She glanced at Jess, who seemed to be in a slight daze, and elbowed her.

She stirred. 'Yeah, it's great.' She picked up her glass. 'I just wish you'd told me this was what you were planning.'

'It only happened this week.'

'But, you know how we were talking about expanding the shop?'

'Yeah.'

'Well, I've already had Toby over to take a look.'

'He mentioned.' Andie nodded, retrieving a chicken from the fridge.

'So, I should just tell him to forget about it?' said Jess.

Andie looked around. 'Why?'

'Well, you're doing this now.'

'Jess, it's only a trial at Viande, and you're only investigating possibilities at the shop,' said Andie. 'We can go ahead with both, take things a step at a time, see how it turns out. I don't want to limit my options anymore.'

'That's very brave talk,' said Jess.

Donna grinned. 'I think it's great.'

'Yes, well, speaking of brave talk, I really blew my own trumpet to Dominic Gerou —'

'You approached him in person?' said Jess.

Andie nodded. 'So the thing is, I absolutely cannot screw up this time.'

'That's why you have to debone twelve chickens?'

'Do you think it's enough?'

Jess gave her a withering look. 'If you can't get it after twelve, you'll never get it.'

'Oh, don't say that,' said Andie. 'I'm determined to get it right.'

'Why do I have the feeling that all my chickens have come home to roost?' muttered Jess. 'Well, we better get you started.' She picked up her glass and joined Andie at the end of the table. 'I assume it's okay for me to drink?'

'As long as you don't think it'll impair your judgement.' Andie gave her a nervous smile.

'Trust me, I'm going to need a drink if we've got to dismember a dozen chooks.'

It wasn't that difficult in the end; as long as Andie followed the steps as Jess showed her, in the exact order, using the correct knife, it was pretty much foolproof. She appeared to have mastered it by the fourth chicken. But Andie wanted to keep practising; she wanted to look like a natural, or a pro, whichever was better.

'So does Ross know about the trial?' Jess asked, as she took a seat at the other end of the table with Donna.

'No, he doesn't,' said Andie, not looking up at either of them. 'It's not really any of his business.'

She hadn't told them the latest with Ross. She hadn't seen Donna, and she'd managed to avoid the topic when Jess came over last week. But she knew she wasn't going to be able to avoid it tonight. She wanted them to know, she did, she just wished she could send them the information telepathically so she wouldn't have to talk about it. And she dreaded having to break the truth, the whole truth, to Donna as well.

'Have you seen him lately?' Donna asked tentatively.

Andie shook her head. 'I haven't seen him at all for a couple of weeks.'

Ross didn't try to contact her for a few days after the fateful telephone call. He must have discovered that Tasha had answered his phone and decided to allow for a cooling-off period. Andie had debated with herself whether she would talk to him if he called, or whether she'd just ignore him. But her confidence was buoyed after her meeting with Dominic Gerou, and Andie decided if she could handle him, she could certainly handle Ross Corcoran.

'I'm sorry I wasn't available when you called the other day,' was his opening line.

What the hell was that? Was he going to make out that the woman who answered was a business associate or something? He was clearly not aware that she'd told Andie he was in the shower.

'Ross, please, for the love of God, will you just stop the bullshit?'

There was silence down the line.

'I know it was Tasha who answered the phone. I know you went to her place after you left here, after you told me you weren't seeing her anymore.'

'You turned me away, Andie, what was I supposed to do?'

For Chrissakes.

Andie looked at Donna. 'There's something I haven't told you – Ross has been having an affair.'

She waited for the reaction, but Donna just looked at her, biting her lip. 'I know,' she said in a small voice.

'You do? How did you find out?'

'I told them,' Jess owned up.

'Them?' said Andie. 'So Toby knows as well?'

She nodded. 'Actually I didn't really tell them, as such.'

'That's right,' said Donna. 'Toby figured it out himself.'

'I only confirmed it,' said Jess.

'I'm just surprised he hasn't mentioned it.'

'He didn't want to upset you,' said Donna.

Andie shrugged. 'Well, he needn't have worried. I'm absolutely fine, and it's definitely over.'

Neither of them said anything, but she could tell by the look on both their faces what they were thinking.

'I assure you, it really is over this time.' Andie held the knife with both hands above the chicken, before plunging it inside and slicing right down the centre of the breastbone. Donna looked vaguely horrified.

'All right, I'll give you the whole story, once and for all, so we can move on,' Andie said, as she began to cut around the bones with the tip of the knife. 'Ross came over the night I moved in. He wanted us to get back together, he told me he wasn't seeing the woman anymore, that he'd do anything. He tried to come on to me, and I almost succumbed.'

'You did?' said Jess.

Andie nodded. 'A girl has needs, you know.'

'What happened?' Donna asked, her eyes wide.

'I couldn't go through with it . . . I thought about him and the woman together, and I got to thinking about all his lies, and how I couldn't tell the lies from the truth anymore. I asked him to leave, and he did, but he'd been drinking and he got into his car, so I ended up worrying about him all night.'

'It wasn't your fault,' said Jess. 'You didn't make him drive.'

'Well, that's not really the issue,' Andie went on. 'I rang the next morning to make sure he'd made it home all right, and the woman answered the phone. Said he was in the shower.'

'Sprung,' said Jess.

'Oh, Andie, I'm so sorry,' said Donna.

'It's okay.' She looked up from the chicken. 'In a funny way I'm actually kind of glad it happened.'

'You are?'

She nodded. 'Obviously I needed another dose of shock therapy to see things for the way they really are. You'd think finding your husband in bed with another woman would do the trick, but I must be a slow learner.'

'Don't be so hard on yourself,' said Jess.

Andie ripped the carcass out of the chicken with a satisfied smile. 'Anyway, the end result is that now I know for sure that I can't believe a word Ross says. That he's lied to me since the beginning of our relationship.'

'He has? What about?' asked Jess.

'It doesn't matter anymore. It's over.'

'So are you going to make it official and file for divorce?' Jess asked.

Andie looked up suddenly. 'Oh, I don't know, I suppose, eventually . . .'

'Andie, if you're serious, and you want Ross to take you seriously, you have to sign off legally, divide the property and assets and be done with him.'

'But I told you I don't care about all that. I don't want a share of the apartment.'

'Why not?' Donna asked.

'Because he slept with the skank in her bed,' Jess said.

'Don't call her a skank,' said Andie, even though she was beginning to think Tasha might actually be one.

'Throw out the bed,' said Jess. 'Burn it, but don't give up a whole apartment.'

'Look, I don't even feel like it's mine to give up. It's all Ross's money in that apartment. I'm only trying to do what's right.'

'That's fine, but let a lawyer figure out what's right, and fair.'

'You think a lawyer's the best person for that?' Andie said wryly, as she proceeded to trim the chicken.

'Why are you so reluctant to deal with this?' Jess persisted.

Andie looked at her. 'I just want to get through the sale of this house – one legal hurdle at a time.'

'You do realise that Ross will have a stake in this too?'

She frowned. 'What are you talking about?'

'Ross will be entitled to a share of your inheritance.'

'No . . .'

'Yes.'

'But he wouldn't go after it,' said Andie. 'He's got more class than that.'

'What about Tasha?'

'Who's Tasha?' asked Donna.

'The skank.'

'Don't call her that,' said Andie.

'Why do you keep saying that?' asked Jess.

'Because we don't know what she's like.'

'That's absolutely true, Andie – she might be Mother Teresa reincarnated, or she might be out for everything she can get her hands on. You don't know. Besides, any family lawyer worth his salt is going to tell Ross he's entitled to a share of your assets as well.'

'But that's not fair.'

'That's why you need to see your own lawyer. If you don't want a share of any of the marital assets, at least protect your own.'

'Okay, I take your point.'

'And while you're at it,' said Jess, 'you might want to protect your friends' jobs? If you just give up everything, we could all be tossed out on our ears.'

Donna spluttered on her wine.

'The shop is in my name, I'm sure Ross couldn't do anything without my say-so,' Andie reassured Donna. 'But you're right, Jess. I'll make an appointment to see a lawyer.'

'Can we drink to that? Sign something in chicken blood, perhaps?' Jess suggested hopefully.

Andie held up a whole filleted chicken with a triumphant smile. 'What do you think?'

'Perfect,' Jess pronounced. 'But honestly, Andie, this chicken smell is beginning to make me gag. You don't have to finish all twelve tonight, have another practice run tomorrow.'

'Of course. Let me just clean all this up, and would you pour me a glass of wine please, Donna? You two better have some good gossip for me, because seriously, I want to talk about something, *anything* else but me.'

'All right,' said Jess. 'I've got something. I'm thinking of getting a Brazilian.'

Andie looked up from wrapping the chicken, and Donna turned around from the fridge. 'What?' they said in unison.

Jess shrugged. 'They're the new black.'

'When have you ever been one to slavishly follow the latest trend?' Andie frowned.

'I'm just sick of guys commenting about it all the time.'

'What kinds of comments?' Donna asked as she topped up Jess's glass.

'Whenever you hook up with a guy these days, as soon as he . . . comes into contact, he has to make some kind of remark.'

'Like what?' Andie wanted to know.

'Oh, like . . . so you go natural? Wow, that's old-school, or brave. Or, are you a hippy? Through to, hey, ever thought of tidying up down there?'

Andie was vigorously wiping down the table. 'That just makes me want to spit.'

'Me too,' said Donna.

'I mean, who decided we have to look like little girls? I think it's demeaning.'

'Some women do it for themselves,' said Jess. 'I've been asking around. They like the feel of it, that it's all clean and fresh.'

Donna frowned. 'But isn't the whole reason we have hair got to do with catching bacteria so it doesn't get into the wrong places?'

'But we don't mind ripping it out from under our arms now, do we?' said Jess.

'Look, if you really want to do this for yourself, Jess, go right ahead,' said Andie. 'But I wish you didn't feel the need to do it to attract men.'

'You know what they say about beggars and choosers.'

'You're not a beggar,' Donna exclaimed.

'In this marketplace I am. Thirtysomething women are passed over all the time for younger models.'

'God, I'm glad I'm married.'

Andie had finished washing her hands and sat down to join them.

'Sorry, that was a bit insensitive,' Donna said with a sheepish look. 'Why?'

'Because . . . you know, your marriage has just . . .'

'Collapsed?'

'Failed, broken down . . . died in the bum?' Jess added.

Andie smiled. 'It's okay, Donna.'

'Well, you're not going to be alone for long,' she said.

'Believe me, the last thing I need is a relationship right now.'

'Why is that?'

Andie took a sip of her wine. 'Let's just say I'm not ready to get a Brazilian.'

December

Andie slipped off her chef's jacket and tossed it into the hamper in the corner of the change room. That was a nice little perk of the job – the jackets were all professionally laundered, returning for the next shift clean, pressed and neatly folded. She was beginning to feel like she belonged now, after nearly two months. Her trial period lasted a couple of weeks, before Tang informed her she had been approved to stay on. Andie was thrilled. She was welcomed as a bonafide member of the crew, she even stayed back regularly for staffy's on Sunday nights; with the restaurant closed for business on Mondays it was the end of their working week and the staff always stayed on for drinks. Tang could not have been lovelier, and had taken her under his wing without making a single comment about her sudden departure, or her equally sudden reappearance. He and Cosmo were the senior sous chefs at Viande and in reality Andie worked for them. Dominic Gerou barely even spoke to her, but she had no reason to take that personally. While the staff all seemed to respect him, even hold him in high regard, they told Andie he rarely mixed with them socially – he never joined them for staffy's, even though he supplied the drinks. He had acknowledged Andie on her first night back with a brisk greeting, and had later given a nod of approval after she expertly deboned a chicken as he watched on. She'd hardly had anything to do with him since.

She was way below his radar anyway – still relegated to the ranks of the apprentices in the bread and salad section – but Andie didn't mind. She was finally working in a real kitchen, talking about food, learning about food. And she was learning so much. Bread and salad was not as basic as it sounded, at least not in a kitchen like this. Andie was all over the bread, given it had been a longstanding specialty at The Corner Gourmet. But the vegetables were a whole new world – the variety of salad greens, heirloom carrots ranging from creamy white through yellow to purple, potatoes similarly in every colour, turnips and radishes sliced into wafer-thin discs for garnish, ribbons of celeriac . . . Andie was given plenty of opportunity to observe Tang or Cosmo as they prepped dishes and plated up, using long Japanese tweezers to place the delicate garnishes in their precise positions. Each and every plate – more than two hundred a night – was a miniature work of art. Andie wondered if the diners appreciated the level of care and attention that went into presenting their food as much as they enjoyed the taste. But she had a feeling it wouldn't have mattered to the chefs anyway, they had their own meticulous standards to meet. Although she wouldn't be allowed anywhere near the pass for some time yet, Andie found it inspirational. She worked hard, trying to take the same care with every task she was given. And she was getting faster all the time, and building muscles in her arms from lifting racks and heavy pans. Her legs ached after every shift, but she fell into bed at night and slept more soundly than she had in a long time. Andie was happy, she didn't need Dominic Gerou's approval, she'd only needed him to give her a job, and he'd already done that.

Though every now and then, she got the feeling she was being watched, and she'd look up to find him staring in her direction, from right across the other side of the kitchen. He always quickly turned away, and Andie assumed he was probably just staring into space, or looking at something else entirely.

She picked up her cardigan from her locker and slipped it on over her T-shirt. The evenings were still cool, even though summer was supposed to have officially begun. Andie slung her bag over her shoulder and walked up the corridor, pushing on the metal rail to release the exit door. As the cool night air hit her, she drew her cardigan more closely around her. She started across the carpark when she heard her name called. She turned to see Ross coming towards her.

'What are you doing here?' she asked him.

'I wanted to talk to you.'

'Why didn't you just call?'

'Because you don't pick up when I call,' he said bluntly, stopping in front of her.

Andie hadn't seen him since the night at the house, and she'd only spoken to him that one time. After that low point she had decided not to bother answering his calls anymore, and she assumed he'd finally given up.

She crossed her arms. 'How did you know to find me here?'

'Brooke told me you were working here again,' he said. 'And I think it's great, Andie. I'm so proud of you.'

Whoopee. That was supposed to mean something to her? 'Look, I've had a long night, Ross, and it's cold out here.'

'Then let's go somewhere we can talk.'

Andie groaned. Better to just get it over with. 'What do you want, Ross?'

He sighed, pushing his hands down into his pockets. He looked tired, he was beginning to show his age.

'My lawyer received a letter from your lawyer,' he said.

She nodded. 'I went to see someone to find out what I have to do —'

'Find out what you have to do?' he sniped. 'How about talk to your husband before you go to a lawyer?'

'Ross,' she sighed, 'what's your actual problem here? Don't you want to be a free man?'

'No, where did you get that idea? When did I ever say that?'

'Oh, so you want to carry on an affair and stay married, is that it?'

'No, not at all. I want my marriage back, and I'll do whatever it takes.'

Andie looked at him. 'Are you still seeing her, Ross?'

He hesitated. 'That's beside the point —'

'No, it isn't,' she exclaimed. 'It's the whole point!'

'Well, if the affair is the whole point, and I end it, then there is no point resorting to lawyers.'

Andie shook her head. 'I can't deal with this right now,' she said wearily, turning to leave.

'Wait.' He grabbed her arm. 'Don't just walk away.'

'Ross, let go of me.'

'Andie . . . are you all right?'

They both looked around. Dominic Gerou was taking halting steps towards them.

'She's fine,' said Ross, releasing her arm. 'It's none of your concern, mate.'

'Andie,' Dominic said again, 'are you all right?'

She couldn't recall him ever saying her name out loud before, she was surprised he remembered it. He stepped into a pool of light, his gaze focused steadily on her, ignoring Ross.

'Mate, I said —'

'Ross!' Andie cut him off. 'Thanks, Chef, I'm okay.'

'Are you sure?'

'Listen,' said Ross, 'I don't know who you think you are, but I'm her husband.'

'He is my boss,' Andie said firmly.

'It's Dominic out here.'

Andie nodded. 'Thank you, Dominic. I'll be fine.'

'Would you like me to walk you to your car?'

'Oh come on —'

'Ross, for crying out loud, would you just shut up!' Andie snapped.

He shrank back at that, finally, bowing his head.

Dominic nodded. 'Looks like you can handle yourself. Goodnight, Andie.'

'Thanks again.' Her voice trailed after him as he walked away back across the carpark. Great, playing out her own little soap opera in front of the boss outside her place of work. And sounding like a piece of trailer trash in the process. Very professional, Andie, well done.

'Wanker.'

'Christ, Ross,' she exclaimed, striding off towards her car. She could hear his footsteps following behind her.

'Andie, wait,' he said. 'We still have to talk about this.'

'I don't have to talk to you, especially when you carry on like a complete Neanderthal.'

'I'm sorry, okay?' he said dramatically, holding his arms out wide. 'I don't know what else I'm supposed to do.'

She reached her car and turned around. 'You could try leaving me alone.'

'So this is how it's going to be?' he said. 'Communicating through our lawyers, ending everything because of one mistake?'

'Not this again,' she sighed. 'Ross, it wasn't one mistake, it was a constant stream of lies with no end in sight. You know, I was actually worried about you that night when you drove off drunk.'

'See, so you do have feelings for me.'

He was shameless. He was utterly and completely without shame. 'Don't worry, any feelings I may have had are rapidly diminishing by the minute.'

He was shaking his head. 'I really didn't think you were this kind of person, Andie. That you'd throw away our whole marriage at the first sign of any trouble.'

'No, Ross, you were the one who did that.'

'I don't want to throw away the marriage,' he said. 'I want to work on it.'

She looked at him. 'So working on it means going back to that woman when I won't obediently fall straight back into your arms?'

'Look, it's nothing, it's a fling, it's not going anywhere. I could end it tomorrow.'

'So end it,' she said. 'Once and for all.'

'I will, if you'll say you're coming back.'

'No, Ross, that's not how it works,' said Andie. 'You end it, and then you prove to me over time that you're prepared to work on the marriage.'

'How can I prove that?'

'Live alone.'

'I am living alone, I haven't moved in with her.'

'And how many nights do you spend in the apartment by yourself?'

He didn't have an answer for that.

'Well, at least you're not lying, that's something.'

'Andie, I'll do whatever it takes.'

'It's not enough, Ross. I can't trust you, and I've lost so much respect for you now that there's nothing left.'

He stared at her. 'So that's it? You're just going to leave it to the lawyers.'

'I think it's best if we cut our losses and move on.'

He sighed, raking his hand through his hair. 'So, you're planning to take me to the cleaners, is that it, Andie?'

'What? No.'

'Your lawyer is asking for full financial disclosure. He wants complete records of all my investments, my —'

'Ross, I don't care about any of that,' she stopped him. 'I don't want anything, except the shop, and that's mine anyway. I'll be getting a share of my father's estate, that's enough for me, as long as you don't expect a cut of it.'

'Of course I wouldn't expect that,' he said, wounded. 'I wouldn't take your father's money from you. How could you think I'd do that?'

Andie sighed. 'Well, what do you know, you do have a shred of decency left in you.'

'I have more than that, Andie. I still love you.'

'It's too late, Ross.'

He looked down at the ground, shaking his head. 'I can't believe this is happening.'

Andie took her keys out of her bag and pressed the remote lock. 'I'll call my lawyer and get him to draw up an agreement that will protect the shop and my inheritance. And I'll withdraw all other claims on you. All right?' She opened the car door.

'I don't want it to be like this, Andie.'

'Well, you should have thought about that before . . .'

What was the point in even finishing the sentence? She climbed into the car and closed the door. He stood there, looking forlorn, as she started the car and drove away.

A week later

Andie arrived at the building site and phoned Joanna from the other side of the cyclone fencing. She had contacted her yesterday to arrange a time she could drop off Christmas presents for the family, but with Joanna working days and Andie working nights, the only alternative in the end was for Andie to visit Joanna at work. At the moment she was on-site most days, as project manager of a medium-density residential development in the eastern suburbs. She told Andie she'd have to wait outside when she arrived, as she'd have to be escorted in.

Andie spotted Joanna coming towards her in a hard hat and a fluoro vest, and carrying a second hat and vest.

'Hi,' Joanna said as she approached. 'You're going to have to wear these.' She had to shout over the sound of machinery. 'OH&S requirements, you know.'

Andie smiled, taking them from her. She put the hat on. 'I feel like Bob the Builder.'

'What's that?' said Joanna, cupping her hand to her ear.

'Never mind!' Andie shouted back as she pulled on the vest.

'Come on,' said Joanna. 'I'll take you to the site office, at least we'll be able to hear each other there.'

They walked across muddy clay, past a series of structures of varying heights and dimensions. It was still largely skeletal, but the scale of the development was impressive.

'This looks pretty big,' Andie shouted.

Joanna nodded. 'Biggest project I've ever worked on.'

Just then they heard a loud wolf-whistle from behind and they both turned. A group of workers on an upper floor all waved.

'You've got some fans,' said Andie.

Joanna smiled at her. 'Oh, that wasn't for me.'

They arrived at a portable building that served as the site office, and Joanna held the door open for Andie as she stepped inside. It was surprisingly roomy; two men were working at computers at one end, there were several filing cabinets, a long couch, fridges, and a table in the centre with plans spread out across it.

'My friend, Andie,' Joanna announced, and the men gave her a nod and a 'Hi'. She turned towards the other end of the office. 'My desk is up here,' she said.

Andie followed her, pausing at a large print posted up on the wall, an artist's impression of the project. It was stunning; there were probably eight buildings of various sizes, each one unique, but complementary, tied together through the use of common materials, timber and corrugated iron mostly, and a harmonising colour palette of greens and greys. They appeared to be tucked amongst groves of trees, gardens, walkways and courtyard spaces.

'This is amazing, Joanna.'

'Yeah, it is pretty special,' she said. 'Not that I'm responsible for the design.'

'But you're responsible for making it a reality,' said Andie.

Joanna nodded. 'I guess so. There are a few other chiefs on-site,' she added. 'Engineers, the building supervisor . . . I have backup.'

Andie looked at her. 'I wonder if a man in your position would be so quick to share the credit around?'

'Probably not,' she admitted. 'It's hard enough being a woman in this industry without blowing your own trumpet too loudly.' She walked around the desk. 'You don't need to wear your hat in here,' she said as she removed hers and sat down, indicating a chair for Andie. 'Can I get you something? Coffee? A cold drink?'

'No, I don't want to take up too much of your time,' she said, setting the bag of presents down on the floor beside her.

'It's fine,' Joanna assured her. 'How are things with you, Andie? You're still at the restaurant?'

'I am. They kept me on after my trial, which is great.'

'So you're permanent?'

'I'm on a six-month contract, same as everybody at my level.'

Joanna nodded. 'Well, congratulations. I'm pleased for you.' She paused. 'And Brooke tells me you're still living over the bridge? That's a bit of a commute.'

'It won't be for much longer.'

The house was scheduled for auction next week, but the real estate agent had already had some serious offers; she didn't see it making it to auction. Andie had considered moving out before it went on the market, but the agent urged her to stay – apparently empty houses lacked warmth, even one person in situ would give it a lived-in feel. So Andie resigned herself to wait it out until it sold, but rentals began to get scarce before Christmas, especially near the beach. She wasn't ready to buy, she wasn't really in the position until the estate was finalised anyway. But that was okay – Andie didn't know where she wanted to settle ultimately, so she wasn't in any rush.

'Do you see Ross?' Joanna asked.

'No, but our lawyers are on speaking terms.'

Joanna shook her head. 'I honestly can't believe how stupid that man is, putting himself through this all over again. I can't help but think the girl must be pretty stupid too.'

'Is that what you used to say about me?' Andie gave her a sly smile.

'No, I didn't actually. But now there's a pattern of behaviour, doesn't this girl see that?' said Joanna. 'I mean, who in their right mind would hook up with a man who has now left two wives for younger women? Does she think she's going to be the one to break the cycle?'

Andie shrugged. 'So you think he'll do it again?'

'Who knows?' said Joanna. 'But his winning streak has to come to an end eventually. Ross isn't rich enough to nab a twentysomething when he's seventy. That takes serious money.'

Andie smiled at that. She'd still felt so awkward around Joanna only six months ago, and now they were sitting here in her office, sharing war stories.

'Do you mind if I ask, Joanna, how did you feel when it was finally over?'

'What do you mean?'

'I guess I'm starting to get the feeling that I'm finally living my own life,' said Andie. 'You were so young when you married, and you were together so long, I imagine that feeling must have been even stronger.'

Joanna seemed thoughtful. 'Yes, but it took so much longer to get to that. When you have children together, you can never be completely free. Just as well you two didn't have any.'

She was right of course, but that didn't stop Andie from wondering what if. She still noticed babies in the street, though not as obsessively as before. There was just sadness now, regret that she could no longer see a baby in her future. Of course it could happen, she wasn't too old yet, but it seemed highly implausible right now. There had to be a man involved, for one thing, and Andie wasn't even looking. And he would have to be a good, decent man who she could trust, and that was going to take a leap of faith in itself. It would take time to achieve that level of trust, time that Andie didn't have. So she was better off resigning herself to never having a family of her own. But the idea still stung.

'Anyway, I can see you're busy, so . . .' Andie reached for the bag at her feet and set it down on the desk in front of Joanna.

'This is really thoughtful, Andie, the kids will appreciate it.' Joanna leaned forward. 'You know they would have liked to have you come over for Christmas.'

'You don't have to say that.'

'I know I don't, but it's true.'

Andie looked at her. 'Even Lauren?'

'Might be a case of the devil you know . . .' Joanna smiled. 'She's not at all impressed that this one's younger than her. All the kids were threatening to boycott Christmas if she came.'

'So what are you going to do?'

'Compromise, as usual,' she said. 'Funny how Ross has never had to compromise on what he wants, but somehow everyone else ends up compromising around him.' She shook her head, as if she was clearing that thought. 'Anyway, he's coming for lunch, and then she'll pick him up afterwards, so that everyone can meet.'

'Oh, you haven't met yet?'

'No, we've been avoiding it,' said Joanna. 'Did you ever end up meeting her?'

'Ah no, not formally,' Andie said with a sheepish grin. 'She was . . . indisposed at the time.'

'Oh God.' Joanna closed her eyes. 'I'd almost forgotten about that.'

'I wish I could.'

'Now, the kids asked me to give you this.' Joanna swivelled her chair around and picked up a flat box wrapped in Christmas paper from the cabinet behind her. She turned back to hand it to Andie.

'Oh . . .' Andie felt a little overcome. 'They didn't have to do that.'

'They wanted to, even Lauren.'

Andie felt tears pricking her eyes as Joanna handed her the gift.

'Of course Brooke organised it, but Lauren was happy to contribute.'

'Please, tell them I'm really touched, and grateful,' Andie said, her voice thick. She composed herself as she got to her feet. 'And now I'll let you get back to it.'

Joanna walked her out to the gate. 'So what are you doing for Christmas, Andie? Will you spend it with your sister?'

Meredith did do the right thing, and asked her to Christmas lunch, but Andie had seen the relief on her face when she offered her apology – that she was sorry, but she already had a previous invitation. Which was true, in fact she'd had a number of invitations, only she wasn't going to accept any of them. Donna and Toby had asked her to their various celebrations, desperate to assure her she wouldn't be tagging along. But as they would be dashing between two sets of parents, as well as another extended family get-together, tagging along was exactly what Andie would be doing if she accepted. So she had politely declined. Jess had also invited her to her family Christmas, but Andie would have felt out of place. It was difficult to explain to her friends; she knew they wanted her to feel welcome, but Andie would have felt more alone knowing this wasn't her family, that she didn't really belong. Perhaps she was just being maudlin.

'I haven't exactly decided what I'm doing for Christmas yet,' Andie said to Joanna. 'Not that I'm short of invitations. You know how people are, they take pity on poor single girls spending Christmas alone.'

Joanna's expression became serious. 'You won't spend it alone though, will you, Andie?'

'Of course not,' she assured her.

Though she really didn't know what she was going to do. If she had the choice, she'd knock herself out for forty-eight hours and wake up when it was all over. She had been counting on work saving her, only to discover that the owner was a deeply religious man who never opened any of his many businesses on Christmas Day. Though some of the staff had suggested it was because he was too tight to pay penalty rates.

Andie slipped off the fluoro vest and removed the hard hat, shaking out her hair. 'Thanks for everything, Joanna.'

As she walked through the gate, she heard another wolf-whistle.

'What did I tell you?' Joanna sang out after her.

Christmas

Andie had set the alarm for eight, which was a bit undignified for any day off, let alone Christmas Day. And last night had been a particularly long and hectic shift. Management made up for not opening on Christmas Day by offering a six-course banquet, which included a gourmet twist on every conceivable festive food that had ever had any association with Christmas.

The staff only stayed back for one quick drink to exchange their Secret Santa gifts; many of them had small children and were going to have to be up again in a few hours, so they weren't keen to linger. Andie felt tired on the long drive home to Roseville, but even so, she diverted her route and meandered through the neighbouring streets, searching out a little Christmas cheer amongst the gaudy lights that decorated the surrounding houses. But all she seemed to be able to think about was the greenhouse gases that were being spent for the sake of the season. Bah humbug. She felt like Scrooge.

Greenhouse gases aside, when she got home she was glad she'd left the lights on inside the house. Although she had achieved quite a remarkable transformation – if she did say so herself – it was still a bit creepy in the dark. All the more because it was almost empty these days. Andie had been quite bemused by the whole selling process. As part of the contract the real estate agent provided an interior decorating service, complete with rented furniture, curtains, lamps, even vases and cushions as required. The decorator had been quite awestruck by the vintage of the existing furniture – and not in a good way. It didn't even have kitsch value for the most part, and so, with Meredith's consent, and in deference to her parents' Catholic background, Andie had contacted Vinnie's, and they sent around a truck. She was a little surprised to discover how picky they were. They wouldn't touch the beds, and they weren't particularly fussed on the wardrobes either – they only took one. But at least they were happy to take most of the furniture throughout the living areas, though for some reason Andie wouldn't let them have the kitchen setting. The decorator had remarked that perhaps a 'vintage' store – in the inner west most likely – might be interested in the laminex table and vinyl chairs. But Andie wanted to keep them, she didn't delve too deeply into the reasons why. She would probably pay to have them stored, along with everything from Brendan's room, because she couldn't bear to part with any of that either.

The house had promptly sold before auction, and settlement was slated for the last week in January. The buyers' children were enrolled in schools in the area, but they were happy to have one last Christmas in their old house. For her part, Andie was glad that a family was moving in, and they seemed very nice, they would make it into a home again. There were two girls and a boy, and Andie had made the mistake of mentioning that there were two girls and a boy in her family also. So of course they started asking questions about how old everyone was now, and what they were doing with their lives, and Andie had to brush over some of the details, she didn't want to talk about Brendan with these strangers.

At least the prompt sale had meant that Andie didn't have to worry about doing up the house for Christmas. The decorator had offered to handle it, she seemed quite enthusiastic about the prospect, she probably didn't get to do many Christmas makeovers. She suggested a huge tree and she showed Andie a whole catalogue of designer bling that she had at her disposal. Andie would have found it all a bit much with only her here.

Her mother had never been big on Christmas. She always displayed a nativity setting on the mantelpiece and they did have a tree, but it couldn't have been more than four feet tall; Andie had outgrown it while she was still in primary school. Present-wise her parents favoured the sensible over the silly, function over fun.

So they usually received clothes, educational games and books, though Brendan did get a bike when he was ten, and he used to let Andie ride it.

She came down the hall past the empty lounge room. The only things remaining now were her dad's armchair and the TV, which the decorator had installed up on the wall, making it less imposing. She assured Andie it was a plus, but warned that it would have to be included in the sale, as people expected it nowadays; it became a fixture of the house, like an oven. Andie was only too happy to be relieved of it.

She walked through to the kitchen and her eyes landed on the gift from Ross's children, where she had placed it next to the small Christmas tree centrepiece – her one concession to festive decorating. She dumped her bag on a chair and crossed to the fridge, taking out a bottle of wine she had opened a couple of nights ago. She never seemed to manage more than one glass when she got home from work, she was always so exhausted it would almost put her to sleep. Andie had reduced everything down to a single cupboard, where she kept a small stash of basic supplies – coffee, sugar, chocolate – and a couple of plates, cups and glasses. She picked up a wineglass and took a seat at the table, poured herself some wine and sat back. She pictured her family sitting around the table. They always had Christmas lunch in the dining room, which was only used for special occasions. But this was where they sat on Christmas morning, and every other morning and evening; their dad at the head, their mother on his right, and Meredith beside her. Brendan sat next to their dad, and opposite their mum, with Andie beside him. Their mother was strict about manners, no elbows on the table, no talking above each other, not much talking at all. Though Brendan usually managed to jolly things along, he always seemed to be able to make their mother smile.

Andie considered the wrapped box. She looked at her watch. It was well after midnight, going on one in fact. She might as well open it now.

'Merry Christmas, Andie,' she said out loud, raising her glass and taking a drink. She slid the gift towards her. The card read, 'To dear Andie, something to help you remember us. Love Brooke, Matty, Lauren and family xxx'

Andie tore back the paper to reveal a flat black box. She opened the lid, and moved back the tissue paper. It was a photo of all three of them, along with James and Emily. The word 'Family' was embossed on the frame, below the picture. A sob caught in her throat and Andie started to cry.

*

She stayed in bed through two snooze cycles of the alarm, not actually snoozing, just reluctant to get out of bed. Then the message beep sounded on her mobile phone and she rolled over to grab it. She turned over onto her back again and held the phone up to read the message. It was from Jess.

Happy xmas beautiful! Wish I was going with you. Have fun. xJ

Hm. Fun? Andie thought that might be a bit optimistic. She was rostered on to serve Christmas lunch at a homeless shelter in the inner city. Jess had signed up soon after Christmas last year – apparently there were waiting lists for volunteers. It was something she'd always wanted to do, but when her mother got wind of it, she'd nearly had a conniption; it was simply not acceptable to miss Christmas dinner. So Jess had transferred her registration to Andie.

She got out of bed and trudged out to the kitchen to put on the kettle. As she spotted the framed photo of the kids propped next to the miniature Christmas tree, she teared up again. It was just as well she had something to occupy her today or it would have been very grim indeed around here. She wasn't convinced that working in a soup kitchen wasn't going to prove a little grim as well, but at least she'd be around people. And out of this house.

*

An hour and a half later, Andie was circling the block in Kings Cross, uncomfortably close to Ross's apartment. It was strange how she didn't even think of the place as hers anymore, maybe because it had never really felt like home to her. She only thought of it when she went to look for something and realised she'd probably left it behind at the apartment. Jess had told her she'd go with her some time to clear out the rest of her stuff – her share of the kitchen items, linen, that kind of thing – but Andie was inclined to leave it. She didn't really want constant reminders from her life with Ross. She would buy her own things when the time came, start fresh.

She eventually found a park, locked the car and walked the few blocks back to the shelter. She was to present herself at the front desk when she arrived to be assigned a work station. The place was a hive of activity already; Andie had read in the pamphlet Jess had given her that they served over a thousand meals on Christmas Day. Jess had been pre-assigned to cooking duties, naturally, and when Andie explained she was a chef as well, there was no need to change that. She stuck the name tag she was given onto her T-shirt as she walked through into the main area, where row upon row of trestle tables were being assembled. A makeshift commercial kitchen had been set up at one end behind a wall of temporary office dividers. They had asked volunteers to bring their own aprons, as they couldn't supply them for everyone, and Andie had also brought a chef's cap to keep her hair out of the way. She got ready in the secure change room provided, stowed her bag away and rejoined the fray. A coordinator directed Andie to the potato-peeling station. Joy. But, she had to remind herself, this was not about her, so she smiled at her compatriots, picked up a potato and began to peel.

'Your first time?' asked the man standing on the opposite side of the bench.

'Does it show?' she asked.

'No, we're first-timers too. I'm Mitchell, my wife, Kirsty,' he said, cocking his head in the direction of the woman beside him.

'I'm Andie.'

'Mandy?'

'No, Andie. It's short for Andrea.'

Mitchell and Kirsty's eyes lit up simultaneously, and they turned to look at each other.

'Ooh, I like that, what do you think?' Kirsty asked her husband.

'Andie's cute.' Mitchell looked at Andie. 'You spell it with an i-e, yeah?'

'That's right,' she said, increasingly bemused by their fascination with her name.

'We're expecting our first,' Kirsty explained, giving her tummy a pat. 'Not quite four months along, so you can't really tell yet.'

'We don't know what we're having,' said Mitchell. 'We think we're going to keep it a surprise . . . Not sure yet.'

'So we have to think about boys' *and* girls' names,' Kirsty continued. 'It's so hard. You want something unique, but not ridiculous.'

'And we don't want weird spelling,' added Mitchell. 'Then you're just condemning the kid to a lifetime of having to spell out their name.'

Kirsty nodded. 'It's a minefield.'

An hour later the potatoes kept on coming, and Mitchell and Kirsty kept on talking. Andie had been fully briefed on all their parenting dilemmas: birthing styles – to drug or not to drug; slings versus prams; whether to give the baby a dummy . . . They seemed like a lovely couple, if a little earnest. But two people committed to each other, so excited about bringing a baby into the world, Andie couldn't help feel a little envious. So she was relieved when the coordinator returned.

'You're a chef, right?' she said to Andie.

'Yes, I am.'

'We could use you over at the coalface, so to speak. Despite what they say, you can never have too many cooks,' she said with a grin.

Andie wished Kirsty and Mitchell all the best with the baby, and followed the coordinator to the other end of the kitchen area. A bank of ovens filled the entire wall, and volunteers were lined up at the facing bench, turning vegetables in baking pans or basting joints of meat.

'The team leader is over this way,' she said to Andie. They walked up behind a tall man in a chef's jacket. 'Brought you more help,' she said loudly.

He turned around. And Andie's mouth dropped open.

'You,' he said.

'It's Andie . . . Chef.'

He considered her for a moment. 'I told you, it's Dominic outside of work.'

'So you two know each other?' the coordinator said cheerfully. 'I'll leave you to it then.'

'What are you doing here?' he asked.

Andie blinked. She didn't know what to say to that. 'Well, I think it's pretty obvious, isn't it?'

'Did you know I was going to be here?'

Whoa, Andie wasn't sure if that was fuelled by ego or paranoia. Either way . . .

'No, I had no idea you were going to be here,' she assured him. 'A friend signed me up, or signed herself up, and then she couldn't make it, and I had nothing better to do.'

'On Christmas Day?'

He looked as though he found that highly dubious. So what was he doing here? This was a very odd conversation.

'Yes, that's right,' Andie replied. 'But looks like you don't either.'

Now he looked confused.

'You don't have anything better to do on Christmas either?' she clarified for him.

He shrugged. 'I do this every year.' He glanced around. 'Okay, let's get on with it then. Over there, vegetables onto baking trays, there should be some tongs around somewhere.'

Andie found tongs and started to load up the trays, trying to decide if this was a good thing or not. It was strange, and certainly unexpected, she knew that much. At least it was a chance to work closely with him, in the same vicinity anyway, prove she was competent and capable and hardworking. As long as she didn't stuff up. But there was nothing she could stuff up here – baking meat and vegetables did not require a great deal of expertise. But then maybe he'd think that was all she was good for?

Sometimes her powers of negative thinking surprised even her.

Despite her direst predictions, Andie picked up the system almost immediately, and worked quickly and efficiently, without having to be told every second thing. In fact, she ended up supervising some of the less experienced volunteers. She was astounded at the scale of the operation, that somehow this disparate group of trained and untrained volunteers – most of whom had probably never worked together before – managed to serve up an impressive Christmas lunch to such a huge number of people. And although it was nonstop, it didn't feel as pressured as working in a regular restaurant. Certainly everybody was enjoying themselves a lot more. Even Chef seemed to relax, cracking a smile now and then. It occurred to Andie that he wasn't bad looking, actually, not bad looking at all. His eyes were quite dark, so they'd always seemed a little foreboding, but when he smiled they softened to a warm brown. His whole face softened in fact. She supposed she'd been too intimidated before to notice, then again, he didn't smile all that often . . . Then again, Andie had not really dwelled on a man's looks for some time . . . Wait, he wasn't a man, he was her *boss*. She shouldn't be dwelling on anything about him, and certainly not his eyes or his smile.

They were finally left with a line-up of full plates, and no one left to serve, so the coordinator said they should finish up now and have something to eat themselves. They each took a plate of food and picked their way among the tables to find an empty seat. Andie was surprised when Chef came up behind her and touched her elbow.

'Over this way,' he said.

She allowed him to lead her to a table and he took a seat opposite her.

'So, no family?' he said, tucking into his lunch.

'Pardon?' said Andie.

He looked up. 'You don't have anywhere to go on Christmas, so I'm assuming that means no family.' He paused, but before she could answer he added, 'Oh, that's right, your father died only recently, didn't he?'

'Yes.'

'That's why you have nowhere to go?'

His style of questioning was a bit blunt, for want of another word. Another word like 'rude', for example.

Andie squared her shoulders. 'I have a sister, a niece and a nephew, friends . . . I had invitations, I just preferred to do this.'

He nodded.

'What about you?' she asked.

'What about me?'

'Do you have any family?'

He was concentrating on his plate, scooping food together with his fork. 'I told you, I do this every year,' he said, without looking up.

'That doesn't actually answer my question.'

He glanced at her then, with a faint smile. 'No, I suppose it doesn't.'

They continued eating, and left the chitchat to other people at the table, who were clearly a lot better at it than they were. But Andie was intrigued now. What was Mr Gerou's story anyway? That name was French, she assumed, and he could pass for French, or European anyway, with his dark hair and eyes. But there was that trace of an English accent . . . Maybe he'd been educated in England? Maybe all his family were in Europe and he didn't have anyone in Australia? He said he volunteered here every year. Didn't he even have any friends?

When Andie was almost finished her meal, more volunteers started bringing around plum pudding and custard.

'Oh, should we be getting back to the kitchen?' Andie said.

Dominic shook his head. 'There'll be a whole new team in there taking care of dessert,' he explained.

She got to her feet. 'Well, I couldn't fit pudding in anyway. I'll go see if I can help.'

'You know, you don't have to stay,' Dominic said to her. 'Fresh volunteers arrive every couple of hours. They'll be starting the clean-up soon.'

Andie shrugged. 'I read that the clean-up is the biggest part. Can't hurt to have another pair of hands.'

He was gazing up at her with a bemused expression, Andie detected perhaps even a tiny hint of approval in his eyes. Good. She made her way back through the tables to the kitchen area, but it was at capacity. Dessert was under control, and a small army had already started cleaning the baking trays and pans and utensils. Andie looked around. She noticed people weaving in and around the tables collecting rubbish into garbage bags, and so she approached one of the coordinators and asked where she could find the bags. Clearing up was easy, and she wasn't that tired, no more tired than after a shift at the restaurant. But there was something very uplifting about this. Andie was glad she'd done it. Chalk one up for new experiences.

She didn't come across Dominic again for the next hour or so, he seemed to be staying put in the kitchen to help with the clean-up there

– something he certainly never had to do at Viande. Andie enjoyed wandering around the tables. The guests who remained were in good spirits and so full of gratitude, Andie found it humbling.

Finally the original coordinator approached Andie. 'Hey, you've been at it all day,' she said. 'We don't want to wear you out. You should feel free to go any time.'

The place really was starting to empty; perhaps the organisers appreciated some time together to debrief at the end of the day. Andie didn't want to outstay her welcome, so she dumped the last full garbage bag into a skip bin at the rear of the building and went back inside to the change room. She took off her apron and pulled the cap from her head, shaking out her hair, before gathering up her things and walking out the door, and almost straight into Dominic Gerou.

'I was looking for you,' he said, taking a step back. 'I thought you must have already gone.'

'No, just leaving now.'

'Is there somewhere you have to be?' he asked.

'Oh, no . . . um, they said I should go, there was nothing much left to do.' She slipped her bag off her shoulder. 'Why, do you need some help?'

He was shaking his head. 'No, that's not why I was asking. I'm finishing up now as well.'

Andie nodded, waiting.

He took a breath. 'I was thinking, if you didn't have to be anywhere . . .' He seemed oddly nervous. 'Well, maybe you'd like to get a drink? You know, for Christmas.'

That was quite possibly the last thing Andie had expected him to say. 'Um . . .' she hesitated.

'Never mind, it's been a long day.' Now he looked embarrassed.

'No, no, it's fine,' she said quickly. 'Sure, why not? Let's go for a drink.'

He seemed relieved now, and there was the hint of a smile in his eyes. 'Good then. Give me a minute to clean up and I'll meet you out front.'

'Okay.'

*

Andie stood waiting on the footpath outside the main entrance. Why did she say yes? This was going to be excruciating. Going out for a drink with Chef . . . Dominic . . . Chef . . . She groaned. If she didn't even feel comfortable calling him by his name, how was she going to sit across a table from him for half an hour . . . though it would probably be longer, wouldn't it? More like an hour. And how would she excuse herself politely? He was her boss, she couldn't just say to him, well, I've had enough of you, time to go. Not that she'd say it like that of course, she wasn't that stupid, but however she put it, he was going to know that's what she was thinking. It would be like when you got stuck talking to someone you didn't know at a party and you ended up having to make some excuse, like getting a drink or going to the loo, when it was quite obvious that you'd exhausted the conversation and you really just wanted to move on.

She sighed inwardly. What was wrong with her? Where was her confidence? It was just that she hadn't dated in a long time . . .

Hold on, she was getting way ahead of herself here. This wasn't a *date*. Why did that term even come into her head? Chef . . . *Dominic* . . . he was a colleague. All right, normally he was her boss, but today they had been coworkers, and they were simply going out for a friendly drink after work. This should be no more awkward or strange than staffy's on a Sunday night.

Yeah, right.

'Andie?'

She looked up. He was standing right in front of her, waving his hand in her face. Oh God, what an idiot, she must have been a million miles away.

'You were a million miles away,' he said.

As she suspected.

'Sorry,' said Andie, with an apologetic smile. 'Are you ready?'

'Yes.' He'd discarded his chef's jacket and was wearing an open shirt over a T-shirt and jeans. Okay, that helped, he looked like a regular person.

'Do you know anywhere around here?' he asked.

Andie shrugged. 'I wonder if anything'll even be open on Christmas Day?' She also wondered if her tone was giving away that she hoped there wouldn't be.

'Oh, there's sure to be something open up in the Cross,' he said. Dandy.

They walked in the direction of the main drag making very small talk, minute talk, in fact. He was really not an easy person to talk to. Maybe his position made it difficult for him to fraternise . . . Oh, why did that particular term have to come to mind?

Anyway, he was the one who had extended the invitation, he was only trying to be friendly, so Andie really needed to give him the benefit of the doubt. Maybe he'd relax over a drink, let his guard down a little. She might even get to know Dominic the man, rather than the chef. Then she might even manage to actually call him Dominic without breaking into a sweat.

He led the way to a bar off William Street. Andie was relieved when they walked in. It was small, but not so small as to feel intimate; quiet, but not so quiet they would have to huddle and speak in hushed tones; there were enough people to mask any potential awkwardness, but not so many that it was crowded. It was just right. Andie was beginning to feel like Goldilocks.

And now she was thinking of bears. Dangerous predatory bears, not cute ones you cuddled in bed.

And now she was thinking of cuddling in bed. She really had to stop thinking.

Dominic went to get the drinks and Andie grabbed a table smack in the middle of the place, well-lit and right out in the open. She watched Dominic at the bar. He wasn't bear-like at all; he was tall, but slim, not skinny. Andie wasn't keen on skinny men. Though what that had to do with the price of fish . . . Sometimes she wished she could just stop the voice in her head from prattling on. It always got worse when she was nervous. He was heading towards the table now with their drinks, thank God, Andie was in dire need of some Dutch courage. She snatched up her glass as soon as he set it down, taking a healthy gulp. Dominic looked a little disconcerted. She probably should have waited for him to sit, raise their glasses. Oh well, faux pas the first. The way she was going it was unlikely to be the last.

She glanced at his drink, a long glass of soda and something. 'So, vodka drinker?'

'I'm sorry?'

'I'm guessing it's vodka in that soda,' she said. 'It doesn't agree with me so much these days, I tend to stick to wine. But vodka and I had some very good times together, back in my twenties —'

'It's just a club soda,' he said, his expression clouding over.

'Oh, you're not having a drink?'

'I am, it just doesn't have any alcohol in it,' he said. 'I have to drive home.'

Andie wondered if her face had gone red. She decided it must have, because his next question was, 'Are you driving?'

She swallowed. 'Yes, but I'll only have this one.'

Yeesh, he looked so . . . disapproving.

'We could go for coffee, if you'd rather?' she offered.

'No, we're here now,' he said. 'I'm sure you won't be over the limit after one glass of wine.'

It sounded like he was trying to reassure himself. At least she had an excuse now to call it a night after one drink. Captain Temperance here would obviously be more than okay with that.

'So . . .' she said, desperately searching for something to say to lighten the mood. And fill in the silence. Why did the man ask her for a drink when he didn't want to drink, and he didn't even seem to have much to say? Why did everything about this have to be weird and uncomfortable?

'How are you enjoying working at Viande?' Dominic asked.

'Very much.' Andie was relieved. Work should be a safe topic. 'Everyone's so nice and helpful.'

He nodded. 'You're doing well. Tang and Cosmo both have good things to say about you.'

'Oh, that's nice.'

Couldn't she think of another word than 'nice'? Hold on, what was that he just said? They reported to him about her? He was interested?

'They're both such great guys,' said Andie.

Great guys? She sounded like a teenage girl. They were her superiors, her mentors, they were professionals, not 'great guys'.

Well, they were great guys, but . . . Why wasn't he saying anything? Because he thought she was a twit probably. God, this was some kind of endurance test. Andie took another gulp of her wine. Keep talking about work, say something intelligent, or at least sensible . . . even fawning would do.

'I haven't had a chance to thank you.'

'That isn't necessary,' said Dominic. 'I was only concerned you were all right, that he wasn't bothering you.'

What was he talking about? 'No one's bothering me,' she assured him. 'Like I said, everyone's been great.'

'Oh . . .' He looked slightly thrown. 'What were you thanking me for?'

'For the second chance,' she said. 'For giving me another trial.'

He nodded. 'Of course.'

'What did you think I was talking about?'

'Nothing, it doesn't matter.' He picked up his glass and took a drink. 'It's none of my business anyway.'

Then it hit Andie. He thought she was referring to the scene in the carpark with Ross.

'Oh, of course, I do want to thank you for that as well,' she said. 'You know, what happened, that night, with my husband . . . my ex-husband.'

'It isn't necessary, really,' he said, staring down at the table again.

This strain between them was such a . . . a *strain*. Andie didn't think she could take much more of this. She decided to be more upfront.

'No,' she said firmly, 'I think it is necessary. I should apologise for bringing my private life to work like that.'

He met her gaze then. 'You didn't bring it, it seemed to me it came looking for you.'

'Hm. Ross, my ex, well, he's not my ex yet . . .'

'Oh?'

'Only a matter of time,' she said. 'It's in the hands of the lawyers as we speak. Well, probably not as we speak, it is Christmas Day after all.'

She smiled, but he didn't. She probably shouldn't make jokes about a pending divorce. Another faux pas. Andie wondered if Dominic was keeping count.

'Anyway,' she went on, 'the thing is, Ross showed up that night because he was upset I'd been to a lawyer. He'd been hoping it wouldn't come to that.'

'It's really none of my business,' said Dominic.

Fine.

'So you're the one ending it?' he asked.

And now it was his business.

'In a manner of speaking,' said Andie. 'I'm ending it because he had an affair. Is still having an affair, as far as I know.'

He looked faintly embarrassed. Too much information? God, she had no idea what to do with this conversation.

'I'm sorry,' he said finally.

'What for?' Andie wasn't following him.

He hesitated. 'Well . . . for your loss, I suppose,' he said. 'I'm not sure how to put it.'

'Oh, thanks.'

'Were you happy?' he asked.

'I thought we were.'

'No, I asked if *you* were happy.'

She looked at him. 'Sure. I thought we'd be together forever.'

'So you have no idea why he decided to have an affair?'

She shrugged. 'Why does any man?'

'Or woman. I don't think it's gender-exclusive.'

'Still, I think men may have the jump on it, statistically,' Andie said wryly.

'Not anymore apparently. Statistically, women are catching up.'

What? Did he make a study of this?

'So you really don't know why your husband had an affair?' said Dominic, returning to his original question.

'No, I don't,' she said tightly. She didn't like his tone. 'What are you implying?'

He looked abashed. 'Nothing, it's none of my business.'

No, it wasn't.

'Only, I was wondering what you think about the theory that an affair is only likely to happen in a marriage that's already troubled?'

She glared at him. 'What exactly are you trying to say?'

'Nothing, really,' he said. 'I didn't mean anything by it.'

'You think it was my fault somehow?'

'No —'

'Look, you can say whatever you like to me at work where you're the boss,' Andie said, flustered. 'But I don't think you have the right to ask me out for a drink and then . . . insult me.'

'That wasn't my intention, I assure you,' he said.

She felt like sculling the rest of her wine, but she wouldn't give him any more ammunition against her. So she took a sedate sip and pushed her glass aside, standing up.

'I have to go. Thanks for the drink,' she said, picking up her bag and heading for the exit. She felt rattled, and embarrassed. Why would he jump to the conclusion that there was something wrong with her marriage? And why did that bother her?

He caught up to her at the door and held it open as she strode out past him.

'Andie, wait,' he said, stepping out onto the footpath.

She turned around, but fixed her gaze down the street, away from him. He didn't say anything, so after a while Andie stole a glance at him. He was just standing there looking bewildered.

'Look, I really do have to go,' she said.

He stirred. 'Can I walk you to your car?'

'No, I'll be fine.' She could not figure him out. 'Thanks again for the drink.' She turned on her heel and started down the street, in the opposite direction they'd come from. She'd have to retrace her steps later, but that was preferable to spending any more time in his company. What an arrogant, opinionated prig he'd turned out to be . . . wait, he'd always been.

When she finally made it back to her car, Andie took out her phone and texted Jess to see where she was. She didn't want to go home to the empty house and sit there stewing about this, which she knew she would. She was hoping things might have wrapped up for Jess and they could meet for a drink.

Her phone eventually beeped in response, and she picked it up off the passenger seat to read the message.

Still at mums! Come rescue me!

*

Jess had apparently been drinking since late morning, so she was in no state to drive herself home, and she had Buckley's of getting a cab, deep in suburban Concord on Christmas Day. It was looking like she was going to have to stay the night, so Andie's message came at the right time. Jess gave her strict instructions not to enter the premises, as she may never make it out again. Andie was worried that might seem rude, but Jess reassured her that no one would even notice, that she should just prank her phone when she arrived and Jess would come out.

'So how was your day?' asked Andie as they drove away down the street.

'Oh, the usual, too much food, way too much Christmas cheer. I'm all familied out,' she groaned, throwing her head back. 'Who invented families, honestly? We should all be born in pods, like in that movie . . . with that guy . . . oh, you know the one, he has absolutely no expression, his face is a blank.'

'*The Matrix*,' said Andie.

'Yeah, but what's his name again?'

'Keanu Reeves.'

'That's it.' She seemed relieved. 'So what were we talking about?'

Andie glanced at her with a smile. 'I have no idea.'

Jess smiled back. 'So, tell me, how did it go at the shelter?'

'It was great, really,' she said. 'I'm so glad I did it. Thanks for giving me the push.'

'You're welcome,' she slurred.

'A funny thing happened, though.'

'Oh?'

'Guess who showed up there today?'

'Not Ross!' Jess said, sitting bolt upright.

'No,' Andie scoffed. 'As if Ross would set foot in a place like that. No, it was my boss, Dominic Gerou.'

'Seriously?'

Andie nodded.

'What was he doing there? Not looking for a feed, I hope?'

That made her laugh. 'No, he was volunteering as well. Apparently he's been doing it for years.'

'Hm . . . small world,' Jess murmured sleepily.

Andie was beginning to wonder if she'd have company tonight after all. 'Where do you want to go, Jess?'

'Oh, just home,' she said. 'I have all those leftovers Mum gave me. We'll be all set.'

Andie couldn't get much out of Jess for the rest of the drive back to her flat, she dozed most of the way. Maybe she'd have to go home by herself after all, it was no less depressing an option than bunking down at Jess's place if she was only going to crash as soon as they got there. But Andie couldn't help feeling disappointed. She wanted to talk to Jess about what happened today. She knew exactly what she'd say – that Dominic was an arrogant wanker and she should just ignore him – but Andie needed to hear her say it. Fortunately, Jess seemed to get a second wind from the car to her flat, and once inside she buzzed around the tiny kitchen, putting out leftovers and opening wine.

'So, you know how I was telling you that my boss was there today?' Andie began.

'Yep.'

'Well, he asked me out for a drink afterwards.'

Jess turned to look at her. 'He asked you out? And you didn't go?'

'No, I did go.'

'Then how are you here now?'

'We only had one drink. I didn't even finish mine,' said Andie.

'Why, what happened?'

'He's just so arrogant,' she said, feeling her hackles rise again.

'He's a chef.' Jess shrugged, like that was a given.

'He asked me out for a drink and then all he did was lecture me.'

'About your job?'

'No, no, that's all fine.' Though how she was going to face him at work again, she had no idea. 'We got to talking about my marriage break-up . . . breakdown . . . ups and downs.'

Jess frowned as she passed Andie a glass of wine. 'What on earth made you go into that murky territory?'

'I was thanking him for the way he stepped in when Ross showed up at work that night.'

'What the hell?' Jess looked shocked.

'Didn't I tell you about that?'

'Tell me about what?'

'It's not a big deal,' Andie dismissed. 'It was a few weeks ago now. Ross waited in the carpark after work to talk to me because I hadn't been answering his calls. Anyway, Dominic happened to come out of the restaurant just as Ross was getting a little . . . worked up.'

'What was he doing?' Jess's voice rose along with her heightened imagination.

'Nothing, honestly. I thought I told you all this?'

'No,' she said airily, 'you never tell me anything anymore.'

Andie ignored that. 'Back to today . . .'

'So you're really not going to tell me what happened with Ross?'

'It's not important. In fact, I haven't even seen him since then.' It was true, she realised as she said it. He'd finally got the hint and backed off – for good, Andie hoped. 'It's all in the hands of the lawyers now.'

'Well, that's something.' Jess picked up her glass and a platter of food and walked into the living area. 'So what about this Dominic?' she said, sitting down on the sofa. 'You two are on first-name basis now?'

'Not really,' said Andie, taking a seat next to her. 'He started asking me all these intrusive questions, and next thing he's implying that I must have done something to make Ross go off and have an affair.'

Jess blinked. 'He actually said that?'

'Yes.' Kind of. Something like that. That was the inference anyway. Wasn't it? God, she didn't even know anymore.

'What a prick,' said Jess. 'He doesn't even know you.'

'I know, right?'

'Where does he get off?'

'Exactly.' Andie felt so much better already. She gulped down half her glass of wine. At least Jess wouldn't have a dig at her drinking habits. Clearly Dominic Gerou had issues left and right. Andie didn't have any issues, she knew exactly what had destroyed her marriage. Her husband had an affair. That was that. Dominic obviously empathised more with Ross because he was a man. He'd probably dumped a string of women with the same excuse – that there was something wrong with the relationship. Piffle. Jess was right. 'Arrogant prick,' she said out loud.

'You didn't say that to him?' Jess looked worried.

'No, I said something like, he didn't have the right to insult me, and I walked out.'

'On your boss?'

Andie's heart dropped. 'Oh shit.'

'Don't worry about it,' said Jess. 'He can't do anything to you – it was outside of work.'

'You think?'

'You didn't abuse him or anything?'

Andie thought about it. 'No, definitely not. I thanked him for the drink and left.'

'You'll be okay then.'

She sighed, resting her chin in her hand. 'You know, during the day I actually thought I might have made a good impression on him.'

'Obviously, if he asked you out,' said Jess.

'He didn't ask me *out* out,' said Andie. 'It was just end-of-the-day, coworker-type drinks.'

'Are you sure?'

'Yes,' she said uncertainly. 'I don't know. How can you tell?'

Jess smiled. 'You've been out of the game a long time, haven't you?'

'No, I'm sure this wasn't anything,' Andie decided. 'He's not like that. He doesn't even hang around at work for staffy's.'

'Yet this was only a friendly coworker drink with you?' Jess raised an eyebrow.

'It had to be,' she insisted. 'Think about it, if he was coming on to me, he had a funny way of showing it. Throwing insults at me about my marriage failing.'

'Hm . . . that is weird,' Jess mused. 'Anyway, it's just as well. Fraternising with the boss is never a good idea.'

'Don't worry, I won't be doing that again in a hurry.'

'Though, I have been meaning to say,' Jess went on, 'you really should be thinking about getting back on the horse, Andie.'

She rolled her eyes and leaned her head back against the sofa.

'I'm serious,' said Jess. 'Put it off and it's only going to get harder. When's the last time you had sex?'

Andie frowned. 'When's the last time *you* had sex?'

'About two weeks ago.'

'Oh, well, it's longer than that.'

'It's months, isn't it?' said Jess. 'You know, if you were a guy, you'd have gone out and picked up someone the very next weekend, if not the next night, to salve your ego.'

'Well, I'm not a guy.'

'You still have needs. You said so yourself.'

'The ink isn't even dry on my divorce papers, Jess . . . Come to think of it, the divorce papers haven't even been printed yet. I'm just not ready.'

'So you're not over Ross?'

'I doubt it.'

'Andie!' Jess sighed.

'I'm only being honest,' she said. 'I'm not pining for him, I have no intention of going back to him. But I guess on some level I must still love him. Feelings don't go away overnight, they need time to fade.'

'Hm, like a rash.' Jess grunted. 'Surely there must be a cream for that?'

Andie snorted a laugh. 'Yeah, vanishing cream, perhaps?'

'What was vanishing cream anyway?' said Jess. 'You never hear of it any more. I wish it was still around, I could use it on my nether regions instead of boiling wax.'

Andie winced. 'So you went through with it?'

'No,' she said. 'You two made me feel like I'd be betraying the sisterhood if I did. But when I'm still single in the nursing home, I'll be cursing you.'

Andie considered her. 'I didn't think you were that bothered about being single.'

Jess shrugged. 'I don't know, maybe I'm getting a bit old for one-nighters, or the one-nighters are getting a bit old.'

Andie was almost shocked. 'Are you telling me you want to settle down?'

'I'm never going to be bored, or old, or crazy enough to get married,' she said. 'But you know, it wouldn't be so bad to have a regular guy, someone you could hang out with on a wet afternoon and watch Netflix, someone you could actually have a conversation with . . . someone just . . . *nice*.'

'Isn't that what gay friends are for?' said Andie.

'Yeah, but they don't like to have sex with girls.'

'Like I always say, you can't have it all.'

Boxing Day

Andie slept pretty soundly on Jess's fold-out, but she woke earlier than she would have preferred on a day off, the street noises around here being somewhat more intrusive than in quiet suburban Roseville. She only had a mild hangover, nothing that a good hot breakfast wouldn't fix, so she went to check out the refrigerator. Not only was it brimming with leftovers from Christmas, there were also eggs and onions and herbs and good cheese – you could always find decent basics in a chef's fridge. When Jess finally emerged, Andie had almost finished cooking a ham and cheese frittata, and a hash she'd made from leftover baked potatoes. Together they made short work of it. It was warming up outside, and they briefly considered going to the beach – until they remembered that Boxing Day was probably the most popular beach day of the year, and the crowds would be horrendous. Andie decided she better just head back to the house.

'It's a good chance to get some more packing done,' she told Jess. 'I still have a couple of boxes of stuff I haven't been through yet.'

'I guess it's an appropriate way to spend Boxing Day,' Jess quipped.

When Andie arrived home and got out of the car, it was really getting quite steamy, but because the house had been shut up since the day before, it was relatively cool inside. She had a quick shower and changed out of the clothes she'd been wearing since yesterday, before dragging the boxes out of the wardrobe. These were the last ones from her mother's things. She sat down cross-legged on the floor and opened the first, lifting out an old concertina-style file. She flicked through the alphabetised sections – they appeared to be full of old bills, receipts, guarantees. She knew the solicitor had the deed for the house and all her father's financial documents, so Andie was pretty sure these were just household records. The whole thing could probably go straight into the recycling, but what if there was something relevant, instructions or a valid warranty, for example? She really didn't feel like sorting through it all now, so she decided she'd hold on to it for a couple of months after the new owners had moved in, and if no issues surfaced she'd toss the lot then. There was another file in the bottom of the box, an old manila folder marked 'Certificates', tied with a thin faded ribbon. Andie lifted it out and laid it on the floor in front of her. She untied the ribbon and opened the folder.

Her heart lurched. On top was an envelope marked 'Death Certificate'. Andie gingerly picked it up, only to reveal another, identical envelope underneath. Oh God, one must be her mother's, the other had to be Brendan's. Andie held them both, just staring at them, her hands trembling. There was no need to open them or look at them, it would only make her sad. She held them close to her chest as her gaze landed on the next document on the pile, titled 'Coroner's Report'. It wasn't in an envelope, it was just lying there, barefaced. Phrases jumped out at her before she could block them . . . compound fracture to the skull . . . death – instant . . . Andie turned away, quickly placing the envelopes aside and the report face-down on top of them. She hoped it wasn't all going to be this depressing. She looked back to the pile, relieved to see their certificates of confirmation and first communion next, printed on pages featuring quaint pictures of angels and the Virgin Mary and Jesus – the anglicised version, with fair hair and blue eyes, in flowing, luminous robes, children clustered around him, all blue-eyed and rosy-cheeked. They looked like characters in an Enid Blyton book, dressed up for a nativity play perhaps. Their baptismal certificates followed, less colourfully adorned, and finally copies of their official birth certificates.

The last few documents were her parents' original birth certificates, and their marriage certificate. Andie picked it up and read the florid script. They were married at the Church of the Holy Redeemer, on the twelfth day of September, nineteen hundred and . . .

That couldn't be right. Meredith was going to be forty next year, the maths was pretty straightforward. Andie sifted back through the documents and found Meredith's birth certificate, checking the year of birth against the date of her parents' wedding. Unless the Registry of Births, Deaths and Marriages had made a mistake, Meredith was born six months after they were married.

Why had they never mentioned it? Andie wondered if Meredith knew, and decided she probably didn't. Her mother had clearly kept it a secret from everyone all these years, like a hidden shame. Andie only ever remembered seeing one photo from their wedding when she was just a girl, it was certainly never put out on display. Her mother had worn quite a severe grey suit, and Andie had asked her why she didn't wear a real bride's dress. She said it would have been a waste of money because you could never wear it again. Andie remembered being perplexed about all the other brides she'd seen in proper wedding dresses that would never be worn again, and wondering whatever happened to them.

If her mother was pregnant she certainly wouldn't have been able to wear the grey suit for much longer either. Andie leaned back against the wardrobe behind her. She believed her parents loved each other, she wanted to believe that, though she supposed she hadn't witnessed much affection between them. There was respect – she couldn't recall her mother ever criticising her husband, and she never heard her father say a bad word about his wife. But if they hadn't really loved each other, if they'd married because they had no choice . . . well, that was just too sad to contemplate.

Her dad had seemed to get joy out of all his children, but Andie was sure Brendan was the only one who brought her mother any joy. She was perennially worried about her daughters, always so insistent that they had to make more of their lives, so she never let her guard down around them, at least not around Andie anyway. She and Meredith seemed to understand each other, to speak the same language. And she was entirely different with Brendan. She must have felt she didn't have to worry about him; he was going to be a man in what she still considered a man's world, he would be all right. No wonder she was so destroyed by his death.

Andie stirred after a while, glancing over at the other box. She wasn't so sure she felt like uncovering any more family history, but she might as well get it over with. She dragged the box closer and opened it. Lying on top was a large dark blue photo album. Andie opened the cover. On the facing page, in her mother's own hand, was neatly written 'Brendan Patrick Lonergan', followed underneath by his date of birth, at St Margaret's Hospital, Darlinghurst. She turned the page, and there were his hospital records, his newborn photo, and his ankle and wrist identification bands, all glued neatly into place. This was Brendan's baby book. Andie had never seen it before, she was surprised her mother had even kept such a thing, she wasn't a sentimental sort at all. Though she was different with Brendan, her beloved son. Perhaps she had worked on this after he died, as a memorial to him, but surely Andie would have noticed, she was with her most of the time throughout her last year.

She lifted the album onto her lap and flipped through the pages. He was such an adorable baby, and then toddler, always grinning mischievously at the camera. All his milestones were recorded faithfully, and once he was at school, his class photos and yearly reports were interspersed with paintings and handwritten stories, tests with impressive scores. The photos and reports continued all the way to Year 12, the last photo taken at his formal. He wore a plain black dinner suit but with a lime-green tie, braces and shoes – he'd had to get them specially dyed, Andie remembered. There were more pages, but they were blank. Brendan had died the following year, so there were no graduation photos or anything else. She wondered if he'd ever seen this album, but she doubted it, he would have told her.

Andie closed the cover and hugged it to her chest, thinking of Brendan in those crazy green shoes. Their mother had pleaded with him to reconsider, but of course in the end he'd cajoled her into going along with what he wanted, as usual. Andie looked down at the album in her arms, she was so relieved she hadn't decided to turf all the boxes without going through them.

She lay it gently on the floor next to her, and leaned forward to lift the next album out of the box. As Andie opened the cover she drew her breath in sharply. Her own details were recorded on the first page, just like Brendan's. Her heart beat faster as she turned page after page. The same meticulous care had been taken recording her milestones, preserving her childhood paintings and stories, handmade Mother's Day cards, school reports, photos. Andie was overcome and tears filled her eyes. Why had her mother never shown her this? Did she plan that they would only be found after her death? But why? What a shame not to share these with her children. Then it occurred to Andie, maybe she hadn't done them for her children at all, maybe she'd done them for herself. Perhaps her own regrets and disappointments faded when she looked at the lives and achievements of the children she'd borne. Andie hoped she'd felt proud, that creating these albums had given her some of the joy that seemed to be missing from her life.

There was one more album at the bottom of the box, and it was Meredith's. Andie quickly flicked through the pages – it was the same as the others, except at the end there was a photo of Meredith graduating from university. At least her mother had been around to see one of her daughters achieve that.

Andie went back through the certificates and separated out Meredith's, slipping them between the pages of her album. She'd pass it on to her next time she saw her. She sorted her and Brendan's certificates and put them inside their respective albums. She didn't think Meredith would mind if she held on to Brendan's, so long as someone did. Andie considered her parents' papers, wondering what to do with them. She didn't want to tell Meredith; her parents had kept it a secret, perhaps from some misplaced sense of shame, but Andie would respect their intention. Besides, what would it achieve telling her? It was the kind of thing that was likely to upset Meredith, so there was nothing to be gained from it. Finally Andie slipped the documents into the back of her own album, and then she packed it back into one of the boxes, along with Brendan's album, and the concertina file. She sealed the box with tape, and wrote 'To Be Kept' across the top, in thick black marker.

Viande

Andie fronted up for work the day after Boxing Day feeling sad and sentimental, but also a sense of peace as well. Her perspective had been radically altered, though she had to admit, largely for the better. She knew one thing for certain – a life shaped by regrets was half a life, if that. Her mother had a solid marriage, and children she obviously loved, but she wouldn't allow herself to get much joy out of any of it. Andie's marriage had failed, and she didn't see herself having a baby now, but she just couldn't let those regrets define her forever. She was lucky enough to find herself in her dream career, and she wasn't going to waste a minute of the opportunity. Even though it wasn't the career her mother had envisaged for her, Andie hoped it would still have made her proud.

So she was keen to get out of the house and back to work – though she was not so keen when she remembered she'd have to face Dominic . . . Chef . . . bloody hell, it was just going to be awkward and uncomfortable, or worse.

It had been stupid to have anything to do with her boss outside of work – this job was too important. Andie should have just said a polite no in the first place. Better to have risked offending his ego ever so slightly than to have this hanging over her. With anyone else, working at the shelter together would have been a bonding experience, but the best Andie could hope for was that things would be as they were before, and they would have very little to do with each other.

As it turned out, she didn't lay eyes on him the entire first shift back at work, Cosmo and Tang ran both the lunch and dinner services. She wondered if Chef was sick, or had gone away . . . or maybe it was something more serious? He couldn't have left outright without there being some sort of announcement, surely?

When he hadn't appeared by halfway through the shift again the following day, Andie decided to ask Tang at her first opportunity. But she had to get the wording right, she didn't want it to seem like she was asking after Dominic, as such.

'So you and Cosmo have had a promotion?' she said to Tang when he came by to collect the vegetables for garnish. 'You're running the place now.'

He smiled at her. 'It's only temporary. Chef's having a week off.'

There. Mystery solved. For the most part. Was it a holiday? Was he visiting family? Was he unwell? Was it any of her business?

Andie put it out of her mind and got on with her week, relieved she'd been given a reprieve for now. The restaurant was open on New Year's Eve and she was more than happy to spend it working . . . and thus avoid the whole dilemma about what to do on New Year's Eve. It had always been a romantic night for her and Ross. They didn't get invited to many parties in the beginning – as a new couple they didn't really fit in with old groups of friends, so they made it a special night for just the two of them. They had watched the fireworks from a suite overlooking Sydney Harbour, relaxed in a luxurious spa retreat in Byron Bay, they had even flown to New York one year. But even the years they spent at home were special – they had each other, they didn't need to be at a big party with lots of people. Though that was exactly what they'd done last year, as it turned out. Ross accepted an invitation to some swanky corporate soirée, and though Andie objected, he said it might be fun for a change. It wasn't. Andie had never been so bored in her life. She kept hinting at Ross to leave and he'd say 'Soon', but they didn't end up getting home until nearly 3 am. It had been her worst New Year's Eve ever, and she had no intention of topping it this year.

Working was by far the best antidote for whatever emotions threatened to surface on the night, especially as they were flat chat the whole time. They only had one sitting for dinner, serving a special degustation menu that carried the diners through to midnight. Andie was given more responsibility, with some of the regular staff on leave; she even got to actually help assemble the *amuse-bouche* – tiny butter puff pastries topped with a single, perfect scallop poached in white wine with lemon and dill. It was as close to plating up as Andie had ever been, and she couldn't believe the thrill it gave her. She worked on New Year's Day as well; again the restaurant only offered one sitting, at lunch, but it was a huge seafood-based feast this time. Chef was still away, and Andie had put the whole thing to the back of her mind, she was so immersed in her work. So she was startled when he turned up on the second day of January – literally startled, because she bumped right into him as she was carrying a large rack of bread across the kitchen.

'Hello, Andie,' he said, with a slight bow of his head.

'Chef.' She nodded. 'You're back.'

'I am.'

They stood for a moment longer in awkward silence, till Andie finally excused herself. 'I best get on with it.'

'Of course.' He moved out of her way. 'Andie,' he called after her.

She looked back.

'Happy New Year.'

She felt her face go hot. 'Same to you, Chef.'

At least he didn't seem angry or pissed at her. Maybe all her worrying had been for nothing and he was going to pretend it had never happened? That suited Andie just fine.

At the end of the shift, she was cleaning her work station after most of the staff had gone for the night. Andie tended to be one of the last to leave; she took her time, never in much of a hurry to get back to the house. She heard someone clearing his throat behind her and she looked around. Dominic was standing at the end of the bench, watching her.

'Oh, you gave me a start,' she said, her heart pounding.

'Sorry, I didn't mean to.'

'Is there something you need?'

He hesitated. 'Could I speak with you for a moment, Andie? I won't hold you up long.'

'Okay.' What was this about? She had a bad feeling.

'Do you mind?' he said, indicating the doors to the restaurant. 'We can talk in there.'

'Sure.' He walked ahead, and Andie followed him. Bugger, was he going to give her the sack or something? Because he felt awkward around her now? That hardly seemed fair. She hadn't done anything wrong; she had as much right to volunteer at the shelter as he did, and he was the one who'd asked her to go for a drink anyway, and he was the one who'd started asking personal questions, and making outrageous assumptions. So she had walked out. All right, maybe that was a bit of an overreaction on her part, maybe he hadn't said anything all that outrageous, but she'd taken her leave politely, and he wasn't bloody royalty. How could that be a sackable offence?

It didn't have to be. When you were employed on a contract basis, a boss only had to take a dislike to you, or decide he felt awkward around you, or that he just didn't like the cut of your jib for whatever arbitrary reason, and he was under no obligation to renew your contract the next time around. Right now Chef could say she wasn't working out, and as her contract was up in a couple of months, maybe she should start looking around . . . There was no use fighting it or she'd never get a job anywhere else. He had all the power, Andie had none. She was best to take it gracefully and hope he'd at least give her a reasonable reference.

She followed him into the main room of the restaurant. The tables were stripped, the chairs stacked on top ready for the cleaners in the morning. She waited as he turned over a couple of chairs and set them down on the floor, then indicated for her to take a seat. Andie felt vaguely nauseous as she stepped forward and sat down.

'Can I get you a drink, or anything?' he asked.

She looked up at him. 'Look, Chef, if you're going to fire me, I'd rather you just cut to the chase.'

'I'm sorry?' he said, as though he wasn't following her. 'I'm not going to fire you.'

'Yeah, okay, you can't actually fire me,' she said. 'But you're letting me know you're not going to renew my contract, right? And you're going to suggest I start looking around for alternatives. It's the same difference.' So much for taking it gracefully.

'Andie, I have no idea what you're talking about,' he said. 'Your position here is perfectly safe.'

She was instantly relieved, and then instantly confused. 'Then what's this about?'

He breathed out. 'May I sit?'

Why was he asking her? She nodded.

He sat down opposite her. Andie would have preferred to have the table between them, some kind of barrier, but he'd placed the chairs at the end of the table, facing each other.

'What this is about . . .' He began hesitantly. He seemed nervous again, like when he asked her for a drink. And that made Andie nervous.

'I wanted to apologise,' he said finally, 'for the other day, after the Christmas lunch. For the things I said.'

She hadn't seen that coming. 'There's no need to apologise.'

'Yes, there is,' he said. 'I upset you, not that I meant to, I was only trying to make conversation.' He paused, he seemed to be thinking about what to say next. 'I'm not very good at this. It's been a long time for me.'

What has? Making conversation?

'When you showed up at the shelter like that, out of the blue, well, it felt like an opportunity was presenting itself . . .'

What was he talking about?

'Sometimes you think these things are meant to be, but I don't know. I don't know if I even believe in fate.' He became lost in thought for a moment. 'But anyhow, I stuffed it up entirely,' he went on. 'I don't have to tell you that, you were there. I offended you somehow, and that was the last thing I intended. And, so . . . well, I'd like to make it up to you.'

What?

'You don't have to do that,' Andie said, feeling uneasy.

'But I want to,' he said quickly. 'What I mean is, what I'm asking is . . . I'd like to know . . . if you would like to go out . . . sometime?'

Her throat went dry. 'What?' she croaked. 'You want to go out . . . with me?'

'Yes,' he said quietly.

Andie would have been less surprised if he had sacked her. 'Why?'

'I'm sorry?'

'Why do you want to go out with me?'

He looked perplexed. 'I'm not sure what you're asking.'

'It's not that difficult,' she said. 'You don't seem to like me very much. You hardly know me. I don't understand why you want to go out with me. If it's just to make up for upsetting me —'

'No, it's not just that,' he said, but then he didn't offer anything else.

'Well, I don't get it,' said Andie, folding her arms.

He stared down at his hands for a moment, clasping and unclasping them. Finally he looked up at her. 'I'm sorry you think that I don't like you,' he said. 'I'm sorry if I've given you that impression. I said I'm not very good at this.'

'That doesn't answer my question,' she muttered.

'I'm attracted to you,' he said bluntly.

Andie just stared at him.

'You're a very attractive woman, Andie. I can't be the first man to have told you that.'

She sighed. 'No, you're not,' she said, her heart sinking. 'And if you're trying to flatter me, sorry, but it's not going to work.' She got to her feet. 'I didn't do anything to look like this, it's not an achievement, and it hasn't done me any favours. I seem to "attract" men who want some kind of trophy, and they get bored with me eventually and dump me . . . sometimes they even break my heart.' She swallowed. 'So if attraction is all you've got, it's not enough. Thanks anyway.'

She started for the door.

'Andie, wait,' said Dominic. 'Please.'

She stopped, but she didn't turn around. She felt embarrassed, and self-conscious, and, weirdly, a vague feeling of disappointment.

'When you first showed up at the restaurant,' he said, 'I thought you were a pretty face and not much more, it's true. Especially the way you ran out that night. But you surprised me when you came back. And you've kept surprising me ever since, by how hard you work, how determined you've been. I noticed, I know I don't mix much with the staff, but I noticed. And then you turned up at the shelter, and you surprised me again.' He took a breath. 'I think there's a lot more to you than just a pretty face, and I would like the chance to get to know you better.' There was a long pause. 'Andie,' he said, 'please turn around.'

She did as he asked, slowly turning to face him again, though she couldn't actually look at him.

'Do you remember when you asked me for a second chance?' he went on. 'You said you weren't prepared the first time. It was the same for me. I wasn't prepared when you turned up at the shelter, and I screwed up. So now I'm asking you for a second chance.'

Andie stood there, trying to breathe normally while her heart nearly pummelled its way out of her rib cage. He was asking her out on a date? Was this for real?

'Is this for real?' she said out loud.

He dropped his gaze for a moment, before looking up at her again. 'I'm sorry, Andie, I didn't mean to make you uncomfortable, or put you on the spot. You can go.'

'It's just, you're my boss, you know?'

'I know. It's okay, please, feel free to go.'

Oh God, he was misunderstanding her, and he looked so crestfallen.

'I'm not saying no, I didn't say no, did I?' she blurted.

He looked confused now.

'I wasn't expecting it, that's all,' she went on, her heart racing. 'After the other day, why would I?'

'I understand,' he said. 'And I apologise —'

'Stop. You didn't do anything wrong, I was being sensitive —'

'No, it was my fault —'

'You don't have to keep apologising,' she interrupted him finally, catching her breath. 'Just give a girl a minute to catch up.'

Andie detected the beginnings of a smile on his face, and something stirred inside her. 'You know,' she said, 'if you could see yourself when you smile, you'd smile a lot more often.'

His eyebrows lifted slightly, and now he looked at once embarrassed, coy, even a little vulnerable. Andie began to think there might be a lot more to Dominic Gerou than the arrogant chef persona he wore so well.

'What are you thinking?' he asked after a while.

This may turn out to be the stupidest thing she'd ever done. Jess would probably freak. But suddenly Andie couldn't help herself. How had he put it before?

'I'm thinking that an opportunity has presented itself . . .'

He smiled then, a proper smile. And that sealed it.

'See, that's not so hard, is it?'

January 4

They had settled on Monday night, their only night off, which meant they had to get through a whole shift on Sunday first. Andie wasn't worried about being fired anymore, now she was only worried about where Dominic was at any given time, if he was watching her, what he was thinking. He smiled at her more in one shift than she'd seen him smile the whole time she'd been working there.

He had said he'd noticed her, a lot, which meant all those times she'd thought he was watching her, he probably was. Andie vacillated between feeling flattered and feeling self-conscious, but mostly she just wondered why she said yes. She'd been beating herself up for even having a drink with him, and now she was going on a proper, not-to-be-mistaken-for-anything-else, real live date? And since when had she decided to date anyone again, let alone her boss? It was too soon, for one thing. Wasn't it? Not that it was serious, not that it was actually anything yet. She had far more important priorities to attend to – like finding her own place and establishing her career – before she even thought about starting a new relationship.

But who said anything about a 'relationship'? It was definitely too soon for that. She'd be crazy to even contemplate it. She needed time and space to get over the last one – the last one being a ten-year-long marriage she'd thought would last forever. This was only a date. It might turn into a few dates, or it might go nowhere. She really needed to chill out. That's what Jess would say, if Andie told her. But Andie hadn't told her because she knew Jess would have a problem with the whole 'fraternising' with the boss thing. She would also remind Andie that she'd thought he was an arrogant prick only a week ago. That was true, this date could turn into an unmitigated disaster of unparalleled awkwardness, given their track record so far. Their track record being one drink, which is where Andie really should have let things lie, if she had any brains . . . But instead she'd been swayed by all his talk about how he noticed her, how she kept surprising him . . . how he wanted to get to know her better . . . the way he smiled . . .

'Are you all right, Andie?'

She stirred, Cosmo was watching her across the table. Somehow she'd made it through the shift today, on autopilot she suspected, and she was getting ready to go home when she noticed everyone was gathering for staffy's. She'd forgotten it was Sunday.

She took a gulp of her drink. 'Sure, I'm fine, thanks, Cosmo. Everything's fine.'

He nodded. 'You seemed a little distracted today.'

Andie's eyes grew wide. 'I'm sorry, did I do something wrong?'

'No, of course not,' he assured her. 'I think you could do most of your regular tasks on autopilot now.'

Just as well.

'You really stepped up over New Year's,' he went on. 'I was impressed. In fact, it's getting time we moved you up. I'll have a talk to Chef.'

'Don't do that,' she blurted.

Cosmo was taken aback. 'Why, what's wrong?'

She starts dating the boss and suddenly gets a promotion, that's what's wrong!

'I just don't think I'm ready,' said Andie. 'It's too soon, isn't it?'

'Why do you say that?'

She hesitated. 'Because it is . . . isn't it?'

Cosmo shook his head. 'I've known chefs who have trained for years, but they don't have that . . . that *something*.'

'What something?'

He was thinking about it. 'It's like the secret ingredient that lifts a dish from the everyday to something special.' He looked at her. 'That's what you have, Andie.'

'I do?' She blinked. She had a secret ingredient? 'Can you tell me what it is?'

Cosmo smiled at her. 'You need to trust your own instincts. You know what you're doing, start believing it.'

*

Cosmo's words were still jangling in her head when Andie woke this morning – D-day. She was actually feeling a little sick . . . Sick enough to cancel? she wondered. Probably not, seeing as she was only feeling sick at the thought of this date. Notwithstanding all the other issues – and there were enough of them – she just hadn't been on a date in so long, more than a decade in fact, as long as she'd been with Ross. And look how that had turned out.

What the hell was the matter with her? She was ten years older – and wiser, she hoped – and Dominic was a mature man . . . who was probably around the same age as Ross when she met him, it just occurred to Andie. She wasn't sure how she felt about that. But then she remembered she was not a naive twentysomething anymore, and besides, Dominic was not Ross . . . and besides *besides*, this was just a date! She really had to stop overthinking it.

She decided to ring Jess, she needed someone to knock some sense into her. But it went straight to voicemail. So she said, 'Call me when you get this,' and hung up. Damn.

Now she had no choice but to get out of bed. She was making herself a cup of tea when her phone rang. She was relieved to see it was Jess calling back.

'What's wrong?' Jess said breathlessly as soon as she picked up. 'What's happened? Are you okay?'

'I'm fine,' Andie reassured her.

'My God, you sounded so grim in your voice message.'

'Did I?'

'Yeah, I've put the "Back in five" sign up and locked the door.'

'Of course, you're at the shop today,' said Andie. 'I forgot, I'm sorry.'

'Forgot you had a shop?' Jess said wryly.

'I know, I really need to come in, very soon.'

'Well, what are you doing today? It's your day off, isn't it?'

Andie sighed. 'That's what I was calling about. I have a date.'

'Whoo! So you're taking my advice, getting right back in the saddle. Good for you.'

'No, you don't understand, it's not good.'

'Why not?'

'Don't freak . . .'

'You're not going out with Ross, are you?'

'No!' she insisted. 'Jess, would you stop always thinking everything is about Ross. I promise you, he's out of my life.'

'Okay. So what's the problem then?'

Andie took a deep breath. 'The date is with Dominic Gerou.' She winced, waiting for her reaction.

'Hold on, I'm confused,' Jess said, her voice surprisingly calm. 'That wouldn't be Dominic Gerou, the same guy you said was an arrogant wanker? The same guy who happens to be your *boss*.'

'All right, I get it, you're going with sarcasm.'

'Are you nuts?'

'Probably.'

'How did this happen? When did he ask you? Why did you say yes? Tell me everything.'

Andie sat down at the kitchen table, jiggling the tea bag in her cup. 'I haven't even seen him since Christmas, he's been off work. He was back Saturday, and he approached me at the end of the shift.'

'Sounds keen.'

'Hm. Anyway, he said he was sorry about the other time, he never intended to offend me, and he'd like another chance.'

'Yikes, now that sounds serious.'

She groaned. 'What am I going to do?'

'Do you like him at all? Even a little bit? Does he do anything for you?'

Andie was flummoxed. 'What's that got to do with it?'

'Well, you are going on a date with him.'

'But the issue is not whether I'm attracted to him.'

'Then what is the issue?'

'That he's my boss!'

She heard Jess sigh. 'Okay, granted, it's probably not the smartest idea to date your boss, but you're not working in some government department where it's against regulations, and you're not a twenty-year-old intern where he's the CEO of the company. This is not exactly unethical, Andie. In this industry, if you don't date people you work with, you don't date.'

'But it's still a minefield,' she said. 'What if he asks me out again?'

'Why don't you wait and see how this one goes first?'

'No,' Andie said decisively. 'I really don't think I should take it any further after tonight.'

'Then, if that's how you really feel, you'll just have to tell him.'

'How am I supposed to do that?' she said. 'If I go out with him, it's uncomfortable, if I don't go out with him, it's going to be uncomfortable. I'm damned either way.'

'Okay . . .' Jess said slowly, thinking about it. 'Then what you have to do is totally kill the attraction.'

Andie frowned. 'How do I do that?'

'Play it cool, act bored, *be* boring, or be outright offensive – swear a lot. Do you think he's the type who'd be turned off by that? A lot of guys are, even if they've got mouths like sewers themselves.'

'I don't know . . .' Andie said vaguely.

'What about his politics, do you know which way he votes? If he's to the right, go full leftie green wingnut, if he's to the left, start complaining about immigrants and say you don't believe in climate change.'

'Jess, don't you think that's all a bit extreme?'

'Maybe, but if you play it right he won't ask you out again.'

'And he probably won't renew my contract either. He'll think I'm a crackpot.'

Jess groaned. 'Then stop stressing. You're only going on a date, do you know how many dates I've been on that have never gone anywhere? That would be most of them. So go, have a nice time. On the bright side, you might even get laid.'

'Oh, don't even say that.'

'Do you good.'

As if things weren't already complicated enough. 'I still think it's too soon,' said Andie. 'I was married to Ross for ten years, I can't just hop into bed with the first guy that comes along.'

'Ross did . . . not with a guy, but you know what I'm saying.'

'Yes, and you think he's a bastard.'

'That's totally different,' said Jess. 'But hey, there's your way out – honesty. Just tell this Dominic that it's too soon. He'll probably run a mile once he realises you're fresh out of a marriage break-up.'

'He already knows, remember, we talked about it over drinks.'

'He is keen then.'

Now Andie groaned.

'You know, Andie, there are worse things than having a guy keen on you.'

'Not when he's your boss,' she said glumly.

'Look, tell me the truth, did you only say yes because you felt pressured?' Jess asked her.

'No,' she sighed, 'he didn't pressure me, he gave me the chance to bow out gracefully.'

'Then why did you say yes?'

Andie thought about it. There was his smile, but that would just sound lame. 'I suppose it was what he said – that I keep surprising him, that he thinks there's a lot more to me than just a pretty face, and he'd like the chance to get to know me better. He said he screwed up, and he asked me if I'd give him a second chance.'

'Sounds like a bit of thought went into all that,' Jess mused.

Andie released a loud sigh.

'Do me a favour, Andie, and stop thinking so much. Just go out and enjoy yourself. It's a date, you're not going in front of a firing squad.'

'Okay, you're right.'

'Yes, I am,' she said firmly. 'Now, enough of this, what are you going to wear?'

'Oh God, I haven't even thought about that.'

She hung up and went to investigate her wardrobe. Most of her 'date' clothes must still be back at the apartment she discovered. She had plenty of clothes for everyday wear or working at the shop, and that was about it. So she made a mad dash to the nearest shopping mall, but once she got there, she had no idea what she was looking for. Dominic had suggested dinner, but that was no help – anything from semi-formal to jeans and a nice top might be acceptable, depending on where they were going. Things were very loose these days, not like in her mother's era when there were rules about what you wore where and when. There was something to be said for all that at a time like this.

Andie went in search of caffeine – she needed it to help her think. She sat in a cafe out of the throng and contemplated her options. It was no use calling Jess again, she didn't know where they were going either. There was only one person who could tell her that. She and Dominic had exchanged mobile numbers the other night – which had felt significant in itself – so she took out her phone and scrolled to find his number. Should she really call him to ask him what to wear? Would it sound ridiculous? Would it be better than looking ridiculous later? She conjured up a mental picture of Dominic in jeans, and her in a formal dress, or her in jeans and him in a suit. She pictured his face. Andie held her breath and pressed *Call*.

He picked up after a few rings. 'Hello, Andie?' He sounded tentative.

'Hi.'

'Is everything all right for tonight?' he asked.

'Yes and no. Please don't think I'm silly, but I don't know what to wear.'

Andie heard a loud sigh, and then he started to laugh.

'Don't laugh at me.'

'I'm not, I'm laughing out of relief. I thought you were calling to cancel.'

He was relieved . . . He was worried she might cancel . . . That was actually quite sweet.

Hold on – exactly how much stock was he putting into this date?

'Casual is fine,' he was saying. 'Or, actually, you can wear whatever you like, if you want to get more dressed up, I'll —'

'I'm happy with casual,' she broke in.

'Okay. So I'll see you at seven?'

'Are you sure you still want to come all the way over here?'

He had insisted on picking her up, even after she told him where she was living. It was quite an act of chivalry, her mother would have been impressed. Then again, Andie wondered later if he was just worried about her drinking and driving.

'It's already settled,' he said. 'See you at seven.'

'Okay.'

*

Andie glanced at the clock again; it was almost seven, only a minute or two away. She'd been ready for forty-five minutes, and that was after several complete changes of hairstyle and one full makeup reapplication. So at a quarter past six she found herself pacing the kitchen floor, wearing the most expensive pair of jeans she'd ever owned in her life, and a much more moderately priced top, and dying for a glass of wine to calm her mounting nerves. But she worried Dominic might be able to smell it on her breath, not that she was assuming he was going to get that close, but alcohol was more noticeable on someone else when you hadn't been drinking yourself. Then she had a debate with herself for ten minutes about what was the problem anyway, and just because he obviously had a thing about drinking and driving didn't mean he was anti-alcohol altogether – he was head chef at a licensed restaurant for godsakes – and so finally she'd that glass of wine and then spent another ten minutes brushing her teeth and rinsing her mouth and applying more perfume so she didn't smell like a toothpaste factory.

Why was she putting herself through this? Dressing up, worrying about her breath, going on a date with her boss . . . Going on a date, full stop.

Finally there was a knock at the door.

It was Dominic, not surprisingly. He was wearing jeans and a dark collared shirt . . . Okay, why was it that he seemed to be getting better looking every time she saw him now? What was that about? Was her mind playing tricks on her?

'Hi.' He smiled at her. 'You look . . . just right.'

Like Goldilocks.

Despite Andie's trepidation, the conversation flowed throughout the drive over the bridge and beyond. Dominic asked her lots of questions about where she grew up, went to school, that kind of thing, with none of the intrusive tone of Christmas Day – giving her the cue to ask similar questions of him, questions that didn't require information about past relationships or anything else potentially touchy. And so they made it all the way to Bondi without any obvious awkwardness. Faux pas count – nil.

Before the road took them down to the beachfront, Dominic pulled over at a small shopping centre, right in front of a restaurant that appeared to be closed. Andie peered out through the car window at the name on the door – Elliot's. She'd heard of this place, it had created quite a buzz. They didn't take bookings, and had people queuing around the block on weekends. There was no queue tonight, and the building was in darkness. Maybe this was just a convenient parking spot, and they were going somewhere further along. Dominic was already walking around to the passenger side, and he held the door open as Andie stepped out onto the kerb. She looked further up the block, but it seemed very quiet. It was a Monday night after all, not exactly a big night for dining out.

'So, here we are,' Dominic announced, turning to face the restaurant.

'It doesn't look like it's open,' said Andie.

He gave her a smile. 'It isn't, at least not to the general public.'

He led her around to the side of the building where a light shone above an alcove and another entrance. Dominic knocked loudly on the door, and Andie heard a muffled call from inside. Presently the door burst open.

'It's about bloody time,' declared the man who appeared in the doorway.

'What are you talking about? It's just on seven thirty now,' Dominic said, glancing at his watch.

'I'm saying it's about bloody time you finally bothered to make an appearance at my restaurant,' he said, with a friendly thump on Dominic's shoulder, to which Dominic responded with a shove, and which finally morphed into a man-hug with the whole mandatory backslapping thing.

Look at that . . . Dominic had a mate?

His friend turned to Andie. 'And you are a bonus, my dear,' he said, taking her hand. 'To whom do I owe the pleasure?'

'Andie Lonergan,' said Dominic, 'I would like to introduce my very charming, and oldest friend in the world, Elliot Mason.'

Andie shook his hand. 'It's great to meet you, Elliot,' she said. 'I've heard wonderful things about this place.'

'Why thank you, and for that I'll even let you inside.'

They bypassed the restaurant proper and followed Elliot into the brightly lit kitchen.

'My, my,' he said, smiling at Andie. 'I can see why you've waited so long, Dom, you were obviously holding out for perfection.'

Andie felt herself blushing, and she didn't know where to look.

'Happy now?' said Dominic. 'You've embarrassed my date.'

'Sorry, Andie,' said Elliot. 'I've always been a sucker for a beautiful woman. You didn't tell me how beautiful, Dom.'

'Oh, I hadn't really noticed.'

Andie smiled at that.

'But speaking of beautiful women, how are Sally and Ava?'

'Exceptional,' Elliot replied. 'Sal wants to know when you're coming to visit your goddaughter, before she grows so much you won't recognise her.'

Dominic turned to Andie. 'Sally is Elliot's wife. She's far too good for him, but thankfully their baby girl, Ava, takes entirely after her mother.'

'You have a baby?' Andie cooed.

'That's code for "you want to see a photo" right?' said Elliot, reaching into his pocket for his wallet. He flipped it open and passed it to Andie.

She gazed at the picture of the blonde blue-eyed infant. 'Oh my God, she's so gorgeous.'

'Told you, she takes after her mother.'

'You'll keep,' Elliot said to Dominic.

'I feel bad that you're here cooking for us on your night off,' said Andie. 'You should be home with your wife and baby.'

'I had the day with them,' he assured her, 'and this boofhead hasn't set foot in my restaurant yet so I had to get him here while I had the chance. But Sal said next time you'll both have to come to our place for dinner.'

Andie glanced sideways at Dominic. What did he think about all this talk of 'next time' and cosy dinners with other couples? He seemed unfazed.

'So what are you going to feed us tonight?' he was asking Elliot.

'Well, I hope you don't mind, Andie, I was planning to experiment a little,' he said. 'It's too good an opportunity with him here, I have to make the most of it.'

'When you say experiment . . .' Dominic said warily.

Elliot launched into a rapturous account of the milk-fed venison he had lately sourced, the cheek of which he planned to gently poach in a stock made from its own marrow, and serve with a crème fraîche blended with Jerusalem artichokes on a bed of truffle soil.

Andie was speechless.

'You enjoyed that, did you, El?' said Dominic. 'Little joke at my expense?'

Now Andie was confused.

'What are you really cooking?' Dominic persisted.

'Paella . . . with my own inimitable twist, of course.'

'That's more like it.'

'So there's no milk-fed venison cheek?' Andie frowned.

'I'm sorry,' Elliot said, 'we shouldn't be having private jokes.'

'You see, Andie,' Dominic explained, 'Elliot favours a rustic style of cooking —'

'Good, honest, time-honoured recipes using real food,' he broke in. 'Whereas Dom is into food as art, the kitchen as laboratory . . .'

'I'm not *into* it,' Dominic defended. 'It's what people expect at the top end of fine dining.'

'If we're going to have this argument again, I better get us drinks first.'

'I'm driving,' said Dominic. 'I'll wait for dinner.'

'Then I hope you'll have a drink with me, Andie?' said Elliot. 'Why didn't you guys just come by cab?'

'That's my fault,' said Andie. 'I live miles away, up in Roseville, though I hope not for much longer.'

'White, red, bubbles?' Elliot asked her, standing in front of the glass-fronted refrigerator.

'You choose, I'll drink anything,' said Andie, before she could stop herself. 'Anything in moderation, of course,' she added lamely.

'Anything it is, then,' said Elliot, grabbing a bottle of white wine. 'So why do you hope you won't be in Roseville for much longer?'

Andie explained the situation in brief, her father dying, and the house needing to be sold, while neatly sidestepping any mention of her marriage collapsing.

'So now I have a few weeks to find somewhere to live,' she said.

'That doesn't give you much time,' said Elliot, passing her a glass of wine.

'I know, but there wasn't any point looking over Christmas, especially around here.'

'You want to move over this way?'

Andie nodded, taking a sip of her wine. 'This is lovely, thank you.'

'I might have a lead for you,' said Elliot. 'Right here in Bondi.'

'Seriously?' said Andie.

'Yeah, one of the young guys working here, he wants to move in with his girlfriend. Her flatmate just left, and she can't afford the place on her own, but he can't break his lease. So they're stuck paying for both places, and she's going to have to get someone in to share again.'

'Why doesn't she just move in with him?'

'Place is too small.' Then Elliot winced. 'Ah, sorry, I should have said, it's only a studio.'

'No, that's perfect,' Andie exclaimed. 'That's exactly what I was looking for.'

'Serendipity,' he said. 'Well, I can't promise anything, but last I heard he was putting the word out for someone to take over his lease. Give me your number before you leave tonight, I'll see what's going on tomorrow and get back to you.'

'That'd be so great, Elliot. Thank you.'

He smiled. 'I aim to please.'

'Do you aim to start cooking any time soon?' said Dominic.

'If you get off your lazy arse and give me a hand.'

'Can I do anything?' Andie asked.

'No, you sit, relax,' said Elliot. 'Traditionally paella is made by men on a Sunday, to give the women a day off from cooking.'

'I didn't know that,' said Andie.

'It's really peasant food,' Elliot was saying. 'They used to cook it up in a big paella pan – the *paellera* – over an open fire outside, and they'd put in anything they had on hand, or that they'd caught in the fields. Originally it included chicken, rabbit, ground snails, even field rats.'

'Oh God, what are you planning to put in it?' Dominic grimaced.

Elliot grinned. 'Don't worry, I haven't been catching rats out in the back alley. Whenever paella is made by the sea, it includes seafood, so as we are by the sea, this paella will have prawns.'

'Not mussels? Aren't they traditional?' said Dominic. 'I remember having paella with mussels in Spain.'

'I'm not as fussed on mussels,' said Elliot. 'I mean they look great in the dish, but then you've got to make a mess pulling them apart. Really, the three most important elements are the broth, the rice, which has to be calasparra, and the saffron. If you get them right, you can bung in anything you like. So along with these fantastic tiger prawns, I'm also going to add chorizo, and – wait to be impressed, Dom – *jamón ibérico de bellota.*'

'Okay, I'm impressed.'

'I'd like to be impressed too,' said Andie, feeling like they were speaking in a foreign language. Which they were, come to think of it.

'It's Spanish ham,' Dominic said. 'Arguably the best in the world.'

'But that's not all, Andie,' said Elliot. 'It only comes from black Iberian pigs that range free in the oak forests on the border of Spain and Portugal, and for the final period before slaughter they're fed solely on acorns.'

Andie frowned. 'Okay, so this is another one of your private jokes?'

They both laughed. 'No,' Elliot assured her. 'Although I know it sounds like something wanky that Dom'd serve, just wait until you taste it.'

Andie sat back, sipping her wine and watching the two men cook as they riffed off each other, bouncing insults and one-liners with the synchronicity that came only after years of friendship.

'Now, the final secret of a good paella is the layer of toasted rice at the bottom of the pan,' said Elliot. 'At the end of cooking, you place the pan over a high flame and listen for the rice toasting. Once the aroma wafts upwards, remove it from the heat,' he said, lifting the pan and setting it down on the bench. He covered it with a tea towel. 'The towel will absorb the remaining broth, and it'll be ready to eat in about five minutes.'

He placed it on the centre of the chef's table and passed around bowls so they could dish up themselves.

'I'd like to serve it like this in the restaurant,' said Elliot. 'To have parties of four or even six order it for the table. I don't know if it'll work.'

'This is so good,' Andie said, savouring her first forkful.

'What'd I tell you?' said Elliot. 'This is real, unadulterated —'

'You can't say it's unadulterated,' Dominic scoffed. 'It has been cooked, it's what separates us from the animals.'

'But, Andie,' Elliot appealed to her, 'isn't this better than eating some indistinguishable, tortured piece of something or other, placed on the plate like a work of sculpture rather than a meal?'

'If you're referring to Dominic's food, I'm the wrong person to ask, because I think it's extraordinary,' said Andie.

'Ha, good choice of word – "extra-ordinary". Out of this world. Like sci-fi, or postmodern art.'

'So what if it's like art?' she said. 'The best art fills the senses, excites, makes you see things in a different way.'

Dominic nudged Elliot. 'What she said.'

'All due respect, I don't know that I agree,' said Elliot. 'I reckon fine dining has become more like those fashion shows. Regular people wouldn't be seen dead in what they parade on the catwalk, in fact, most of it's unwearable.'

'Maybe,' said Andie, 'but surely there's room for both – food that nurtures and satisfies and feels comforting and familiar. And food that pushes the boundaries, and offers an experience that simpler food can never achieve?'

Elliot looked at Dominic. 'She's very diplomatic.'

Andie smiled. 'So how do you two know each other?' she asked.

'I had the misfortune of meeting Elliot at high school,' said Dominic.

'What are you talking about?' he retorted. 'You only survived high school because of me.'

'That's true actually.'

'He was such a nancy boy,' said Elliot, 'straight off the boat from England. If not for me he would have been beaten up on a daily basis.'

'Really?'

'I'm afraid so,' Dominic admitted. 'I had to pay him protection money.'

'No,' said Andie, 'I mean, you immigrated from England when you were in high school?' So that really was an accent, he wasn't just being pompous. 'Were you one of those Ten Pound Poms?'

'How old do you think I am?' he objected.

But Elliot just laughed. 'Can you imagine if your old man heard that? That'd make his aristocratic blood boil.'

'Gerou doesn't sound very English?' Andie asked, curious.

'It isn't,' said Dominic. 'It's my mother's name, actually. An odd blend of French and Greek, of all things, but a long way back.'

'He was still Dominic Chamberlain when I first met him,' said Elliot.

'Why did you change it?'

He hesitated. 'My father and I didn't see eye to eye on much back then. So in a fit of youthful petulance, I dropped his name for my mother's. Just to piss him off, really.'

He couldn't just leave that hanging in the air. To Andie's surprise, he didn't.

'My father was a QC,' Dominic went on. 'I was expected to follow the same path. So I took law at university, but I wasn't very good at it, so I dropped out.'

'You hated it,' said Elliot.

'But I wasn't doing well.'

'Because you hated it.'

'Did you always want to be a chef?' Andie asked Dominic.

Elliot laughed at that. 'He needed a job once he got kicked out of home.'

'They didn't kick me out,' Dominic said. 'My father just gave me some ultimatums that I chose not to meet.'

'Now who's being diplomatic,' Elliot muttered.

'It's the truth. Besides, they were going back to England, and I wanted to stay . . .'

'I was an apprentice chef at the time,' said Elliot, 'and Dom was sleeping on my couch. I got him a job as a kitchenhand so at least he could pay for his own food.'

'That's how you got started?' said Andie.

Dominic nodded, with a faint, almost sheepish smile.

She was amazed. He wasn't some elite, cordon bleu career chef, he was almost an accidental chef. 'So then you fell in love with it?'

Dominic and Elliot exchanged a glance.

'It was a job,' Dominic said with a shrug, 'no better or worse than anything else I could have got at the time. I needed to support myself.'

'He worked really hard,' Elliot said. 'Never complained, did every shitty job given to him, which was impressive for a boy with blue blood running through his veins. My boss ended up putting him on as an apprentice, and the rest,' he said grandly, 'as they say, is history.'

*

'Thank you for a wonderful meal, I had such a great time,' Andie sad as Elliot saw them out the side door.

They agreed to finally call it a night when they noticed it was past eleven. They all had to work tomorrow, and Dominic had to do the round trip across the bridge and back to take Andie home.

'Thank you for getting this guy to finally come to my restaurant,' said Elliot.

'It had nothing to do with me.'

'Oh, I think it might have,' he said, giving Dominic a thump on the arm. 'So, Sal will give you a call, Dom, we'll make a night at our place. I'll look forward to seeing you again then, Andie.'

Elliot stood in the doorway as they walked down the side of the building towards the street where the car was parked. 'And I'll be in touch about that apartment,' he called after them.

'Thank you, I appreciate it.'

'He's great,' Andie said after they drove away.

Dominic nodded. 'I thought you'd like him. He's been a good friend to me, the best.'

'I could see that.'

He glanced at her. 'I hope you didn't mind sharing the date with him?'

'No, of course not.'

Sharing the date with Elliot in fact had been a revelation. Dominic was the most relaxed she'd ever seen him, and she was certain she wouldn't have learned so much about his background if Elliot hadn't been there, goading him along and filling in the gaps. It was so different to the Christmas lunch where he couldn't, or wouldn't, answer a straight question. Now she knew a lot more about him, and she found herself wanting to know even more.

'Do you mind if I ask you a question?' she said as they joined the expressway that would take them to the bridge.

He glanced at her. 'Go ahead.'

'Do you have a problem with drinking?'

Now he turned his head fully to look at her.

Andie winced. 'Sorry, that sounded like I was asking if you're a problem drinker.'

'I don't have a problem with drinking,' he said with a sigh. 'Though I think this country might have a problem with drinking. It seems that if you're moderate you're immediately suspect.'

'I'm sorry, you're right. I shouldn't have brought it up.'

'It's okay,' he said kindly. 'I don't mind telling you that in my deep dark past I made some stupid mistakes that I'm lucky to have lived through. Nowadays I just don't like that feeling of being out of control, I suppose it brings back too many bad memories, those that I can remember, at least.'

'You have a deep dark past?' Andie raised an eyebrow.

He gave her a cryptic smile. 'Did I say that?'

*

When he pulled up outside her house, he jumped out of the car so quickly he was opening the door for her before Andie had picked up her handbag. She wondered if he was hoping to be invited inside, but he seemed too . . . reserved, or gentlemanly, or something, to be expecting to bed her at the first opportunity. Whatever Jess had to say about getting laid, it really would complicate things. He was still her boss. Andie decided she was going to have to say something.

He was standing holding the door now, offering her his hand. Andie took it as she stepped out of the car, but as soon as she was on her own two feet, he released her hand again.

'I had a really nice time tonight, Dominic,' she said.

'Me too.' He had that nervous look about him again. Maybe he was the kind of guy who wanted to jump into bed on the first date?

'So, I was wondering . . . well —'

'I would ask you in,' Andie said quickly, 'but it's my parents' house and —'

'No, no.' He looked almost shocked. 'I wasn't suggesting, I wouldn't suggest . . .'

'Okay,' said Andie.

'I was only wondering if you'd like to do this again,' he said. 'Go out, again . . . sometime.'

She hesitated. 'Oh.'

He was watching her. 'I see. I'm sorry, I thought it went well.'

'No, it did,' she assured him. 'I really did have a nice time.'

'But?' he prompted.

Just say it. 'You're my boss, Dominic. I still feel uncomfortable about this.'

He nodded. 'I don't want to make light of your feelings, Andie, but I just don't think it's an issue. You got the job through your own persistence and determination, and you've earned it on your own merits. Keeping it isn't reliant on you making nice with the boss.'

Andie was thinking. 'All right. But what if you decide, well, that you don't want to see me anymore, or I don't want to see you, or it just ends . . . for whatever reason. We work together, it'd be awkward.'

'Well, then you would have to leave.'

Her eyes widened, but he was smiling down at her.

'I'm kidding,' he said. 'Andie, do you think, before we worry about messy break-ups and things getting awkward at work, that perhaps we could go out on a second date?'

She gave him a coy smile.

'Are you usually given to such negative thought patterns?' he asked.

'I don't know, I've been told I have a tendency to overthink things.'

'Well, I'd like to assure you, right now, that I wouldn't let anything that happens between us away from work compromise your position at Viande.' He paused. 'Okay?'

She nodded. 'Okay.'

They stood there, facing each other. Andie sensed an air of expectation. What now? Was he going to kiss her? Probably. It was a first date, and they'd just decided on a second, it was customary . . .

'Would you like me to walk you to the door?' Dominic said, breaking the silence.

'It's okay, it's just there,' she said. 'I can find my way.'

His face dropped. 'All right then.'

Oh, blast, that was part of the etiquette, wasn't it? He had to walk her to the door to kiss her goodnight, and she'd more or less turned him down. Andie was so out of practice she had no idea. But she could hardly turn around now and say, yes, okay, walk me to the door.

'Well, I best get going then,' he said.

'Thank you, again,' said Andie. And then impulsively she took a step closer and reached up to kiss him. She had been aiming for his cheek but he turned his head slightly and their mouths met. It seemed to surprise them both and they hesitated, allowing their lips just to linger against each other, as his hand felt for hers. It was really a bare whisper of a kiss, but it still made Andie feel lightheaded. After a few moments, she drew back again, and he gave her hand a gentle squeeze before releasing it. 'Goodnight, Andie.'

'Goodnight.' She turned to walk up the path. When she got to the door she looked back, and he was standing in the same spot, watching her. Andie raised her hand in a wave, he waved back, and she opened the door. He still hadn't moved when she closed the door behind her.

The next day

Andie was finishing a cup of coffee as she pottered around, getting ready to leave for work, when her phone rang. It would be Jess, no doubt, calling for a debrief. But when she looked at the screen, she didn't recognise the number.

'Hello?' she asked.

'Hi, Andie? It's Elliot.'

'Oh hello, Elliot, how are you?'

'Great. I wanted to call straightaway,' he said. 'I've just talked to Stan, the kid I was telling you about, with the apartment?'

'Yes?'

'Well, he jumped at it. He said you should give him a call to organise a time to go see the place. I've got his number.'

'Wow, that was quick.'

'Yeah, well, like I told you, he's desperate.'

'This is fantastic, Elliot,' said Andie. 'You don't know how much I've been dreading flat-hunting. I've heard nightmare stories about people lining up for inspections, bidding wars. I can't believe I won't have to go through any of that.'

'Hey, maybe you shouldn't count your chickens, you know, at least until you've seen the place,' he warned. 'I've never been there, but I told Stan that you're a class act, and it better not be a dump. He assured me it's in very good condition, and it's in a great location, only a couple of blocks back from the beach.'

'I'm so excited,' said Andie. 'I don't know how to thank you.'

'Aah, stop it, happy to help.' He paused. 'Though there is one thing.'

'Oh?'

'Promise me you'll give Dom a chance,' he said.

Her heart skipped a beat. 'I'm sorry?'

'Look, I don't know where things are between you two,' said Elliot, 'and I'm probably stepping way over the line, but I don't know if you realise what a huge deal it was that he brought you to meet me last night.'

'It was?'

'Dom doesn't date lightly . . . by that I mean he hardly dates at all. So it was such a relief to meet you, you seem so nice and normal,' he said.

'Thanks . . .' Andie said warily.

'Now I've freaked you out.'

'No . . .' Maybe a little.

'Shit, I shouldn't have said anything. Sal'll kill me if I've stuffed it up. She's worried about him.'

Andie didn't know what to say, or think. This was all a little perplexing.

'And now I've got you thinking there's something wrong with him.' Elliot sighed. 'There isn't, I promise you. It's only that he's been burned in the past, haven't we all?'

She could hardly argue with that.

'Dom is a great guy, Andie, the best. All I was really trying to say is give him a chance. He might take some time to crack, but it'll be worth it.'

A week later

'Well, hello there, stranger,' Jess said when Andie walked in through the back of the shop just after opening, the following Monday.

'I know, I deserve that. I'm sorry,' she said. 'Things have been crazy lately.'

Andie went to see the apartment the morning after Elliot phoned. It was perfect. Although it was only a studio, it was roomier than Andie had imagined, though that might have been an optical illusion created by the large picture window that dominated the main wall, and looked out over the surrounding buildings to the ocean beyond. It was clean and well-kept, with a relatively new bathroom and kitchenette. That's all you could really call the bank of cupboards that housed a sink, small oven and hotplates, with room for only a bar fridge under the bench. But that didn't bother her; she worked in a kitchen every day, this would do for home. There was something right about the place, Andie felt immediately comfortable. Stan was as keen as she was to get the ball rolling, he was virtually living at his girlfriend's already, so things went into overdrive. He notified the real estate agent, who, after a seeming mountain of paperwork, approved Andie to sublet the place until the lease was up, and then to have first dibs after that. Stan organised a mate with a ute to help him move the following weekend, and said Andie could start moving her stuff in as soon as she liked.

'I'm *sooo* glad you're here,' Jess said in a rush. 'We really need to go through some stuff . . . Oh, and while I think of it, that Spanish ham you asked me to order came in, and —'

'I've found an apartment,' Andie said. She wanted to get it out before they got distracted by business.

'Wow,' Jess exclaimed. 'Well, that's great, I didn't realise you'd even started looking.'

'I didn't have to, this one landed right in my lap, through a friend of a friend, of a friend, from work. It was too good to pass up. It's in Bondi, it's only a studio, but it's really roomy, and clean and modern. It even has ocean glimpses.'

Jess looked impressed. 'That does sound too good to pass up. Well done you. So when do you move in?'

'Next weekend.'

'I see what you mean about things being crazy.'

'Right? Actually, I could have moved in yesterday,' said Andie, 'but you know, I wanted to clean it myself. The guy left it in really good shape, but —'

'— it's not the same,' Jess agreed. 'Okay, so when do I get to see it?'

'Well, if you didn't have to run the shop today, you could have come and helped me clean,' Andie said. 'As it is, you'll have to wait till Saturday when I move, I'll be at work all week.'

'Oh bugger, I'm going away this weekend,' said Jess. 'I promised to help my friends – remember Rod and Alison? They have that restaurant in the Blue Mountains, and they've got a wedding Saturday.'

'Don't worry about it,' said Andie. 'Toby's going to give me a hand, and I'm taking the whole weekend off work, so along with my regular day off Monday, I'll have three straight days to move and settle in.'

'That's great,' Jess said. 'So apart from missing my face, what brings you here today?'

Andie smiled. 'I've been a terrible slacker, I really need to get up to speed around here, catch up on some paperwork.'

'You don't have to worry, I'm keeping up with everything,' Jess assured her.

'I know, you're a marvel, but it's not fair to leave it all up to you,' she said. 'Besides, I also need to use the computer. I have a flat to furnish – I figure it might be quicker to do it online and have it delivered.'

'You're really not going to take anything from your apartment?'

'Ross's apartment,' Andie corrected her. Jess went to protest but Andie spoke over the top of her. 'The property settlement has been finalised, it's going through the court – he can't touch the shop or my inheritance, and I can't touch anything of his. Okay?'

In the midst of everything, papers had arrived by registered mail detailing the property settlement. The conditions had been accepted by Ross and his lawyers, and once Andie signed the papers, a consent order would be granted by the court, which carried the full weight of the law. Fortunately there was no need for either of them to attend the court in person.

'So when do we celebrate?' said Jess.

'I don't know that it's something to celebrate,' Andie said. 'Maybe when I'm all moved in we can crack open a bottle and celebrate my independence?'

'Absolutely.' Jess leaned back against the bench, folding her arms. 'How long do you think you'll be at the new place today? I could pop round after I close up here.'

Andie hesitated. Dominic was meeting her there later, they were going out to get a bite to eat if she felt up to it.

Jess was watching her. 'Why are you blushing?'

'I'm not blushing.'

'Are too.'

The bell above the door sounded out in the shop. 'You have a customer,' said Andie.

'Literally saved by the bell,' Jess said wryly. 'We'll pick this up again in a minute,' she added over her shoulder as she walked through to the shop.

Andie sighed as she sat down in front of the computer. Jess wouldn't let it go regardless, but it would be good to talk to her. They'd had a quick debrief about her date with Dominic last week, but Andie hadn't told her much, because there wasn't all that much to tell. She mainly talked about meeting Elliot, and the amazing meal . . . though she had admitted she'd agreed to a second date.

She hadn't told Jess about the cryptic phone call with Elliot because she didn't really know what to make of it herself. So, there was baggage, even skeletons, in Dominic's closet; Andie was hardly in a position to be touchy about that, she didn't have the room in her closet for all the skeletons and baggage from her past. But that was only part of what was bothering her.

Her lawyer had mentioned that it was customary to process the divorce and property settlement together, however, you had to wait twelve months after the date of separation to file for divorce. Andie couldn't help feeling guilty, or at least uneasy, that she wasn't yet entitled to a divorce under the law and here she was gallivanting around with another man. Not that there had been much gallivanting to speak of. Although she saw Dominic every day at work, they were naturally being discreet. He'd walked her to her car a couple of nights, when they were both leaving at the same time and no one was around. However, there had definitely been no kissing – that would hardly be discreet in the staff carpark. But as the memory of that one kiss faded, Andie's doubts and misgivings had rushed in, and she was driving herself dotty.

She was scrolling idly through the Ikea catalogue online when Jess returned to the back room.

'Okay, out with it,' she said. 'Does the blush have anything to do with a certain chef?'

Andie sighed, swivelling in the chair to face Jess. 'He's meeting me at the apartment later on.'

'So, things are moving along?'

'I guess.' Andie hesitated. 'But I've been thinking . . .'

Jess sighed heavily and pulled a stool over to sit. 'You do way too much of that, you know.'

'That may be true, but just hear me out.'

'I'm all ears.'

Andie sat forward. 'Look, all right, I admit I like him. It's not him, it's me.'

'This'll be good,' Jess said, leaning her chin in her hand.

'The thing is, I'm beginning to see a pattern,' Andie began. 'Think about it – I started going out with Ross after I lost my brother and then my mother. I overlooked the very glaring fact that he was married —'

'Is the chef married?' Jess blurted.

Andie blinked. 'What? No! God, Jess, do you really think I'd be that stupid again?'

She looked relieved. 'Well, what has Ross being married before got to do with you and the chef?'

'I'm getting to that,' said Andie. 'I ignored the reasons I shouldn't have been with Ross because I needed him, he filled a gap, I suppose. And I'm worried I'm doing the same thing all over again. I lost my husband and my father within days of each other, I've even lost the chance to have a family of my own. And so now I'm overlooking the fact that Dominic is my boss, and all the issues that come with dating him . . . and, well, I can't help thinking, am I really so afraid to face my own demons, deal with my grief . . . be on my own?'

Jess was frowning. 'Wow, psychoanalysing yourself there much, Andie?'

She sighed. 'I just wonder if it mightn't have been better to have some time alone before I started a new relationship?'

'Well, yes . . . no . . . maybe . . . God, I don't know,' said Jess. 'If we could plot out our lives to follow a nice, smooth path maybe that would be the right way to do it . . . But —'

The bell above the door sounded again.

'Now you've been saved by the bell,' said Andie.

'No,' Jess insisted. 'It just gives me thinking time. I'll be right back.'

Andie sat staring at the screen, she couldn't even be bothered scrolling. She stared so long at a sofa called 'GLØNK' the word started to look weird. Wait, the word was weird. She heard the bell sound again. She sincerely hoped that was the customer leaving, not another one coming in. Which was not a great attitude for the owner of the business to have.

Jess appeared in the doorway again. 'Okay, here's what I think.'

Andie looked at her expectantly.

'It's not some psycho pattern to need, or want, to attach to someone after losing significant people in your life. I think it's actually pretty normal, certainly understandable, and probably healthy.'

'I don't know,' Andie muttered.

'Listen,' said Jess, sitting down in front of her again, 'weren't you always worried about your dad being on his own? Wouldn't it have been better if he'd found someone to share his life with, even just a casual companion?'

That was a very good point. One she couldn't really argue with.

'The timing wasn't the problem with Ross,' Jess went on, 'the problem was you lost yourself and became Mrs Ross Corcoran. You totally relinquished control of your life to him, until I could hardly recognise you anymore.'

Andie was thinking about it. 'But isn't that all the more reason I should be on my own for a while? So I can get my act together?'

'Being on your own is overrated,' Jess said drily. 'Besides, your act isn't so bad, Andie. Why don't you try it out on the chef? Just be yourself. Own your own life, don't give it away, and don't let him take it over.'

'He wouldn't do that. He's not like Ross.'

'Glad to hear it.'

'You know, I thought he was so arrogant at first, but I think that's just awkwardness, even a bit of shyness. He's actually quite sweet . . . Not that I really know him all that well.'

'Isn't that what dating's for?' said Jess. 'To get to know each other?'

'Yeah . . .'

'In fact, isn't that what he said about you – that he wanted to get to know you better?'

Andie nodded thoughtfully.

'So let him.'

*

Andie had spent the rest of the morning picking out furniture for the apartment, with Jess popping in and out between customers to throw in her two cents' worth. Andie welcomed her input; she'd never done anything like this before, it felt impulsive and a little indulgent . . . no, a lot indulgent. But Jess kept reminding her that the place was hers and hers alone, she was the only one who had to like what she put in it because she was the only one who had to live with it. So, if she wanted a purple couch, she should have a purple couch. She didn't, but it was incredibly liberating to have the choice. It was also time-consuming – she had intended to catch up on paperwork, but Jess assured her again that everything was up to date, and when Andie did a quick scan through the orders, wages and accounts, she could see that it was.

'I should be paying you more,' she said as she got ready to leave.

'One day I'll call in the favour,' said Jess.

'Oh, what did you want to talk to me about?' Andie asked, remembering. 'You mentioned it when I first arrived.'

But Jess waved it off. 'It'll keep. You won't have any time to clean the apartment before the Love Chef gets there.'

Andie pulled a face. 'That's not going to become a thing, is it?'

*

As it turned out, there was plenty of time. Andie cleaned every square inch of the place, carpets and tiles and woodwork, inside and out of every cupboard, she even washed all the windows and polished the mirrors, but the place was so small it only took her a couple of hours. She finally had a nice long, cooling shower in her shiny clean bathroom, dressed in the change of clothes she'd brought with her, dabbed on a little makeup, and it was barely five o'clock. Dominic had said to give him a call when she was done, but would she seem too eager?

Bugger it. In for a penny . . .

'It's . . . compact,' Dominic remarked when he arrived, looking around.

Andie smiled. 'It is, but it's all I need,' she said. 'And look at this view.'

'That is quite a view,' he agreed, stopping in front of the window. 'But how are you going to fit all your stuff in here?'

'All what stuff?'

'Well, you sold up the family home, didn't you say?'

'Yeah, but I'm not bringing anything from there. We gave most of the contents to charity, anyway.'

The kitchen setting was going into storage along with Brendan's things. Andie had thought about bringing it to the apartment, considering her weirdly sentimental attachment to it, but it was too big for the space. So she really only had her own personal items and clothing, which all fitted into her huge wheelie case and an overnight bag. The remaining bits and pieces she would take from the house – some linen, things from the kitchen, the albums – would be lucky to fill a few boxes, so Andie would simply bring it all over in her car on Saturday.

'It's pretty impressive that you can fit all your worldly possessions into the back of a car,' Dominic said when she explained the situation.

Andie frowned. 'Why is that impressive?'

'Maybe I used the wrong term,' he said. 'I just mean that most of us are weighed down by all the stuff we own. It must be nice for your life to be so . . . portable.'

'Well, it's not anymore. I just weighed myself down all over again buying furniture online. But what can I do? I need a bed and something to sit on, at least.'

'Of course.' He was gazing down at her with an odd look on his face. 'I hope you don't mind me asking . . . but is everything okay, Andie, are you okay?'

She felt a little uncomfortable. 'Sure, what are you getting at?'

'Look, it's none of my business . . .' He took a breath. 'But I know your husband was well-off, and now . . . Well, when you told me you needed the job, I didn't realise things were quite so bad.'

Andie glanced around the apartment. This tiny empty space said nothing about her. How could it? It was the proverbial blank slate. She'd felt as though she didn't know much about Dominic, but it occurred to Andie that Dominic knew very little about her. As Jess had suggested, it was time to let him get to know her.

'There's something I'd like to show you,' said Andie.

*

A short while later they pulled up outside The Corner Gourmet. Dominic looked at her expectantly. 'What are we doing here?'

'You'll see.'

He stood behind her as Andie unlocked the front door.

'You have a key to the place?' he said.

She smiled, standing aside for him to pass. He gave her a curious frown as he stepped inside. She followed him in and closed the door again.

'Am I supposed to guess?' he said, turning to look at her.

Andie smiled. 'This belongs to me.'

'You own this shop?' he said, surprised.

'Lock, stock.' She nodded. 'So, hungry?'

Andie proceeded to make up an antipasto platter while she filled Dominic in on the history of the place. Or at least her history with the place.

'So that's how I ended up running a shop instead of being a chef,' she said finally, setting the platter down on the table in the back room and offering him a seat.

'This looks superb,' he said, pulling out a chair while Andie fetched them plates and forks and napkins.

'Try the olives,' she said over her shoulder. 'We have this supplier in the Southern Highlands, the lemon and garlic are my favourite.'

'They are good,' he agreed, after tasting a couple.

She sat down opposite him. 'And this La Luna cheese is to die for,' she said, picking up the knife to slice him a piece. 'Oh, I better get you something to drink.'

'Andie —'

But she was already up. She grabbed some Italian mineral water out of the fridge and a couple of glasses and rejoined him at the table.

'Are you going to stop now?' Dominic said.

She smiled. She did feel a little flushed, she supposed she was trying to impress him.

'The cheese is very good,' he said to her. 'It's goat's cheese, right?'

She nodded. 'One of the few made in Australia in the soft-curd style.'

'Where does it come from?'

'Tasmania,' she said. 'It's quite a small family operation. They're not very well known on the mainland.'

'You'll have to give me their details.'

Andie imagined telling the supplier that the executive chef from Viande in Sydney was interested in their cheese.

'You mustn't get a chance to spend much time here now,' said Dominic. 'Not with your hours at the restaurant.'

'My best friend Jess is virtually running the place,' Andie explained. 'It's in very good hands.'

'And you don't miss it?' he persisted.

She shook her head as she bit into a stuffed bell pepper.

'Not even the hours?' said Dominic. 'There's something to be said for working nine to five.'

Andie shrugged. 'But then I couldn't cook.'

'It means that much to you?'

She nodded.

'Then why did you give it up in the first place?'

'Like I told you earlier, my husband didn't like the hours.'

'He sounds . . . controlling.'

'I suppose he was, but it didn't seem that way to me at the time,' she said. 'I mean, it's not as though he ever used force, or temper, he did it all with charm. I always thought he wanted me to be happy, I didn't realise that was only if it suited him. I was naive, I guess.'

'You were a lot younger,' said Dominic. 'Do you mind me asking . . . when you first came to the restaurant, wasn't it your husband who organised the trial for you? What made him change his mind?'

'He was suddenly very keen for me to be occupied at night.'

Dominic frowned. 'Oh, that's right, he had an affair, you said. I'm sorry.'

Andie looked at him. 'You remember my first night at the restaurant, when I ran out of the place like a teenage girl?'

'Oh, vaguely,' he said, but she could see the smile in his eyes.

'Well, Ross didn't expect me home so soon, obviously,' said Andie, 'and I walked in on him with the woman.'

Dominic looked confused. 'Wait a minute, you mean they were in your house?'

'Apartment, actually. But yes.'

'Bloody hell,' he exclaimed. 'That's . . . well, I mean . . . fuck.'

'Hm, I believe that's what they were doing at the time.'

Andie smiled at Dominic, and his face relaxed into a smile as well. And suddenly they were both laughing.

'At least you can laugh about it now,' he said. 'That shows resilience.'

Andie shrugged. 'What do they say, if you don't laugh you'll cry. But really, I was so naive, and too ready to believe anything Ross told me. I needed the shock of seeing it with my own eyes.' She didn't have to mention right now that she'd actually needed an aftershock as well to finally be convinced.

'So it's over now, between you and your husband?'

Andie nodded. 'We can't actually get a divorce until twelve months have passed, it's only been about six or seven. But the property settlement has gone through the court, and I elected not to take anything of his, which is why my life looks so "portable". But he can't touch this place, or my inheritance from my father.'

'Oh, of course, your father died in the middle of all that as well.' Dominic shook his head. 'I take it you have no other family, because you sold the house?'

'I have a sister,' said Andie. 'We're not very close, unfortunately. I was close to my brother, but he died young, and then my mother died a year later.'

Dominic looked astounded. 'My God, it's a wonder you're still standing.'

'It was a long time ago.' She shrugged, sliding an olive into her mouth.

He was watching her. 'Seriously, Andie, the way you've managed to carry on with your life, well, it's quite . . . inspirational.'

She gave a little cough to clear her throat as she transferred the olive pip onto a napkin. 'I think that might be overstating it.'

'Cosmo mentioned to me that he thinks you're ready to move up.'

Andie looked up suddenly. 'I don't think that's such a good idea.'

'Why not?'

'Why do you think?'

'It has nothing to do with you and me,' he said firmly.

'Yet that's the first thing that came into your head,' she pointed out.

He sighed. 'Andie, I can understand why you want to avoid the appearance of favouritism, but I won't allow you to end up worse off because you're seeing me. I'm going to instruct Cosmo and Tang to go ahead and move you up as soon as they see fit.'

Andie went to protest but he kept talking.

'By the time everyone knows about us you'll be established in your own right, just as you deserve. Seriously, Andie, after everything you've been through, I'd like to be one thing in your life that isn't negative.'

She was just staring at him. Her throat had gone dry.

Dominic dropped his head, rubbing his eyes with his hand. 'Oh God . . . I didn't mean to assume . . .' He looked up at her again. 'I'm sorry, Andie. I was making the assumption that we – you and I – will continue to see each other . . . socially, that is . . . which is an assumption I have no right to make.'

His accent became more pronounced when he was flustered, his language more formal, Andie found it quite endearing. She had to put him out of his misery. She reached across the table and squeezed his hand, smiling at him. 'I think it's a pretty reasonable assumption . . . at least for the foreseeable future.'

He met her gaze then, smiling faintly as he squeezed her hand in return. Andie was suddenly distracted by the curve of his mouth, imagining what it would be like to kiss him, really kiss him, to have him hold her close in his arms . . . It occurred to her that she might not have to wait long to find out. She'd just agreed that they'd keep seeing each other, and that was bound to involve some kissing. And probably more . . . Her heart started to race.

'Andie?' Dominic prompted. 'What do you think?'

She stirred. 'Hm?'

'I was just saying, this was a perfect appetiser,' he said, glancing at the almost empty platter. 'Shall we move on to mains somewhere else?'

'Yes, sure. Of course.' Andie wasn't as sure she could eat, but she didn't want the night to end now. She reached for the platter, but Dominic picked it up first.

'I'll get it.' He stood up and crossed to the sink to rinse off the platter. Andie was still a little mesmerised, watching him. She had to snap out of it.

She flicked off the lights as they walked out to the front of the shop. The streetlights shone through the glass door as she fumbled with the keys. She couldn't stop thinking about the very real fact that there would be kissing later on, and wondering how she was going to get through dinner staring slack-jawed at his lips the whole time. She could feel him standing behind her, quite close, she would only have to turn around . . . Her heart was thumping now.

'Are you having trouble with the lock?' Dominic asked, over her shoulder.

'No . . .' He said he was attracted to her because she kept surprising him, didn't he? Andie turned around. 'It's not the lock. I just . . . well, I just want to get this out of the way.'

She reached up and hooked her arm around his neck as she planted her lips directly onto his. He wasn't expecting it, of course, and he kind of froze on contact, but it only took him a moment to thaw, then she felt his arms slide around her, drawing her in close to him . . . Oh, this was very nice . . . his mouth, the taste of him, his tongue, now tentatively working around her lips, her tongue. It was a very long kiss, perhaps more correctly a series of kisses; their lips did break and reconnect every so often, if only for a second. Andie was becoming faintly, agreeably aroused, but they were standing in the door of the shop, for goodness sake. This couldn't go anywhere . . . not right now anyway. It was an appetiser, like the platter they'd just eaten . . . just enough to take the edge off the hunger.

Andie drew back reluctantly, and Dominic smiled down at her, glassy-eyed.

'I guess we should go.' She turned again to unlock the door. The bell sounded as they stepped out into the street, and he took her hand in his.

Bondi

'So what do you think?' Andie said, holding her arms out wide.

Donna and Toby stood just inside the doorway gazing around the apartment. Toby's face broke into a broad smile.

'It's awesome, Andie,' he said, as he walked past her over to the window. 'Look at that view!'

Donna was wandering around with a frown on her face. 'Where's the bedroom?'

'You're standing in it.'

'But isn't this the living room?'

'And the bedroom, and the dining room.'

Donna looked confused.

'I told you it was a studio, love,' Toby said. 'That's a one-room apartment.'

'I thought it was a one-*bedroom* apartment,' she said. 'Are you sure you're going to be all right here, Andie? I mean, how will you get any privacy?'

'Who does she need privacy from, herself?' said Toby.

Andie was smiling. 'He's right, Donna, it's just me here. It's like my own little cosy cocoon. I can do whatever I like, I can have things just the way I want, I don't have to run it by anyone, or compromise about anything. It feels so indulgent.'

'That does sound pretty wonderful,' Donna said dreamily.

'Hey, stop giving her ideas,' said Toby.

There was a knock behind them, and Andie turned around to see a man in the doorway, wearing a fluoro safety vest and holding a clipboard; if he wasn't a delivery man he was doing a damn fine impression of one. She'd been told her furniture would arrive any time after eight this morning so she'd been here since before that, and it was now going on eleven. So she certainly hoped he was the real thing.

'Is there a Ms Lonergan here?' he asked.

'That's me. Are you from Ikea?'

'Yes, ma'am,' he said. 'If you'll just give me your autograph, then we'll start bringing your goods up.'

'I better get out while I still can,' said Donna, ducking past them. 'I'll see you in a few hours. Have fun.'

She had to get back to Max, but Toby was staying to give Andie a hand assembling the furniture. Everything except the sofa was in flat packs, and Andie had thought she'd be able to manage it on her own. The website certainly made it look as though all you needed was an allen key and a free afternoon. But when she mentioned that in front of Toby, he'd insisted on coming over to help.

'DIY is a crock,' he said. 'One free afternoon and all you'll have to show for it is a bookcase on a lean. Leave it to the professionals.'

*

Several hours and many more swearwords later, they had managed to put together the bed, the bookcase, one of the side tables, a small drop-sided dining table, and two of the four chairs Andie had bought.

'Oh my God,' Andie sighed. 'You were right, Toby, I would never have been able to do this without you.'

'Don't worry about it,' he said. 'Someone should write an exposé about the myth of the allen key.'

Andie laughed lazily. They were sitting on the floor, their backs against the wall, having a beer each, after breaking into the case Andie had bought for Toby and chilling a six-pack in the tiny bar fridge that Stan had left for her, for a very fair price.

'I'm going to have to buy you another case of beer,' Andie said. 'What am I saying, I owe you a truckload of beer after all you've done today.'

'Stop it,' said Toby. 'You don't owe me anything. We're family.' She smiled at him.

'Brendan'd be proud of you, you know,' he said.

'What, for getting my own place, finally?'

'No, for being brave.'

'Because I left Ross?'

Toby nodded, taking a swig of his beer.

'Brendan would never have been happy that I was with him in the first place,' said Andie.

'Exactly. So imagine how happy he'd be that you left him?'

'Hm,' she mused. 'Do you miss him?'

'Every day.'

'You two were so close, just like brothers.'

'I've never had a mate like him, before or since,' said Toby. 'It'd feel kind of weird, like I was cheating on him or something.'

There was a pause as they both took another drink.

'That sounded kind of gay, didn't it?'

Andie laughed, elbowing him. 'No, I know what you mean, how can you replace Brendan? He's the only brother I'll ever have,' she said.

'Except for me.'

'Except for you.' It was true, Toby was the closest thing she had to a brother, to a sibling even. Meredith had called during the week, and had even suggested popping over before Andie left the house to say goodbye. Andie had considered reminding her that she wasn't moving to another country, but she let it go. They had settled back into a polite rapport, no doubt helped by the fact that the house had fetched a very good price – well above the reserve set for the auction – and that Andie had done all the work to get it there. They were never going to have a sisterly relationship, they never had, so how were they supposed to start now? Meredith had her own family, she didn't need Andie. And that was okay, because Andie had people like Toby in her life.

She looked at him now. If Brendan were here, she'd have told him about Dominic by now. Things were right on the verge, teetering on the precipice . . . They hadn't had any time alone since Monday night, and they hadn't gone beyond kissing. After dinner Dominic had offered to drive her home to Roseville, until she reminded him that she'd driven herself to the apartment earlier in the day. When he dropped her back to her car, they'd made out like a pair of teenagers, steaming up the windows and leaving them both breathless and wanting. The tension between them was electric. Andie had to admit there was something quite exquisite about it, though she certainly didn't want to draw it out any longer than was absolutely necessary. He'd phoned her this morning to wish her well for the move, and suggested that if she was all settled in by Monday, they should get together. Settled or not, they were getting together, Andie was going to make sure of that.

So before things went any further, she wanted Toby to at least be aware of Dominic's existence.

'There's something I want to tell you, Toby,' she said.

He turned side on to face her. 'Should I be worried?'

'No, no,' she reassured him. 'It's nothing bad. It's only . . . well, I'm kind of seeing someone.'

His face broke into a smile. 'Good for you.'

'You think?'

'Why wouldn't I?' he said. 'Unless . . . he's not married, is he?'

'No!'

'Then it's all good.'

She glanced at him. 'You don't think it's too soon?'

'Nope.'

'You seem very definite about that.'

'Look, Ross was already at it while you were still together,' he said flatly. 'If he gets to be with someone, why shouldn't you? I don't like thinking of you on your own.'

'I'm fine, Toby,' she insisted. 'It's not an entirely bad thing to spend some time alone, have a little breather.'

'So you've had your little breather,' he said. 'Who's the lucky guy?'

Andie smiled. 'It's not serious or anything . . . it's not even anything yet.'

'It's something, or you wouldn't be telling me,' said Toby. 'It's okay, Andie, come on, give it up. Who is he, where'd you meet him?'

'At work,' she said. 'See that's the other thing . . . he's my boss. I don't know if it's appropriate.'

He shrugged. 'How old is he?'

'Oh, I don't know, it's often hard to tell with guys. But I'd say he's not much older than me.'

'Then I don't see the problem.'

Andie frowned. 'What's his age got to do with it?'

'Well, it's not like he's some old guy taking advantage of a young trainee.'

'Hm, Jess said something like that.'

'So now you've got a second opinion.' Toby took a swig of his beer. 'I suppose it comes down to whether you feel intimidated or uncomfortable, or under any kind of pressure to go out with him?'

'No, not anymore. Maybe a little at first,' she admitted, 'because I wasn't sure of him, and in a way I didn't feel like I could turn him down. But it's different now.'

Toby nudged her. 'So, what's he like?'

Andie thought about it. 'Well, when I first met him I thought he was arrogant, and opinionated, and then he seemed pretty awkward socially . . .'

'You're not doing a great sell there, Andie.'

She laughed at herself. 'Now that I've got to know him better, I realise it was never arrogance, more that he's a little shy, or maybe reserved . . . but I don't even know if that's how I'd describe him.' Composed might be a better word than reserved. There was something very solid about Dominic, Andie decided, he had a quiet dignity that she found very appealing. 'He's just different to Ross, he's not brash and egocentric.' She looked at Toby. 'I think you'll like him.'

'If you do, I will.'

Andie raised an eyebrow. 'That didn't actually work with Ross, did it?'

'Ah, but you said he was different to Ross,' he reminded her. 'Speaking of the devil, does he know you're seeing someone?'

She shook her head. 'I haven't had anything to do with him for a while now. It's all been handled by the lawyers.'

'Good, as long as you're getting your fair share,' said Toby.

'I am,' she said. 'Jess reckons I should have gone for more, but I want to be free of him. And I don't want any hassle.'

'Fair enough,' he said. 'But are you going to be all right, you know, financially?'

'Absolutely,' she assured him. 'The shop is mine, free and clear. And he can't touch my inheritance from Dad.'

'He wouldn't bloody want to,' Toby declared.

'But he could have, if I'd gone after more,' she said. 'It's better this way, trust me.'

'I trust you, I just wouldn't trust Ross as far as I could throw him.' He paused, taking a slurp of his beer. 'The shop'll give you security. In fact I reckon it could really take off with some of the things Jess has planned.'

Andie gave him a vacant look.

'What?' Toby frowned. 'She said she'd spoken to you, that you gave her the go-ahead. I've been there and measured it up for a quote – seriously, she hasn't talked about it with you yet?'

Damn, Andie had cut her off the other day. She'd have to find time to go and see her, show some interest. 'No, she absolutely talked about it, I've just been caught up with the move.'

There was a knock at the door before it suddenly flew open and Max charged in, carrying a big yellow bucket and spade. He stopped short when he spotted Andie and gasped, struggling to manoeuvre the bucket around behind his back. Donna closed the door and plonked some bags on the kitchen bench. 'Hey, things are looking good in here, you guys,' she remarked. 'Max, show Aunty Andie what you've got there.'

'Arnee Andie,' Max said proudly, 'I haves a present for your new house.'

'Aww, Maxy,' she cried. 'That's so nice of you.'

He nodded, standing there, still holding the bucket awkwardly behind him.

'Are you going to show me?' Andie prompted.

He took a step towards her and brought the bucket around in front, presenting it to her. 'It's for the beach, because that's where you lives now.'

'It's perfect, Max!' she said.

'Do you haves one orready?' he asked.
'No, I don't. And you know what else I don't have?'
He shook his head.
'A hug.'
He smiled shyly and then fell forward into her arms.
'I brought food,' Donna announced.
'You little beauty,' said Toby, getting up from the floor. 'I could eat a horse and chase its rider.'
'Well, you won't have to. I think I may have brought enough to feed a horse, actually.'

Sunday

Andie lay in her bed, staring out the window to the arc of blue sea visible beyond the rooftops. She had been woken at some ungodly hour by the sun as it rose up out of the ocean, above the rooftops, to shine right onto her face. She would have to close the blinds in future if she had any hope of sleeping in, but she couldn't bring herself to close them last night when she'd finally fallen into bed, exhausted. She wanted to gaze out at the sky and listen to the faint roll of the waves, just audible above the hubbub of the surrounding bars and restaurants, doors slamming and cars coming and going, voices in the street, loud, laughing, sometimes even singing – it was a Saturday night, after all, and this was Bondi. It was a lot noisier than Roseville, but Andie didn't mind. She felt a deep sense of contentment, of being home, that she hadn't felt in a very long time. And although she'd woken at daybreak, she had drifted easily back to sleep – after burying her head under a pillow to block out the light.

She rolled over and looked around the apartment. She loved that she could see it all from this vantage point – well, all but the bathroom. It was little more than a cubicle comprising a sink, shower and toilet, but it was clean and functional and it was all she needed. A bath might have been nice, but Andie was not going to dwell on what she didn't have. What she did have was a place of her own, finally. She supposed the apartment she shared with Ross should have felt like hers, but it never really had. Ross had always had very strong opinions about what went in it, and Andie had never quibbled, he was paying for it all, what right did she have to impose her taste on him? But sometimes it felt like she was staying with Ross in his apartment . . . That had never really occurred to her until now, gazing around at this space that was totally hers. She felt like queen of her very own, very small castle.

Toby had insisted on finishing the rest of the furniture last night, and fortunately they didn't run into any more allen key glitches. Two more dining chairs, a coffee table, and the second bedside table had all been assembled with a minimum of fuss and not one swearword, probably because Max was within earshot. The dear little boy had eventually fallen fast asleep on Andie's new bed, giving Toby time to take all the cardboard packaging down to his ute to dispose of later.

'You've done enough,' Andie had tried to protest.

'Job's not finished till the cleaning up's done,' was all he said in response.

They finally left, a sleeping Max slung over his father's shoulder as they whispered their goodbyes, and then made their way down the stairs to the street. Although she was bone-tired, her brain was too revved up, and Andie couldn't think about sleeping. She unpacked her clothes into the built-in wardrobe, arranged her things in the bathroom, and put away the few kitchen items she'd brought with her. Along the way she found a couple of Stan's things, a jumper stuck right up the back of the top shelf in the wardrobe, and a plastic container in the kitchen cupboard. She could drop them off to him tomorrow; she would have to go shopping for more crockery and glasses and cutlery, food of course, and she might just check out some of the funky little homewares shops in the area, buy some scatter cushions, storage baskets . . . whatever took her fancy, really. It was going to be fun.

Finally, when there really was nothing left to do, Andie had collapsed into bed and slept like a dead person.

Her phone started ringing now, and she shimmied over to pick it up from the bedside table where it sat beside two framed photos, the one of her and Brendan, and the one of Ross's children. Andie smiled when she looked at the screen of her phone. It was Dominic.

'Good morning,' she said.

'Good morning to you,' he replied. 'I was just about to leave for work, thought I'd call to see how the big move went.'

'It went great, thanks,' she said. 'Toby was amazing, he put together every stick of furniture and even took away all the packaging. The place looks almost normal.'

'Great, so maybe you can make it into work after all?'

'Oh . . .' Andie hesitated. 'I do have a few more things to organise . . .'

'I was joking,' he assured her. 'So do you think you'll be ready for a break tomorrow?'

'Why, what did you have in mind?'

'I wanted to ask you over for dinner.'

Her heart skipped a beat. 'Over where?'

'Over to my house.'

'Oh.' His house . . . the two of them alone . . . He wasn't mucking around.

'I thought you might enjoy having dinner cooked for you after all your hard work,' he said.

'But you have to cook all day every day,' said Andie. 'You don't want to do it on your day off.'

'I haven't cooked for you. And I'd like to have you over . . . here.'

Hm. 'Then I'd like to come.'

'Good,' he said. 'Is six too early? We both have to work the next day.'

'Six should be fine,' she said. 'I just have to call in to the shop after closing, so I might be a little later.'

'No rush, I'll see you when you get here.'

'And exactly where is here?'

'Pardon?'

'I need your address.'

*

Andie got on with her day, and her shopping spree. She had fun for a while, but she flagged after a couple of hours. She found shopping malls overwhelming – the artificial lighting, the piped music, the crowds. She had planned to do more, but she'd bought all the essentials on her list. Most importantly, she had a new kettle, and she really just wanted to go home and make herself a cup of tea.

When she got back to the car, she saw the plastic bag on the front seat and remembered she needed to go by Elliot's and return Stan's things. She might as well get it out of the way, as she'd be driving right past. She parked the car around the corner and walked back to the restaurant. She thought about knocking at the side entrance, but that might be a little presumptuous, so she went around to the front like a regular patron, and pushed open the main door. The place appeared to be pretty full, she hoped this wasn't a bad time. She was fishing in her bag for her phone to check the time when Stan walked up to her, dressed in his waiter's garb.

'Hello, Andie.'

'Hi, Stan,' she said.

'Is there a problem with the apartment?' he asked, looking worried.

'No, no, it's great,' she assured him. 'I'm all moved in, it feels like home already.'

'That's a relief.' He smiled. 'So, what can I do for you?'

'Oh, you left some stuff behind,' she said, passing him the plastic bag.

Stan shook his head, peering into the bag. 'Sorry, I was in such a hurry. It was good of you to come and drop it off specially.'

'I was passing,' Andie dismissed.

'Well, you better come say hi to the boss while you're here.'

'Oh, no, I don't want to interrupt, it's obviously busy.'

'Service is finished for the day,' said Stan. 'And he'll have my hide if he finds out you were here and I didn't bring you back to say hello.'

She followed Stan out to the kitchen where Elliot was sitting back on a chair with his hands clasped behind his head and his feet propped on the edge of a bench – service was clearly over – obviously sharing a joke with the rest of the kitchen staff. He jumped up as soon as he saw her.

'Hello, Andie,' he said warmly, coming over to give her a kiss on the cheek like they were old friends. 'This is a nice surprise, what brings you here?'

'I had to return some of Stan's things,' she said.

'Are you hungry? We could rustle up something —'

But she was already holding up her hand to stop him. 'No, no, I'm fine, I've eaten,' she assured him.

'Hey guys,' he said to the rest of the crew, 'this is Andie. She's my best friend's girl, as the song goes.'

They responded with a haphazard chorus of 'Hey Andie'.

She smiled. 'Hi everyone.'

'Coffee?' he said. 'I was just about to make myself one.'

'Oh, I don't want to interrupt.'

'You'll give me an excuse to get out of cleaning.' He winked at her. 'All right, you lot,' he said loudly, 'enough slacking off and get on with it. Andie and I are retiring to the courtyard.'

There were some good-natured groans as the staff dispersed to their work stations. When Elliot had made the coffee he showed her out to the tiny courtyard. There was just enough room for a small wrought-iron table and two chairs, tucked inside the U formed by three high brick walls, lined top to bottom with shelves of potted herbs.

'This is great,' said Andie.

'Yep, the only way to ensure really fresh herbs is to grow them on-site. And,' said Elliot, indicating for her to sit, 'it's a nice little oasis from the heat of the kitchen.'

'I imagine it is.'

'How come you're not at work today?' he asked.

'I had the weekend off to move into the apartment.'

'Of course.' He nodded. 'How'd it go?'

'Great, I love it,' she said. 'I've just been shopping for supplies – nesting, you know.'

He smiled. 'So how's my man Dom?'

'He's fine, I think,' she said. 'He sounded fine on the phone this morning.'

Elliot nodded. 'So you're hanging in there, I didn't put you off altogether?'

Andie smiled. 'No, you didn't put me off.'

'Good, Sal will be relieved. She's dying to meet you,' he said. 'You know, I've been thinking about it ever since. Dom must be pretty serious about you, bringing you to meet me, because he knows what I'm like, he knows I'll push him to keep seeing you. It was like he wanted a witness so that he'd go through with it.'

Go through with it? Was it that hard for him?

'I'm doing it again, aren't I?' Elliot said, watching her.

Andie shrugged. 'I'm just beginning to wonder about his deep dark past.'

'It's not that deep or dark,' he said. 'A marriage break-up is pretty normal these days.'

'He was married?'

Elliot looked at her. 'He hasn't mentioned it?'

She shook her head. 'Was this recent?'

'No, it was a long time ago, he was barely more than a kid,' he said. 'But are you saying it's never even come up that he was married?'

'Nope.'

Elliot was rubbing his jaw, frowning. 'I don't know how much I should say.'

'You don't have to say anything, really.' This felt a bit weird.

'Oh look, there isn't really anything much to say,' he assured her. 'He married young, in haste, and he's repented at leisure.'

'And he still hardly ever dates after all this time?' said Andie. 'Sounds like he never got over her.'

'Oh, no, he got over her all right,' said Elliot. 'She was just a bit . . . full-on. I think she scared him off relationships.'

Andie wondered exactly what 'full-on' meant. 'She must have scared him pretty bad if he's been single all this time.'

'If you want to know the truth, I think Dom's married to his work. He wouldn't be the only chef who is,' he added. 'But it's not good for him. All I can say is that you're the best thing that's happened to Dom in a very long time.'

Andie was at once flattered and a little overwhelmed.

'I should get going,' she said, standing up. 'I've still got so much to do at the flat.'

Elliot showed her out via the side exit. 'I hope we see you soon.'

'Me too.' She waved as she headed down the alley to the street.

Monday

Andie walked through the front door of the shop, setting the bell off and summoning Jess from the back.

'Hello!' she said, surprised. 'Two weeks in a row, this is a record.'

'I promise you now that I've moved you're going to see a lot more of me.'

'I'm seeing a whole lot more of you right now in that top,' Jess remarked.

Andie glanced down at herself. The top she was wearing was made of a filmy fabric that draped loosely over her, held up by a pair of gossamer-fine straps, so she couldn't really wear a bra. She supposed it was pretty revealing. 'Oh, is it too much?'

'No, it's definitely not too *much*,' said Jess. 'Where are you off to, anyway?'

'I have to go out,' she said, 'and I was just trying to find something cool to wear, it's so hot out there.'

'Oh, you're going out?' Jess pulled a face. 'I was just about to give you a call actually. I was hoping I could come around and check out your new digs.'

'Sorry,' said Andie. 'You'll have to come soon though.'

'So why are you here?'

She walked around the counter. 'Toby told me you had him around to measure up —'

'You said it was all right.'

'I know I did, and it is.'

'I was going to tell you.'

'But you couldn't get a word in, right?' said Andie with a sigh. 'All I do is talk about myself lately. And I'm sorry about that.'

Jess smiled. 'Listen, I manage to get plenty of words in,' she said. 'Telling you what to do with your life, imparting all my worldly wisdom.'

'Which I couldn't do without,' Andie insisted. 'But enough about me, are you going to show me what you've been up to?'

Jess quickly locked the front door and turned over the closed sign before leading her out the back to the computer. 'I'll show you Toby's preliminary plans,' she said.

'They're on the computer?'

'It's all done on computer now,' said Jess. 'He emailed them to me.'

She sat beside Andie at the desk as she took her through the plans. They weren't extravagant changes, but they were enough to make a big difference to what could be achieved in the kitchen. They included the installation of a new double oven and professional cooktop, and a range hood with a commercial-grade exhaust duct system; a large island bench unit incorporating a pastry-making slab; and there were plans to replace some of the older style kitchen cupboard units with more serviceable shelves and wire racks.

'So will this have to go through council?' Andie asked her.

'No,' said Jess. 'Nothing's being changed externally, or to the structure of the building. I've been madly checking that everything meets commercial standards and complies with health and fire regulations, that kind of thing, but Toby's up on all that anyway.'

'And so what do you hope to do once this is all in place?'

Jess sat back to look at her. 'Well, I'd like to start by offering a limited range of restaurant-quality takeaway meals. It'll work best in the winter months, with casseroles, pasta dishes, pies, that kind of thing. We could see how it goes and take it from there.'

Andie was nodding slowly. 'You've really put a lot of thought into this. And it sounds completely doable, but you have to realise, Jess, I'm not going to be able to be very involved, I only have one day off a week.'

'I know that, Andie. But I think I can manage this myself, with the support of the regular staff, of course.'

'What if you get more restaurant shifts?'

She sighed. 'I really haven't been doing much of that for a while now, I'm here most of the time.'

'And you don't mind that?'

'That's the whole thing, I don't mind at all,' Jess said plainly. 'In fact, I'm enjoying it. I know you're loving working in a kitchen right now, but I've been doing it for over ten years. If I had a permanent, ongoing position somewhere, even just a couple of nights a week, I could make my own mark. But as it is, I'm only ever filling in someone else's shoes. This is a chance for me to do my own thing . . .' She hesitated. 'Sorry, Andie, I shouldn't presume. I know you have to think about this, the expense involved. But I've been doing some costing of my own and if it works out, it's going to pay for itself, and hopefully turn a profit before long. Plus the renovations are a tax write-off for the business.'

Andie was just sitting staring at the computer screen.

'I don't mean to push you,' said Jess. 'Toby should have the quote ready any day, and then you'll have more information to help you decide.'

'No, I want you to go ahead with it,' said Andie.

'What?'

'I think it's a great idea, and if you want to do it —'

'Just like that?' Jess blinked.

'It's not just like that,' said Andie. 'You and I have talked about this kind of thing before, perhaps not on this scale. But now I have the money to do it.'

'You mean your inheritance?'

'That's right.'

'But, Andie, that's your future, your security,' said Jess. 'You have to buy your own place, put some away in super —'

'I'll still be able to buy my own place,' Andie assured her. 'But this is my place too, and my security, and I should invest in it. I haven't spent anything on the business in a very long time, and this seems to me to be a pretty smart move.' She looked directly at Jess. 'Seriously, what have I got to lose? Toby's doing the renovations, so that's in good hands, and where would I get someone of your calibre and experience to run something like this?' She paused. 'You know, the more I sit here and think about it, the more I realise I'd be a bloody fool not to go ahead with this. It's a brilliant opportunity.'

Jess's eyes were glassy. 'So that's it? You're happy for us to run with it?'

'Yep. Keep me posted, of course. But you and Toby are the two people I trust most in the world, so I think I'm in safe hands.' She glanced at her watch. 'Now, I really have to get going.'

She stood up and Jess jumped to her feet. 'I don't know what to say. Just . . . thank you.' She threw her arms around her.

Andie hugged her back. 'It's my pleasure. It might make up a little for everything you've done for me.'

Jess drew back, giving her eyes a quick wipe with the back of her hand. 'So you didn't say, where are you off to, anyway?'

'Dinner with Dominic.'

'Ooh, where's he taking you?'

'His place.'

Jess raised her eyebrows. 'Dominic Gerou is cooking you dinner? That's not too shabby,' she said. 'And that explains the saucy top. So tonight's the night, or has that ship already sailed?'

'Not yet,' said Andie. 'But let's just say we've pulled up the anchor and we're ready to go.'

Jess winced. 'Okay, let's not take that metaphor any further. So, have you got protection?'

'Against what?'

'Don't play dumb.'

'I'm still on the pill,' Andie said with a shrug.

'Andie, honestly, do I have to spell it out for you? The pill doesn't ward off an STD.'

'I know that.' She screwed up her nose. 'But isn't that his responsibility?'

Jess walked over to her handbag, shaking her head. 'You really have been out of the game for a long time. It's your body, your responsibility.' She fished around in her bag and pulled out a strip of condoms.

Andie grimaced. 'I don't know if I feel comfortable taking your condoms.'

'It's not as if they're used!' she said, slapping them into Andie's hand. 'Besides, I hate to bring this up, but have you been tested yourself?'

'What? I haven't been with anyone but . . . Oh shit.'

'Exactly,' said Jess. 'Did Ross use condoms with you?'

'No, that would have been a bit of a giveaway.'

'Don't worry, he probably used them with her, married men having affairs tend to be careful,' she said. 'But you can never be too careful. You should make an appointment to get tested.'

'Way to put a downer on the evening,' Andie said glumly as Jess walked her to the door.

'Oh, come on, don't let it spoil it for you,' said Jess, giving her arm a rub. 'Now let me look at you.'

Andie turned to face her.

'Gorgeous,' Jess declared. 'He won't be able to keep his hands off you. Go, enjoy yourself.'

*

Andie knew Jess was only looking after her best interests – and she certainly appreciated that someone was – but she felt a little sleazy on the drive to Dominic's, packing condoms in her purse and wearing a top that left very little to the imagination. She was glad she'd brought a light cardigan with her, she would put it on before she left the car, despite the sweltering conditions outside. She hoped Dominic's house was cool.

What made things worse was that the exchange with Jess had brought Ross back into the forefront of her mind, at a time when she really didn't need Ross anywhere near her mind. Especially not the image of him with that woman. She found herself trying to remember if she'd noticed a condom, which was patently ridiculous, considering the position he was in at the time. But Jess was right, married men were likely to be cautious. Ross had used condoms early in their relationship, until he actually physically left Joanna. Andie hadn't really thought about it at the time, but it probably meant he was still having sex with Joanna, when he'd claimed they hadn't had sex in years.

She groaned inwardly. She'd been in a good mood on the way to the shop, anticipating the night ahead, excited. Now it felt like a tawdry rendezvous. But it wasn't that, was it? She was formally separated, Dominic was single, they were adults . . . Whatever, she was going to have to tell him she hadn't been tested, it was the right thing to do. Bloody Ross was still somehow managing to have control over her life when he wasn't even in her life anymore. Remote control.

Andie turned into Dominic's street in Paddington and inched along until she spotted the number of his house. It was a neat restored terrace in a row of similarly neat restored terraces that stepped their way down a gentle incline. Dominic's was about halfway along. Andie found a park nearby and pulled on her cardigan before getting out of the car. She was feeling jittery as she walked back up to his house and in through the front gate, past the pocket-handkerchief front garden. She stepped up onto the porch and pressed the buzzer. Her heart seemed to be thudding in time with the footsteps she could hear approaching up the hall. Then the door opened and Dominic was standing there smiling at her, and Andie felt seventeen different emotions just seeing his face.

'Hi, come in,' he said. 'Did you find the place all right?'

'Yes, no problem.'

He sounded a little nervous as well, which oddly made her relax as she walked inside. Then he bent to kiss her, just softly, one hand resting on her cheek, and Andie felt jittery all over again, but in a good way.

He straightened. 'I missed you . . . at the restaurant, you know. I'm used to seeing you there.'

She smiled. 'I missed being there.'

'Well, come on through,' he said, leading the way. She followed him past a narrow staircase on the right, and what looked like a sitting room on the left, though she only caught a glimpse as they passed. The floor had been stripped to timber, and all the walls were white, but the original features remained – deep skirting boards, ornate plasterwork. They walked through into a large open space that was obviously a new extension. It comprised a large kitchen and eating area, with a wall of glass facing the courtyard off the back. It was all white and stainless steel, sparsely furnished with a white glass-topped dining table and white chairs.

'This is stunning,' said Andie. 'How long have you lived here?'

'A few years now,' he said, as he walked around the long, sleek island bench topped with white marble. 'It was mostly as you see it when I bought it, I just put in a new kitchen. Hazard of the profession, though I don't get to use it much. Can I get you a drink?'

'Yes, thanks, though I am driving, I'll have to keep track,' she added demurely.

'Well, you can always catch a taxi home . . . or whatever.'

Her heart jumped and he turned away abruptly to open the fridge. They both knew what 'whatever' meant. It was strange, going through the paces, knowing what was likely to happen before the night was out. She felt tingly and breathless already. She really needed a drink to calm her down.

'White wine?' Dominic offered, peering into the fridge. 'Or I have beer, or I could open a red?'

'White wine's good, thanks.'

'So how's the new apartment?' he asked as he poured the wine.

'It's wonderful,' she said. 'I feel at home already.'

He passed her a glass before picking up his. 'To feeling at home,' he toasted.

They clinked glasses and Andie drank from hers. 'So, what's for dinner?' she asked.

'Hamburgers and chips,' he said plainly.

She lifted an eyebrow. 'Oh?'

He nodded, smiling. 'I hope you're hungry.'

Andie was well aware of the trend, even in high-end restaurants, of including gourmet hamburgers on the menu. They certainly wouldn't be served at Viande, which was cutting edge, but always classy; fine dining, not funky. It would be interesting to see just how far Dominic could slum it.

'I'm very hungry,' she lied. Right at the moment, she wasn't at all sure she would manage to eat.

'Then let's get started,' he said. 'Do you mind helping?'

Even better than having Dominic Gerou cook her dinner was to be able to cook alongside him. He'd already prepared the patties and they were chilling in the refrigerator, so he took her through the process of making the sauce, a reduction of heritage tomatoes with fresh herbs. He'd cheated with the buns, he said, having picked up some brioche from a local bakery that morning.

'So we only have to get started on the chips.'

'Are you going to use the method of cooking them three times over?'

He nodded. 'So you know it?'

'I know of it,' she said. 'I've never tried it myself.'

Dominic had already completed the first stage, steaming the thick-cut chips until they were half-cooked. They were cooling in the refrigerator. He instructed Andie to wrap them in a tea towel to remove all traces of moisture while he heated the oil, testing it with a thermometer. They proceeded to fry the chips in batches until they were pale yellow, before draining them and returning them to the fridge again, while they prepared everything else.

'I think you can't go past iceberg lettuce on a burger,' Dominic said, fishing one out of the crisper and passing it to Andie.

'Really?'

'There are stronger-tasting lettuces but they're usually bitter, which is great in a salad with dressing, but they just compete with the other flavours on a hamburger.' He handed her a stalk of truss tomatoes, then grabbed a slab of cheese and a bowl, closing the fridge door with his elbow. 'And knowing the Australian obsession with beetroot, I roasted some for you earlier,' he said, revealing the reddish-purple bulbs in the bowl.

Andie clapped her hands together. 'I love beetroot on hamburgers.'

'Hm, just as I thought.'

The chips would only need about another five minutes of frying, so it was time to start the meat. Dominic fired up the barbecue plate on the wondrous cooktop – the kind Andie had only seen in magazines, with every function imaginable: gas jets, induction elements and stone hotplates.

'I believe I can leave the buns and the salad to you,' he said.

'Yes you can,' Andie said. 'I know everything there is to know about bread and salad.'

'Which is why you're moving on to main meal prep as of tomorrow.'

She turned to look at him, wide-eyed. 'Dominic, I —'

'We've already been over this, Andie. Cosmo and Tang came to me, I simply gave them the go-ahead, like I do for anyone they recommend.'

'But —'

He leaned across to give her a light kiss on the lips before she could say anything else. 'Congratulations,' he said.

Andie had to let it go for now, as the final stage of cooking got underway. The aroma was incredible. Dominic admitted that he'd gone the full gourmet route and used wagyu beef because it really did make the best hamburger patties. He added a wafer-thin slice of Gruyère right at the end of cooking, so it just melted onto the beef. It was all in the timing with burgers – buns had to be toasted and still warm, ready for the patties, vegetables waiting, sliced and shredded, and the chips needed to be served hot at the same time. Dominic left Andie to lift the chips from the oil in batches and drain them on absorbent paper, while he plated up the burgers with the same care and attention to detail he showed at the restaurant. She watched him spoon an elegant smear of the sauce over each perfectly circular patty, then fuss over the exact placement of each tomato and beetroot slice and every shred of lettuce. The result was sublime. Andie had never seen such a perfect hamburger – except in commercials, but she knew stylists had to do weird things to food to make it look right, usually rendering it inedible. The burger in front of her was anything but. Andie felt like she was living in some parallel universe, sitting opposite a renowned, award-winning chef in his kitchen, eating the most luscious wagyu hamburgers. And the best chips ever.

'They are good,' Dominic agreed after she waxed lyrical. 'But in the end it's just potatoes and oil, the same as they use in any corner takeaway. Goes to show what you can achieve with a little attention to technique.'

'Is that what you like about cooking?' Andie asked him. 'The technique, or the process? I mean, what you do now is so meticulous, so precise. Makes me wonder if you were into making models when you were a kid?'

He smiled, shaking his head. 'No, I don't recall ever making models.'

'Do you recall what you wanted to be?'

He shrugged. 'Probably all the regular things when I was very young – you know, fireman, astronaut . . . But as I got older, well, it was such a foregone conclusion that I'd go into law, I didn't really think about what else I might have wanted to do.'

'It must have been a pretty big deal then, to drop out?'

He nodded. 'Big deal is putting it mildly.'

Andie paused, giving Dominic the opportunity to go on, she was beginning to feel like she was interrogating him. But he just picked up his burger and took another bite.

'I know what it's like for a parent's expectations to override your own,' Andie said carefully. 'My mother was desperate for her daughters to go to uni because she missed out herself. She thought cooking was for housewives.'

He wiped the corners of his mouth with a napkin. 'Yet here you are, a chef.'

'I did start uni, but I didn't go back after she died,' said Andie. 'My dad said life was too short . . .' She paused, becoming wistful. 'I just wish my mother had realised that her disappointment didn't come purely from missing out on an education, at the heart of it was that she didn't get to fulfil the dreams that mattered to her – whatever they might have been. I know she meant well, but she was forcing the same frustration and disappointment onto me.'

'But are you at peace now that you are following your dream?'

'I am.' She nodded. 'What about you? When we were at Elliot's it sounded like cooking had never been your dream, or your passion.'

'It wasn't at the beginning.'

'But it is now?'

He thought about it. 'I don't know about passion, it's more like a very long marriage – albeit a successful one, where you'll probably grow old together but the thrill has gone.'

'Then what makes you stay?'

'The same reason anyone stays in a long marriage: security, familiarity, loyalty.' He looked at her. 'Honestly, it's probably ego as much as anything. You get to a certain level and you're expected to stay there, maintain that standard, or you're deemed a failure.'

Andie shook her head. 'This is a tough enough industry to survive in if you don't really love it.'

'Don't get me wrong, it does give me a great deal of satisfaction. The kitchen is the place I feel most in control.'

'What do you mean?'

'Well, it's a highly controlled environment. There's cause and effect – you take a set of ingredients in the right quantities, you follow a method and you get a result. If you're disciplined, and precise, and you pay attention, you can duplicate those same results, again and again.'

'But us ordinary humans make mistakes,' said Andie.

He gave her a wry smile. 'Everyone makes mistakes, it's working at minimising them that helps you improve.'

'But don't you think you learn from your mistakes?'

'Of course, you learn not to make them again.'

'You've never made the same mistake twice?' Andie wanted to know.

'I've made plenty of mistakes. You'd be surprised.'

'Try me.'

He looked at her. 'You seem to be fishing for something.'

'I'm just interested,' said Andie. 'I've told you a lot about myself now, but you seem a little cagey about your deep dark past.'

He frowned slightly.

'That's what you called it on our way home from Elliot's.'

'Yes, I did,' he said. 'Look, I went off the rails for a few years back in my youth, that's all.'

'So apart from drinking too much, which you've already confessed, what else did you do that was so bad?'

'What didn't I do, is probably a better question.' He pushed his plate to the side. 'Yes, there was a lot of drinking and partying, I spent my parents' money like there was no tomorrow, I wouldn't go home for days at a time, I wrecked a car, you name it . . . I was really just a spoiled rich kid, totally out of control.'

Andie found that image difficult to marry with the man hunched over the kitchen bench earlier, painstakingly arranging shreds of lettuce with a pair of tweezers.

'So what happened?'

'I fell in love,' he said. 'Or I thought I'd fallen in love. I didn't really know which way was up let alone what love was. But when you're twenty you know everything, right?'

She smiled. 'Well, I don't know about you, but I certainly did.'

Dominic smiled back at her. 'Her name was Justine, and I thought she was the most incredible, free, extraordinary person I'd ever met. She dyed her hair crazy colours, all at once sometimes; she had piercings, a tattoo – before they became a fashion statement. Her philosophy of life was "If in doubt, do it", to hell with the consequences. You can imagine the effect she had on a sheltered, stitched-up English boy.'

'Doesn't sound like you were all that stitched-up by then?'

'That's true, I was already on a downward spiral, and she took me the rest of the way. My parents were naturally horrified, they tried to do everything to break us apart. But of course, that only pushed us closer together.'

'Because you were twenty, and you knew everything.'

He nodded. 'They forced the issue, said they were going back to England, I had no choice but to go with them. So Justine and I got married.'

Andie's eyes grew wide. 'That's who you were married to?'

Dominic gave her an odd look.

She didn't want to act like she didn't know. 'Elliot mentioned . . .'

'Elliot mentioned I was married? When?'

'The other day. Stan, the guy who had the apartment before me, he left some things behind, and I dropped in to Elliot's to return them. We got to talking, Elliot and I —'

'And he told you about my marriage?' He seemed rattled.

'No,' Andie assured him. 'He told me you'd been married, a long time ago, and that it ended unhappily. That's all. I didn't want to pretend I didn't know that much.'

Dominic nodded faintly.

'I'm sorry.'

'No, it's fine. It's not a secret, it's just not something I talk about, it was hardly my finest hour.' He sighed. 'My parents were devastated, but there was nothing they could do. They returned to England, taking their money with them. So I had to get a job.'

'That's when you started working with Elliot?'

'Yes. And that's when reality started to bite. I wasn't quite so appealing to Justine when my parents weren't funding our lifestyle. She hated the depressing little flat that was all we could afford, the hours I had to work . . . It's hard being with someone who's not in the industry, they really don't get it.'

'I know.'

'Justine partied on, but I was too tired to join her most of the time. I had to work double shifts, she spent money faster than I could earn it.'

'Why did you put up with it?'

'I didn't feel like I had a choice,' he said. 'She'd done me a favour, marrying me, I felt like I owed her. And what else could I do? I certainly wasn't going to go running to my parents, prove they were right.'

'So what did you do?'

'I threw myself into my work. I thought that once I had qualifications, at least I'd make a bit more money, things would settle down. But they never did. At first I worked because I had to, then I worked because it was all I had.' He stopped to take a drink of his wine. 'Justine came and went. She'd stay away for a weekend, then it was weeks at a time, then longer. I started praying she wouldn't come back, but eventually she'd run out of money or options, and I'd wake up one morning and she'd be there, crashed out on the bed beside me.'

'Why did you keep taking her back?' said Andie. 'You must have known . . .'

'That she was with other men?' he finished. 'Of course. But she'd say that I was the only one she loved, promise me things would be different. And they would be, for a while . . .'

'And then?'

'I finally faced the truth that she was never going to change, and things were never going to be different.' He paused. 'One time she hadn't been home for a week or so, I gave notice at work, and on the flat, packed up her things and left them with a friend of hers, and then I went as far away as I could get, so that she couldn't find me.'

'Where did you go?'

'Europe,' he said. 'I stayed away the best part of a decade. I had to support myself, so I worked in restaurants right across the continent. Plied my trade.'

'Were you able to mend things with your parents?'

'With my mother.' He nodded. 'Not that she'd ever given up on me. I think mothers will forgive their sons almost anything.'

'Did you ever see Justine again?'

He shook his head, he looked a little wistful. 'I tried to find her after I returned to Australia. We really needed to finalise things, get a divorce, but I wanted to make sure she was all right. I was in the position by then to help her out if she needed anything. I felt I owed her that much.' He paused. 'Someone told me she'd died, fell off the back of a motorbike, drunk. I had a solicitor look into it for me, sadly it was true.' He became thoughtful. 'Sometimes I think people like Justine are destined to die young.' He took another drink, then seemed to snap himself out of it. 'So there you have it, my deep dark past.'

No wonder he'd been scared off relationships. But now he was taking a chance on her. Andie was caught between worrying what expectations he had of her, and wanting to fulfil every one of them.

'And,' he said suddenly, getting to his feet, 'your glass is empty.'

He walked over to the fridge and Andie picked up their plates and came around the bench at the opposite end.

'More wine?' he asked.

'Oh . . . I don't know,' she said, setting the plates down in the sink. 'I should keep an eye on the time, we both have to work tomorrow.'

He closed the fridge door. 'Andie, it isn't even eight o'clock,' he said, walking towards her. 'Have I frightened you away?'

'No, no, of course not,' she said.

'Then what's the matter?' he asked gently, standing right in front of her.

'Nothing, nothing's the matter, really.'

He lifted her chin so she had to look at him. 'Now I feel like I shouldn't have told you any of that.'

'No,' she assured him. 'I don't think worse of you. Why would I? You were loyal and decent. You're a good person, Dominic.'

He grimaced faintly. 'That doesn't sound very promising.'

Andie laughed lightly, taking his hand between both of hers. 'Elliot did say something else.'

'Bloody Elliot strikes again.'

'Don't be cross with him,' she said. 'He just said it was unusual that you were seeing someone.'

'I told you that myself, that it had been a long time.'

'Since Justine?'

'Good heavens no, I'm not a monk,' he said. 'There have been women over the years, just no one serious, or long term. I haven't felt . . . I haven't felt anything, for anyone, for a very long time. Until now.'

Andie took a deep breath. 'Then I guess I'm feeling the weight of expectation.'

'Andie,' he sighed, 'I don't expect anything of you. I just like you . . . I like you so much. I like being around you.'

'I like being around you too, Dominic, I really do.'

'But?'

She thought about how to put it. 'I've just come out of a marriage, and I lost myself for a long time. I don't want to get swallowed up in something else right away.'

'I understand.' He looped his arms around her waist, planting a soft kiss on her forehead. 'May I make a suggestion?'

Andie looked up at him, waiting.

'Why don't we just relax and enjoy ourselves, allow things to run their own course. And I promise I won't expect any more than that. Does that work for you?'

She smiled. 'Yes, that works.'

He brought his lips to hers and they kissed. It was slow and gentle at first, but it soon became more urgent. They weren't standing in the doorway of the shop now, there was nothing to stop them taking this further. And Andie was ready, she was so ready. She felt his hands on the bare skin of her waist, under the flimsy fabric of her top.

'Andie . . .' he murmured, his lips barely leaving hers. 'I have a very comfortable bed, just up the stairs. Would it be presumptuous of me to suggest . . .'

She smiled. Always the polite Englishman. 'Lead the way.'

He took her by the hand, and Andie followed him back up the hall, and up the stairs, and into his bedroom. It was all white walls in here as well, but the lighting was mercifully more subdued. He turned to face her, and they stood, looking at each other, a little tentatively.

'We seem to have lost momentum,' he said.

Andie smiled, stepping closer and circling her arms around him. 'I'm sure we can find it again.'

Dominic reached for the clip holding her hair up and released it, then he raked his fingers through her hair to shake it free.

'I love your hair. I never get to see it, it's always tucked up under your cap.' He was gazing down at her, his expression tender, even a little soulful.

'What is it?' she asked.

'Nothing . . . I'm just glad you're here.'

'Me too.'

His mouth covered hers again, his fingers grazing her skin as he slipped her cardigan down over her shoulders. Andie dropped her arms to her side, allowing it to fall to the floor, while Dominic held her close, cradling the back of her head in one hand as he kissed her, and pressing into the small of her back with his other hand so her pelvis jutted up against his. Andie felt lightheaded, her skin prickled all over as his lips moved down her throat, across her shoulders, sliding the fine straps out the way. Oh, they had quite clearly found their momentum again. She reached up to unbutton his shirt, opening it up and smoothing her hands over the bare skin of his chest. He shuddered under her touch, lifting the scrap of fabric that was her top easily over her head, and tossing it aside. His breathing was ragged as he stared at her, a little stunned. She reached for his hand and brought it to her breast.

'Andie,' he said thickly, pulling her close again and kissing her hard. He eased her down onto the bed, pushing his knee between hers. Andie felt a longing for him that was almost agonising, arching herself towards him, but he was not going to be rushed. He ran his hand slowly down her torso, his mouth following the trail, until his fingers slipped under her waistband. She could feel his tongue sliding across the skin of her belly as he worked on the button of her jeans . . .

Andie grabbed his shoulders. 'Wait!'

Dominic lifted his head to look at her. 'What is it?'

She swallowed. 'I haven't been tested.'

'Pardon?'

'I haven't been with anyone since Ross,' she stammered, 'but he's been with her, so . . .'

Dominic looked faintly confused, as he brought himself back up beside her. 'Are you having problems of some kind?'

'Oh, no, I'm fine.' She sighed. 'I just . . . you know, I should have been better prepared. Once I started dating again I should have had a check-up, tests, it's what a responsible person would do.'

He stroked her hair. 'Andie, it's okay, I have protection.'

'So do I.'

He smiled. 'So you were at least a little prepared?' he murmured, his lips close to hers again.

She could only manage a squeak from somewhere in her throat in response, as her mouth opened against his and they kissed again, now more frantically, their tongues entwining, hands caressing as they freed each other from the last of their clothes, and there was nothing but skin against skin, limbs locking, bodies writhing . . . and finally, Andie felt him thrust up inside her, filling her, quenching the ache, over and over. She arched back with a soft cry, pulling him close to her. They seemed to drift into slow motion, rocking in unison, her legs wrapped around him, drawing his body further up into hers, till they were fused, climaxing together, and then falling again, gently, stroking, kissing, replete.

Dominic eventually shifted onto his side, bringing her with him.

'Oh my God,' he breathed.

She stifled a giggle into his neck.

'That was worth waiting for,' he said in a low voice.

'Yes, it was.' Andie felt somehow free, free of the last vestiges of Ross's hold on her life. She was her own person. She'd just made love to a good man, a wonderful man. Someone who was going to give her the time she needed. Who wasn't going to expect more of her than this, right now, lying together in each other's arms, content.

Dominic drew back to look at her. 'There's something I want to say, and you have to let me say it.'

Andie gazed up at him. 'What?'

'You really are very beautiful, Andie.'

She smiled.

'I wanted to say it before, but I know you don't like it. But you have to let me say it, in this context.'

'In this context, you're allowed to say it.'

He sighed deeply, bringing his hand up to smooth her hair away from her face and stroke her cheek. 'I'm so glad this has finally happened. I've been imagining it since the first time we met.'

She blinked. 'Really?'

'No, sorry, not the first time. Since the time you came in asking for another chance.'

'But you were so ominous. You really made me work for it.'

'That's because you made me literally go weak at the knees,' he said. 'I was only trying to resist you. You think I wanted that kind of distraction in my kitchen?'

'So why did you say yes?'

He gazed down at her. 'Because I couldn't say no.'

Potts Point

'Rossie, I'm bored, why can't we go out?' Tasha pouted.

'Because I told you, I'm tired, Tash,' said Ross. 'And it's a Monday night. Who goes out on a Monday night?' He checked his watch. 'At ten o'clock?'

'People under thirty,' she muttered.

'What did you say?'

'Nothing.'

Life with Ross was not working out quite the way Tasha had pictured. She thought that moving into his apartment would be a step up, that they'd finally be a couple, that she would accompany him to his business dinners, cocktail parties, big glitzy corporate bashes. She thought he'd want to show off his much younger partner, that he'd be proud of her. He insisted he was, but he'd 'been there, done that' with the whole social scene and he found it a crashing bore most of the time. He'd rather cuddle up at home with her.

Excitement city.

It was all very well to have an adoring man, but Ross was an adoring *older* man, and he was so stuck in his ways. He used to say he loved her energy and her vitality, that it made him feel young. Well, you'd never know it. Lately he was always tired, going to bed early, complaining about random aches and pains, like Tasha really needed, or wanted, to know. Next thing he'd be asking her to fill his hot water bottle for him. Ugh.

She'd finally had to give him an ultimatum and insist on moving in here, especially after the ex had taken him to court. Well, not literally – Tasha didn't get how it worked, the lawyers handled the whole thing apparently. It seemed weird to her that you could divorce someone without even facing up to them in court, all those American legal shows must make it up just for the drama. Ross wouldn't talk to her about the settlement, he said it was none of her concern. When she baulked at that, he said he meant he didn't want to concern her. Was there something to be concerned about? she'd asked him then. He'd assured her there wasn't, that Andie had actually settled for less than she was entitled to. Hm, Tasha found that hard to believe. Did Ross even know what her father's estate was worth? No, he didn't, and it was none of his business, he said. Yeah, well, no wonder she slipped away so quietly. Tasha was sure that if things were split down the middle, Ross may well have got himself a piece of that inheritance, and she told him so.

But he had just closed his eyes and given his head a shake. Tasha hated when he did that, like she was a naughty child.

She picked up the remote and turned on the TV.

'Oh good,' said Ross, 'we can catch the last half of *Q&A*.'

Tasha pulled a face. 'Ah, I don't think so, Ross. You don't get to call the shots on everything.' She flicked the channel and plonked herself onto the chesterfield. God, she hated the thing, it was like sitting on a padded brick, but when she'd suggested getting rid of it, Ross had nearly had a heart attack. He said he'd waited all his life to get a chesterfield, Tasha said he ought to dream bigger. It was a couch. But not just any couch, he'd insisted. Then he'd carried on about the kid leather and the studding done by hand, and the waiting list he'd had to go on, and how much it cost and that it was an investment, till Tasha was bored shitless. She asked him what she *could* change or get rid of in the apartment. He told her there was no reason to throw out perfectly good furniture. She was welcome to put her personal things around – photos and knick-knacks and the like – and she could buy some new cushions if she wanted, but he'd prefer not to go to unnecessary expense right now.

'What about the bed? Can we move my bed over at least, to replace yours?'

He had winced slightly. 'My bed's a lot more comfortable than yours, it's much better quality . . .'

'It's your marriage bed!' she cried.

'That didn't seem to bother you the night you seduced me on it.'

That hadn't ended well. They slept in their own beds for the next couple of nights, until Ross had shown up on her doorstep with flowers and expensive champagne, and a proposal that they buy a whole new bed, which would be their bed. He always knew how to get back into her good books.

Her show was coming on after the ads.

'What's this?' said Ross, frowning at the screen.

'*Keeping up with the Kardashians.*'

He groaned as he got up from his armchair. 'I'm going to bed.'

'Don't forget we've got gym in the morning,' she called after him.

Morning

Andie blinked a few times. She could feel the sun warm on her face, and she could feel Dominic's body warm against her back, and she could feel his lips, warm on her shoulder, leaving a trail of soft kisses. It was a very nice way to wake up.

'What time is it?' she asked sleepily.

'Time to get up,' he murmured. 'We have to get ready for work, you have a big day ahead of you.'

She frowned for a moment, until she realised what he was referring to. She shifted around to face him. 'We have to talk about that.'

'There's nothing to talk about.'

'You have to tell Cosmo I can't move up right now.'

'I don't have to do any such thing,' he insisted.

'Dominic, look at me! I'm in your bed. Naked. I am naked in your bed. I simply cannot be seen to be getting an advantage.'

'But no one can see you.'

'Dominic!'

He sighed heavily, propping his head up with his hand. 'Andie, this really has to stop. I didn't whisper in anyone's ear, I didn't single you out, I didn't make the recommendation. Cosmo came to me, Tang agreed, it's time for you to move up, whether you happen to grace my bed naked or not. Now can that be the end of it, once and for all?'

Andie suppressed a smile. 'You don't have to be so bossy,' she muttered.

'Well, now you're just being insubordinate,' he said, shifting so that he was above her. 'You may have to be disciplined.'

Andie giggled as he buried his face into her neck. 'Don't we have to get ready for work?'

'We have time,' he murmured in her ear. 'Besides, you're with the boss, doesn't matter if you're late.'

'Dominic —' But he covered her mouth with his own, and before long Andie forgot about work, forgot about anything but the feel of his body against hers. There was already an easy synchronicity between them that Andie hadn't expected. They fitted somehow. Last night was wonderful. They had come downstairs in the middle of the night, and Dominic had made her the most divine pancakes. He already had strawberries marinating, he'd planned to serve them for dessert with mascarpone cream, but by then they needed something more substantial. They fed each other pancakes and strawberries between long, languid kisses, until they couldn't hold back any longer, and they returned upstairs to make love once more, finally falling asleep in each other's arms, completely spent.

And now, again . . . Dominic was obviously making up for lost time, and Andie wasn't about to complain. She should have felt tired, but instead she felt energised.

Afterwards he was lying tucked into her side, his head resting against her breasts. She wondered if he was falling asleep. She stroked his hair. 'Dominic?'

'Hm.'

'I will have to get going, I'll have to call by my place to change my clothes.'

'There's plenty of time,' he said, lifting himself up to look down at her. 'I woke you early. Do you want to have a shower here?'

'No, I might as well shower at home, I have to change anyway.'

'All right, well, I'll go and start breakfast.' He kissed her lightly on the lips before he got out of bed to get dressed.

'Don't worry about breakfast, Dominic, you have to get ready for work yourself.'

'I can do that after you leave, but we both have to eat.'

'Thank you,' she called as he walked out of the room, pulling a T-shirt over his head.

She could get used to this. Although she loved to cook herself, it was quite a novelty to have a man cook for her – a three-hatted chef, no less. She really hoped everything was going to be all right at work. She wanted to stay at Viande, and she had to admit, she wanted to work with Dominic, or at least close by. And she was excited to be moving up, if not for this development she would have been champing at the bit for the challenge. But Dominic was right, she was ready, and she had earned it. So she was just going to have to work harder than ever, and leave no room for anyone to doubt that.

But now she really had to get up. She automatically reached over to the bedside table to feel for her phone to check the time. But of course it wasn't there, it was still in her handbag downstairs. She got out of bed and dressed in her clothes from last night – it was a long time since she'd had to do the walk of shame the morning after. Not that she could say she felt any shame. After all her misgivings yesterday, her nerves, the frayed remnants of Catholic guilt, this morning Andie felt free and lighter somehow – like she'd cast off old baggage for good. And she felt no pressure, just a pure kind of happiness that was exhilarating.

She almost skipped down the stairs and down the hall into the kitchen. Dominic was whisking eggs in a bowl and Andie walked straight up to him.

'Here you are. Thought I'd do scrambled eggs, they're —'

She cut him off with a kiss, circling her arms around his neck.

'What was that for?' he asked when she pulled back. He was still holding the bowl and the whisk.

She shrugged, smiling. 'For everything.'

There was such a rush of tenderness in his eyes that Andie just wanted to hug him. So she did. Dominic put down the bowl and folded his arms around her, and they stood, holding each other tight, just hugging. It was possibly the most intimate moment they'd shared yet.

'Much as I could stay like this all day,' Dominic said, pulling back after a while, 'we really do have to get a move on.'

She smiled, planting a kiss on his lips. 'Did you see where I left my handbag?'

'I think it's over on one of the dining chairs.'

'Ah.' She walked across and picked up her bag, setting it down on the table as she felt for her phone. 'That's odd,' she said when she checked the screen.

'What is?' Dominic asked.

'Ross's daughter has tried to call a few times this morning,' she said.

'Already?'

'I know, that's what's odd. She's still on holidays from uni, she wouldn't usually be up this early.' Andie felt an uncomfortable niggle. She looked over at Dominic. 'Do you mind if I call her back?'

'No, of course not.'

Andie pressed *Call* and waited until the phone rang out. 'Damn, she's not answering,' she said, hanging up.

'Why didn't you leave a message?' Dominic asked, passing her a glass of freshly squeezed juice.

'Thanks,' said Andie. 'Brooke doesn't have voicemail, none of the kids do anymore, they think it's old hat.'

He shook his head. 'Young people today . . .'

She was typing a text message when the phone started to ring. It was Brooke.

'Hi,' said Andie. 'I just tried to call you.'

'Yeah, I saw, I had my phone on silent. I had to come outside to make the call – Mum gets mad if I use my phone inside the hospital.'

'What are you doing at the hospital?'

Dominic looked up.

'You haven't heard anything yet?' said Brooke.

'No,' Andie said. This was starting to worry her.

'That bitch,' she muttered. 'Sorry, Andie, but I thought it was weird you hadn't turned up, that's why I called you.'

'Brooke, what are you talking about?' she said urgently. 'Why are you at the hospital?'

'It's Dad, Andie,' she said. 'He had a heart attack.'

Andie couldn't catch her breath, it was like all the air had suddenly been sucked out of the room. 'Is he all right? Is he . . .?'

'They're just trying to stabilise him for now, but they think he's going to need surgery.'

'Oh my God, they have to do a bypass?'

'No, they said something about implanting some kind of device to stop his heart from racing.'

'A pacemaker?'

'I don't know what it's called, we really haven't been told much yet.'

'Where are you, Brooke? Which hospital?'

'St Luke's.'

At least that was close. 'Okay, I'll get there as fast as I can.'

'Great, see you soon.'

Andie hung up the phone.

'What's going on?' asked Dominic, coming around the bench to her.

'It's Ross, my ex,' she said, her voice wavering. 'He had a heart attack, but it doesn't sound like a regular heart attack. I don't really understand, his heart was racing or something,' she said. 'And apparently they're going to have to implant some kind of device.'

Dominic was nodding. 'An uncle of mine had that. Arrhythmia, I think it's called.'

'Did he have the thing implanted?' Andie asked.

'Yes, he did, as a matter of fact.'

'How did it go?'

'Well, he's dead now —'

That was it, the banks burst and Andie started to sob uncontrollably.

'Andie . . . Andie,' Dominic held her by the shoulders and tried to get her attention above the sobs. 'Listen to me, you didn't let me finish. He died years later, it was a long time ago now.' He brought his arms around her and held her close, and she started to calm down.

'I'm sorry,' she said. 'It's just a shock.'

'Of course it is,' said Dominic. 'So where is he? Which hospital?'

'St Luke's.'

'Do you want me to take you there?'

'No, you have to go to work . . . What am I saying? I have to go to work.'

'Don't worry about it.'

She looked up at him. 'You can't give me special treatment, Dominic.'

'Andie, this is a family emergency,' he said. 'I'm not giving you special treatment, I wouldn't expect anyone to turn up at work under these circumstances.'

'Okay,' she relented. 'Then I might just be a bit late, I'll come as soon I find out what's going on.'

'Andie,' he said, taking her hands in his, 'don't worry about work. You're upset, you need to get to the hospital and find out what's happening. One thing at a time, okay?'

'Okay.'

'I can drop you off on the way.'

She took a deep breath. 'No, I better drive myself, then I'll have my car, whatever I decide to do.'

'Are you sure?'

She nodded. 'I'm sure.'

'I can make those eggs up quickly, if you like?'

'No, thanks, I don't think I could eat now anyway.'

'All right, well, finish your juice at least,' he said, passing her the glass. 'It'll bring up your blood sugar.'

Andie gave him a grateful smile, and drank the rest of the juice. She glanced down at herself. 'Oh God, I can't go looking like this to the hospital. I must have left my cardigan upstairs. I better find it.' She bolted up the stairs and looked frantically around the room, spotting it on the floor halfway under the bed, along with her hairclip. She grabbed them both and gave the cardigan a shake, pulled the flimsy top up over her head and slipped on the cardigan, buttoning it all the way as she stood in front of the mirror. That would have to do. She twisted her hair and caught it up with the clip. When she hurried back down the stairs, Dominic was waiting at the front door.

'Does this look all right?' she said, pushing up the sleeves. She hoped she wouldn't get too hot, but it would be air-conditioned at the hospital.

'You look fine,' he said, touching her cheek. 'Maybe a little flushed. You need to slow down, take a breath.'

She did as he suggested. 'I'm sorry about this, Dominic.'

'You don't have to apologise.'

'Still . . .' She took a step closer. 'I just want you to know I had a wonderful time last night.'

He smiled down at her. 'I did too,' he said, kissing her gently on the lips. 'Call me when you know what's happening?'

'I will.'

'Drive safe.'

*

Andie did her best to stay calm, but as the traffic snarled and knotted the closer she got to the hospital she could feel her anxiety building. She finally parked several floors up in the parking station and made her way back out to the main entrance of the hospital. She hurried through the doors and was immediately confronted by a barrage of signage that only served to confuse her. It was quicker to ask someone.

She was directed up a couple of floors, left towards some wing, right when she got to the end of the corridor, and on it went. Why did hospitals always have such hopelessly complex layouts? Wasn't there some kind of imperative to make it as easy as possible to find your way around, considering all the sick, anxious, stressed people who frequented the place?

She had to ask again twice along the way, but she finally made it to the waiting room of the cardiac ward, spotting Brooke immediately, over by a window.

'Andie!' she called. Joanna and Matty turned in their seats, standing up when they caught sight of her. They all rushed at her at once, and Andie braced herself – do they hug, kiss, what? Brooke just barrelled straight at her, throwing her arms around her. Andie felt a little self-conscious; she hadn't showered, she could still feel Dominic on her skin.

'I'm so glad you're here, Andie,' said Brooke. 'Maybe you can deal with Stalin McHitler-face in there.'

'What?'

'Hi, Andie,' said Joanna. 'She's referring to Tasha.'

'Oh.' Andie turned to Matty who was standing awkwardly to the side. 'Hi mate, have you grown, like, another foot taller?' she said.

He smiled shyly and stooped to give her a quick, clumsy half a hug. 'It's good to see you, Andie.'

'So what's happening?' she asked, looking at Joanna.

'What we've been told, so far, is that Ross collapsed at the gym, and then apparently his heart went into arrhythmia, which is when it speeds up to a dangerous rate. They had to use those paddles on him and put him on a ventilator to get him to the hospital.'

Andie brought her hand to her mouth.

'He's on a heart monitor and oxygen still, we think. They were trying to stabilise him, I'm not even sure if he's conscious.'

'How long has he been here?'

'A couple of hours now,' Joanna said, glancing at her watch.

'And they can't tell you any more than that?'

'I told you,' said Brooke, '*Trasha* won't let us anywhere near him.'

'How does she have the right to do that?' said Andie.

'He's in the high-dependency unit,' Joanna explained. 'They're only letting in one visitor at a time, and she's refusing to leave his side.'

'And the doctor won't tell you anything else?'

'She's controlling the whole show,' said Brooke. 'We get bits of information from the nurses coming in and out. You have to do something, Andie.'

She blinked. 'What do you expect me to do?' Shouldn't Joanna be the one in charge? She was the first wife, and the mother of his children. Besides, she had a far more credible aura about her – Andie had never been good in these kinds of situations, she crumpled before authority.

'We've just been wondering what her legal standing is,' said Joanna. 'She has moved in with Ross, but it's only been a month or two, so that doesn't really give her de facto status. Someone might have to sign consent if they have to operate. I don't know if there's a grey area after a divorce, where you still have some rights.'

'We're not divorced,' said Andie.

'You're not?' everyone seemed to say at once.

'But you said it was with the lawyers last time we spoke?' said Joanna.

'The property settlement was,' Andie explained, 'but we have to wait twelve months from the date of separation before we can file for divorce.'

'Oh my God,' said Joanna, 'you're right. Andie, you're still his current wife, you have all the legal rights – and responsibilities – of next of kin.'

'Excellent,' Brooke exclaimed, hooking her arm through Andie's. 'Let's go put out the *trash*.'

'Brooke,' Andie and Joanna chided at the same time.

'What?'

'Tasha is probably in shock,' said Joanna. 'She was there when it happened, so let's show a bit of empathy?'

They approached the nurses' station and a woman looked up. 'Can I help you?'

'Hello,' said Andie. 'My . . . husband has been admitted. Apparently he's in the high-dependency unit?'

She turned to the computer screen. 'Name?'

'Ross Corcoran.'

The woman looked up again. 'You're his wife?'

'Yes.'

'Someone came in with him . . .' she said tentatively.

'That would be his girlfriend,' said Andie. 'It's okay, we're separated, but I am still his legal wife, and these are his children, and they'd really like to see their dad.'

'Of course, Mrs Corcoran,' she said. 'I'm afraid I do have to ask, do you have some kind of proof, ID?'

Andie frowned. 'I don't carry around my marriage certificate.'

She smiled. 'A driver's licence will do. Is it in your married name?'

It was. Andie had gone to the RTA to change her address, and thought she might as well revert back to her own name at the same time, but they were not so amenable to the idea. She was told she would need three forms of identification, but as all of her ID was in her married name, except for her birth certificate, she didn't know how that would even be possible. So she put it in the too-hard basket and decided to wait until after the divorce.

She handed her licence to the nurse, who nodded. 'That's fine, Mrs Corcoran.'

It didn't mean she necessarily wanted to go by that name. 'Please, it's Andie.'

The nurse looked up at her. 'You're Andie?'

'Yes.'

She glanced back at the driver's licence.

'It's short for Andrea,' Andie explained.

'He was asking for you when they brought him in,' said the nurse.

'He was?'

'He was still quite out of it, we couldn't get much sense out of him, we thought it was his son, or a brother maybe . . .'

Brooke squeezed her arm.

'After you've been in to see him, there are some forms that need filling out, basic information, medical history, that kind of thing, and we need to know his health fund. His, ah . . . companion didn't seem to have much information.' She came around the desk. 'Follow me,' she said, glancing at her entourage. Andie wasn't going to explain who Joanna was right now, things were complicated enough.

'You know he can only have one visitor at a time,' the nurse told her.

'What about his . . . companion?' said Andie.

'Don't worry, you outrank her.'

They followed her down the corridor to a set of double doors. She turned to face them. 'You have to turn off all mobile phones and electronic equipment before entering,' she said.

'That's *off*, not silent, you two,' Joanna warned Brooke and Matty, as they all scrambled in bags and pockets for their phones.

The nurse had to swipe a card for the doors to open. Inside resembled a command-control centre. There was a long desk directly in front of them which housed, along with assorted computers and phones, an angled panel with rows of buttons and lights, some of them flashing. Staff in scrubs and masks strode around purposefully, in and out of the glass-walled cubicles that ran the length of the opposite wall; they were so full of high-tech equipment you could barely make out the hospital bed within. The place had a distinctly sci-fi atmosphere, which made it somewhat intimidating.

'I'll just go ahead and sort this out,' the nurse said to Andie. 'You all need to stay back here, behind the desk. You can't wander around in this area.'

She walked across the main floor, stopping briefly to talk to another nurse, before entering one of the cubicles through an automatic sliding door. It wasn't long before a young woman came marching out of the same doors. Her dark hair was tied back in a ponytail and she was wearing leggings, trainers and a very tight, hot pink singlet with the slogan 'Life's a Game, Play It!' emblazoned across the chest. Andie sighed inwardly. The top left nothing to the imagination, and she wasn't wearing a bra. Andie would recognise those breasts anywhere.

Tasha came to an abrupt halt in front of them. Andie was shocked to see how young she was close up.

'Joanna.' She nodded curtly. 'Brooke, Matthew.' Then her gaze landed on Andie, and her contempt was palpable.

'I'm Andie,' she piped up, she wasn't going to be fazed. 'Thanks, the kids really want to see their father.'

Tasha shrugged. 'I need to get home to shower and change anyway,' she said tartly. 'I'll be back as soon as I can.'

'Um, one thing, Tasha,' Andie stopped her.

She raised an eyebrow.

'Could you have a look for Ross's health fund papers? Bring them with you when you come back?'

'I have no idea where he keeps that kind of thing,' she sniffed.

'The desk in the living room, over in the corner?' Andie prompted her. 'Is it still there?'

'I guess.'

'It has file drawers, you could try checking there.'

'I won't have much time,' she said.

'It's just that the hospital's asking for them,' Andie said, keeping her cool.

'I'll see what I can do.' She turned on her heel and headed for the double doors, her trainers squeaking on the vinyl floor.

'Piece. Of. Work,' said Brooke.

'Okay, which one of you wants to go in first?' said Andie.

The nurse had rejoined them. 'I think you should go in first, Mrs Corcoran . . . Andie.'

'Oh . . .' She hesitated, glancing at Brooke and Matty.

'I told Mr Corcoran you were on your way in,' the nurse explained. 'He was very relieved.'

'It's fine, Andie,' said Brooke, 'you should go.'

'Well, I won't stay long,' she said. 'Then you two can spend some time with him.'

Andie followed the nurse across to the cubicle, but she stopped in front of the door. 'You need to prepare yourself,' she said. 'There are a lot of tubes going in and out of his arms and his chest, providing oxygen and pain relief, and wires that are monitoring his heart and other vital signs. They all help to keep him stable, as well as the staff informed of exactly what is happening. He's also very pale, unnaturally pale, but don't be alarmed, it's completely normal after a heart episode such as this.'

But his heart 'episode' could hardly be described as normal.

'Can he speak?' asked Andie.

'Oh, yes, oxygen is being administered via a nasal tube, his mouth and airways are not obstructed.'

'So he is conscious?'

'Yes, but extremely fatigued, as you can imagine. The main thing is not to overtax him, keep him calm.'

She pressed a button on the wall and the door slid open. 'I'm Sue, by the way. Sing out if you need anything. You can go in.'

Andie stepped tentatively into the cubicle. The bed was surrounded by assorted machines on trolleys, beeping and pulsing and flashing – they were vaguely menacing. She looked past them to the bed, and the figure of Ross, pale and shrunken into the pillow. He looked like an old man. He stirred, opening his eyes.

'Andie.' He mouthed her name, his voice barely making it out of his throat.

'I'm here,' she said, coming closer. She took hold of his hand, and she felt him squeeze hers, though there was hardly any strength behind it. 'What have you done to yourself?' she chided gently.

He gave her a wan smile.

'How are you feeling?'

'How do I look?' he rasped.

She smiled then.

'Like shit, eh?' he said.

'I've seen you look better.'

He fixed his eyes on her. They had lost their vividness, they looked washed out, she wanted to say lifeless . . . but then again, she really didn't.

'You've never looked so good to me,' he managed to say.

'So, Brooke and Matty are both outside waiting,' Andie said, steering him away from wherever he was heading with that remark. 'Do you think you're up to seeing them?'

'Don't go,' he said.

'They won't let you have more than one visitor, Ross.'

'Don't go, Andie,' he repeated.

'I won't go yet.'

'Don't leave me.'

'Ross . . .'

He started to cry. Oh shit. She held his hand between both of hers and leaned closer. 'It's okay, Ross, I won't go anywhere. But you have to stay calm. They'll make me leave if they think I'm upsetting you.'

There were tears streaming down his face. Andie reached over and grabbed a tissue from a box fixed on the wall above the bed. She gently dabbed his cheeks while he stared up at her.

'I miss you, Andie.'

'Shh.'

'I was a fool.'

'Ross, not now,' she said. 'You're not to let yourself get upset.'

He nodded faintly. 'But you'll stay?'

'The kids want to see you.'

'Yes, but you won't leave the hospital?'

She sighed. 'No, Ross, I won't leave the hospital right now.'

'You'll come back and sit with me after the kids have been in?'

'Ross, Tasha's not going to want me hanging around when she gets back,' she said.

He seemed to be thinking about that. 'You'll come again tomorrow?'

'I have to work, Ross.'

His eyes teared up again.

'I'll visit whenever I can manage, I promise.'

'Okay.'

'I'm going to get Brooke now, she's very anxious to see you.'

He nodded. 'Will you come back and see me before you go?'

'All right.'

'Andie?'

'Hm?'

'Can I have a kiss?'

'Ross . . .'

'Please, just a peck.'

Andie bent down and kissed his cheek, holding her face against his for a moment. 'Everything's going to be all right, Ross,' she said near his ear. 'But you have to promise me you'll stay calm.'

Andie left the cubicle and walked back across the main area. Brooke and Joanna had taken a seat on the chairs lined up along the wall.

'He's waiting for you, Brooke,' she said. 'Don't get a shock when you see him. He's very pale, this has really knocked it out of him.'

Brooke looked apprehensive.

'It'll be okay,' her mother assured her. 'He'll be better for seeing you.'

'Where's Matty?' she asked Joanna after Brooke left them.

'Off to find a toilet,' she said, as Andie took a seat next to her. 'How is he, honestly?'

'I'm not going to lie to you, Joanna . . . he looks like death.'

'But he's conscious, talking?'

'Oh yes, he's quite coherent. But he's very emotional, he started to cry.'

'That's not uncommon after a life-threatening event, especially involving the heart.'

'Really?'

She nodded. 'My father had a couple of heart attacks . . . He used to be a crusty old man, never mean exactly, but definitely not in touch with his emotions. Afterwards he was like a big marshmallow.'

'Mrs Corcoran?'

They both looked up and said 'Yes' simultaneously.

The doctor looked confused. Andie assumed he was the doctor, given that he was wearing a white coat and was flanked by two young, earnest-looking attendants, also in white coats.

'She's the current Mrs Corcoran,' said Joanna, standing up.

'Not really,' Andie muttered as she got to her feet.

Now the doctor looked more confused.

'Sorry,' said Andie. 'It's complicated. I'm his . . . we're both family.'

'Okay,' he said. 'I'm Dr Jorgenson, I'm the surgeon responsible for your husband . . . I mean, Mr Corcoran's care. Doctors Bain and Lee are the registrars assisting me,' he added, indicating his two shadows. 'I don't know how much has been explained to you so far?'

'Not much at all,' said Andie. 'You can start from the beginning.'

'Okay, your hus—'

'Ross,' said Andie.

He nodded. 'Ross collapsed from an episode of cardiac arrhythmia, which is where the heartbeat increases to above a hundred beats per minute. In Ross's case his heart went into ventricular fibrillation, what we refer to as V-fib, which is life-threatening. He's a very lucky man that there was actually a nurse and a paramedic at the gym at the time. They administered effective cardiopulmonary resuscitation until an ambulance arrived and the officers were able to defibrillate.'

'But he's okay now,' said Andie. 'I was just talking to him.'

'He's alive, yes, but we have to prevent this from happening again,' said Dr Jorgenson. 'V-fib usually indicates an underlying medical condition, so we are in the process of evaluating that with further tests, but there's no doubt in my mind that he will need to have defibrillator implant surgery.'

'That sounds serious,' said Joanna.

'We're dealing with the heart here, so it is major surgery,' he said. 'But at the same time I want to assure you that it's a relatively routine procedure. A device, called an implantable cardioverter defibrillator – or ICD – is implanted in the chest area. In case of an irregular heart rhythm, it sends out mild electrical impulses to restore normal heartbeats. If the heart is still not functioning properly, the ICD gives a shock to the heart, after which normal heartbeat is resumed.'

Andie took a deep breath. 'But how long will it be before Ross is able to handle surgery?'

'As I said, we have a number of tests to run first to ensure that he is strong enough, after today's episode. By the same token, the sooner we implant the ICD, the sooner he can begin to recover fully.' He paused. 'Do you have any questions?'

Andie glanced at Joanna, just as Brooke rejoined them.

'It's a lot to take in,' said Andie.

'I understand,' said Dr Jorgenson. 'I'm going to check on him now. We'll speak again after that, when you've had time to digest everything.'

'Oh, Mum,' Brooke said tearfully after the doctors walked away, 'he's really sick.'

'I know, sweetheart,' said Joanna, putting an arm around her daughter. 'But he's in good hands here. They know what they're doing, and they know how to make him better.'

'You should have heard the doctor,' Andie added. 'He was talking like it's all very routine. He's not concerned.'

Brooke seemed relieved.

'Look, this might be a good time,' said Andie. 'I need to make a phone call, I'll be back.'

Joanna nodded, and Andie walked over to the double doors and pressed a button on the wall. As they slid open, Matty was standing on the other side, looking perplexed. 'I didn't know how to get back in,' he said.

Andie smiled at him. 'Go on through, Matty, you'll be able to see your dad soon. I'm just going to make a phone call.'

She walked back to the nurses' station but Sue wasn't there, another nurse was now manning the desk.

'Excuse me,' said Andie. 'I have to make a phone call on my mobile. Do I need to go back to the entrance and outside before I can turn on my phone?'

The nurse directed her to an outside balcony where Andie could use her phone. She was relieved she didn't have to go all the way out of the building, she would have needed to leave a trail of breadcrumbs to find her way back again. She pushed on the doors at the end of the corridor and stepped out onto the soulless concrete balcony. She turned on her phone and checked the time. It would be busy at the restaurant – deliveries came in all morning, and they would be prepping for lunch service, she wondered if Dominic would be able to take her call. She pressed his number and waited, but it went straight to voicemail.

'Hi, it's me, Andie,' she said. 'Um . . . I know you're busy. If you get the chance, could you call me back? Oh, I can't have my phone on inside . . . I'll wait for a bit, um, maybe five, ten minutes? If you get this soon, could you call me? Thanks.'

She hung up and breathed out heavily, leaning against the railing as she looked out at the view across the uni and the racecourse. She felt . . . overwhelmed was the only word to describe it. Ross was very ill, she'd never seen him look so frail, so old, or so vulnerable. Andie didn't know what was going to happen now. She was still his wife, maybe only on paper, but she couldn't just walk away. She might have to act or answer on his behalf, she might have to give consent, sign papers. She had a legal responsibility, and she couldn't help thinking she had a moral one as well.

And then there was Tasha. Andie wondered how devoted she would turn out to be, when push came to shove. She was very young, and this was a lot for anyone to take on, let alone someone so young. She'd only known him . . . Andie was not entirely sure how long, but probably less than a year.

More than anything, Andie was just frightened. Frightened for Ross, frightened about what this was going to mean for her —

Her phone rang. It was Dominic. 'Hello?'

'Hi, Andie, I just got your message. What's happening?'

A lump rose in her throat at hearing his voice, but she needed to keep it together. This must be weird for him . . .

'Andie?'

'Yes, um, well, Ross is still in the high-dependency ward, they're trying to keep him stable.'

'Was it arrhythmia?'

'Uh-huh, he collapsed at the gym, and he had to be resuscitated . . .' Her voice started to break. She swallowed, clearing her throat. 'So they're going to do some tests, and they'll have to operate in the next few days, I gather.'

'Are you all right?'

She sniffed. 'Sure, I saw him, he's . . . okay. He's in good hands, his family are here as well.'

'But are you all right?' he asked again.

She blinked back tears. He didn't know any of these people, he was only concerned about her. Andie appreciated that right now there was someone who cared about her in the scheme of things. 'I'm fine, thanks, Dominic. I'm just not sure when I'll make it into work.'

'It's okay,' he assured her. 'I've already called in a casual. Don't even think about that.'

She sighed. 'Thank you for being so understanding.'

'Of course I understand,' he said. 'You know that . . . don't you?'

She nodded, which was useless on the phone, but she couldn't seem to find her voice.

'Andie?'

'Yes, I'm here,' she managed to say.

'Listen, I have to go.'

'Of course, sorry, I didn't mean to hold you up.'

'You didn't hold me up,' he said. 'Keep in touch, okay?'

'I will.'

'Talk to you later.'

She ended the call and held the phone for a minute, before turning it off and walking inside, and all the way back down the long corridor. Brooke and Matty and Joanna were waiting near the nurses' station.

'What's going on?' said Andie. 'Why are you all out here?'

'Trasha's back,' Brooke said glumly.

'She shooed us all out,' Joanna added.

Andie looked at Matty. 'Did you get to see your dad?' she asked him.

He nodded. Poor kid, his eyes were all swollen and red.

'You can go back in there now, Andie,' said Brooke. 'Tell her to piss off, she's not wanted.'

Andie didn't know what to say, but Joanna spoke for her.

'You can't expect Andie to do that, Brooke. Whether we like it or not, Tasha has a right to be with him. Your father would want that.'

'No, he wouldn't,' she insisted. 'He asked me to make sure Andie came back, after he saw Matty.'

'He asked me too,' Matty said in a gravelly voice.

Andie didn't know what to do. 'Did you talk to the doctor again, Joanna?'

She nodded. 'He was with me when Tasha got back. He said Ross was stable, that they would continue to monitor him overnight, and run some tests tomorrow. He said we should all go home and try to get some rest.'

'Well,' Andie said. 'Doctor's orders . . .'

'But *she* went back into his room,' said Brooke. 'You have to do something, Andie.'

'The main thing now is not to upset your dad.'

'Andie's right,' said Joanna. 'We can't do anything about Tasha. The staff will ask her to leave eventually.'

'Excuse me, Mrs Corcoran?' It was Sue, she was back at the nurses' station. 'I need to get you to fill out those papers.'

'Of course.' She looked at Joanna. 'Did Tasha say anything about Ross's health fund?'

Joanna shook her head. 'I didn't ask her.'

Andie turned back to Sue. 'Did Ms . . .' She realised she didn't even know Tasha's surname.

'Vassallo,' said Joanna.

'Thanks. Did Ms Vassallo leave his health fund details with you?'

She flipped through some pages and shook her head. 'No, I'm afraid there's nothing here.'

Andie took the papers from the nurse and asked Joanna to help her. She simply didn't know a lot about Ross's medical history – he had been in good health throughout their marriage, had never been hospitalised, so it hadn't come up before. Tasha had made a start of the basic information form, filling in his name and address and gender. But Andie had to smile when she came to his date of birth. She nudged Joanna and pointed it out to her.

Joanna shook her head. 'So Ross is getting younger by the year?'

Tasha had also put herself as next of kin, but a clean line had been ruled through that, and Andie's name written above it, by the nurse, Sue, she imagined. She stared at it now, feeling the weight on her shoulders.

After they had completed the forms Andie returned them to Sue at the desk. 'I think we covered everything,' she said. 'We're just waiting on the health fund details.'

'Look, we don't need actual documentation,' said Sue. 'If you can remember which fund he's in, we can contact them and take it from there.'

'Well, in that case,' said Joanna, 'it's probably the same one we've always been in.'

'It's worth a try.'

Joanna gave Sue the details, and Andie felt a little annoyed with herself. She recalled having a conversation about health insurance when they were first married. Ross was doing some paperwork one night, he asked her if she was in a health fund and she told him no. She was only young and had never had much money, so it hadn't been a priority. He'd muttered something about taking care of it, and it never came up again. Ross tended to handle that kind of thing, but whenever he got Andie to sign anything, she always checked it thoroughly. She was uneasy enough about being a kept woman, let alone a clueless kept woman. But she honestly couldn't remember ever signing anything regarding a health fund.

Lauren arrived at the hospital soon after; she'd wanted to avoid bringing the baby in, and James had been in transit from Singapore on a business trip earlier in the day. She was quite worked up and very anxious to see her father, so Andie had to call on Sue and pull rank again.

This time Tasha had nowhere to go when she came out of Ross's room. She paced back and forth for a while, clearly agitated.

'Oh, by the way,' she turned to no one in particular, 'I had a quick look for those papers, but I couldn't find anything.'

In other words, she'd opened a drawer in the filing cabinet and when they didn't jump out at her, she'd given up.

'No problem,' said Andie. 'Joanna sorted it.'

Tasha folded her arms and marched off to the other end of the waiting area to lean against the wall.

When Lauren came out from seeing her father, she did not mince words. 'Dad said he wants to see Andie, that you should go take a break, Tasha.'

The thunder rolled in across her face, then just as quickly blew over again. 'Good, I was desperate for a coffee anyway,' she declared as she turned and flounced off.

When Andie walked into Ross's room, she wasn't sure if he was looking a little better or she was just more prepared now.

'I want you to stay, Andie,' he said.

'I can't be here all the time, Ross, I have a job.'

'I've told the kids, they all agree,' he went on as though he hadn't heard her. 'You can tell Tasha she doesn't need to hang around.'

'Oh no, Ross, I'm not going to do your dirty work for you,' said Andie. 'If you don't want Tasha here, you tell her yourself.' She paused. 'But I think that would be mean, to be honest.'

'Why?'

'Ross, what is wrong with you?' said Andie. 'You're living with the woman. You made your bed, buddy . . .'

'I know, I've made mistakes —'

'Not now, Ross.'

'Just give me some hope, Andie.'

She gave him a stern look. 'You have to stop this, Ross, it isn't fair. You can't ask me questions like that at a time like this.'

'But this is exactly the time those questions need to be asked.'

'Ross, I don't want to upset you.'

'So your answer would upset me,' he said, despondent.

Andie sighed. 'It's just that I'm making a life for myself, I've got my own place now, I've got a job . . .' She wouldn't mention that she was seeing someone, no need to rub salt in. 'Do you have any idea how lucky you are, Ross? You have three kids who are all here for you, even though you haven't always done the same for them. You have a woman who's barely left your bedside, you have me, you even have your first wife here as well.'

'Joanna's out there?'

Andie nodded. 'She brought the kids, she's been here all day.'

'I'd like to see her, afterwards.'

Ross and his harem, how much stroking did his ego need?

'I'll tell Joanna,' she said. 'Now you need to get some rest.'

*

It was late afternoon when Andie walked in the door of her apartment and dumped her bag on the table. She was exhausted, and hot and sticky. She opened the windows to get some air into the place. There was a storm forecast for later, she'd heard on the radio in the car on the way home, and she could smell it in the air. She peeled off the cardigan and tossed it aside, she couldn't wait to get under the shower. But first she better let Dominic know what was going on. She sent him a text message to say she was home and that she would definitely be at work tomorrow. She didn't expect a response, she was sure he wouldn't have his phone on him anyway, they would be gearing up for dinner service and he'd be flat out. She stripped off and stood under the shower for ages, directing the stream of water squarely onto the crown of her head, as though it could somehow wash away the chaos in her mind. This morning she had felt so free and happy, and in only a few short hours everything had been turned upside down. She was still Ross's wife, with all the duties and obligations and responsibilities that went with it. In sickness and in health. She was no more free of him than she was free to fly to the moon.

*

Andie woke with a start. Her phone was ringing and she reached for it on the bedside table, but it wasn't there. She blinked rapidly, waiting for her eyes to adjust. The apartment was in darkness, the blinds rattling wildly against the window frames, and she was lying sprawled across the bed, stark-naked.

The phone stopped ringing, followed almost immediately by a knock at the door. 'Andie, it's me, Dominic,' she heard from the other side. 'Are you there?'

Everything flooded back, Ross, the hospital, the drive home in the heat . . . When she'd finally stepped out of the shower it was still so hot in the apartment she couldn't stand to put on any clothes, or even to dry herself, so she had lain down on her towel on the bed to wait for the storm . . . and had obviously fallen into a very deep sleep.

Andie pulled herself upright. 'Just give me a minute, Dominic,' she called, giving her head a shake to clear the cobwebs. She turned on the bedside light so she could see, and spotted her bathrobe at the end of the bed, hastily slipping it on as she scooted over to the windows to pull them shut. The blinds sagged and were finally still. Andie tied the sash of her robe firmly around her waist as she turned for the door. 'Coming!' She gave her hair a shake, it was still damp. She must look a sight.

She opened the door and Dominic was standing there, a tentative smile on his face. She was so very glad to see that face.

'Were you sleeping?' he said. 'I'm sorry. I knocked for a while, when there was no answer I thought maybe you were back at the hospital, so I rang your mobile.'

'Oh, that was you?'

'I could hear it ringing, so I knew you had to be inside. I didn't mean to disturb you.'

'Oh, no, Dominic, you're not disturbing me, really,' said Andie.

'But maybe I should let you get back to sleep?'

'No, please, come in.'

'Okay, just for a minute.'

Andie closed the door behind him as he walked inside. She was so happy to see him she had to restrain herself from jumping straight into his arms. She really hoped he'd stay longer than a minute.

He turned around and held up a bag. 'I thought you might not have eaten, so I brought you some food.'

All right, that was it, her eyes filled with tears. She didn't want him to think she was crying for Ross, although that was probably partly true, but it was so much more that she couldn't begin to explain . . .

'Andie?'

'Thank you for the food . . .' A sob caught in her throat, she tried to swallow it down but it was no use. Dominic set the bag on the kitchen bench and came over to her, gathering her in his arms and holding her close.

'I'm sorry,' she whimpered into his chest. 'I'm just feeling very overwhelmed.'

'It's okay,' he said tenderly. 'Do you want me to go?'

'No.' She looked up at him. 'Do you have to be somewhere?'

He shook his head. 'Why do you ask?'

'You said you'd only come in for a minute.'

'I didn't want to impose.'

'You're so not imposing.'

He smiled faintly. 'Then I'll stay as long as you want me to.' He drew her close again. 'Is there anything I can do?'

She sighed. 'Just this, what you're doing right now.'

He tightened his arms around her, planting a kiss on the top of the head. 'Well, I can do this . . . for a very long time.'

*

An hour later Dominic was still holding her, spooned into her back as they lay on the bed, facing the window. The storm had finally hit and there was rain sheeting across the window.

'Do you remember when you told me that you didn't believe in fate?' Andie asked him.

'Hm,' he murmured next to her ear. 'I think I said I wasn't sure . . . Why?'

She sighed. 'I keep thinking, if I hadn't run out of the restaurant that night, I might never have discovered that Ross was having an affair, and it might not have amounted to anything, and it might have even been over by now.'

Dominic rested his chin on her shoulder. 'What are you saying?'

'It's just, without that one little twist of fate, I would be entirely responsible for Ross now. I feel almost guilty, like I dodged a bullet that was meant for me.'

'I really don't understand how you could feel guilty, or responsible.'

Andie turned over to lie on her back, looking up at him. 'Ross is still my husband, I am actually legally responsible for him, I discovered today. So maybe I haven't dodged a bullet after all. Maybe instead I'm being punished.'

'What for?' Dominic frowned. 'You're not making a lot of sense, Andie. If anyone's being punished, isn't it more likely to be Ross, considering he's the one who's been cheating on everybody, and he's the one lying there in the hospital bed?'

'I guess.' She sighed. 'The thing is, Ross always maintained that he wanted me back, and I said I could never trust him again. But even so, I wasn't really prepared to give it a try.'

Dominic was staring intently at her. 'Andie, are you having second thoughts about this . . . about us?'

'No,' she insisted. 'Not at all.' She wanted to tell him he was the only thing she was sure about, the only thing that made sense right now. But was that too much? She didn't want to jinx it, or put any pressure on him. They were supposed to be going with the flow, no complications. So much for that. Andie felt as though her life was hanging in a very delicate balance. One false move . . .

She stroked his arm. 'Don't mind me,' she said. 'I was brought up Catholic, guilt is my default response.'

Wednesday

Dominic stayed the night with her, but he left early to go home and change for work. Andie waited until he was gone before she rang the hospital to check on Ross. She didn't want to bring Dominic into this any more than she already had. He had been understanding beyond the call, but she didn't want to test his patience.

The nurse on the phone reported that Ross had had an uneventful night, and they were currently preparing him for his tests. Andie called Joanna to let her know.

'I wasn't sure whether they'd tell you much over the phone,' she said.

'Thanks,' said Joanna. 'Actually, Lauren is going to clarify they are his kids, so that they'll be kept informed as well. Should take some of the pressure off you.'

That was something.

'Be careful, Andie,' she went on. 'Don't get sucked back in . . . You know, Ross made his own bed . . .'

'I've already said those exact words to him,' Andie assured her. 'Are you going in to the hospital today, Joanna?'

'No, I have to work,' she said. 'Lauren is coming over to pick up Brooke and Matty soon, they'll go in together.'

That put Andie's mind at ease. There would be plenty of people around for Ross, he wouldn't miss her. Besides, she had her own responsibilities. Dominic had assured her that yesterday was but a blip on the radar, and that Cosmo was expecting to begin her training today.

*

Main meal prep meant handling a lot of meat. Quite a lot of meat. Andie spent the morning slicing, dicing, filleting, trimming, rolling, dressing, and – an old favourite – deboning. Preparing the very fiddly garnishes had really honed her skills with a knife, so once she got into a rhythm, Andie's mind drifted. She wondered how Ross was doing today, what tests he was having, when his surgery would be scheduled. And most worrying, what was going to happen after that.

But she didn't stop all day. Whenever there was a lull, Cosmo would take the opportunity to demonstrate another technique, or teach her about the cuts of meat they commonly used in the restaurant. So Andie didn't get to check her phone until the staff dinner break in the late afternoon, only to find there were no messages. She briefly wondered if she should ring the hospital herself, but she resisted. No news is good news, and Andie did not need a progress report.

Dinner service flew by in a blur. Both sittings were fully booked, and there was a group in the larger private dining room – otherwise known as the VIP room, because anyone who could afford to book it had to be from the upper echelons. Andie was cleaning her work station when it occurred to her she hadn't sighted Dominic for a while. She wondered if he'd gone home already, without saying goodbye . . .

Cosmo turned around from the bench in front of her. 'Andie, you should finish up and go home.'

She surveyed the kitchen. There were still waitstaff hanging around, so that meant there were still diners in the restaurant. 'Are you sure? Isn't there anything else I can do?'

He shook his head. 'I'm going to have to stay for a while anyway. There's a group of mining execs in the VIP room, they've just ordered a forty-year-old Cognac and invited Chef to join them. I think it's going to be a long night,' he said. 'You should get out of here. You've had a big day, you must be tired.'

Andie was tired, but when she got home, she felt oddly restless. She really wished she'd got to see Dominic before she left, just to make sure they were still all right. Besides, she missed him. What a wuss she was turning out to be.

She finally forced herself to switch off the TV that she wasn't even watching, turn off the lights and get into bed. Then her phone rang. She switched on the bedside lamp and picked it up. She felt her heart jump when she saw it was Dominic.

'I didn't wake you, did I?' he asked.

'No, I was only just going to bed.'

'Well, I'm only just leaving work, I'm calling you from the car. I couldn't get away from the VIP room.'

'How was it?'

'The usual. They were all drunk and fawning, but they just wouldn't leave. The attitude of entitlement people seem to have when they throw money around . . . I hate keeping the waitstaff late on a weeknight.'

Andie smiled. He was a decent boss, no wonder the staff were so loyal to him.

'Cosmo said you did well today,' he went on.

'Oh, that's good, he's a wonderful teacher.'

'So, any news from the hospital?'

'No, but I'm sure everything must be fine. I was too busy to worry about it today.' That was only a very little lie, hardly a lie at all.

'Well, I just wanted to say goodnight,' said Dominic.

Andie would have loved to ask him over, but it was late, and she didn't want to sound needy. Definitely not needy. She couldn't expect the man to keep dropping everything to be at her beck and call.

'Goodnight, Dominic.'

'Sleep well.'

Thursday

In fact Andie slept like the proverbial log until the phone rang at seven, waking her. Who rings at seven o'clock in the morning? Her eyes were too bleary to focus on the screen of the phone, but if it was anyone she knew their name would have come up in letters big enough for her to read. Then she had a sick feeling. She quickly cleared her throat and answered the phone.

'Hello?'

'Mrs Corcoran?'

'Um . . . yes?'

'It's Dr Jorgenson, we met briefly the other day.'

'Yes, of course. Is Ross okay, did something happen?'

'No, he's doing really well, actually. We're waiting on a couple more test results but we're not expecting any surprises. I'm booking him in for surgery tomorrow.'

'Oh. So soon?'

'The sooner the better,' he said. 'Someone will call you today to confirm the time.'

Why, Andie wanted to say. Why was he even calling her in the first place?

'I want to assure you that your husband will be fine, Mrs Corcoran.'

Oh, that was why. Andie pictured her name printed in clear, block letters under 'next of kin'.

'It is heart surgery, as I explained, but it's routine, and his indicators are all very good at present,' he said. 'All going well, he should be home after a couple of days.'

'Really, that quickly?'

'Patients do much better out of the hospital and in their own homes. It can place more of a burden on the family looking after them, perhaps, but usually they're happy to have them home as well. There will be some things you'll have to be aware of regarding his post-operative care, but I'll explain more about that after his surgery tomorrow.'

So that meant he expected to see her there. 'Okay. Thanks for the call, Doctor,' she said, hanging up the phone. She supposed she didn't mind being there, she'd certainly want to know that Ross was all right. So she just had to hope the surgery would be scheduled for early in the morning. She was going to have to coordinate with the kids, so someone was there at least, if she couldn't hang around. And of course, there was always Tasha. For now, Andie had to get to work and focus; tomorrow she might have to ask for some leeway.

*

It was another nonstop day at the restaurant and Andie was unable to check her phone again until the late afternoon. There were a couple of missed calls – one from hospital administration, with details of Ross's surgery. It was scheduled for seven in the morning, she was glad to hear. The other call was from Brooke, with a rather plaintive request to call her back.

'Hi, Brooke, what's up?' Andie asked when she picked up.

'I was just wondering if you're going to visit Dad today?'

'I can't, honey, I'm at work.'

'Oh . . .'

'Is there something wrong?'

'He's just a little down. He was upset that he didn't see you at all yesterday.'

Andie sighed. 'But he knows I had to go to work, I told him.'

'He thought you might come after work.'

Ross never did get restaurant hours. 'Brooke, I don't finish until ten, or later. But look, I was going to call you anyway. I don't know if you heard, but his surgery's been scheduled for seven in the morning.'

'Yeah, they came and told Dad.'

'Well, you can tell him I'm coming in first thing to see him before he goes into theatre.'

'He'll be so happy,' said Brooke, relieved.

'But I don't know if I'll be able to stay afterwards,' said Andie. 'It depends how long the surgery takes. So at least one of you should plan to be there.'

'I think that'll be too early for Lauren with the baby. But I don't start work until after lunch tomorrow, and I'll see what Matty's up to. He's got a job for the holidays too, but it's only casual.'

'Okay,' said Andie. 'And look, unless you particularly want to see your father before he goes into theatre, you won't have to get to the hospital till about nine. I doubt you'll be able to see him before that, at least.'

She heard a tap on the door and turned around. Dominic was standing in the doorway.

'Listen, Brooke, I have to go, okay?'

'No worries, I'll see you tomorrow.'

Andie hung up the phone.

'Is everything all right?' he asked.

She swallowed. 'I'm on a break, Cosmo said it was okay —'

'Andie, I'm not checking up on you,' he said. 'You can make personal calls on your own phone during your break without answering to me.'

She smiled faintly. He was leaning against the doorjamb, and he kept glancing down the corridor.

'Are you on lookout or something?' she asked him.

'Yes, actually, I am,' he said seriously.

'Oh, right.' Andie put her phone back in her locker and walked across the room towards him.

'I'm only trying to keep you happy,' he said. 'Be discreet.'

'I see, this is just to keep me happy?'

'Well, it certainly isn't for me,' he said, his eyes trained down the corridor. 'What would make me happy right now would be to lock this door and have my way with you.'

She grinned. 'Just exactly what is involved in "having your way with me"?'

He glanced at her then, and Andie could see the glint in his eyes. 'It's hard to explain, I really have to show you.'

She had a sudden mental flash of Dominic having his way with her up against the lockers . . . She felt a little lightheaded.

'So I was thinking,' he went on, 'it's a normal service tonight, no private parties, so I should be able to get away on time.' He looked down the corridor again. 'Perhaps you'd like to come back to my place . . . I could make pancakes again . . . I think you said they were orgasmic the other night.'

'I don't think I was talking about the pancakes.'

He gave her a look that could best be described as smouldering. It was those dark eyes. She was picturing them in his kitchen, feeding each other pancakes and stumbling their way back up the stairs to bed to make love again . . . and waking up with him in the morning . . .

'Oh bugger.'

'What's wrong?' Dominic turned to look at her.

Andie sighed. 'Ross's operation is scheduled for seven tomorrow morning, I said I'd be there before he went into theatre.'

He nodded. 'Of course, no problem.'

'We could still have pancakes tonight?'

He was staring down at the floor. 'It might be safer for you to go straight home, you know, with such an early start.'

Andie pressed her lips together to stop them from trembling. She felt bitterly disappointed . . . or bitter with disappointment, more likely.

'Can I have a raincheck?' she asked.

'Absolutely. So I take it you'll be late to work tomorrow?'

'No, I don't plan to be, I was going to come straight from the hospital.'

'Still you should probably mention it to Cosmo in case.'

'Sure.'

He glanced down the corridor again. 'I better get back.'

And then he was gone. Andie's heart dropped into the pit of her stomach. One more day, and this would all be over.

6.30 am

Ross had been moved to a private room on the same floor as the high-dependency unit, not far from the nurses' station. Tasha was waiting outside and she actually rolled her eyes and sighed as Andie approached. She felt like she was in one of those teen movies about mean girls at high school. This was going to be excruciating.

'Hello, Tasha.'

She just nodded in response.

'What's going on?'

'They asked me to step out for a minute while they get Ross ready for surgery.'

Andie settled herself against the wall on the other side of the door to Tasha. That way there was distance between them, but they weren't facing each other. Presently a nurse appeared, holding the door open while an orderly wheeled Ross out on a gurney, and another nurse followed behind.

'Andie?' Ross lifted one hand as he passed her, but Tasha swooped in and fell in beside him, taking hold of his hand.

'I'm coming, Ross,' said Andie, walking a few paces behind. She watched, faintly amused, as Tasha tottered along on her towering heels. They all packed into the elevator, Tasha still clutching onto his hand, while Andie tucked herself into a corner.

Ross raised his head. 'Hi, Andie, I'm so glad you came.'

'Of course, not a problem,' she said briskly.

Andie noticed the two nurses exchange a bemused look. The atmosphere in the elevator was so thick it was a wonder anyone could breathe. When the doors opened again, the orderly pushed the gurney through and Tasha had to release Ross's hand momentarily, dashing forward again to plant a possessive hand on his arm. Andie dropped back behind the two nurses, happy to keep her distance. When they arrived outside the theatres, the orderly parked the gurney by the wall, and one of the nurses took his chart over to the desk. Ross lifted his head again, beckoning to Andie. She came closer.

'Give us a sec, will you, Tash?' he said, patting the hand that was still clamped firmly on his arm.

Andie didn't look at her as she stepped back from the bed, she didn't dare.

Ross reached for her hand. He was looking a good deal better, there was colour in his face again, and his eyes were not so washed out.

'Thanks for being here, Andie,' he said. 'Will I see you after?'

'Depends how long it takes, Ross, I have to go to work.'

'When will I see you then?'

'I'm not sure, it's the weekend, it's very busy at the restaurant.'

He started to tear up. Oh God. 'I don't think I can get through this without you, Andie.'

'Ross,' she chided. She hoped Tasha couldn't hear any of this. 'You're going to be fine, better than fine, in fact, slightly bionic after this. You might end up with superpowers.'

He managed a smile then. 'Do I get a kiss for luck?'

'You don't need luck.' And he wasn't going to be left out here to face Tasha. So Andie popped a quick kiss on his forehead, before backing away from the bed. Tasha swooped on him again, leaning right over him. Andie turned away.

A theatre nurse came through the plastic swing doors. 'It's time,' she said, touching Tasha on the arm. Tasha stepped back and they wheeled the gurney through the swing doors and out of sight.

Andie looked over at Tasha. This was so awkward. She'd given up pancakes and sex for this.

'I'm going to get coffee, Tasha,' she announced. She didn't want to actually invite her to join her, but she wanted to be civil at least. 'Can I get you something?'

'No, I'm right.' And she flounced off without so much as a glance in Andie's direction, or a 'thanks anyway'.

Andie decided she could risk staying in the café for at least an hour, she remembered Dr Jorgenson had said the operation was likely to take around two hours. She finally bought a newspaper and wandered back down to the waiting room. She spotted Tasha over the far side, fiddling with her phone. She didn't look up, but Andie thought it would be rude not to acknowledge her. She walked over and sat down in the adjacent row of seats. 'Hi.'

Tasha's head bobbed up. 'Oh, hi,' she murmured, returning her attention to her phone.

'Haven't heard anything yet, I take it?' Andie persisted.

'Nuh,' Tasha said without looking up, her thumbs flying across the screen.

She shouldn't really have her phone on in here, but Andie wasn't going to be the one to tell her. She sat back and opened up the paper. She heard a snort and looked across at Tasha.

'You still read the newspaper?' she muttered, not making eye contact. 'Like, hard copy? That's so old-school. Ross loves his newspapers . . . so lame,' she sighed.

God, Andie hoped Brooke and Matty weren't far away.

As it turned out they weren't, they arrived about twenty minutes later. They came straight over to Andie and both gave her a hug, all but ignoring Tasha.

'Have you heard anything?' Brooke asked.

'Not yet, but I don't think it'll be much longer.'

It was barely nine o'clock when Dr Jorgenson came out to inform them that the operation had been a success.

'It was all very routine,' he said. 'He's in recovery now, you should be able to see him in about half an hour. So I want to just talk to you about what to expect from here on in.'

He pulled a chair over, and they formed a loose circle around him. 'As I explained the other day, the ICD will send a shock to Ross's heart if he goes into arrhythmia again.'

'Is it painful?' Andie asked.

'According to people who have an ICD fitted, it feels like a sudden thump in the chest area. So he shouldn't drive for a couple of weeks at least, and he really has to take it easy for a while.'

'Can you see it in his chest?' Matty asked, wide-eyed.

'Yes, you can,' said Dr Jorgenson. 'There's a lump about the size of the lid of a bottle of tablets protruding from this area here,' he said, touching Matty's chest, 'just below the collarbone.'

'Cool,' said Matty. 'Will it go off when he goes through a security scanner at the airport?'

The things boys thought to ask.

'It can, so he'll always have to let them know he has an ICD,' said Dr Jorgenson. 'There's also some concern about mobile phones, so he should always take a call on the opposite side, and obviously he shouldn't keep his phone in his breast pocket.'

'And he'll have this . . . device, inside him forever?' asked Tasha, barely containing a grimace.

'Yes, though it will have to be replaced eventually,' he said. 'But for now, there are a few basic guidelines to follow. He must not raise his right arm up over his shoulder or lift anything heavy for six weeks. And obviously he should avoid stress. A physio will see him tomorrow, she'll be able to explain more, and she'll give you lots of literature that you can refer to once you take him home,' he added, looking at Andie.

Don't look at me, she felt like saying.

'You all need to be aware that during this adjustment period there is increased incidence of anxiety in the patient, and depression rates are higher as well. He needs plenty of reassurance that his future is bright, that things will be back to normal in time.'

'How much longer will he stay in hospital?' Tasha asked.

'He should be able to go home in a couple of days, all going well,' said Dr Jorgenson. 'We just have to run some checks on the device before we let him leave.'

Andie glanced across at Tasha. She looked pale, was she going to be up for this? But it was none of Andie's business. And yet it was. In sickness and in health, the phrase kept playing on a loop, like a line from a song you can't get out of your head.

'As I said, you should be able to see him in about half an hour,' he said finally, getting to his feet.

They all stood except for Tasha. She just sat there, still pale, staring ahead of her.

'Thanks so much for everything, Dr Jorgenson,' said Andie, and Brooke and Matty murmured in agreement. 'I'll have to go now too,' Andie added, after the doctor took his leave. 'You guys will be right?'

'I start work in about an hour,' said Matty. 'Should be just enough time to put shit on Dad for his robot heart.'

Brooke elbowed him. 'I'll be here till one. And Lauren's going to come in tonight.'

'Okay, well, we'll keep in touch,' said Andie. She glanced over at Tasha, still sitting in the same spot. She hadn't moved or said anything. 'Bye, Tasha.' But she didn't get a response.

Andie hurried out of the building to the parking station. She turned on her phone to discover there was a run of missed calls from Meredith, of all people. She sighed. She hadn't spoken to her sister since she'd moved out of the house, and this really wasn't a good time. But she had developed a pathological fear of ignoring Meredith's calls, given past experience, so she pressed *Call* and set a brisk pace back to her car. She was not going to be late for work for anything.

'Andrea, finally,' Meredith said when she answered. 'I really don't understand why someone has a mobile phone that they constantly leave turned off!'

Andie went to reply but Meredith was not finished.

'I mean, you're as bad as the children. Their phones are supposed to be for emergencies and yet any time I really have to contact one of them, I can never get through. They always have an excuse – they're out of credit, or out of charge, or in class . . . it drives me mad. So when you didn't answer, I looked you up on the White Pages online, but you're not listed, at least there's no A. Corcoran in Bondi, that's all I had to go on because I don't have your address, which is the whole reason I was calling in the first place. I'm sending out invitations for my fortieth birthday, and I didn't know where to send yours. Honestly, all the means of communication we have at our disposal and all I have for my own sister is a mobile phone number you rarely seem to answer.'

That was a breath, she had finally taken a breath.

'I had to turn it off in the hospital,' Andie said quickly, grabbing the opportunity.

'Why are you at the hospital? What's going on? Are you all right?'

'Yes, I'm fine. It's Ross.'

'Is it something serious?' She actually sounded concerned.

'Yes, he had a heart attack.'

'Oh my goodness,' said Meredith. 'Isn't he a bit young?'

'It wasn't a coronary, he has arrhythmia, he just came out of surgery —'

'They implanted an ICD, I gather?'

'That's right.'

'They are very effective, they've been shown to decrease mortality rates significantly. You don't have to worry, Andrea, he'll still have a long life ahead of him.'

Andie knew Meredith had a degree in some field of medical research, but did she have to know everything about everything?

'So I gather you two have reconciled then?' Meredith asked.

'No, at least not in the way you think,' said Andie. 'I have been here for him, obviously, it was the right thing to do.'

'Of course it's the right thing to do, Andrea,' Meredith declared. 'For heaven's sake, he's your husband. How would you feel if this was reversed, and you were completely on your own, needing medical care, and he didn't give a damn? This is when duty overrides personal feelings, Andrea. It's why we have the institution of marriage, it protects us. What do you think Mum would have to say about this?'

Plenty, no doubt.

'Ross is not on his own, Meredith.' Andie had had to wait until she'd drawn breath again to get a word in. 'While he was in theatre, I sat in the waiting room with his new, very young girlfriend, so please don't lecture me about duty, because I think I've gone beyond the call.'

Meredith had nothing to say to that.

'Now I have to go, I'm on my way to work,' said Andie, as she got to her car. 'I'll text you my address.'

*

Andie made it to the restaurant comfortably on time, and was determined to put everything behind her and focus on her work. She didn't even mind that she'd been assigned a list of jobs that included some of her least favourite tasks, including clarifying a sizeable quantity of butter this afternoon. It was so tedious and painstaking, but that was okay. Tedious was good – anything apart from being in that hospital, and talking about Ross, and dealing with Tasha, was, in fact, excellent.

But her mind kept drifting, recalling the stunned-mullet expression on Tasha's face at the hospital. Andie had to wonder if the girl had even thought through the ramifications. Was she prepared to take time off work to care for Ross? Was she able to? She couldn't just leave him to fend for himself all day, that was simply not an option, at least not for the first week or two. Andie didn't want to butt her nose in any further than she already had, and she could hardly tell Tasha what to do. She'd have to discuss it with the kids. True, they couldn't stand Tasha, especially Brooke, but Ross was their father, and they had the right to insist that he receive proper care, even if they had to provide it themselves. There wasn't going to be much Andie could do to help, Mondays were her only day off . . .

'Andie?'

She jumped. Dominic was leaning over the bench to get her attention.

'Sorry, I was . . . concentrating.' Not so much on her job though. She glanced down at the piece of pork belly she was working on; it was okay, she hadn't hacked it. She had to keep her wits about her.

'How is everything?' Dominic asked.

'Everything's good, really good,' she said brightly.

'Your ex-husband is out of surgery?'

She nodded. 'It all went well, and he should be going home in a couple of days. So now things can get back to normal, thank God.'

He gave her a curious look.

Great, that sounded compassionate. 'I didn't mean —'

'I know what you meant,' he said.

Andie glanced at him, lowering her voice. 'Maybe I can take you up on that raincheck later?' she suggested, her heart fluttering inside her chest.

'Maybe . . .' He gave her a smile, just a small one, but it did go as far as his eyes. 'Anyway, I'll leave you to it for now.'

Andie watched him walk back along the bench towards his office, and breathed a sigh of relief. She returned her attention to the pork belly as her phone started to vibrate in her pocket. Damn. She shouldn't even have it on her, it was expressly against kitchen policy to take calls on the floor, but Andie couldn't bring herself to leave it in her locker. Ross was still in recovery when she'd left the hospital, it didn't feel right to be out of contact.

She worked quickly but carefully through the pork, cutting it into the perfect cubes required for the dish. She carried the finished tray to the next station and went to wash her hands. She couldn't see Dominic anywhere, and Cosmo and Tang were occupied gearing up for lunch service, so Andie slipped out to the change room to check her phone. There was a missed call from Brooke. She pressed to call back.

'Hi, it's me,' Andie said when she answered. 'What's going on, is your father all right?'

'Yeah, he's still pretty out of it,' she said.

'I think that's normal, and it's good for him to rest.'

'He keeps asking for you.'

That must be going down well with Tasha. 'I'm at work, Brooke.'

'I know, that's what I told him. It's just . . .'

'What?'

'Well, Matty's already left, and I have to go soon. I just feel bad leaving Dad alone all afternoon, right after he's had surgery.'

Andie sighed. 'Brooke, you really have to stop being so dismissive of Tasha. He won't be alone, she'll be with him.'

'Tasha's not here, Andie.'

'What? When did she leave?'

'She didn't even wait until they brought Dad out of recovery.'

'She didn't?' said Andie, her mind racing. 'Well, I suppose she must have had to go to work, she's been off the whole week with this.' But it seemed funny to bother to go back on a Friday, especially the day of his surgery.

'Listen, Brooke, he'll be all right. Just tell him Lauren will be in later. You said he's really out of it, he's probably not going to even notice.'

After she hung up, Andie slipped her phone back into her pocket. She had to be contactable, she really didn't have a choice now. She went back to the kitchen and got on with her work, but her mind wasn't in gear. Where the hell was Tasha? They couldn't get rid of her before, and now she'd skipped off after his operation without even waiting to see him? Andie was beginning to get a bad feeling about this.

But she couldn't do anything about it right now, especially once service was underway and they were all run off their feet, as ever. Friday was the day of the long lunch, the busiest lunch service of the week. Andie felt her phone vibrating in her pocket a couple of times, but she had to ignore it. She was finally able to duck out after the last order was away, returning to the change room to check the missed calls.

The first left a voicemail, it was Ross's bank. What the hell? The woman said something about the security division, and left a number for a direct line, asking Andie to call back at her earliest convenience. The other call had come from the hospital.

'Your husband is a little distressed after his operation,' the nurse told Andie when she rang back.

'Is he in pain?'

'No, we're managing that. But he's quite emotional, which is not unusual after surgery. It's just that he's alone, so he's feeling it more. He asked me to call you to find out when you're coming in. I wanted to put his mind at rest.'

'Look, I'm sorry, I'm at work, and Ross knew I wasn't able to come in. I gather Ms Vassallo isn't around?'

'No one's been here since his daughter left earlier.'

'Well, his other daughter will be in this evening. Maybe you can remind him.'

'I will, thanks, Mrs Corcoran.'

Andie hung up with a heavy sigh. Why was this happening? Her fingers were trembling as she returned the call to the bank.

'Thank you for getting back to us, Mrs Corcoran,' the woman said. 'We have been trying to get in touch directly with your husband —'

'He's in the hospital right now.'

'Oh, I see.'

'What's this about?'

'There has been some unusual activity on Mr Corcoran's accounts in the last few hours.'

Andie felt sick in the stomach. 'What do you mean, "unusual activity"?'

'There have been several large credit transactions, as well as a substantial cash advance, all within the space of an hour or two.'

Shit. 'Can you put a stop on the credit cards?'

'Do you have reason to believe the cards have been stolen?'

'Um, well . . . it's complicated. Can't you just put a stop on them?'

'Not without Mr Corcoran's authorisation, unless you're prepared to officially report the cards as stolen.'

Andie thought about it. She had no idea what Tasha was doing, but Ross would have given her the cards, so Andie couldn't accuse her of stealing.

'No, I don't want to do that. I'll see what I can find out, and I'll get back to you.'

'You have my direct number.'

Cosmo popped his head around the door. 'There you are, Andie. I need that clarified butter.'

'Yes, goodbye,' she said, hanging up quickly. 'Of course, Cosmo, sorry about that.'

She raced back to her station and got to work chopping up the butter and placing it in a large pot. Her head was spinning. So Tasha had disappeared, and was in the process of maxing out Ross's credit cards. Andie wondered how many she had, what kind of limit was on them. Ross had always been very generous with her, but they were married. She hoped he'd been a little more judicious with someone he hadn't known so long. But it was unlikely. He was a bit of a show-off with his money, he liked to splash it around.

Andie tried to calm down, think it through rationally. So Tasha had left the hospital without waiting to see Ross after his operation, it didn't mean she was never going back. She might have been relieved, gone off and had a bit of a spending spree; she may even have been buying something for him . . . to help with his recovery.

Yeah, right. Not likely. Andie wasn't going to stress about it, it wasn't her problem. Ross could afford it, and it was his own stupid fault anyway.

It suddenly occurred to her – who was going to look after him after he left the hospital if Tasha was gone? He couldn't go back to the apartment alone. *Shit.* Matty and Brooke were going to have to stay with him, take turns. That was the only way. Andie refused to be roped into this, it just wasn't possible anyway; she had a job, she had a life of her own —

'Andie, what are you doing?'

It was Cosmo, in front of her. The butter was foaming up almost out of the pot. *Shit.* She quickly moved it off the flame. 'Oh my God, I'm so sorry.'

He peered into the pot. 'It's no good, you'll have to discard that batch and start again.'

'Cosmo.' It was Dominic, right behind her. 'Have one of the others take over. Andie, can I see you in my office?'

Shit. Shit.

She followed him into the office and he closed the door behind her. 'Take a seat,' he said.

He was being very formal, so Andie followed suit.

'I apologise, Chef,' she said. 'It was a mistake, it won't happen again.' After all, he didn't believe people should make mistakes twice.

'Are you sure, Andie?' Dominic said gravely, as he walked around his desk and sat down. 'You have to decide if you're up to this right now. I noticed you missing from the floor a couple of times today. You said everything was over with. It doesn't appear to be.'

'I really do apologise, Chef —'

'Andie, it's me, Dominic,' he said. 'Talk to me.'

She sighed. 'There have been some . . . unexpected developments today.'

'Is your ex-husband all right?'

'He's fine. It's, um . . .' Andie looked at him. She really wasn't sure she should go into it with him.

'You have to tell me what's going on, Andie.'

She took a breath. 'Ross's girlfriend has decided she's not up for this, so she's taken off, and it looks like she's spent the day maxing out his credit cards. He's going to be released from hospital as soon as the day after tomorrow and I don't know who's going to look after him, or what's going to happen, quite frankly.'

There was a pause before he spoke. 'Then I think you should take a few days off to sort it out.'

'No, Dominic, I don't need to. Really, it's not my problem anymore.'

'It sounds as though it's very much your problem, Andie.'

'Look, I'll leave my phone in my locker from now on, I'll deal with it after work.'

'You had your phone on the floor?' he said darkly.

'I didn't take any calls —'

'It's expressly forbidden, and you know it is. You're the one who didn't want special treatment, and now you're taking calls on the floor —'

'I wasn't on the floor,' she cried.

'But you should have been,' he snapped back at her, raising his voice above hers.

Andie just stared at him.

'Take a few days,' he said levelly. 'And I'm sorry, Andie, but that's not a suggestion.'

'No,' she said, 'it sounds like an order. You're Chef again, right? Not Dominic.'

'Don't be like that,' he returned. 'I just can not have this kind of disruption in my kitchen.'

'No, that would never do, would it?'

He frowned at her. 'So now you're pissed at me? Seriously, Andie?'

She bristled. 'It's just that you should know there are some things more important than trying to create the perfect dish. This kitchen, the way it works, it's not like real life.'

'No, it's a place of work, where there are standards and expectations.'

'It was just a pot of butter, for Chrissakes, I'll pay for it. Nobody died, Chef.'

'Okay, that's quite enough,' he said harshly. 'Now, please leave as I asked . . . and try to restrain yourself from running out this time, show some decorum.'

Andie was mortified. She got up and walked out the door without looking at him again.

*

She was shaking when she got back to her car, and she had to sit for a while to pull herself together. What the hell was that? Where was the Dominic of only a day or two ago, offering her comfort, reassuring her he'd be there for her? But not in his precious bloody kitchen.

Oh God, maybe she was expecting special treatment. Not consciously, but she knew the rules, and she'd consciously broken them. And Dominic was right, she had acted pissed off with him for daring to challenge her about it. Damn! It was an impossible situation, she should never have gone out with him in the first place . . . She felt a stabbing sensation in her heart with the realisation. It was hopeless.

Andie started the car and drove out of the carpark, and she had the strongest feeling it would be the last time. She couldn't come back, how could she work here and have a relationship with Dominic? And now she wasn't sure she could have that either, it was spoiled like that blasted butter in the bottom of the pot. Tears welled in her eyes and spilled over onto her cheeks. She drove aimlessly through the city, she didn't know what to do, or where to go. One thing, she wasn't going to see Ross, she was in no state to deal with his pathetic mooning over her. No wonder Tasha had had enough of him.

Then Andie knew what she had to do – confront the woman and find out what was going on. Get her to see sense, face up to her responsibilities. It was probably hopeless, but she had to do something to try to sort out this mess. She wiped her eyes and looked around to get her bearings. She turned down the next street and headed in the direction of Ross's apartment.

*

Andie parked outside the apartment block and checked her face in the rearview mirror. She wiped the smudges from under her eyes and fixed her hair, still flattened from the stupid chef's hat. Well, she wouldn't have to worry about that anymore. She got out of the car and walked wearily up to the entrance. She had no idea if Tasha would even be there, but if she really was doing a runner, she had to come back some time, and she would assume the coast was clear for the next couple of days. Andie still had keys to the apartment, she had meant to give them back to Ross, but the opportunity had never presented itself. So if there was no answer she would just let herself in and wait, see if she could get any clues as to what was going on. Andie had vowed never to set foot in the place again, but desperate times . . .

She pressed the button on the intercom at the entrance and waited. Her heart lurched when she heard the click and Tasha's voice came through the speaker. 'Who is it?'

She cleared her throat. 'Tasha, it's me, Andie.'

There was no response, but she didn't hang up either.

'I need to speak to you,' Andie persisted.

'Is Ross all right?'

'Well, no, actually. He's very upset that you haven't been to see him.'

'I doubt that he's asking for me,' she said bluntly.

'Tasha, we have to talk.'

'I have nothing to say to you.'

'Look, I still have keys to the apartment, but I gave you the courtesy of not just barging in on you. But I will, if you won't let me in.'

There was a long pause.

'I only want to talk,' said Andie. 'It's not as though I can force you to do anything you don't want to do.'

There was another pause, and finally the buzz sounded, releasing the door. Andie pushed it open and stepped into the foyer. She caught the lift up, and as she walked out into the hall, she could see the door of the apartment was ajar. Andie stood tentatively in the doorway and knocked.

'I'm in here,' Tasha called.

God, she expected Andie to have this out with her in the bedroom? She sighed. 'Okay.' She picked her way slowly across the living room. She wondered if Tasha would have tidied up if she realised she was going to have company, but somehow Andie doubted it. Clothes were strewn across chairs, shoes scattered around the floor, cups, glasses and plates of half-eaten food were spread across the kitchen bench. She couldn't help noticing the splashes of hot pink and purple – garish picture frames, a lava lamp, and some ridiculous fluffy cushions tossed on the chesterfield; she was surprised Ross tolerated that, the thing was sacrosanct.

Andie took a breath as she approached the bedroom door. It was open. 'Tasha?'

'Yeah.'

As she walked in, she saw two large suitcases lying open on the bed – a different bed, not their marital bed, the one they'd defiled. Tasha was busy folding clothes.

'So you're actually leaving him?' said Andie.

'What does it look like?' She glanced across at Andie without really looking at her. 'Look, I don't have much time, so just say whatever you came here to say.'

'What are you doing, Tasha? You're really going to leave him at a time like this?'

She sighed. 'You can think whatever you want to about me, you will anyway. But the fact is, I didn't sign up for this.'

'You hooked up with a man thirty years your senior,' Andie pointed out. 'It was on the cards.'

'Ross is, or was, an extremely fit, healthy man,' she returned. 'I didn't see this coming.'

'And you don't feel any responsibility?'

She turned to look at Andie. 'For his heart attack?'

'No, for him as a person,' she said. 'A person you are in love with, that you're in a relationship with.'

'He doesn't love me,' she said squarely. 'He's still in love with you.'

'No, he isn't. It's just talk.'

She rolled her eyes. 'It's not just talk. I've had to put up with it all week. I was the one there every day, sitting by his bedside, and all he could talk about was you, when you were coming in, why you couldn't take time off work to be with him. And then that doctor saying he'll have to be looked after for another couple of weeks, longer, that he can't drive, that he's going to have anxiety, depression . . .' She shook her head. 'And I'm the one who's supposed to put up with all that? Take more time off work while he mopes around for you? I can't do it. And I'm not going to.'

'Okay,' said Andie.

Tasha frowned at her.

'Okay, I understand.'

'No offence, but I really don't give a fuck whether you understand or not.'

Andie took a deep breath. 'I'm just saying that I get why you're angry. I'm afraid Ross has always been self-centred. It's not that he loves me more than you, he just wants everyone fussing over him.'

Tasha returned to her packing, bustling around the room. Andie wasn't even sure she was listening.

'This just seems very sudden, Tasha. You were still hanging on to him this morning before his surgery. You must have feelings for him. I can't help thinking you're going to regret this.'

'I don't believe in regrets.'

Nice to have the luxury.

'All I'm suggesting is, why don't you take a couple of days off, have a break from all of this? Then you could sort out something with the kids. If you have to work, they can come and stay with him, I'll even help when I can. Ross does need to have someone with him at first, but it doesn't have to be you all the time.'

Tasha had actually stopped halfway through to listen. Andie only hoped she was getting through to her.

But suddenly she shook her head. 'No, I think a clean break is best.' She pranced off into the bathroom, returning a moment later with a bag of toiletries she must have packed earlier.

Now Andie was just pissed off. 'So a clean break involves maxing out his credit cards before you leave him in the lurch?' she accused.

Tasha narrowed her eyes. 'How do you know about that?'

'The bank called. Unfortunately I'm still his legal wife.'

She shrugged. 'I paid some bills, and I ordered some furniture, stuff I'm going to need to set myself up again. I gave up a lot to be with Ross, and I'm just reimbursing myself for my losses. I can do it the simple way, like this, or I can get a lawyer afterwards, like you did.'

'That was entirely different, Tasha. We were married for ten years.'

'Yes, and you were pretty quick to cut and run.'

'I'm sorry?' said Andie.

'You didn't waste any time arranging that property settlement. And you made sure it all went your way.'

Andie steeled herself. 'I don't know what Ross told you, Tasha, but I didn't take anything of his, I didn't want anything.'

'But now you've got your inheritance all to yourself. He was entitled to some of that, you know.'

'I didn't hide it from him,' Andie said, almost gritting her teeth. 'Ross ran everything by his lawyers . . .' She really didn't want to be discussing this with Tasha, it wasn't any of her business anyway.

Tasha was glaring at her. 'Do you really think Ross would begrudge me this? You know what he's like. If I asked for a cash settlement, he'd give it to me.'

She was right. Part showing off, part guilt money, probably.

'Now, as you can see, I'm very busy, so if you've said everything you came to say . . .'

'Just one more thing,' said Andie. 'Are you going to go and see him, tell him yourself?'

She shrugged. 'I wasn't planning to.'

'Tasha, that's really unfair to put it onto the kids to tell him.'

'Then you tell him.'

'It's not my responsibility!'
'Fine,' she retorted. 'I'll send him a text.'
Andie blinked. 'Are you serious?'
'Don't worry, I'll make it a long one.'

Saturday morning

Andie rolled over in bed, hugging her pillow and staring out the window. She was going to have to visit Ross today, she couldn't put it off any longer. She wasn't up to dealing with him last night, and it had occurred to her that she didn't have to. Everyone would be assuming she was at work, so that meant she could at least have one lousy night to herself.

How had her life come to this? A couple of days ago she had a great job, a blossoming relationship, and now she was unemployed and alone, and not only that, she was going to have to coordinate her ex-husband's post-operative care. When she wasn't able to get onto either Brooke or Matty yesterday, she'd finally called Joanna.

'Sorry to bother you,' Andie said when she answered. 'I was wondering if you've talked to Ross?'

'No, but Brooke called,' she explained, 'said he was sulking that you didn't stay to see him after his operation. Oh, and apparently Tasha has gone MIA.'

'So Ross hasn't heard anything from her? Not even a text message?'

'He doesn't have his phone, as far as I know,' said Joanna.

Of course. They wouldn't have let him have it in the high-dependency unit, with all that equipment around, and now he had to be careful about mobile phones near the implant. Andie hadn't expected Tasha to text him immediately, but it didn't matter, he wasn't going to get her break-up message anyway.

'Is there anything wrong, Andie?' Joanna was asking.

She took a deep breath. 'I have something to tell you . . .'

*

Joanna had insisted that she would break the news to Ross about Tasha, bless her. Andie thought it was her own responsibility, as she was the one who'd got it from the horse's mouth, so to speak, but Joanna assured her that she was the best person to handle Ross. She'd be sympathetic, but she wouldn't take any nonsense, and nonsense was all Andie was likely to get from him. Joanna had reminded her again to keep her guard up, that now Ross would be more desperate than before to get her back. He would play on her feelings of guilt and responsibility, and they both knew how convincing he could be.

Andie was startled now by a knock on the door. She glanced at the time. It wasn't even eight thirty. There was another knock, a couple of knocks, louder this time.

'Just a minute,' she called, scrambling off the bed. Hold your horses.

'Andie, it's me, Dominic.'

She froze, standing in the middle of the room.

'I have to talk to you.' There was a pause. 'Just for a minute. Can you let me in, please?'

She had to deal with him sometime, and she had a feeling he wouldn't go away until she did.

'All right, I'm coming.' She grabbed her robe and tied the sash around her waist. Her heart was pounding as she opened the door.

'Thank you,' he said. He looked weary, like he hadn't had much sleep.

Andie stood back to let him in and closed the door, turning around to face him.

'I'm sorry,' he said, 'I know it's early, but I had to come before work. And you won't answer my calls.'

She had turned off her phone when she got home yesterday. She hadn't purposely not answered his calls, she just hadn't wanted to deal with anyone last night.

Dominic started to pace the floor in front of her. 'Look, I'm sorry about the way things happened yesterday, but it couldn't be helped.'

'You don't think so?'

He stopped to look at her. 'What are you saying?'

'You promised me you wouldn't let anything that happened between us, outside of work, compromise my position at Viande.'

'And I haven't. But can you say the same thing, Andie?'

She sighed heavily. 'I don't know, maybe not.' She perched on the arm of the sofa. 'But just tell me something, Dominic, if you didn't know what was going on in my life, if I was just another member of staff, a hardworking member of staff in good standing, and I accidentally spoilt a batch of clarified butter, would you have fired me then?'

'I didn't fire you, Andie,' he insisted. 'Your job is safe.'

'For now,' she muttered. 'Let me put it another way. Would you have treated another staff member the same, effectively suspending them?'

'I think you're being unfair,' said Dominic, 'and I think you are expecting different treatment, Andie. A member of staff who kept leaving the floor to make calls and was distracted to the point of ruining food and wasting everyone's time, might well get the sack, depending on the situation. I'd hear them out, and if the problem was reasonable they might be given another chance, but I don't know how many would actually be granted a few days off to sort out their personal lives.'

Andie gazed up at him sadly. 'You think a few days is going to do it, Dominic?'

He frowned. 'What do you mean?'

'In case you hadn't noticed, my life is kind of out of control at the moment. I might get the immediate problems sorted in a couple of days, but it's not going to end there.' She paused. 'The truth is, I have baggage, I have an ex-husband. I may not love him anymore, but I still have a responsibility to him, and more importantly, I have a responsibility to his children, who I do love, very much.'

Dominic was listening, staring down at the carpet. 'Are you sure you don't love him anymore?' he asked after a while.

'Quite sure.'

He sighed. 'Well, I wish I could be so sure of that.' He started to pace again. 'All that talk about feeling guilty and responsible the other night, about how maybe you should have taken him back —'

'That's not what I was saying, Dominic.'

He looked at her. 'You know, I tried to ignore what I was feeling for you for a very long time,' he said. 'I knew your marriage had just broken up, that you'd be on the rebound, and I knew I shouldn't risk it. It appears as though I was right.'

Andie felt a cramp in her chest. 'Does that make you feel better?' she said ruefully.

He frowned. 'No. How can you say that? You think I'm happy you'd choose him over me?'

'I'm not choosing him,' she insisted. 'I don't want to be with Ross.'

'I don't think you know what you want,' he said squarely.

'And what do you want from me, Dominic?'

'I know I don't want this . . . this uncertainty.'

She nodded. 'You want everything under control and predictable. And I can't give you that right now.' She paused, she could feel tears pricking at the corners of her eyes. 'This isn't working, Dominic, and I don't see how it can work.' Her voice caught in her throat and she swallowed. 'You're absolutely right, you shouldn't have risked it with me, it's too soon, I had the same concerns myself. There are too many loose ends, and if you can't deal with them, if it's all too messy for you, then you are better off without me.'

He looked at her for a long time, she could see the hurt in his eyes. 'Okay, if that's the way you want it, I won't bother you anymore.' He crossed to the door. 'Good luck, Andie.'

Newtown

'I never should have gone out with the boss, I told you.' Andie pointed her finger and shook her head emphatically. 'Big mistake, and Dominic Gerou does not tolerate mistakes.'

She'd turned up on Jess's doorstep that afternoon with an armful of wine bottles and a resolution to get drunk. Jess had nothing against that, per se, but she had never seen Andie like this. She poured glass after glass and guzzled it down, railing against men, and chefs, and skanky women, and even heart attacks. Which was an odd thing to rail against. She hadn't fallen apart even after what Ross had done to her; Jess had waited for it, had even hoped she would so she could be sure she'd got him out of her system, but Andie had remained strangely composed. Except for that day at the cemetery, and that had all been about Brendan. Because Andie loved her brother, fiercely. So what was all this about? Was she so heartbroken about this Dominic character, or was she finally letting go about everything? Maybe it was a bit of both.

'If we weren't seeing each other,' Andie went on, slurring her words, 'he'd know nothing about me, he wouldn't know any of what was going on, and he wouldn't have fired me just for spoiling a batch of butter, for fuck's sake. It's only fucking butter! I even said I'd fucking pay for it!'

'But did he actually fire you?' Jess asked, getting confused now. 'I thought you said he told you just to take a few days —'

'Same diff,' she muttered. 'He was just being a coward.'

The whole thing didn't make sense to Jess, but she doubted she was going to get any sense from Andie tonight. She watched her splash more wine into her glass . . . and some onto the table, before she passed her the bottle. Jess poured just a mouthful into her own glass and then took the bottle to the kitchen. Andie wouldn't have realised it was still half full. Jess ran the tap as she tipped the rest out in the sink, and quietly slipped the one remaining bottle out of the fridge, hiding it in a cupboard.

'What are you doing?' Andie called.

'Just getting a cloth,' she said, coming back out of the kitchen and proceeding to wipe down the coffee table.

'Oh, no, was that me?' said Andie. 'I'm so sorry . . .' She started to sob.

Oh God, here she goes. Andie was just not much of a drinker, she hardly ever got this bad. Jess could remember a couple of times when they were students, maybe once or twice afterwards, but not for years and years.

She lowered herself down onto the floor next to Andie and put her arm around her shoulders. 'Now, come on, no point crying over spilled wine.'

Andie gave a tremulous sigh. 'Bloody Ross, why did he have to go and get . . . athingy-mia in the first place? As if a twentysomething wants an old man with a heart-starter sticking out of his chest. What was he thinking?'

'Well, I don't think he planned it.'

'Why are you defending Ross?'

'I'm not defending Ross.'

'And you shouldn't either, because Ross can . . . he can go fuck himself.'

That was the other thing. Andie turned into a gutter-mouth when she'd had too much to drink.

'Maybe I should get you to bed,' said Jess.

'Why, I haven't got anything to get up for, I don't even have a lousy job anymore.' The tears welled again. 'Because my boyfriend fired me,' she cried. 'What sort of a boyfriend does that?'

Jess got to her feet. 'All right, I'm calling last drinks,' she said, snatching the glass out of Andie's hand. 'You'll thank me tomorrow.'

Andie didn't argue with her, she just sat in a crumpled heap in the middle of the floor, sobbing quietly, defeated. Eventually Jess coaxed her into the bathroom, seizing the opportunity to quickly set up the sofa bed, in the hope that Andie would pretty much fall into it when she came out again. Which was exactly what she did. Jess got her to drink some water, and then she pulled the covers over her and sat beside her, stroking her head, until she fell asleep. Jess glanced down at her now, she was out for the count. She didn't envy how Andie was going to feel in the morning. Hopefully she'd sleep the worst of it off. Jess got up off the sofa bed, switched off the light, and took herself off to her room.

The morning after

Andie opened her eyes and blinked a few times to focus. She was at Jess's, she remembered now. She turned her head to look for the time, and that was when it hit her. Her brain swirled inside her head at the slightest movement, making her nauseous. She closed her eyes, but she wasn't fooling anyone. Oh dear God, what had she done to herself?

She heard a click as the front door lock released, and watched Jess creep in and close it again quietly behind her.

'Hi,' Andie croaked.

She jumped. 'Fuck, give me a heart attack, why don't you?'

'Sorry.'

'It's okay. How are you feeling?'

'Don't ask.'

'I brought you a hangover breakfast,' Jess said, waving a giant paper bag from one of the worst of the takeaway chains. 'Full of greasy goodness!'

'God bless you,' said Andie, struggling to sit up, and breaking out in a cold sweat as she did. 'Oh, I don't know if I'm going to be able to stomach it.'

'Oh, but you must,' Jess insisted, plonking down beside her.

'Ugh, please be gentle,' Andie whimpered.

Jess laid out the food picnic-style across the bed. Andie picked up a bacon and egg burger concoction and bit into it gingerly.

'Here,' said Jess, 'wash it down with this.' She passed her an orange juice. 'I'll make you a strong coffee after you get some food into you.'

'Thanks.' She chewed slowly and eventually swallowed. Okay, that seemed to be staying down. 'So how bad was I last night?'

'On a scale of one to ten, around a forty-seven,' said Jess. 'Lots of swearing, lots of "fucks" in particular. You sounded like me. You said Ross should go fuck himself.'

'Maybe if he could he wouldn't keep screwing with everyone else.'

'Ha, look at that, you made a joke, despite your severe mental incapacity.'

'Hm. I wonder just how many brain cells I managed to kill off?'

'That's a myth, you know,' Jess said, chomping into her breakfast burger.

'Is it?'

She nodded, swallowing. 'I read it somewhere, I don't remember all the details, but I do remember that much – you cannot kill brain cells. Maybe you can shrink them, or disable them, but you can't kill the buggers.'

Andie sipped her juice. 'I don't know, I don't even remember much after I got here.'

'Do you remember what happened before you got here?'

She nodded. 'Tasha left Ross, so now he's my responsibility.'

'He really isn't.'

'He really is,' said Andie. 'I told you I'm still his wife, legally.'

'Pffft, and I told *you* you should have put through those divorce papers.'

'And I told *you* I couldn't,' she said. 'Not for a year.'

'We could have fudged the date, I would totally have signed off on that.'

'Well, much as I appreciate that you'd perjure yourself for me, it's too late now.'

Jess looked at her. 'So what are you going to do?'

'I'll have to talk to the kids, work out something,' said Andie. 'I'm going to have to help out, I don't have the excuse of a job anymore. Or a boyfriend. Or a life.'

Jess wiped her hands on a napkin and sat back, drawing her arm around her.

Andie leaned her head on her shoulder. 'I went against my instincts again and again – give it time, wait until you've been on your own for a while, don't date the boss.' She sighed. 'Now it's all blown up in my face and I've got no one to blame but myself.'

'Well, I don't know about that,' said Jess. 'I kind of egged you on.'

'It's not your fault. What did you say to me? My body, my responsibility?' Andie lifted her head. 'It just sucks so much,' she said. 'I was really starting to get somewhere at work. I haven't seen you to tell you, but I was just put up to main meal prep. It was only a matter of time before I'd actually be starting to cook – in a three-hatted restaurant! And now that's all over.'

'What about Dominic?' Jess asked tentatively.

Andie stared out ahead. 'I really liked him, I still really like him. But it doesn't matter, I've ruined it for good.'

'You were blaming it all on him last night.'

'Oh, he's certainly got issues, but it wasn't his fault. I shouldn't have kept my phone on me, and left the floor to take calls. It's against the rules, and I shouldn't have done it. I put him in a difficult position. And now I've lost him.'

Andie didn't want to admit how much he meant to her, and how she wished he'd fought for her. But he didn't, and that hurt her more than she could say.

Jess rubbed her arm. 'Just promise me you won't go back to Ross.'

'What?' Andie turned to look at her. 'I'm heartbroken, alone, and unemployed . . . but I'm not desperate.'

'And you're not unemployed. You own a shop, remember?'

'So I do.'

Jess shifted to face her. 'I know you're not in the mood to hear it now, but by the time the dust settles, we'll be up and running. I'm working on the menu right now.'

Andie gave her a weak smile. 'I suppose you could use an extra pair of hands.'

'Are you kidding?' she said, growing visibly more excited. 'Do you know how much I would love to do this with you? We haven't worked together, not cooking anyway, in how long?'

'Long.'

'Remember we used to say we'd open our own restaurant one day? I know this isn't the same, but maybe it's the next best thing.'

Potts Point

That phrase was still echoing in Andie's head the next day. She had a feeling it was going to become her mantra, or was it motto? Perhaps it would be her eulogy – Andie didn't really get the life she wanted, but she got the next best thing.

Ross had developed his own mantra.

'This is the first day of the rest of my life,' he said to Andie and Brooke when they brought him home to the apartment. 'I'm not going to worry anymore about what's happened in the past. I've got my life back. This is my second chance, and I'm not going to waste it.'

He'd been spouting platitudes like that since yesterday afternoon, after the doctors had run his device through its paces and given him a clean bill of health. Andie didn't know whether Ross was just delirious from the painkillers or what, but he seemed totally unfazed that his girlfriend had abandoned him and run up a bill of over ten thousand dollars on the same day, at least some of it while he was still under anaesthetic.

Brooke couldn't stay, so Andie was on duty until Matty came to take over this evening. They had worked out a roster between the three of them, and Joanna and Lauren were happy to be on standby. Ross didn't need someone with him 24/7 anyway, he could survive an hour or two at a time by himself. Andie had only one condition, she would not stay overnight. While she didn't have a choice about relaxing her rule never to step foot in the apartment again, she had to draw the line somewhere.

Andie made Ross a cup of tea and brought it over to him. He'd deposited himself in an armchair looking out at the view.

'Sit with me?' he said.

She didn't have much else to do, so she might as well. She had to start planning how to make use of the time while she was here or else she'd go batty. At the very least, she could use Ross's computer to keep up with the business side of things at the shop. She was prepared to give this two weeks, tops. If Ross still needed help after that, he could hire a nurse.

'Look at this view,' he was saying. 'I'd stopped noticing it. But you know, coming so close to death, you start to notice everything. It helps you work out what's important in life, Andie.'

She suppressed a yawn. Here he goes again.

'It's a gift,' he went on. 'I'll never look at things the same way again. I can't get even the slightest bit interested in work. Tony rang the other day – you remember Tony?'

'Of course, Ross, you've worked together almost the entire time I've known you.'

He nodded. 'So anyway, he was reassuring me about my various projects, and clients, and I really didn't care. Someone else is looking after them, and that's all right with me.'

'Well, that's good,' said Andie. 'You don't want to be stressing about work. When you're ready to go back, you'll have to find a way to ease into it slowly, maybe even part-time.'

He was shaking his head. 'I don't know if I'll ever go back, Andie.'

She raised an eyebrow.

'I was having a talk to the doctor about this. He agreed that my lifestyle might not be compatible with my medical condition, as he put it, that I should think about making some changes. I need to simplify my life.' He paused. 'I'm thinking about moving to the country.'

'Really?'

He looked at her. 'Yes, really.'

'What would you do in the country, Ross?'

'Relax, get away from it all, live a simpler life.'

The man who couldn't wait to get out of the relative peace of the Shire for the inner city, who couldn't wait not to have a backyard anymore.

'Come with me, Andie,' Ross said suddenly.

'Pardon?'

'I'm serious. We could open up a little restaurant in the Southern Highlands, like we used to talk about. Remember how much we loved the Southern Highlands?'

'We used to love the Southern Highlands,' she agreed. 'We also used to love each other.'

'I still love you,' he said.

She sighed. 'Ross . . .'

'And you still love me.'

She shook her head.

'Admit it, Andie,' he persisted, leaning forward. 'You rushed to my bedside as soon as you heard what happened. Why else would you do that?'

'Obligation,' she said bluntly.

'You don't have to be cruel.'

'I'm not meaning to be cruel, Ross,' she said. 'It was obligation, because I do care about you —'

'See, you can't deny you still have feelings.'

'I feel *for* you, Ross, there's a difference.'

'It's enough to start over,' he said. 'Think about it, Andie. This happened for a reason. You and I weren't even speaking, you were never going to set foot in this apartment again. And here you are. Can't you see this was meant to be?'

She didn't even know how to begin to respond to that. For a long time Andie had taken it for granted that she did still love Ross, on some level. She didn't know what it would feel like not to love him. But she knew now. She couldn't love him anymore, this man, so full of swagger, so full of self-confidence that a mere heart attack could never have been the end of him. She was mildly surprised that she had loved him once, but then again, the sheer force of his personality had overwhelmed her. And Andie had been easily overwhelmed, back then.

'How can you just turn your back on ten years?' he said, reaching over to cover her hand with his.

'You were the one who turned your back, Ross,' said Andie. 'You gave up on me long before I gave up on you.'

'I was never serious about Tasha,' he dismissed. 'Circumstances conspired to push us together, or else it never would have come to anything, I swear. And look what she turned out to be. I told you, didn't I, that she was unhinged . . .'

Had Andie really fallen for this kind of manipulation in the past? Back then she'd called it 'charm'. More fool her. She slipped her hand out from under his.

'I'm not blaming you,' he said quickly. 'I didn't mean it to sound that way. I'm just desperate, Andie. I've come to realise through all this that I love you more than anything —'

'That's enough, Ross!' she said sharply, cutting him off. She wasn't going to be able to stand this for two weeks. 'Can't you see that it's too late?'

'It's never too late, darling.'

Another cliché. 'Actually, sometimes it is too late, I don't even know why that's a saying.' She turned to look at him. 'We're in different places now, Ross. I still want to be a chef, I even still want a baby, not that I expect that's ever going to happen. But the point is, I want so many things that aren't compatible with what you want or need in your life. And I certainly don't want to semi-retire in the country.'

'We don't have to do that,' he said. 'We can do anything you want.'

'I want to do my own thing. I put my life on hold for you, Ross. I lived your life, not my own.'

'Andie, I made a mistake. I'm not going to make it again. I'd be mad.'

'Then you must be mad, because you've already made the same mistake twice. You left Joanna for me, then you left me for Tasha.' She stood up. 'It's over, Ross. I don't want to talk about it again, and if you do keep talking about it, then I won't come here anymore. Is that understood?'

Killara

Meredith had chosen to have a Sunday luncheon for her fortieth birthday, at home, though she had it fully catered. It was a subdued affair, to say the least. Andie felt a little out of place with all the sciencey bods – they were nice, but dull, or a little intense, or a little odd. She could have used a few drinks, but she had to drive. She had wanted to make the effort, to maintain some connection with her only sister, her only family. Besides, she had something to give her, and this seemed like an appropriate occasion.

Andie glanced out at the terrace and saw Philippa and Tristan. They looked decidedly bored. She knew how they felt, so she wandered out to join them.

'Hi guys,' she said, smiling.

'Hello, Aunty Andrea,' Philippa said politely. Tristan just gave her an awkward shrug.

'So, lunch was nice,' she said. 'Did you get plenty to eat?'

They both nodded.

She had no idea what to say to them, she didn't really know them. She pulled a chair over and sat down.

'So, how's school?' she tried next. 'Are you in high school yet, Tristan?'

He reddened a little. 'Next year.'

She should have known that.

'And Philippa, you must be in year . . .'

'Nine,' she finished for Andie.

'That means you're taking electives this year, right?'

She nodded.

'So, what did you choose?'

'Well, Mum and Dad insisted on a language, of course,' Philippa said. 'But my school makes you do one anyway. I'm taking French.'

'It's a beautiful language.'

'Oh, do you speak it?'

'No,' said Andie. 'I took it at school, but I wasn't very good. There are a lot of French terms in cooking though,' she added.

Philippa had nothing to say to that.

'What else did you choose?' Andie persisted.

'Drama.'

'That must be fun?'

'Mum thinks it's a massive waste of time,' said Philippa. Then she looked sideways at Andie. 'But I love it.'

Andie had to restrain herself from saying 'You go, girl!' Instead, she asked, 'Are you likely to have any productions during the year?'

'Oh, yes, my school's quite big on that. We're going to do *A Midsummer Night's Dream* in term three.'

'I love that play,' said Andie.

'Oh, you know it?'

Yes, even lowly cooks like her aunty knew a little Shakespeare.

'Could you make sure you let me know when it's on?' said Andie. 'I'd love to come and see it.'

She looked bemused. 'Would you really?'

'Yes, really.'

And then she smiled, and Andie suddenly saw her mother. 'Philippa, you look a little like Grandma, has anyone ever told you that?'

'No,' she said.

'Philippa, Tristan,' Neville called from the doorway. 'Come say goodbye to Nanna and Aunty.'

Philippa jumped to her feet. 'I'll make sure Mum tells you when the play's on,' she said.

'I'll look forward to it,' said Andie.

She wandered back inside after them, standing over in a corner while the guests took their leave. It appeared to be a mass exodus, clearly no one wanted to be the last to leave in this group.

Eventually Meredith came back down the hall into the empty room. 'Oh, Andrea, you're still here.'

'Yes.'

'Well, that's nice,' she said. 'I'm sorry I haven't had a chance to talk to you all day.'

'It's always difficult at your own party to get around to everyone.'

'Yes.' She nodded. 'But you don't have to run off, do you? Let's have a drink.'

'Oh, I'm driving . . .'

'Have you had much to drink yet?'

'No, I only had a champagne for the toast.'

'Well, then you can have a glass now,' she said. 'What would you like?'

'Oh, wine, I guess, whatever you're having.'

'Neville,' she called into the kitchen, 'bring Andrea and me a glass of wine, would you? Come and sit down.'

Andie followed her over to the sofa as Neville appeared with two glasses of red.

'Thanks, Neville,' said Andie, when he passed her one.

'Andrea and I are going to have a nice catch-up, Neville,' said Meredith, taking her glass.

He took the hint. 'I'll leave you to it then.' He smiled, walking back to the kitchen.

Andie noticed Meredith's cheeks were quite pink, and her eyes glassy. She must have had a few of these already today, and they'd loosened her up. Andie had never seen her quite so relaxed.

She held up her glass. 'Happy birthday, Meredith.'

'Thank you.' She smiled, clinking her glass against Andie's. 'And thank you for coming, I really appreciate it.'

'Oh,' said Andie, remembering. 'I have something for you.' She set her glass down on the coffee table. 'Just a minute.'

She scooted up the hall to the main bedroom where they had been invited to leave their bags. Andie picked up the gift box and took it back down to the sitting room. She passed it to Meredith.

'Oh my goodness, what's this?' she said as Andie sat down next to her.

'I didn't get the chance to give it to you before I left the house,' she said. 'I've been holding on to it for you, I found it among Mum's things.'

Meredith opened the box and lifted out the album, a curious look on her face. Andie realised she must never have seen it either.

She opened the album and started going through the pages. 'Oh my, you found this at the house?'

Andie nodded. 'There was one for me and Brendan as well. You never saw it before?'

Meredith shook her head. 'I had no idea,' she said quietly, turning the pages, her eyes misting over. 'This is a surprise.'

The album was opened on a page with a picture of her in primary school.

'Look how cute you were,' said Andie.

Meredith looked at her sideways. 'You're joking?'

'No I'm not,' she insisted.

'You and Brendan got all the looks,' she said, but not unkindly. 'I got the brains, as Mum was always telling me. But, she used to say, you really have to try and do something with yourself, Meredith, if you want to get a husband one day. Look at your sister, she won't have any trouble.'

Andie frowned. 'She said that to you?'

Meredith nodded with a sigh, turning over to a photo of herself in high school. 'And is it any wonder?'

It was probably not her best look – braces, pimples, a bad haircut.

'All I ever got was how I had to improve myself,' said Andie. 'That a pretty face wasn't everything. That I didn't have brains like you.'

Meredith shook her head.

'I went past the old house on the way,' said Andie, picking up her glass again. 'It looks good, they've spruced it up a bit.'

There was a young boy riding a bike in the driveway, and Andie had teared up seeing him.

'I haven't been able to go there since you left,' said Meredith. 'I miss Dad terribly. I know I didn't go and see him enough, I just took for granted he'd always be there, when I had time.' She shook her head regretfully. 'I feel so guilty.'

Andie reached her hand across to cover her sister's. 'Oh, Meredith, I don't think guilt does anyone any good.'

Meredith looked at her. 'I'm so glad you came today, Andrea.'

'I'm glad too.'

The Corner Gourmet

'I want to begin by thanking you all for coming,' said Jess, getting everyone's attention.

They had decided to hold a launch before they kicked off the takeaway menu next week. It wasn't a marketing exercise, they didn't even invite anyone from the local rag. It was just a private party to celebrate their new venture and thank everyone who had helped along the way.

'This is something Andie and I dreamed of doing for a long time,' Jess went on, 'in one form or another. And to be honest, the way it's turned out is beyond any of my wildest dreams.

'So we have some special people to thank – and the most special of all, I think you'll agree, is Mr Toby Miller, for the amazing renovations!'

That elicited a big cheer and applause, and Toby raised his hand as though he was acknowledging his disciples.

'Yeah, they know who you are, Toby,' said Jess. 'You've been handing out business cards all night.' There was a ripple of laughter before she went on. 'We also want to thank the lovely Donna, and Steph, and Angela . . . and the rest of the casual staff – I'm sure to leave someone out if I try to remember all your names, but you're getting free drinks tonight, so deal with it. But we are really grateful to you all for picking up the slack and keeping the place running while Andie and I have been otherwise occupied.

'Which brings me to the main person I want to thank tonight, and that's the woman standing right beside me. Like she has been for over a dozen years now. Everyone who has ever worked at The Corner Gourmet knows that Andie is about the best boss you could ever ask for – and not just because she's a complete pushover.'

That raised another laugh.

'But also because she's generous to a fault, and I'm not just saying that. She gave me the nod to go ahead with all this while she was still working full-time as a chef, because it was something I wanted. She left it all to me, trusted me to make the decisions, gave me a blank cheque. Now her circumstances have changed and I couldn't be happier that we're going to be working together again.' She turned to Andie and raised her glass. 'To my best friend, Andie.'

'To Andie,' the crowd repeated.

'And to Jess,' said Andie, holding up her glass.

'And to The Corner Gourmet!' Jess added.

People converged to offer their congratulations, but eventually Andie pushed her way through the throng. She had spotted Brooke standing on her own, and she hadn't really had the chance to talk to her yet, except to offer a quick hello when they first arrived.

'Where's your mum?' Andie asked when she got to her.

'Oh, she saw someone she knew,' said Brooke. 'I think she's out front in the shop.'

Andie nodded. 'So, how are you?'

'Not too bad,' she said. 'Mid-semester break is over Easter, then I don't think I'll be coming up for air.'

'And Matty?'

'Oh, he sent his apologies,' she said. 'He didn't think it would be quite his scene.'

Andie smiled. 'It's okay, I didn't really expect him to come.' She paused. 'And so to the inevitable, how's your dad?'

'He's really well, almost back to normal, he reckons. He's back at work on reduced hours, but he hasn't gone back to the gym, I don't know if he ever will.'

'Can't say I blame him.'

Brooke nodded, but she was frowning. 'Andie, I wanted to tell you something, before you heard it from someone else.'

Andie could guess what it was before Brooke confirmed it.

'Dad's seeing someone. She's younger than you, but older than Tasha, and Lauren, which is a relief.'

Andie waited for some sensation, a pang, but nothing came. 'Thanks for telling me,' she said. 'But it's okay. I really am over him.'

Brooke sighed. 'You know, when Tasha left I thought maybe you two would get back together.'

'Brooke —'

'No, it's okay, I understand. He brought it on himself,' she said. 'It's just . . .' Her eyes teared up. 'He's my dad, and it's getting a little bit pathetic.'

Andie put an arm around her. 'Promise me something?'

Brooke nodded, brushing a tear away with the back of her hand.

She thought about how to put it. 'Well, promise me that you won't think the worst of men because of this, there really are some good ones out there, believe me. But the mistakes fathers make can screw up their daughters forever. I'd feel partly responsible if that happened.'

'Why would you feel responsible?'

'I broke up your family in the first place, Brooke.'

She was shaking her head. 'No you didn't. Dad did that. It was his family to break.' She paused. 'Anyway, we're not broken.'

'No, you're not, you're absolutely right,' said Andie. 'You're a wonderful family, always hold on to that.'

Joanna walked up to join them. 'What a great night, Andie,' she said. 'And the place is fabulous, I think it's going to be a raging success.'

'Thanks, Joanna.'

'I'm afraid we have to get going,' she said, nudging Brooke. 'Hey, chicken?'

'Early class tomorrow,' Brooke said, pulling a face.

'Ah, I almost forgot, I have something for you, Andie,' said Joanna, rooting around in her bag. 'Emily is turning one next month.'

'Oh my God,' said Andie, 'she's one already?'

'I know – crazy, right?' said Brooke.

Joanna held out an envelope. 'This is an invitation to her birthday party.'

Andie just stared at it.

'It's okay, it's from Lauren,' Joanna assured her.

She accepted the envelope gingerly. 'That's so nice, tell her thank you.'

'Great,' said Brooke. 'So we'll see you there. It's only in a couple of weeks away.'

Andie looked at Joanna. 'Are you sure it'll be okay?'

'You're invited,' said Joanna. 'You're family, for heaven's sake, you always will be.'

They said their goodbyes and Andie watched them make their way through the shop. Toby came up behind her.

'Was that Ross's daughter?' he asked.

Andie nodded. 'And her mum.'

'You mean his first wife?'

'Yep.' She looked up at him. 'We're family, and we always will be.'

Toby frowned. 'Have you seen Ross?'

'No, I haven't, not for a while,' said Andie. 'And I have no intention of seeing him, so you can relax. Brooke just told me he's got someone new.'

'You are kidding me?' said Toby.

Andie smiled. 'What do they say? There's a sucker born every minute.'

'How about you?' he asked. 'Are you still seeing that bloke you told me about?'

Andie was glad Toby and Donna didn't know all that much about Dominic.

'No, that didn't go anywhere,' she said. And there was the pang, the one she couldn't muster at the news of Ross.

Toby put his arm around her shoulder and gave her a squeeze. 'Oh, well, there's plenty more fish in the ocean – and you are quite a catch, after all.'

Andie just looked at him.

'I can't believe I just said that. I am actually turning into my father.'

Donna walked over with Max perched on her hip.

'I blame him,' said Toby, as Donna passed Max over.

'What for?' Donna frowned.

'For turning me into a dad.'

'Don't try and follow the logic,' Andie said to Donna.

'I think we're going to have to go,' said Donna. 'Max is tired.'

His head was drooping on his father's shoulder.

'Thanks for everything,' said Andie. 'Really, I couldn't get by without you two. I hope you know that.'

'Stop it,' said Toby. 'You want me to start crying? Ruin the burly builder thing I've been working on all night?'

*

It was only just after ten when Jess saw the last of the guests out the front door of the shop, locking it behind them. But the two of them had been at it since before seven this morning. Andie did all the canapés, borrowing quite a few ideas from Viande, while Jess made three of the dishes that were going to be on the inaugural takeaway menu – a Sri Lankan beef curry, a Moroccan-inspired chicken casserole, and a vegetarian mushroom and leek risotto – served in tiny individual bowls with tiny bamboo forks that were recyclable and compostable and whatever else – Jess was taking a very green approach to the whole thing.

She came out from the front, waving a bottle of champagne. 'Time to celebrate,' she said.

'Should we open another bottle now?' said Andie. 'Just for the two of us?'

'Seriously, can you remember finishing even one glass tonight? We were run off our feet. Now we can relax.'

'You're right. Open away.'

Jess popped the cork and poured them both a glass. 'To us!'

Andie smiled, raising hers and taking a drink.

Jess was watching her. 'Okay, spill, Andie.'

'What?'

'There's something wrong.'

'No there isn't.'

'Oh yes there is. You don't seem very happy. There's no spring in your step.'

'That's because I've been on my feet all day,' she protested, swinging them up now to plant them on a nearby chair.

Jess shook her head. 'No, you've been like this all week. Longer. I've been jumping out of my skin, but you've just been going through the motions, I could tell. And I'm worried about you.'

'I'm just tired.'

'Andie,' she said, 'I'm your best friend, right?'

'Of course.'

'Then stop the bullshit and tell me what's wrong.'

Andie sighed heavily, thinking about it. 'When I was still with Ross, and I kept trying out new things here, I'd get into it for a while, but then I'd lose interest. I remember Ross once said I was flitting about, but in the end, it just wasn't enough . . . But every single day at the restaurant, even when I was doing the most mundane tasks, I was still just thrilled to be there, every dinner and lunch service, being even a small part of creating each and every one of those meals that went out. Even the last day I was still learning something new . . .'

There was that pang again, when she thought of the last day, the last time she drove out of the carpark at Viande, tears streaming down her face.

'Then you have to go back,' Jess said simply.

'No, I can't —'

'Why not?'

'Because we've got this up and running now, and it's great, really. Don't worry, I'll get into it, in time.'

'I'm afraid that's not good enough,' said Jess.

Andie looked at her. 'What do you mean?'

'If you don't feel the same excitement I'm feeling about this, then this is not where you should be.'

'It doesn't matter anyway, I can't go back to Viande.'

'Then get a job somewhere else,' said Jess. 'But you have to do it right now, while your experience is still relevant and you can put it in your résumé. You can't wait around another ten years, I won't let you.'

Andie frowned, biting her lip. 'I feel like I'd be letting you down.'

Jess covered her hand. 'You'll only be letting me down if you don't do it.'

'But how can you run all this on your own?'

'I won't,' she said. 'I'll get somebody in on a casual basis. I know chefs that would be happy to pick up extra shifts.'

Andie took a sip of her champagne, thinking.

'You have to do it, Andie,' Jess said seriously. 'This place will always be here – it can be your fallback position. Not that I think you're going to need it.'

She gave Jess a small, tentative smile. 'But I am going to need a reference.'

Viande

Andie sipped her coffee as she gazed across the carpark to the entrance. She was waiting for Dominic to arrive for work. She had to talk to him before anyone else got here, and she needed to see him alone.

It wasn't long before his black BMW swept around the corner of the building and pulled into its regular spot. Andie's heart began to race. Breathe deeply, she told herself. Stay in control. She hadn't seen him since that day in her apartment, and she wasn't sure how she was going to cope seeing him now. But she had to do this.

She watched Dominic get out of the car, and there was that pang again. She took a gulp of her coffee. He hooked his bag over his shoulder and headed for the entrance, unlocked the door and pushed it open, and it swung closed behind him as he walked through. Andie waited for him to reappear, which he did moments later, dropping the chuck and kicking it under the door to wedge it open. Then he went back inside.

She stepped out of the car. Shoving her hands in the pockets of her jacket, she crossed the carpark to the entrance. Autumn had well and truly arrived, the mornings were getting cooler now. She walked straight through the open doorway into the building. No need to sneak up the corridor this time. As she made her way through the kitchen she glanced over at the office, but he wasn't there. He preferred to make his calls out in the restaurant, before anyone was around. Andie headed for the double doors, walking straight through the first set, and not hesitating as she pushed through the next. Dominic was pacing the floor, his phone to his ear. He stopped mid-sentence as she entered. He looked surprised, which she supposed he had every right to be.

'I'll have to call you back,' he said, before dropping his phone into his pocket. 'Andie . . .'

'It's okay, Dominic,' she said quickly. 'I'm not staying, and I'm not here to beg or plead or throw myself at you, so don't worry.'

His expression softened, with sadness, or maybe it was regret.

'I came to ask you a favour,' she pushed on. 'It's not a big favour, in fact I'm sure you'll find it's quite reasonable. You see, I need a reference.'

'You're looking for a job?'

She nodded. 'I've been working at the deli. We've expanded, we're making gourmet takeaway now. It was all Jess's idea. But it's not enough for me. I physically miss being in the kitchen.'

'You still have a job here if you want it.'

'I can't come back,' said Andie, 'we both know that. I've started looking around, but it's pretty competitive out there. So a recommendation from you would go a long way. Not that I'm asking you to say anything that isn't true, you understand.'

He was just staring at her. 'Andie, I . . .'

'Look, if it's a problem, I didn't mean to put you on the spot. Maybe you could ask Cosmo or Tang if they wouldn't mind?'

'It's not a problem,' he assured her. 'Of course I'll write you a reference.'

'You don't have to write it, usually they just want a phone number, so they can call you.'

'Of course. Do you still have my contact numbers?'

'Yes, I do.' She hadn't been able to bring herself to delete them.

He nodded. 'Well, feel free to give them to anyone who asks. And I'll write something for you as well, in case.'

'Thank you, I appreciate it.'

There was a pause before he asked, 'So, how are you?'

'I'm okay. Busy, you know, with the shop.'

'Everyone has been asking after you. They . . . we . . . miss you.'

She nodded. 'I should drop in some time for staffy's, say hi.'

'You should.'

'How are you, Dominic?'

He looked as though that was the hardest question in the world to answer. So he just shrugged. Andie couldn't help it, she felt a rush of tenderness towards him.

She took a breath. 'Before I go . . . there's something I have to say.'

'Go ahead.'

She took a moment. She'd been rehearsing this, she needed to say it, it needed to be said. He was watching her, waiting.

'Look, I'm sorry I messed up, Dominic, I really am,' she began. 'I think you were right, that maybe I was expecting an advantage, not consciously —'

'Andie, no, I was —'

'Please, Dominic,' she said. 'Just let me get this out?'

He nodded faintly, gazing at her.

'I wanted to apologise, because I know what a mess your life was all those years ago, and how important having control is to you. And I brought a whole lot of chaos into your life that you didn't ask for.' She paused. 'But the thing is, life is messy, Dominic, people are messy, relationships are messy. And wonderful. I don't know whether you can have one without the other. It's just like the best food. I remember you told me once that it needs contrast, of flavours and textures, or else it just ends up bland.'

He was staring down at the floor now.

'Anyway, I don't want to take up any more of your time,' said Andie. 'I just wanted you to know I'll always appreciate the chance you gave me. It changed my life.'

She turned and walked to the doorway.

'Andie . . .'

She stopped, looking back at him.

'I'll write you the reference.'

'Thank you.' She turned again and walked out of the restaurant.

Easter

'What are you wearing?' asked Jess.

'What does it look like?' said Andie.

'Seriously? Bunny ears?'

'They have a function,' she defended. 'They help keep my hair back.'

'You've gone soft in the head.'

'Ah, bah humbug.'

'That has to do with Christmas,' said Jess.

'You're still being a Scroogey McScrooge Face,' said Andie.

They had decided to officially launch the takeaway menu over the Easter long weekend. They thought it might be a good opportunity while other businesses were closed, or only operating on reduced hours. It had paid off, they could barely keep up with the demand. So today Jess had called in the casual chef she'd hired, who turned out to be a rather handsome young man called Ben, who was not only a good cook, he was good with the customers as well.

'Where did you find Ben?' Andie asked in a low voice.

'Around the traps,' Jess answered demurely. 'I've known him for a while,' she added, and Andie noticed the sparkle in her eyes.

'And just how well do you know him?'

'Let's just say he likes to watch Netflix on a rainy afternoon.' She winked.

Andie smiled, stirring the risotto. 'We're going to need more takeaway containers,' she said.

'Coming right up.'

Jess walked into the storeroom and inspected the boxes stacked on the shelves. She thought she heard knocking and she craned her head around into the corridor that led to the back entrance. She could see a figure through the frosted glass.

'Can someone get the back door?' she called into the shop.

No one responded. Jess sighed, and went to open it. They weren't expecting any deliveries today, but the guy standing on the other side of the door didn't look like a delivery man. 'Can I help you?'

'I hope so,' he said. 'I'm looking for Andie Lonergan.'

He didn't sound like a delivery man either, he had a bit of a toffee accent. 'In regards to?' said Jess in her best officious voice.

He cleared his throat. 'She used to work . . . We used to work together.'

'Oh, okay.' That seemed innocent enough. 'Can I give her a name?'

'Tell her it's Dominic.'

Jess blinked. 'You're Dominic? Dominic Gerou? From Viande?'

'Yes.'

'Well, it's nice to meet you!' she said with a wide smile. 'I'm Jess.'

He shook her outstretched hand. 'Jess,' he nodded, 'Andie talked about you.'

'Then you can't say you haven't been warned.'

He smiled. 'I hope you don't mind that I came round the back, there's a queue at the front door.'

'I know, isn't it great?'

'Yes, yes it is.'

'We just started the takeaway this weekend, we weren't sure how it was going to go at Easter.'

'Seems like you made the right decision.'

He was quite good-looking, Jess decided, nice eyes. He had that dark, smouldering thing happening. Though right now he was looking a little nervous, like he was going for a job interview or something.

'Um . . . so is Andie about?' he prompted her.

She stirred. 'Oh yeah, sure. Sorry. I'll just go grab her.'

Jess ducked back through to the kitchen. Andie was standing at the stove, still stirring the risotto.

'Andie, someone for you at the back door.'

'What?' She frowned. 'Who is it?'

Jess shrugged. 'Someone who wants to see you.'

She sighed. 'Well, I can't leave this.'

'Yes you can.'

'Then you'll have to take over.'

'No I can't.'

'Why not?'

'Ahh . . . I'm in the middle of something,' she said. 'Just take it off the jet for a sec, it'll be okay.'

Andie looked at her. 'Why are you acting weird?'

'I'm not acting weird, just hurry.'

She moved the pot and Jess ushered her through the storeroom and hovered behind as she went for the door. Andie turned around. 'Didn't you say you were in the middle of something?'

'Just open the door, will you?'

'Fine.' She grabbed the handle and opened the door.

'Hello, Andie,' said Dominic.

She couldn't speak, she just stared at him. His gaze drifted to the top of her head, and Andie quickly grabbed the rabbit ears and yanked them off, thrusting them at Jess.

'Hi,' she said, flustered.

'I can see you're busy,' he said, 'so I don't want to hold you up. I just came to drop this off.' She noticed then that he was holding an envelope. 'It's the reference you asked for.'

'Oh, you didn't have to bring it over in person, you could have mailed it.'

'I wanted to make sure you got it.' He hesitated. 'Actually, do you have a minute?'

'She has five,' said Jess. 'Take ten.' She shoved Andie out the door and closed it behind her.

Andie looked up at Dominic. 'Apparently I do have a minute.'

He smiled. She'd missed that smile.

'You're not at work today?' she said.

'Religious holiday, restaurant's closed.'

'Of course.' Andie nodded. 'So, um, well, thanks for the reference.'

He was still clutching the envelope. He seemed nervous. Like when he asked her out the first time.

'I was hoping you might read it, while I'm here, check if it's all right,' he said finally.

'I'm sure it'll be fine.'

'But I want to make sure I've said everything . . . that needs to be said.'

Andie felt nervous now, her heart started to flutter in her chest uncomfortably. What the hell was this about?

He handed her the envelope. 'Would you read it, please?'

'Sure.'

She slipped the folded paper out of the envelope as Dominic retreated down a couple of stairs and leaned against the railing, watching her. Andie decided it might be best to sit down, so she settled herself on the top step, unfolded the sheet of paper, and read.

To whom it concerns,

Andrea Lonergan has been an employee of Viande for over six months. While this may not seem enough time to get to know someone, let me assure you that it is.

That was an odd thing to say . . . in a reference.

Ms Lonergan, known to us as Andie, began on a trial basis in August of last year, but quickly established her competence to earn a place on our staff. Working under the direct supervision of the senior sous chefs, she was soon moved from bread and salad to main meal prep. Andie is a talented chef who takes on any task given to her with enthusiasm. She is hardworking and reliable, and she became a valuable member of the team at Viande.

But there is so much more to Andie than this. She is very brave, and fiercely honest, and she's warm and wonderful and generous. She's also very beautiful, but she doesn't like anyone to focus on that, because more than anything she wants to be seen for the person she is underneath. I lost sight of that person for a while. I doubted her, and I didn't fight to keep her, because clearly I'm an idiot. I have no other explanation or excuse. I was wrong, and I have come to regret it more than I can express here.

So for these reasons, and many, many more, I'm afraid I cannot recommend Ms Lonergan for any position, because I don't want to let her go, ever again.

Regards,
Dominic Gerou
Executive Chef
Viande

Andie sat staring at the letter, breathing hard.

'You're not saying anything,' Dominic said after a while.

He obviously didn't realise how hard it was for her to speak right now.

'Andie . . . what are you thinking?'

'Well, I'm not going to be able to give this to any prospective employers,' she said, meeting his gaze. 'You'll have to write me another one.'

'Oh . . .'

His face, it had that crestfallen look that always got to her.

'I'm sorry,' he said. 'I'll do it again. Give it to me.'

'Oh, you're not getting it back,' said Andie, standing up. 'I have it in writing that you admit you're an idiot, and that you were wrong. I'm keeping this.'

He sighed, managing a small smile. 'Andie, I've missed you, every single day. I didn't think I had the right, after everything . . . I thought I should leave you alone. But then when you came to the restaurant the other day . . .' He paused, taking a breath. 'I had to see you again. I had to ask you. Please come back to Viande.'

Andie was shaking her head. 'I can't come back, Dominic.'

There was that look again.

'Don't you get it? I don't want to make the same mistake twice.'

'So you think it would be a mistake,' he said, defeated.

She was going to have to spell it out for him. 'Yes, Dominic, it would be a mistake to have a relationship with my boss again,' she said. 'So that's why I can't come back to work at Viande, for you.'

She watched his expression go from bewildered to enlightened as the penny dropped. And then he smiled.

'So,' Andie said, 'are you coming in?'

He stirred. 'Pardon?'

'I have to get back inside. Are you coming?'

'Oh, I don't know . . . I don't want to be in the way.'

Andie looked at him. 'Let me rephrase that – you are coming in.'

'I am?'

'We're flat out, we could use the help.' She held out her hand to him. 'I should say though, it's pretty messy in there, in fact it's chaos.'

Dominic smiled, taking her hand. 'I don't mind . . . I don't mind at all.'

Acknowledgements

I have to begin this time with thanks in retrospect, as some of the team have moved on since my last book. Top of the list is Cate Paterson – my amazing publisher who plucked my first manuscript off the slush pile and has nurtured, guided and mentored me for more than ten years. She is deservedly now the Publishing Director at Pan Macmillan. I have said it before, but it bears repeating – I will never be able to thank her enough for everything she has done for me.

Louise Bourke was her assistant for the last few years, and was always incredibly patient and hardworking as she shepherded my novels through to publication. I hope she knows how much I valued her contribution, and that I wish her all the very best on her new path.

Thanks to my new publisher, Alex Nahlous, who stepped up to the plate and guided me to the finish line – or perhaps dragged? (late again!) My structural editor, Julia Stiles, did an amazing job as usual, helping me wrangle this book into shape. I couldn't have done it without her intelligent insight and her empathy. Thanks to Libby Turner who replaced Lou, and brought the same passionate commitment to transforming the manuscript into the finished book that you have in your hands.

My sons always deserve a special thank you. This time, Pat was my primary sounding board, helping me thrash out ideas early on, and putting up with more than his fair share of my doubts and emotional ups and downs – so much so he left the country for four months of R&R in south-east Asia! Joel leapt to my aid and read the first draft at a very busy time for him, and came back with his trademark insight and spot-on suggestions. And I'm grateful to Zac for being such an easygoing kid, and to Dane for never failing to surprise and inspire.

Thanks to Diane Stubbings for reading my longwinded emails full of writerly angst, and taking the time to give me thoughtful feedback and understanding, and thanks to Desley Hennessy for the long walks and a listening ear. And I am always appreciative of the friendship, support and encouragement of fellow authors, especially Tony Park and his lovely wife Nicola, and Ber Carroll and Liane Moriarty.

And last, but never least, thanks to my wonderful readers. It has been a genuine privilege to meet so many of you this past year at library and bookshop talks, and on Facebook and Twitter. Your unwavering loyalty and enthusiasm are the reason I keep writing.

More Titles from Dianne Blacklock

About Call Waiting

Of course Meg was a success: she planned, she set goals, she made lists. Ally never made lists.

Ally Tasker is trapped in a dead-end teaching job and a relationship that's going nowhere. Her college friend Meg has a fabulous job in advertising, a doting husband and a gorgeous baby boy. Why did Ally's life seem to be permanently on hold?

When her grandfather and sole relative dies, Ally has to return to the Southern Highlands. As she sets to restoring the rundown home of her childhood, the past unravels, and Ally realises the choice to be happy has been in her hands all along.

Meanwhile Meg's life is not as idyllic as Ally imagines. She longs to inject more passion and spontaneity into her life, but at what cost to her career, and more importantly, to the people she loves most in the world?

Sometimes you have to risk all you have to realise what is worth saving.

Find out more at: books2read.com/callwaiting

About Wife for Hire

When she was a little girl, all Samantha Driscoll ever wanted was to be somebody's wife. She would marry a man called Tod or Brad and she would have two perfect children. But instead she married a Jeff and he's just confessed to having an affair.

Desperate times indeed. Sam has to find a way to support her kids and keep her dream house, but she has no qualifications, having given up any career aspirations she might have had to become the consummate wife. So much for that. Then she finds the job she was born for: Wife for Hire - a service offering everything from domestic help to personal shopping to planning social events for people who don't have the time - people who need a wife.

Surrounded by a gaggle of girlfriends, an eccentric sister, a mother who brings whole new meaning to the word 'demanding', and two teenagers discovering their dad has hormones too, Sam successfully manages a cast of clients from the sublime to the ridiculous, including American businessman Hal Buchanan, who insists he doesn't need her services even if they are part of his executive package. If that's the case, why does he keep hanging around?

Sam may be a born organiser, but there are some things in life that do not go to schedule.

Find out more at: books2read.com/wifeforhire

About Almost Perfect

It's no big deal to love someone who's perfect ... The trick is to love someone despite the fact they're not.

With a beautiful house in an upscale Sydney suburb and two successful careers, anyone would think that Mac and Anna have the perfect life. But their marriage is cracking under the strain of infertility. Consumed by her dream of having a child, Anna cannot see how her pain and disappointment are driving Mac away.

Close by, in a beachside suburb, Georgie Reading and her sister-in-law have made their bookstore, The Reading Rooms, an unqualified success - unlike Georgie's love life. In her thirties, with a deadbeat roommate and no romantic prospects in sight, her beloved brother Nick suggests that maybe she's waiting for someone she was never going to find - the mythical perfect man.

Then Liam walks into the bookstore, and Georgie thinks she has finally found just that. Well, he's perfect for her, anyway. ... At the same time Mac and Anna reach breaking point, putting Mac on a path that will have unforeseen consequences for them all.

Find out more at: books2read.com/almostperfectblacklock

About False Advertising

Helen and Gemma, two women who couldn't be more different, are thrown together when their lives take an unexpected turn.

Helen always tries to be a good person - she recycles, she is even polite to telemarketers. As a mother, wife, daughter and nurse, Helen is used to putting everyone's needs before her own. But it only takes one momentary lapse of concentration to shatter her life forever.

There was no such momentary lapse for Gemma, she had never done anything by halves, and she had certainly never been quiet about it. So when she barges unceremoniously into Helen's life - pregnant, alone, estranged from her family, with a once-promising career in advertising in tatters - things will never be the same again for either of them.

FALSE ADVERTISING is about loss and grief and second chances, it's about knowing when to hang on, and knowing when to move on. And it's about realising that when life falls short of our expectations, it was all just false advertising anyway.

Find out more at: books2read.com/falseadvertising

About Crossing Paths

Jo had learned the hard way that life was not mystical, or magical; it was hard and grey and cold most of the time. Much better to see it for what it is than to be perennially disappointed.

It's not as though Jo Liddell never had dreams. She was going to be a journalist and travel the world, but life had a way of stealing her dreams right out from under her. Okay, she had her column, but heaven forbid she had an opinion about anything that mattered. And now that she's saddled herself with a hefty mortgage, Jo has resigned herself to living a less-than-perfect life.

That is, until she crosses paths with Joe Bannister - a celebrated foreign correspondent, returning home to care for his dying father, take the pressure off his long-suffering sister and maybe pull his recalcitrant brother into line. He did not expect to find himself falling for a headstrong woman who seems to resent him.

But after devastating news, Joe is forced to make an impossible choice, and Jo must fight hard for everything she never believed in - success, self-acceptance, and above all, real love.

Find out more at: books2read.com/crossingpaths

About Three's a Crowd

'Well, we're different, we lead such different lives. I'm not sure how we'll go now without Annie. She was like Carrie, you know, in Sex and the City. Annie was our Carrie.'

Without Annie, friends Catherine, Lexie and Rachel are lost. How will they fill the void? Will their friendship survive?

Catherine is characteristically unfazed, forging ahead in her high-flying career while struggling to connect to her unfathomable teenage daughter. But secrets from the past emerge to shatter her carefully constructed image, and threaten all the relationships she holds dear.

Meanwhile Lexie is juggling the demands of her young family and the ego of her hardworking husband, while taking the first tentative steps to achieving her own dreams. She just wished Annie was around to talk to - Catherine is so bossy, and Rachel ... well, her head seems be more in the clouds now than ever.

Rachel knows what her friends think of her - but what they don't know is that she's currently in the thrall of a new relationship. And she doesn't want them to know, because when the truth comes out, fragile friendships will be put to the test all over again ...

Find out more at: books2read.com/threesacrowd

About The Right Time

The Beckett sisters need to shake things up.

Emma has been planning her dream wedding even since she was a little girl, and she's determined to get her happy ending. Just as soon as her boyfriend Blake gets around to proposing …

Liz is a well respected and successful doctor and supposedly the brains of the family, yet she still believes her married colleague will leave his wife for her, one day …

Evie is cheerfully married to Craig, but after three children, things have stagnated. When Craig suggests a way to spice up their relationship, Evie is horrified - but she always tries so desperately to please …

And Ellen, the eldest sister and the anchor of the family, is dealing with the end of her marriage and getting back into the dating game. But she wonders if she'll ever be able to get naked in front of another man, let alone open her heart to love again.

When their parents drop a bombshell that affects them all, and one sister must make a life-changing decision, it's the right time for the Beckett sisters to band together and face the challenges head-on.

Find out more at: books2read.com/therighttime

About The Best Man

Is the best man always the right man?

With American fiancé, Henry Darrow, publicist Madeleine has at last found the yin to her yang - or whichever way round it is. The calm to her storm, the stillness to her constant motion. Balance.

Her boss, Liv, had to be talked into marriage, which predictably ended in divorce. Liv knows that she and her twins are better off on their own anyway. She just wished everyone would stop telling her to 'put herself out there', whatever that's supposed to mean.

However, when Henry's best man arrives from the US to meet Madeleine for the first time, and Liv has a spontaneous chat with a stranger, the settled lives these women thought they had finally achieved are thrown into chaos. Secrets are unravelled and new doors are opened.

May the best man win.

Find out more at: books2read.com/thebestman